ONE FOR SORROW,
TWO FOR JOY

ONE FOR SORROW, TWO FOR JOY

Madison C. Brightwell

ONE FOR SORROW, TWO FOR JOY

iUniverse books may be ordered through booksellers or by contacting:

iUniverse
1663 Liberty Drive
Bloomington, IN 47403
www.iuniverse.com
1-800-Authors (1-800-288-4677)

ISBN: 978-1-4917-5151-0 (sc)
ISBN: 978-1-4917-5152-7 (e)

Library of Congress Control Number: 2014918968

Printed in the United States of America.

iUniverse rev. date: 11/25/2014

For my dear brothers and sisters

Contents

Chapter One

THIRTY YEARS AGO. That's when it all began. It seems extraordinary that I can stretch my mind back thirty years, and still the memories are more luminous than the events of yesterday. But that's how memories are. The important ones linger, etched permanently on the cortex as with a knife on glass, while insignificant remembrances are quickly blown away like sand by the winds of time.

You may dismiss my tale as just an adventure, entertaining perhaps, certainly remarkable if only because it really happened. That's not why I'm writing about it. I tell you because it's necessary that I pass on the message. I promised to pass on Clair's message and that's what I'll do. Although the story is mine alone, the message it contains is for everyone. Whether or not you believe it is up to you.

But I will begin at the beginning and record the events, just as they happened.

The year was 1995 when my story commences. My brother Clair and I were twins, both reaching six years of age in the October of that year. Everyone who saw us remarked on our physical similarity - we were like two sides of the same coin, one male and one female. We each had the same white complexion giving the impression of having been dusted with chalk, the same straight dark hair that emphasized our pallor, the same green eyes that looked out on the world with an identical expression of hopeful trust, the same way of twittering together like a couple of birds as we told each other secrets no one else knew.

Wherever I went, Clair was there, holding my hand as I tottered gleefully along a narrow pavement ridge; patting my head with a sympathetic gesture he'd learnt from Mother when I scraped my knee; admonishing me gently when I forgot to wear my hat outdoors on a cold winter's day. We shared everything, because to us the world consisted of two people, him and I. Mother called us her little magpies, because of the way we would hoard the sweets she gave us and share them out to each other later in exactly equal portions.

"You bite first, Ally", he would say when handing me the last chocolate in the box, "then give me the rest." I would study the sweet intently to find the halfway mark then bite, feeling the lovely gooey sweetness oozing on to my tongue, and - restraining myself from eating any more than my share - take it from my mouth and pop it into his with a sigh, watching him screw up his eyes tight and poke his chin forward as he enjoyed the delights of a cherry cream surprise.

How could I have foreseen that there would come a day when Clair wouldn't exist? Clair couldn't die. He was my twin brother - he was my world. There was no world without him. Yet, he did die. Although it took me nearly two years even to admit he had gone, to stop laying the table by his chair, waking in the night expecting to feel his hand in mine, asking Mother when he would return - to her exasperation. After he'd died, of course, nothing was ever the same again. I felt as though my childhood had ended, although I was only six years old.

It was a Sunday. The month was November. In the morning Mother asked me to take Clair his "health drink", as she called it, a revolting-looking concoction of fresh fruit and vegetable juices that Mother had whipped up in the blender, convinced that its daily consumption would give her son more vitality. Clair was sitting up in bed propped against two large white pillows, reading his favorite Narnia book by C.S. Lewis, tracing the words along the line with an index finger and silently mouthing phrases in accompaniment. His small body, always slimmer and slighter than mine even at birth, now appeared emaciated from the ravages of the illness and I could see the ribs in his chest sticking out where his dressing gown hung open at the front.

I banged the drink down on the bedside table and hopped on to the bed beside him, lightly tickling him on the arm with my fingernail to get his attention, and giggling in response to his shiver. He dropped his hands and put the book face down on the coverlet, then turned to me with a placid smile, his big eyes shining with inner joy. "It's so wonderful" he said, referring to the book. "I could read it again and again. I'd never get bored."

"I'm bored," I complained, pushing my lips forward into a pout. "It's boring without you, Clarey. I wish you'd play with me." I elongated the words in a petulant whine and hunched my shoulders to my ears in preparation for disappointment.

"What do you want to play?" said Clair. "I'll put my book away now." He reached over and grasped the tumbler

3

containing his health drink, miraculously it seemed to me not wrinkling his nose in disgust at the foul taste, as he drank the entire glassful - slowly because of his debility, and closing his eyes in concentration - then replaced the glass on the table.

"Let's play jigsaws!" I suggested, bouncing up and down on the bed in my eagerness to begin.

"All right" Clair replied.

I ran to the cupboard in the corner of the bedroom, flung open the top drawer and grabbed the first jigsaw puzzle I could find, a cartoon picture of Tom and Jerry with the cat about to catch the mouse by its tail. I raced back to Clair's bed with my prize, opened the box and threw all the pieces out on to the coverlet, spraying many of them on to the carpet so that Clair had to reach out of bed to retrieve the important edge pieces. For over an hour we pored over the puzzle, hardly speaking in our mutual concentration on the task, assembling the picture together in the lid of the box. Sometimes I would look for a piece and Clair would hand it to me, knowing it was the one I was searching for. I could hear Clair's hoarse breathing in my ear as he struggled with the symptoms of his illness, but he never complained or asked to rest.

I remember that morning vividly because it was the last time we ever played together, and so it's carved forever on my memory like a name on the bark of a tree. Even though just a child, I could see a radiance around Clair in those last few days before he died. His serenity seemed to affect us all. It was as if he'd already glimpsed the white tunnel into death and had no fear of it, was ready to pass into the unknown with no doubt or trepidation. I didn't understand then what it meant to die, I just knew that Clair was happy and therefore so was I.

That afternoon, I remember Mother listening to the radio, to Harry Nillson singing *Without You*, while she loaded up the washing machine with our dirty clothes. She was singing along, her voice quavering, not with emotion but with the effort of bending down to sort out the whites from the coloreds, distracted as she always was when doing any domestic chore. I played with a lump of cold pastry on the kitchen table, kneading it into animal shapes as if it were play dough. I was enjoying myself. So much so that I'd almost forgotten about Clair, asleep in the next room.

Clair had been in bed for more than a month. Why weren't we more worried? Perhaps Mother thought it was just a normal childhood illness - like mumps or chickenpox - that had to be endured, giving no cause for especial alarm. The doctor had visited two or three times, calling round again earlier that week. He'd told us little; merely claiming the illness was a viral infection that antibiotics couldn't help. "Plenty of rest and liquids", was his refrain, as he shook the thermometer after taking Clair's temperature for the third time, made a note of the abnormally high reading and collected his black bag with a slightly puzzled air.

The doctor didn't want to admit, as we later discovered, that he had no idea what was wrong with Clair. Because Clair was one of the very first people to be taken ill with the sickness, before anybody even knew what it was. It was several years before medical experts even put a name to the mysterious disease, and quite a while after that before it began to be written about in newspapers and described as the "catastrophe that could wipe out an entire British generation". Nowadays - when practically everyone you meet in Britain has a relative or friend who died in their late twenties or early thirties during the first two decades of the 21st century - it's hard to imagine a time when nobody had heard of Level 3.

I remember when they began screening us every three months, to check whether we had yet succumbed. That was in 2017, just after news of the extent of the disaster broke and started to impinge on the public's consciousness. At first, my regular visits to the clinic seemed rather an irritating chore dreamed up by doctors to increase their prestige. Then it became a national pastime to ask friends how they were each time you spoke to them, the subtext being, "What was the result of your latest test?" I heard children as young as Clair was when he died reciting the stages, as if they'd learnt them in school like ten times table: Level 1 - virus present in cells but dormant, asymptomatic; Level 2 - virus present in cells and active, some symptoms, curable if caught early; Level 3 - virus present and dominant in cells, incurable, gradual but certain progression with worsening symptoms, prognosis three months or two years at most with drug therapy.

There wasn't anything Mother or I or any of the doctors could have done to help Clair, who was suffering from classic symptoms of the disease. None of us were aware of that, during the mid-90's. While today everybody knows that the few children who presented with the disease early in its pathology stood even less chance than their later adult counterparts of withstanding that vicious predator, back then we were unprepared, with no idea that death could strike so swiftly. In less than three months Clair went from a normal, healthy little boy to a pale shadow, skeletally thin, coughing up blood, too weak to move or even hardly eat. Only his eyes shone bright in his haggard face, their enthusiasm undimmed by illness when Mother read to him his favorite stories and I sat by him, his wispy hand clutched in mine.

I don't know if Clair felt the agonizing pains people talk of in connection with the initial onslaught of Level 3. He never complained, but he wouldn't have anyway, being ever stoical. I've met many other sufferers in these last few years, as I've watched so many of my school friends die, and they've described what it's like. Once their bodies were full of the drugs which alleviated the terrible symptoms, they told me how the pains eased and they became enervated with a delicious weakness as in convalescent days after a bad bout of 'flu. The illness lulled them peacefully into death by imitating a long, tranquil sleep and their strength gradually ebbed away, as if the will to live was being slowly sucked out of their body.

I wonder if it was like that for Clair. Although he didn't take any of the drug therapy that I.C.A.L. now provide - there wasn't any in those days - he certainly appeared peaceful. I don't think I will ever be peaceful: I will rage against the dying of the light and have to be dragged kicking and screaming out of the sunshine. But that's where we differed, my brother and I. Clair always accepted things as they were. But I could never accept, never be still, never stop searching and fighting for something. His calm and my strength, balanced each other somehow. But without him I was like the sun without the moon, incomplete, with nothing to fight for.

The day Clair died was just like any other day. Mother asked me to take him his glass of milk and cookies on a tray at teatime and I did so, careful not to spill any of the liquid in the overfull tumbler, as I reached up to open the bedroom door. Clair still lay propped up on the pillows with his head drooping towards the window, but to my surprise he was no longer reading and his eyes were shut.

"Clarey, Clarey" I piped in my most winsome voice. As a child I was easily bored on my own and I needed my companion back. Wanting my brother to wake up and play with me, I put the tray down on the bedside table and clambered on to the bed, sitting astride him and gently pummeling his chest with my fists. His body was so limp; I thought he must be fast asleep. I was cross with him for not waking when I wanted to play, for not taking any notice of me. I put my head on his chest in a familiar gesture, and gripped his slender waist with my arms, squeezing as tightly as I could. But it wasn't tight enough.

Clair's head lolled to one side on the pillow, with his mass of tousled brown hair partially obscuring his face. On the nape of his neck was the red burn mark made by an accident he'd had with a hot coal one Sunday when it had leapt out of the barbecue pan and scorched him. The once-livid weal had now faded to a dusky pink of slightly raised skin in a small s-shape. With the insensitiveness of children, I prodded the old wound with my finger, hoping that the painful sensation would wake my brother. But still he lay motionless. It was no good - he wasn't going to wake up without some extra assistance.

I ran back into the kitchen and jumped up and down in front of Mother, hoping to attract her attention. "Clarey won't wake up! He won't wake up."

"Maybe he's tired", she replied in an irritable voice.

"But he won't wake up. I want him to play."

"He doesn't want to play, Al. Let him be."

"Why doesn't he wake up?"

"Look - I'll come in a sec."

"No - now! Now!"

"Oh Alice - can't you leave me in peace for a minute!"

I was an impossible child. Mother knew that the easiest plan was to yield to my hectoring. She threw a heap of washing on to the ground and followed me into Clair's bedroom, pulled there by my fat, insistent little hand.

"There. Look!"

Mother went to the bed and touched Clair's damp forehead gently with her hand. "Are you all right, darling?" she murmured, brushing his cheek with her fingers.

I followed her and sat on the other side of the bed, staring at my brother to see what effect Mother's efforts would produce. I remember thinking that he must be sleeping very comfortably because I could no longer hear the rasping sound he usually made as he breathed.

But when I looked up at Mother to remark on this she looked different, with an expression I'd never seen before, her lips parted and her hand hovering over Clair's face. The color had drained from her cheeks and all the lines in her face seemed to be pulling it down. She struck me suddenly as an old woman, not the Mother I knew in the flowery print dress, laughing as she rode with us on a rollercoaster ride, pushing her rebellious long blonde hair out of her eyes, but somebody old - as old as my grandmother might have been - a lady I'd never encountered before. And I was suddenly afraid.

"Oh no. No, please God. It can't be", she said softly to herself, almost in a whisper.

"Make him wake up" I pleaded, but Mother took no heed of me, her eyes on Clair. To my surprise, she didn't try to wake him up. She bent over his motionless face and kissed the closed eyelids. Then I saw her eyes, which were wide and staring and fixed on his countenance, fill with tears and her body shook with choking sobs as she leaned over Clair, lying so inert. "I'm sorry, I'm sorry...I should have...known, should have...done ...something" she moaned in lamentation.

Her emotion terrified me. I knew something terrible and enormous had happened, something beyond any adult's control, but I didn't know what.

A couple of days later, when some men came with a big box and lifted Clair into it, I tried to stop them. I thought they were attempting to steal my brother while he was sleeping. I screamed and screamed and bit one of the men on the leg. The other man laughed and called me a little wildcat. Mother was furious with me and locked me in my room for the rest of the day, with no supper. I felt no more remorse than I had knowledge of what I'd done wrong.

And so, to my amazement, for twenty-four years after Clair's death, I, his beloved twin sister, carried on living. My life wasn't all that much different from other people's. I went to school and made friends, hated lessons, loved summer holidays and took trips to the seaside. Mother and I never went further than Brighton or Southend, and when friends boasted to me about their trips abroad I never envied them, finding England perfectly acceptable.

Mother had a few boyfriends but she never married any of them, claiming that marriage was an outdated concept. None of the boyfriends ever stayed for long, perhaps because she didn't want them to. My father was an itinerant Irish fisherman Mother had encountered one summer on holiday on the West coast of Ireland. Clair and I never met him because he died in an ocean storm about a month after we were born. But Mother would talk of him fondly sometimes and say how like him we were, with our dark hair and pale skin and vivid emerald eyes.

I scraped through my exams, was unemployed for a year, then landed a "good" though boring job, which I clung on to for want of anything better. I drifted through several relationships with men, none actively unpleasant but none touching me in the deep way one expects of "love".

When I turned thirty, Mother suddenly realized she was old, and started to act it. Out of sheer laziness, I suppose, I hadn't bothered to leave home, and now I found that I couldn't, saddled as I was with a Mother too frail to look after herself and a wage packet too small to pay for her entry into an old people's home. If she'd only decided to go into a wheelchair before the National Health Service was abandoned in 2018, I could have got her off my hands, but Mother's sense of timing had always been inconvenient. I didn't feel resentful, however. I owed Mother something, after her years of sacrifice for me. Perhaps I secretly enjoyed having someone to be responsible for. After all, I didn't have much else in my life.

What had happened to my fighting spirit? - You may ask. I think I lost my spirit somewhere on the day Clair died, to remain just a small unheard voice submerged beneath layers and layers of pain.

I never spoke to Mother about Clair. In fact, there was only one person among my friends and acquaintances who I ever talked to about anything important to me, and that was Genevieve.

Genevieve was the strangest looking woman I ever saw. She was unbelievably tall, with a bony body balanced precariously on narrow feet, and a lean face with a pointed nose perched on a long slender neck, which she swathed perpetually in an Indian scarf. Her hair - grey roots inexpertly covered by a vivid red dye - would either be scraped away from her face in a tight bun, or sticking out in a frizzy halo around her head. She had very wrinkled skin of a nutty brown color, as if she'd spent years in a sunny climate. Possibly in her late sixties or early seventies, the most amazing thing about Genevieve was her eyes. She had the eyes of a young girl. They were large and aqueous and pale blue, with no lines around them and with an expression of immense sweetness and innocence giving the impression that their owner had stepped into this world from another planet where distrust and pain and grief didn't exist. Strange as she was and older than my own mother, I think I really loved Genevieve. She was the only person I'd ever loved, apart from Clair.

We met at a party given by one of the girls from work, a "resting actress" called Jan who'd temped with us at I.C.A.L. for a few weeks. Jan had taken instantly to me - as people generally do, because I'm unprepossessing and easy to talk to - and had decided to broaden my mind by introducing me to her collection of bizarre friends. I found most of them pretentious and downright boring, obsessed with their own huge egos and unable to talk about anything but auditions and theatre jobs and the foibles of their favorite directors. But Genevieve was an outsider like me, and so we formed an unlikely alliance - conventional young secretary and unorthodox elderly woman.

When I meet a person for the first time I know at once whether we'll become friends. That's how it was with Genevieve, her company instantly inducing feelings of comfortable familiarity. Nevertheless, when I asked about her occupation she bemused me by divulging that she was a "clairvoyant". I stifled a laugh, but her air of confidence and authority - as if telling me she worked in a shop or taught in a primary school - stifled my incredulity.

Compared to hers, my work sounded even more dull and uninspired than when I'd earlier admitted to Jan's actor friends with a self-deprecating shrug: "I work at I.C.A.L., as a sort of secretary". My ten years of employment at I.C.A.L. hadn't seen me rise to great heights within the company - probably through lack of ambition on my part - although I did now work for the Sales Director and I earned a reasonable salary. As Mother often pointed out, I was very lucky to have any job at all, to save me joining the ranks of the five million unemployed.

"I am sure you won't be there for ever" Genevieve remarked with a smile. "Your job doesn't suit you."

I didn't agree with her. As far as I was concerned, I was an ordinary person and my ordinary job suited me fine.

13

After that party, Genevieve and I decided to keep in touch, and she persuaded me to try one of her "sessions". Not knowing what to expect, I must admit I only volunteered for the event out of politeness and a twinge of curiosity. And when I went along the first time, I didn't exactly enjoy it - it was too confusing and beyond the realms of anything I'd come across before. But something about the experience drew me in a way that nothing else had.

I started going to see Genevieve on a regular basis: at first once every month or so, and then once a fortnight and then almost once a week. Out of embarrassment at what my straight-laced I.C.A.L. friends would think of me, I pretended that Genevieve and I went out to the movies or the pub. I was ashamed of admitting my interest in this new world that was opening up for me, "the world of the spirit", as Genevieve called it. Genevieve told me that she could communicate with dead people, because their spirits remained in this world and were accessible to those who were able to hear.

Maybe subconsciously I was waiting for her to speak with Clair, although I didn't concede this to myself. I'd locked away my memory of him in the deepest recesses of my heart and stored it there, like a jewel in a box hidden from the light. I don't know how she found out, but Genevieve knew of my loss before I'd had a chance to tell her. She could read it in my face, she said. As soon as she'd divined this, my memories came spilling out in a flood I couldn't contain, and with them all the grief that I'd hidden for years from my mother and my friends, not wanting them to realize how empty I was inside.

And so, Genevieve became my closest friend. The last time I saw her was the most important night of my life, and the beginning of my real journey. But I should describe it in detail because, as you will see, it has enormous significance to the rest of the story.

CHAPTER TWO

IT WAS NEW Year's Eve, 2020. There was a heightened atmosphere of anticipation, as we approached the end of the year. You could almost feel the street buzzing with it, as you walked out on that crisp December night. People all over London were having parties and celebrations; there was a spectacular fireworks display at Hyde Park and a street carnival in Notting Hill Gate with a lavish parade; the television schedules were full of commemorative programs and King William was due to give a speech at Westminster Cathedral. I.C.A.L. - being such a huge and successful pharmaceutical company - had laid on a special evening's entertainment for its thousand or so employees, at its plush headquarters in London Docklands.

I was quite looking forward to the bash. Mother - in unusually co-operative mood - had told me to forget about her for once and go out and enjoy myself. She had in fact been invited out to an event of her own, organized by the Differently Abled Women's Association, but she preferred to sit it out. Mother never celebrated New Year, and this one would be no exception, she said. In fact, she believed the chaos would be even worse than at most year ends. So I left her - sitting serenely in front of the television set, awaiting the Euro-2020 Song Contest - and set off for Genevieve's.

Mother and I dwelled in a fairly salubrious apartment block in the Docklands area of London, quite close to the gleaming I.C.A.L. building where I worked. In fact, most of the residents of our block were I.C.A.L. employees of one sort or another, ranging from Dr. Hooper the Head of the Research Department who owned his penthouse with river view on the top floor to Mother and I who rented our tiny studio flat on the ground floor at a reasonable price from the I.C.A.L. management. Genevieve lived on the other side of town, and I had to catch an underground train and struggle through hordes of jostling, excited partygoers, to reach her little semi-detached house in West Acton. I had been intending to cancel our meeting that night, but Genevieve had rung me at work to say it was essential I go because she had something important to tell me. I couldn't imagine what was so important that she had to tell me on New Year's Eve of all nights. But Genevieve was my friend and I couldn't let her down.

I reached West Acton at about 8 o'clock. From the house across the street loud music was blaring - the *New Vision 2020* CD that had been advertised interminably on the television since before Christmas that year - and people kept pulling up in cars and pouring out, laughing and singing and honking their horns. By contrast, Genevieve's house was like an oasis of calm in a world gone mad: no fairy lights, no champagne awaiting the big moment, just the usual mood music playing on an old CD system and a joss stick perfuming the air.

"Do you want some herbal tea?" Genevieve offered, as I took up my habitual position on the sofa in her front room.

"No thanks" I declined. "I'm sure I'll be drinking loads later on…" I was going to tell her about the I.C.A.L. rave-up, the foods I was expecting and the entertainment I'd heard had been laid on, but she was staring at me so intently that I stopped in my tracks.

"There's an aura around you tonight" Genevieve said. "It's as if you're waiting for something."

I was in the mood to be lighthearted, and her stare discomfited me. "Well of course I'm waiting for something," I replied flippantly, "It's the year 2020 in just over four hours."

"It isn't that." Her eyes were serious. I'd never seen that expression in them before, so sad and tender. They reminded me of Mother's eyes on the day Clair died. Genevieve took my hands in hers and perched beside me on the sofa.

"Your hands are cold, little Alice."

I didn't reply. She looked down and stroked my hands with her own, as if trying to infuse warmth into them. I could see the veins showing beneath the translucent skin, the age spots on her long fingers bedecked with rings. "Shall we begin?" Her voice was soft and dulcet.

I nodded. Moving away, Genevieve settled herself in the armchair opposite me, swallowed from a glass of water on the occasional table beside her, and leaned back with closed eyes, her slender arms resting on the high sides of the chair. I watched as she breathed deeply for a minute or two and I felt my body become calm and still, soothed by the music and the serenity of her presence. As I observed my friend, her figure seemed to change shape and to grow wider and taller.

She raised herself slightly in the chair and began to speak in a low-pitched voice, steadily, almost intoning the words.

"Something's coming. Something especially for you. Someone." Her mouth twitched in a smile, her eyes still closed. "Do you know who it is?"

"No" I replied.

"Who is it you want to see? Who, more than anyone, would you wish to see if you could? That is the person who is waiting for you on the star."

"He has a message for you."

"Message?" I whispered.

"He hasn't forgotten you. He never left you. But he's here in another form. He wants you to find him. He has a message for you, that will help you and the others like you." *The others like me? Could Genevieve know about that?*

"My guide says your brother is here now," she said. "He's waiting for you."

I didn't know what she meant - *Here now? In some invisible form?*

"He has incarnated into another body," she answered, as if in reply to my silent question. "He doesn't look the same as he did before, so you may not recognize him at first. But he wants you to find him."

I didn't know whether to believe her. *In another body! How could Genevieve possibly know that?* It all seemed so fantastic. Nonetheless, I kept listening.

"Do you want to find him?"

"Yes" I acknowledged. This much was certainly true.

"Then you must go on a journey. It will not be easy, and it will take some time. You will have to be strong. But you will find him if you look hard enough."

19

"What sort of journey...?"

"You must travel to many different countries before you can find him. And you must go alone."

"Oh." I couldn't keep the tone of anxiety out of my voice. "Why do I have to do this to find him? If he's here and he knows where I am, can't he just come and find me?"

Genevieve regarded my face as if viewing me for the first time that evening. "It will be all right," she said, attempting to console me with her smile. "It won't be as unpleasant as you think."

"But I've never been anywhere" I complained. "I've certainly never been anywhere on my own. How will I manage? Can't you come too?"

"It's your journey, Alice, and only you can take it." And now Genevieve appeared troubled, and for the first time a shadow passed over her face. "But I know why you're so worried. You're not well." It was at once a statement and a question.

I hadn't wanted to tell Genevieve. I hadn't even told Mother, intending to wait until I could catch her at an opportune moment so that I could break the news to her gently. I couldn't bear to burden her with the knowledge that both her children would die of the same disease before she had reached her dotage.

But now I was relieved to unburden myself to someone. It had been hard keeping the knowledge to myself, like a guilty secret, over the past couple of weeks since my last fateful blood test. "Yes, you're right. The doctor said I've developed Level 3 since the last time I saw him..."

Before I could say more, Genevieve intervened, in an urgent tone: "You haven't told me about this before, have you, my dear?"

I shook my head miserably.

"I thought you may be afflicted too, but I didn't think it would happen so soon. So soon" she repeated with something like desperation in her voice. "Then you must start immediately, you really must. There's no time to be lost. What a good thing you came tonight." Genevieve rose from her chair and moved away, keeping her back to me.

I lowered my head and stared at my hands, which now lay cold and lonely on my lap. I felt suddenly the oppressive presence of my illness, like a tangible thing, lying in wait for me. I had seen what happened to others so I knew exactly what was coming, knew there was no chance of escape. I hadn't let myself think about the illness until this moment, preferring to bury my head in the sand and pretend nothing was wrong. I could do nothing to help myself anyway, so I didn't see the use of anxiety and mental preparation. Nobody survived who reached Level 3, and there was no cure, only drugs that could alleviate the symptoms for a couple of years. That was all there was to it. All I could do was give in as gracefully as I could.

I heard a sharp intake of breath and turned to look at Genevieve, who was standing in front of the gilded mirror on her wall, staring at me, her eyes full of tears. "I try not to think about it. These things have to happen and I must learn to accept. It's not up to me to decide who suffers. But sometimes it makes me feel so angry. What a waste of young lives - and what for?" I'd never seen Genevieve talk so passionately about anything. Her young eyes shone in the gloom and glittered with tears. "I keep asking why. I know it's not a judgment, although it feels like one. But we have to learn the lessons before we can save ourselves. Do you understand?"

"Not really." I felt I must be stupid, but I had no idea what she was talking about. I had never pondered the whys and wherefores of the sickness. The disease had descended on Britain and one day the doctors would find a cure for it, like the plague of the old days, then all the people of my generation would stop dying.

It wasn't anybody's fault that the virus had infected a batch of baby's milk in 1989, thereby planting a time bomb virus in the cells of about 75% of the babies born in that year, primed to explode about thirty years later. It had simply been an accident, a terrible accident. Of course, sales of the particular brand of the milk had been halted immediately the doctors suspected there was a link between it and the hitherto rare viral condition, but by then it was already too late. The experts had thought that only a few isolated cases, like Clair, would succumb to the virus as children. They hadn't known that this virus was so devilish, it was prepared to wait three decades to launch its attack, lulling its victims into a false sense of security and then proceeding to virtually wipe out a generation of British people with terrifying swiftness, before anyone had time to find a cure that would stop people dying or do any more than alleviate the symptoms and stave off death for a couple of years.

Genevieve sat down beside me and took my hands again, kneading them in her own, and staring at me with an intensity that was unnerving. "It's up to you to learn the lessons and find the message, the cure to help all the others."

All this talk of lessons and messages was making me feel tired and inadequate. "Me? But why me? Surely there are other people, better...I don't know... more qualified..."

Genevieve didn't answer but she looked so sad that I put an arm around her shoulder, and was surprised at how thin and brittle she felt, like an old twig that may snap at any moment.

"It doesn't hurt or anything" I said, hoping to cheer her. "I'm taking the drugs. I get a special price deal because I'm an I.C.A.L. employee. And I feel perfectly normal at the moment. It's amazing, really."

"I know. They say the drugs can take all the pain away. But I almost think that's the worst thing. People just slip away without complaining."

I thought of Clair, lying so peacefully on his bed. My memory evoked Genevieve's previous words. "You said...he has a message for me. What is the message?"

My friend smiled, and gently dried the corners of her eyes with the edge of her chiffon scarf. "It's your message to find, little one. I don't know what it will be. When you find him he'll tell you."

"But how can I find him?" Neither of us mentioned his name, as if his invocation would break the spell Genevieve had weaved around us. She got up and left the room, her long skirt making a swishing noise as it brushed the wooden floor, and I was left with the softly droning music and the smell of incense.

I began to feel desperate, my mind thronging with anxious questions: what was the import of Genevieve's words? why did she always speak in riddles that I would never be intelligent enough to unravel? what was the use of knowing that Clair was here, if I didn't know how to find him? how on earth could I find him, in all the big wide world? why had she set me such an impossible task?

In a few moments, Genevieve returned, clutching a slim black box about the size of a letter. She placed it on the sofa between us and I looked at it, and then stroked its smooth, shiny surface with my fingers. It was cold to the touch and made out of some substance I'd never seen before, a sort of hybrid of metal and plastic.

"Pick it up" Genevieve encouraged, so I did so. I was surprised at how light the box was - it can't have been any heavier than an ordinary envelope. There were clasps at either end, also black and worked in an ornate filigree as fine as a spider's web.

"It will help you."

"What is it?" I shook the box slightly and heard the rattle of its contents. Intrigued, I started to unhinge the clasps, but Genevieve put a warning hand on mine: "Don't open it until tomorrow."

"But why ever not--?"

"I know you're impatient, dear one. But remember this. Don't seek to know too much before time. Promise me you won't open it until tomorrow."

I started to protest, then sighed and gave in. "All right." There was no question of my disobeying her instructions. Genevieve had such an air of mysterious power that I was sure she'd know if I went against her. Even if I was far away, somehow Genevieve would see what I'd done and the enchantment - or whatever it was - which would lead me to Clair would be dissolved. But it was killing me not to know more. I was being eaten up with questions I wanted to ask.

What was in the box? How would it help me? What was I supposed to do with it? With a great effort of will, I bit back all my queries and quelled my tongue.

"I know it's difficult for you" said Genevieve, laying a sympathetic hand on my arm, "but you must try to accept things for once and trust what I tell you."

I clutched the box to me. My fingers tingled with some energy coming from it: it felt almost alive. The nearest thing I'd ever felt to that before was the sensation of static electricity coming from my computer after a day at work in front of the monitor. But the impression wasn't even like that. The box was like an animal, breathing with life, waiting to pounce. I put the article under my sweater and held it there, and the box felt warm next to my heart.

"You're going to find him. I'm sure of it."

"Do you really think so?" My task seemed almost possible, now that I had the box, which I judged would confer some miraculous power on me. I felt hope and desire tugging at my sleeve and sending little ripples of excitement into my stomach.

"Yes, if you try hard enough. But, my dear, it won't be easy and you must be patient."

"I'll try" I responded, but I wasn't really listening to my friend. I was preoccupied with happy visions of Clair and myself reunited and walking in the sunshine, just as we had done as children.

"Remember that the message he gives you will help you and the others like you."

The import of Genevieve's words began to sink in and I dismissed my daydream and turned to face her: "You mean, this has all got something to do with the disease, with Level 3?"

"Yes."

"Does he know the cure that can save us?"

"Yes, I think he does."

"Because that was what he died of too?"

"Yes. But also. There are some other things I have to tell you, which will help you to find him. As I said, he will look different, so it may be difficult for you to recognize him. Remember that he's in a different form now."

"What form?"

"I don't know. That's for you to find out. But his name will begin with an S and there's an s somewhere on his body. That I do know. And when you open the box tomorrow, you will see some other clues. They are there to guide you. Believe that what they say is true. They are there to show you something. So you should go wherever they guide you to go."

I nodded, impatience now building up in me to see what lay inside the box. I didn't know if I'd be able to restrain myself from opening it until the next day.

"And there are two things to remember. Firstly, there's a warning. Be wary of what you wish for. Because whatever you wish for will happen. And secondly, there's a consolation. Your fear is worse than the thing you fear. If you bear in mind these two precepts, it will make your journey easier."

Genevieve squeezed my hands in hers, and the old grandfather clock in the hall started to chime ten o'clock, in a voice echoey with age.

"I have to go." I had been brought back to present reality by the sound of the hour, and I realized that I was already late.

"I know you must."

"I promised Mother I'd pop home and feed Marmalade, and I have to get changed for the office party."

"Of course."

"And I must get there before twelve, or I'll miss the champagne and sandwiches. And there's going to be an enormous cake." My eyes grew large with the thought of the food I'd shortly be consuming.

Genevieve laughed her light, tinkly laugh - I always thought it sounded like the laugh of the Good Witch in one of those animated fairy stories - and guided me to the front door.

As I stood on her doorstep, feeling the cold pinch my cheeks and hearing once again the noises of parties all along the street, I was aware of a strange sweet perfume I'd never smelt before. It seemed to be coming not from Genevieve herself but from the air around her, and it was an odor of spring flowers like jasmine and hyacinth and gardenia all mixed together, which was incongruous on that winter's night.

And later, when I thought about it, I wished I'd asked Genevieve in that moment, how she knew that was to be our last meeting. But she wouldn't have answered me anyway, I know she wouldn't. She preferred to preserve her mystery, and perhaps it was better that way. My friend was more like a guiding spirit or a guardian angel than a flesh and blood human being. Even without her physical presence, I often feel her with me, even now, as some people say they can feel the spirit of their dead loved ones, hovering ghostly around them.

I hurried back to our small apartment in the Docklands area of London. Mother was propped up in her wheelchair in front of the television, perfectly happy. In fact she didn't take much notice of me when I came in, so I busied myself putting on my new red dress and slapping on some make-up.

Marmalade was sitting on the window-ledge in my room, intrigued by the flash of fireworks being exploded all over the city. I called him in with a bowl of food, and shut the window to keep out the chill night air. Then I departed, closing my bedroom door behind me. The night was cold so I wore my heavy winter jacket over my dress, and put the box Genevieve had given me in the inside pocket, not wanting to part from the precious object for a second. I knew Mother didn't like to be bothered by Marmalade crawling over her while she watched television, and I decided that although the cat may be bored for a few hours, I could always let him out again when I came back later that night. Marmalade was a big red tabby cat that we'd had for five years, the most placid, affectionate and sweet-natured animal imaginable. The only time he showed his feral nature was when he gnashed his teeth while looking at birds or flies through the window. He purred when I plonked him down in front of his food.

By the time I got to the party, it was half past eleven, and most of the other guests were merrily drunk. Barnaby staggered past me clutching a silver tray on which a few glasses of champagne slithered like dancers on an ice rink. "So you made it then" he burbled over the din.

Whenever I came to one of these I.C.A.L. events, I always secretly hoped it would be different - not the usual inane gossip and shoptalk - but it never was. When I thought about it, it made sense. The sort of people who worked for I.C.A.L. - which stood for Independent Care Association Ltd. - were concerned only with the amount of money in their bank balances and the size of their properties in the country. It was not a job that attracted the thinking man or woman or anyone who was concerned about the deeper things in life. And while I enjoyed the company of my colleagues when I was with them, there was always a part of me that longed for something else, something more, although I'd never actually had the courage to go out and search for it.

That was the sort of thing I was idly pondering as I sat and listened to the thud of music and watched the laughing faces and munched on my chicken quarter. And when Nigel - who worked alongside me as a computer operator in the Sales department - came and squatted down next to me, and I offered him some of my chicken as a friendly gesture, and we pulled the wishbone together with giggles and fingers slippery with chicken-fat, I found myself wishing fervently and with all my heart: "I wish, I wish, that all this would change, everything I have come to know, I wish it would change utterly and beyond recognition." The wish slipped into my thoughts like an unbidden guest, and I felt slightly ashamed and guilty to realize how discontented with my life I was, when after all it wasn't so bad.

Nigel covered his mouth with his hand and giggled.

"Bet I know what you wished for" I said.

Nigel raised his eyebrows and looked down his nose at me ironically. "Just what are you insinuating?"

"Don't be coy, Nige. I know what you're like. Our nice hunky new research student? Hooper's blue-eyed boy, Martin Blenkinsop?"

Nigel pursed his lips and looked away meaningfully.

"He's certainly got a cute bum. But you're wasting your time inviting him for drinkies, if you ask me. I don't think he's that way inclined."

"I'm not asking you, love. Anyway, there's only one way to tell. I'm just waiting to put him to the test." Nigel licked his lips salaciously.

"You're a dirty bugger. I'm going to tell Martin you've got dishonorable intentions towards him," I teased.

"You can leave me to show him that, girl... Anyway, his attraction isn't purely physical. The boy's got brains."

"Sure, sure." I started to demolish a ham and cheese roll, opening my eyes wide with the effort of stuffing the huge wedge of bread into my gaping mouth.

"No, really" countered Nigel. "We were having a fascinating chat today at lunch, me and the delectable Martin. Where were you, by the way? I looked for you in the canteen."

"Grainger gave me a load of urgent letters to do at quarter to one, so I just grabbed a sandwich from the tray" I replied, mumbling through my sandwich.

"I can see you're making up for lost time now" Nigel commented wryly. "But no, anyway, Martin was telling me..." Here, Nigel suddenly stopped speaking, looked around him in a comical parody of conspiratorial discretion, leaned in towards me and pressed his mouth to my ear. "For your ears only, this is. Don't spread it around."

Entering into the spirit of the game, I whispered: "Mum's the word. I can keep a secret. You know I'm discreet."

"Oh yes, about as discreet as a gossip column in the tabloid press, love. Well, hark at this. You know, of course, that Martin works mainly under Dr. Hooper--"

"Not literally under him, I hope."

Nigel graced me with his best disapproving matron look. "Don't be rude. The point is, Martin's made friends with the other research student in Hooper's department, a boy called Sylvester who started work about the same time. According to Martin, Sylvester is not what he seems."

"In what way?" I shrugged.

"Sylvester's not really interested in pharmacology."

I pulled the corners of my mouth down in disbelief: "What's he doing working here then?"

"Oh, he is a genuine medical student. He's on a sandwich course from university, just like Martin. Not that I'd want him in my sandwich..."

I tutted and shook my head: "Cut to the chase, Nigel. I want a dance in a minute."

"Sorry, I digress. Martin told me he's found out that Sylvester's not just an innocent student, he's also working undercover for some sort of terrorist organization."

I snorted in disbelief. "You're kidding. Terrorist? How could he get away with that?"

"Maybe it does sound too outrageous to be true, but remember I've got this straight from the horse's mouth--"

I tittered: "So to speak."

"All right, jest away. But this is no laughing matter. That's what Martin told me, and he wouldn't have any reason to lie. He says he and Sylvester got horrendously drunk one night in the pub and Syl spilled the beans. Totally confidential, of course, swore Martin to secrecy..."

"And then Martin immediately went and told you. How loyal to his mate!"

"Well, hardly immediately. He's been agonizing over whether to tell anybody for days. And they're hardly mates, just fairly friendly work colleagues."

"O.K. What is this terrorist organization, then?"

"They call themselves the Animals Liberation Army."

I stopped in the middle of helping myself to a plump cherry tomato, my hand hovering over the paper plate. "I think I've heard of them. They're pretty violent, aren't they? I saw something on the news. Aren't they against animal experiments or something?"

"Precisely."

"What on earth is Sylvester doing working for Dr. Hooper, then? Jesus! Everybody knows Hooper's outspoken views on that subject. He's not exactly reticent about it, is he? I remember something on the telly a few months ago when Hooper was really slagging them off. The A.L.A., I mean. Saying the animal rights people are all loonies who should be put in jail and animal experiments are a necessary part of medical research."

"Well, think about it. What better way to get to the man at the top than to infiltrate the organization he works for and pretend to be helping him."

"Pretend?" I frowned, slowly. "You don't mean..."

"I certainly do mean... This Sylvester fellow has not got I.C.A.L.'s best interests at heart, not by a long chalk."

"But, it's crazy!" I spluttered. "How can they let people just walk in here and...? I mean, doesn't Hooper take any precautions? Aren't there any screening procedures when the research department takes on new staff, to stop this sort of thing?"

"Your guess is as good as mine, girl. Ask Personnel. I don't know. Maybe there are screening procedures, but Sylvester was so credible that he fooled everybody."

I knitted my brows and considered Nigel's news for a moment. "So what's Martin going to do now? There's not a lot of point telling you, is there? I mean, he needs to speak to somebody in authority, doesn't he, and get this bloke sacked before he does any damage?"

"Martin asked me what I thought he should do. I must say I was flattered that he came to me but, as you say, I'm not exactly the best person to help him. I suggested exactly the same as you, that he should tell one of the big wigs like Grainger perhaps or someone at his level, and make sure Sylvester gets given the push. But it's not quite as simple as that, apparently. Sylvester's denying the whole thing, now that he's sober. Martin hasn't got any actual proof of Syl's connection with the organization, just his suspicions and the chap's confession, which nobody else heard. If Martin goes straight to the bosses they might think he's just trying to sabotage a fellow employee's reputation for his own personal gain..."

"That's ridiculous!"

"Jobs are so hard to come by these days. Especially prestigious and well-paid jobs like a research assistant at I.C.A.L. And, as you know, only one of these students on medical sandwich courses can actually be offered the full-time assistant's post at the end of their training year, which will leave the other one out in the cold and back on the dole queues waiting for another opportunity."

"Oh my God. I hadn't thought of that."

"Neither had I. But when Martin explained it to me I could see it put him in quite a tricky position."

"Is there anything we can do?"

"No, not a lot." Nigel put the tips of his fingers together in a pyramid and brought them to his nose. "I just wanted to give you a little tip. It occurred to me that it would be very easy for Sylvester to have found out Dr. Hooper's address - all the staff details are on the internal computer network, after all - and the A.L.A. might decide to go after Dr. Hooper at his home."

"What do you mean, go after him?" I demanded, aghast at Nigel's suggestion. "Physical violence?"

"Ssh, keep your voice down!" ordered Nigel in a forceful whisper. Then he added softly: "That's what they do, isn't it, these terrorist type people?"

"Surely they wouldn't go that far!" I countered, nevertheless feeling butterflies in the pit of my stomach. I had never before considered the possibility of my life containing the threat of actual physical danger.

"Why ever not? Hooper's the devil incarnate to them, after all. He's got that whole laboratory full of animals which he tortures on a daily basis..."

"He doesn't torture them" I replied hotly, wondering why I was defending Hooper who I didn't much like. Perhaps because I felt I ought to have some loyalty towards the company that had employed me for ten years. "Anyway, it's in a good cause."

"That's not how the A.L.A. see it" commented Nigel.

I made a sarcastic noise in the back of my throat and tipped back a good swallow of wine from my glass. "I bet if one of the A.L.A. people was dying of Level 3, they'd be happy to use the I.C.A.L. drugs that Dr. Hooper invented with his research."

Nigel scratched his chin. "They probably wouldn't, actually. Some of them are so fanatical they'd be prepared to die for the cause. There's even some of them who don't believe in the drugs at all."

"What do you mean, don't believe in them? Don't believe they exist?"

"Don't believe they work."

"Of course they work!" I scoffed. "Haven't thousands of people been taking them over the past few years and getting relief from their symptoms?" Me, for one, I wanted to add, but didn't.

"Just temporary pain relief, they say. Not a cure."

"Temporary pain relief's a hell of a lot better than nothing at all" I blustered.

"Believe me, I think they're as crazy as you do. I'm just reporting what they say. Some of these fanatics - paranoid hippy types, if you ask me - actually say that I.C.A.L.'s drugs don't just not cure people with Level 3, they kill them in the end."

"How on earth can they say that? They've got no evidence at all."

"As I say, I think they're a bunch of rampant schizophrenics. But some people will believe the most ludicrous crap imaginable if it fits into their world view."

"You're telling me!"

"The point is, although personally I couldn't give a bugger - excuse my French - if they did get Hooper because I think he's a sour faced git anyway, it occurs to me that you live in the same building as him. So I think you had better be careful."

"God! Do you think they're going to be wandering around the communal car park with machine guns or something, waiting for Hooper to come out of his apartment?"

"Heaven knows. I just think you should be aware of the possibilities and...sort of...keep your wits about you."

"Bloody hell. It's like being in one of those American film thrillers."

"Not quite so glamorous, I'm afraid."

Suddenly, our conversation was interrupted by the whine of microphone feedback as somebody started to announce: "Gather round for the big moment, everybody, it's nearly midnight" and the music was switched off. I looked at my watch and saw that it was five to twelve, and felt relief that the party side of the evening was about to begin. I didn't read newspapers or have any interest in politics, and Nigel's fears seemed downright overblown to me.

People were grouping themselves into an enormous circle around the fringes of the hall and I elected to join the jollity. I dragged Nigel into the coil, where he stood clutching my left hand, while my right was grasped by a gormless young girl in a shiny yellow dress who shone me a vacuous smile, as if feeling she ought to know me but couldn't quite remember who I was. I grinned back at her and at the others across the cordon, who were so far away - snaking across the rim of the great hall in their hundreds - that I could hardly make out their faces. The champagne had sent its bubbles up to my brain and my mood was now one of beneficence to the entire world. The music switched abruptly to Auld Lang Syne and several hundred arms began to sway up and down to the rhythm. Then I became aware that David Grainger - the head of our section and my immediate boss - had entered the hub of our huge wheel, and his frame was practically obliterated by an enormous bunch of balloons in different colors, which were tied together with nylon string. Grainger was so convulsed with laughter that his torso was bent double under the press of balloons, which seemed to be bludgeoning him as they struggled to break free of their ties. I saw now that my boss was attempting to cut all the strings with a pair of scissors and some of the balloons started wafting into the air.

I shadowed a balloon with my eyes as it ascended to the ceiling. I remember that yellow balloon with its comical cartoon design of a smiling face. I can still picture it vividly in my mind's eye, because what happened next was such a shock that all the circumstances leading up to that moment were imprinted on my memory with indelible force, and events from then on seemed to unravel in slow motion, in the way it is claimed they do when one comes close to death.

Beneath me the floor quivered briefly, then I was hurled off my feet and thrown backwards on to the floor by the force of a gigantic bang, which seemed to explode all around me. Blinking the dust from my eyes I squirmed on the floor, my back momentarily sore from its recent impact, then raised myself painfully on to one elbow. My first instinct was to wonder dazedly if all the balloons had burst at once, and I looked up at the ceiling expecting to see colored rubber fragments come floating down. Instead, to my horror and utter amazement, I saw a huge crack appear in the plaster which grew wider and wider, then debris from the wreckage began cascading on to my head and I realized that any moment the whole roof would come crashing down. In perplexity I gazed around the room, and apprehended with a jolt of fear that all the people who had been standing beside me moments before were now strewn over the floor, the air was full of choking smoke and the screams of delighted laughter had turned into screams of terror.

Turning my head to the right, I saw that my hand still clutched that of the girl who had stood next to me in the circle but her figure lay sprawled under a large wooden table and the hand I held was lifeless and cold as dead meat. I sprang away in horror, and scrabbled through the chaos of broken crockery, fallen detritus and writhing bodies, searching frantically for the doorway. I realized with consternation that we were now in almost total darkness. The force of the blast - or whatever it was - must have blown out all the electricity at a stroke. Glimpsing a shaft of light, I struggled desperately towards it. The people around me were moaning and screaming, their weak arms waving in the air pleading for help. Splashes of blood dotted the once-pristine parquet floor. But in my panic and confusion I could think only of my own escape and of getting out of the building as fast as possible before the whole structure collapsed.

When I attained the shaft of light, I saw to my relief that it did indeed emanate from the main doorway, and I pushed my way through the heavy glass door into the freezing night air. Now I beheld what had created the glow in the sky which had proved my ally in helping me locate the exit to the I.C.A.L. building, and to my consternation I realized that it was not the splendor of a thousand happy fireworks announcing the birth of a new year, but the incandescence of huge high buildings, apartment blocks across the river, which were burning like a beacon in the sky. From the direction of the gleam, I was well aware which buildings these must be, but I didn't yet want to face what I knew to be true.

I lurched across the street, screaming in my distress, "Fire, fire!" hardly caring that there was no one to listen. Hearing an almighty crash behind me, I swiveled round and saw the huge I.C.A.L. building now being consumed by greedy tongues of fire and belching out black smoke from the uppermost windows. I held my throat with one hand and retched into the bushes by the side of the road, coughing and spluttering with the combined effects of choking smoke and shock at what I had just encountered.

CHAPTER THREE

G ATHERING ALL MY strength now, I raced down the street in the general direction of the apartment block where I had left Mother and Marmalade at home in the flat. It was a good two or three miles back to my home across the river, and I hoped desperately that some vehicle would pass me - a bus or a cab or even a car with a sympathetic driver from whom I could hitch a lift. My thoughts were jumbled and incoherent and I don't know what I planned to do when I arrived at the apartment block, but I felt compelled to reach my home as quickly as possible.

When I'd run a couple of hundred yards I heard the welcome engine noise of a London bus rounding the corner behind me, and I stood in the middle of the road and waved my arms so frenziedly that the driver pulled over, ignoring the fact that I wasn't at an official bus stop. "Where you headed, love?" the driver asked, his round black face and cockney accent seeming the warmest and friendliest things in the world at that moment.

"Isle of Dogs" I gasped. "Are you going through the tunnel?"

"Yep. Hop in."

Amazed and grateful that the driver hadn't asked me for the fare, having left my handbag with all my cash back in the I.C.A.L. building, I slumped into a seat on the front bench and gazed around me. I felt lost and bewildered, as if events were happening in a film I was watching or a dream from which I would soon awake. Observing the faces of the other passengers, their expressions mirrored my own emotions: they seemed scared and shell-shocked like people trapped in a nightmare. I noticed a young man sitting on the other bench across from me. He wore faded blue jeans and a moth-eaten jumper two sizes too big for him. His black hair stuck out wildly from his face and he sat hunched over with his chin jutting out. He was staring at me with deep dark eyes of an indeterminate color, but on this night his behavior didn't appear impolite or intrusive.

"It's like the war" remarked an elderly woman in a stunned voice, as the bus trundled through the dark night, lit by the flames of the huge burning I.C.A.L. complex of buildings, which glimmered devilishly on the surface of the River Thames.

"D'you know what's going on?" I asked the young man who was looking at me. I'm not sure why I believed he'd have more information than I, but I was desperate to communicate with someone.

"Terrorists" he said flatly, not taking his eyes from me. "The anti-I.C.A.L. people. They've been planning this for months. Have you heard of the Animals Liberation Army?"

"Y...yes, I have actually" I stuttered in reply, the word terrorists sparking off a dim memory of Nigel talking about that very thing just before we got up to join the big circle of merrymakers at the I.C.A.L. party...just before... I pushed the horrible images from my mind.

"They've planted bombs at all the locations connected to I.C.A.L., the headquarters, the drug-making factory... It's an extremist faction of the A.L.A. They've been protesting for years, trying to get the plant shut down. Saying it's unethical, all the experiments I.C.A.L. do...did do... on animals to try and find a cure for Level 3. But nobody listened to them. So now they're taking direct action. They're out to destroy the whole company."

"How do you know all this?" I asked, unable to keep a tone of suspicion out of my voice.

The young man glared at me, his eyes darkening. "Don't go accusing me, lady. It's in all the papers, there for anybody to see if they're interested in current events. The bomb squad knew something like this was going to happen."

"Why didn't they do something to prevent it, then? Evacuate the area?"

The young man shrugged and looked out of the window. "Search me. Maybe they got some of their information wrong. It happens."

Snippets of Nigel's earlier conversation kept coming back to me and I tried to grab hold of them but they floated about in the fog of confusion in my mind. "That's...awful" I remarked slowly, almost to myself.

"Haven't you been reading the papers?" the young man demanded suddenly, fixing me again with his intense stare.

"I heard something about it," I admitted, miserably. "But I don't read newspapers generally."

"Well, why should you care then?" The young man seemed to lose interest in me now, and drew his jean-clad legs up beside him on the seat, scuffing the plastic covering with his large muddy boots.

I looked at him for a moment before replying in a small voice: "I do care, I care a lot. You see, I work for...I used to work for I.C.A.L. I was at the party when the bomb went off."

"Bloody hell!" The young man expostulated, obviously impressed at my involvement in such dramatic events.

"My flat's in the I.C.A.L. block on the Isle of Dogs. My mother's still there...at least...I hope she is" I whispered with a slight shiver. I gazed out of the window, but there was nothing to see but golden orbs of light flashing past, as we were now passing through the tunnel under the river.

"I'm really sorry. Hope she's O.K." The young man's demeanor was all embarrassed sympathy now.

I sighed, and we sat for a few moments in companionable silence. The bus was crawling along at a snail's pace, taking no account of the fact that the roads were virtually clear of other traffic, but perhaps it was just my own impatience to reach my destination that made everything seem to happen too slowly. We emerged through the mouth of the tunnel on to the other side of the river, and I comforted myself with the thought that we hadn't much farther to go.

All at once, the young man leaned towards me and spoke in a confidential whisper: "If I were you, I wouldn't tell anybody about your having worked for I.C.A.L. You know it's been exposed, what I.C.A.L. were up to. I read about it in *The Independent*. They're making huge amounts of money out of their drugs for Level 3. And it doesn't even cure anybody, does it? Some people say it was them that created the disease in the first place, so they could make a lot of money out of supposedly relieving people's misery."

"Oh now that's completely ridiculous! I know for certain that's not true." I was starting to feel annoyed by the young man's intensity and to wish that he'd just leave me alone. First Nigel and now he were throwing crazy notions at me - about the I.C.A.L. drugs (which I for one depended upon) not being effective and the organization I'd worked for, for the last ten years being corrupt - and I didn't want to have all my conceptions of the world suddenly overturned when I had enough to cope with worrying whether Mother and Marmalade were all right. I sat at right angles to my companion now, and stared fixedly ahead through the front window, willing the bus driver to propel us faster towards home.

"Well, you believe what you like" the young man replied, sitting back. "But I wouldn't put it past them. It's what you get with monopolies. They get power mad and money hungry and nobody can stop them. I'm getting out of this country. I'm not sticking around to watch them screwing up our lives. If you've got any sense you'll get out too. Unless you're profiting too, of course."

"No of course I'm not profiting" I snapped. "I'm just an employee, just a... a humble worker bee. I've never even met Dr. Hooper."

Nevertheless, the young man looked at me suspiciously, at my posh red dress and my expensively tousled hair, and I could see him thinking that I was one of the enemy, a rich yuppie who collected her wage packet and asked no questions. He fell into a tense silence, but I ignored his stare.

Nigel must have been right when he'd said those things about the A.L.A. and their vendetta against my erstwhile employers. What was the other thing he'd said? *The A.L.A. might decide to go after Dr. Hooper at his home.* My heart started to pound in horror, as I realized the implication of his words, which corresponded with the sight of the burning buildings I'd viewed from across the river. Dr. Hooper lived on the top floor of our very building. Anybody who worked at I.C.A.L. could easily verify that. The best way to kill the doctor would be to plant a bomb that would destroy the whole of our building...

As the bus pulled into my street, the smoke from the fires grew so intense that we could hardly see anything through the windows. Ambulance sirens wailed in the distance and the sound of people shouting and yelling filled the air, along with the acrid smell of burning plastic and metal. It was an eerie experience, cruising through the melee in our stately bus, none of us bus passengers daring to utter a word, mute witnesses to the tragedy unfolding before us.

My emotions had been so numbed by the impact of preceding events that when I descended from the bus and stood in front of my apartment block - which was a blazing inferno - I was surprised at my equanimity. Around me people were screaming or clutching each other, rushing to and fro with buckets of water or struggling with fire hydrants. Their sorrows or struggles appeared puny and futile against the backdrop of that massive complex of apartments, thirty stories high, whose every floor was currently being devastated by flourishing sheets of flame.

To my joy I noticed that a fire engine had arrived on the scene, and men and women in yellow helmets were issuing instructions to the onlookers to stand back, while attempting to organize the chaos surrounding the burning building. Some of the firemen held a long hose, which was shooting a jet of water - glowing silver in the moonlight - on to the rush of flames, and great billows of black smoke were pouring out into the air. Others were scaling the walls of the apartment block on long ladders, their bodies silhouetted against the flaming glow of the fire.

I stood motionless for a few moments - the only still creature in all the excitement - trying to take in the scene and comprehend what had happened. Now I was here, I had no idea what to do next. I felt powerless and small and as if I was in some crazy nightmare with no end.

I attempted to peer through the blanket of smoke to ascertain the extent of damage to the ground floor, where my flat - which faced the front of the building - was located. Heedless of the pandemonium about me, I wandered round the edge of the building on legs that felt shaky and weak as pins, praying to catch a glimpse of Mother or some sign that she had miraculously escaped the fire. But I couldn't even be sure which was our apartment, so thick was the smoke and the confusion. Recollecting how I had locked the front door of our flat on leaving that evening, I fought down my conviction that Mother and Marmalade must have been trapped inside the four small walls.

I wasn't prepared to accept what my head told me was an inescapable truth. In my sudden panic and pain, I ran straight towards the front door of the blazing edifice, ignoring the yells of the people around me who were aware of my suicidal attempt.

When I reached a spot a few feet away from the front entrance the heat of the conflagration was so intense that it almost swept me back against my will, but I was determined not to be stalled. Shielding my face from the searing fire with my arms, I attempted to hurl myself through the door. Just then, strong arms gripped my waist so tightly that all the air was expelled from my lungs, and I was picked up and carried back into the cold, dark street. I stood bent over and coughed for a few moments, wiping my streaming and burning eyes with the back of one coat sleeve.

My rescuer - one of the firemen, an older chap with a weary, careworn face that had witnessed a hundred similar situations - admonished me gently: "That was a stupid thing to do, wasn't it?"

I nodded, dumbly grateful.

"Got someone in there, have you?"

"My mother" I panted, "and my cat."

"Why don't you go and join the others?" the fireman suggested gently, pointing to a group of people standing on the pavement, their eyes trained on the burning apartment block and the efforts of the rescuers. "Everybody's waiting for someone. But it'll take time for us to put this out, maybe a few hours. There's nothing you can do."

"When did the fire start?" I demanded, uncalmed by his attempts to soothe me. "Did anybody escape?"

"Yes, we got quite a few people out. They'll have been taken to hospital. No sense you trying to kill yourself to rescue them. That's what we're here for, isn't it?" He patted my shoulder, encouragingly. "You see that police car over there?" I nodded in mute reply, spotting a blue and white police car with red lights flashing. "There's a chap there with a list of names of the people who've been taken in the ambulance. Your mother's probably one of them. If she's not,

47

we'll do our best to get her out along with everybody else, don't you worry."

I thanked him and walked over to the police car, where a young policeman leant against the side clutching a clipboard with a list of names. When I introduced myself and told him of my plight, the officer looked down his list of residents from our apartment block and was glad to cross my name off as accounted for.

"Have you got a Mrs. Carpenter on your list?" I asked in trepidation.

"Mrs.? That your mum?"

"Yes."

"Yes, she's on the list. Apartment 24 - that right? She's not been crossed off, though. Oh no, hang on a minute." He consulted another list, which was pinned beneath the first, a shorter list with the names marked in red ink. "Oh gosh! Apartment 24 - that's on the ground floor, isn't it?"

I nodded, dreading his next words.

"I'm dreadfully sorry. It was right next to the source of the blast, there. They planted the bomb in the rubbish bins, you see, next to the lift."

I compressed my lips to stop them from trembling. "Is she dead?" My voice sounded choked and hoarse.

The young police officer cleared his throat, and put a hand on my shoulder. "I'm very sorry, miss. It says here a body was retrieved from that apartment, too badly...burned to be identified, I'm afraid. I'm so sorry."

"It's O.K." I whispered, feeling suddenly faint.

"D'you want to sit down a minute? Here - sit in the car, it's a bit warmer in there."

"No, it's all right." I swayed and clutched the side of the car to steady myself. "How did she...? Did you get... anyone else...anything else...out of...? Oh my God!" My legs suddenly gave way beneath me and the policeman caught me before I swooned to the ground.

"Here, sit down." He placed me gently in the driver's seat of the car and knelt down beside me, patting my hand.

I'd been thinking of Marmalade, but the police officer had obviously got the wrong end of the stick: "Just her... wheelchair, was it? It was quite damaged; apparently, the heat must have twisted the metal. I think she was still sitting in it when... Perhaps she'd fallen asleep. I think she would have gone quite quickly."

His words didn't convince me, but I was grateful for his compassion. I breathed deeply and kept seeing the dreadful scene in my mind's eye: my mother sitting in her chair, hearing the screams, smelling the smoke, perhaps hearing the crackling of the approaching fire, and unable to raise herself from her wheelchair, maybe calling out for help to people in the other flats, and Marmalade meanwhile sitting on the window ledge looking out, or maybe crouching under the bed in the knowledge that something terrifying was happening.

My mother was dead. She was dead and gone, killed in the fire. And Marmalade too. They had both died while I'd been at the I.C.A.L. party, perhaps at the very moment that I'd been chatting to Nigel.

I tried to take it in. But nothing seemed real. I couldn't believe any of it.

"Is there anyone you'd like me to call?" asked the policeman.

I shook my head, wondering vaguely why I wasn't crying. Surely I should be crying.

"Do you have anywhere else to go?"

Not knowing how to respond, I made no reply. Perhaps there were places I could go, the houses of friends or relations, but I was unable to make any decisions as to what to do next. I felt as if everything had inexplicably come to a halt and there were no rules for me to abide by, no predetermined plans of action that would help me to know what to do. So I just sat there, shaking my head.

"Well, you can stay here in the car for as long as you like. There is a Bereavement Counseling Service that's been set up for relatives of the victims, if you'd like me to give you the number?"

I nodded dumbly, hoping to stem the tide of solicitous questions, which I had no strength to answer.

I followed him briefly with my eyes and watched him become embroiled in another crisis as two girls ran up to him sobbing and crying hysterically. Although I couldn't hear their words clearly, it was obvious that they were asking if he had news of some friend or relation of theirs, and I realized all at once that there were many other people in the same boat as me and that I had no more claim on the policeman's attention than they had.

I couldn't sit in the police car and keep out of the cold. I couldn't sit down anywhere. I returned to my spot in front of the burning building and stared hypnotically at the leaping flames, half-believing my trance could magic the shape of Mother in her wheelchair to appear silhouetted in the doorway or the prancing form of Marmalade to slink up to my feet and rub his purring fur against my thigh.

But my logical mind was cognizant they were lost for good. I would never see Mother or Marmalade ever again. There could be no mistaking the body the firemen had pulled out of Apartment 24, encased as it had been in the twisted steel of Mother's former wheelchair. And as for Marmalade, the fact that he hadn't been mentioned confirmed my fears that firemen wouldn't bother with a cat, when there were human beings in greater need of their assistance.

Once more I wanted to cry, but no tears would come. I felt numb and separated from my emotions, as if I were acting in a play where nothing touched me in a real way.

Images swam before my eyes, haunting in their intensity, as I tried to make sense of events by enacting what must have happened that dreadful evening in my mind. Mother would have taken her sleeping pills at about ten o'clock, as was her habit. Perhaps not even the sounds of screaming or the smell of fire had broken her slumber. I preferred that version to the one where she awoke in time to appreciate the horror of her danger and the imminence of her demise, knowing that she could do nothing, incapacitated as she was, to break down a locked door.

But my guilt was pricked more at the thought of Marmalade and the part I had played in his destruction. He was a cat - able to fend for himself if I hadn't locked him in the bedroom and closed the windows, thus trapping him inside an incinerator - fit and young and in the peak of condition. He had trusted me and depended on me to protect him and I had let him down. If only I hadn't locked those windows. If only I had left a window open, despite the cold, to give Marmalade a chance to rescue himself. I saw again his face and heard his soft contented purr as I put him down next to his bowl, and my culpability clawed at me with greedy fingers and constricted my stomach, giving me a pain in my heart.

I stood outside the blazing apartment block for two hours, until I finally relented and submitted to a ride in the police van to the hospital, where a kindly young nurse gave me treatment for shock. "Why not go and stay with a friend till the morning," she suggested in a sympathetic voice, as she discharged me. "I'm sorry but we don't have any spare beds, or I'd ask you to stay in overnight. Are you sure you'll be O.K.?" I nodded glumly. I didn't have a friend in mind to contact, but I knew I couldn't stay at the hospital. The whole place was teeming with walking wounded and charred bodies that had been recovered from the wreckage of my erstwhile home.

And now, at last, my weeping began. It seemed that once I had opened the floodgates I was unable to stem the river of tears which streamed inexhaustibly down my face as I wandered the streets that night, attempting to drown my emotions with fatigue, oblivious of where I was going or anything around me.

Finally looking up and taking note of my surroundings, I was surprised to see that it was daylight and I must have been tramping around the center of London in a daze for several hours. I regarded my watch and saw that it was 8.15 am on January 1st, the year 2020. The sight of the date gave me a bitter pang, as I reflected on the significance of the previous night's events, and regretted how much of my joy and hopeful anticipation had turned to misery and pain.

Gazing around me as if waking for the first time that day, I could see I was nearly at Victoria Railway Station and there were huge numbers of people milling about in all directions seemingly uncertain what to do. I wandered inside the station where a male voice was making announcements over the tannoy system, but it was impossible to make out his words over the cacophony of voices. Victoria Station was normally seething with a hectic bustle, but today the atmosphere had a qualitative difference about it. No longer did I hear the buzz of a thousand people with lives to lead, but a warning note of confusion and alarm, chaos and fear. I felt suddenly that I was in a world where all the familiar barriers had been lifted; the safety gates swept away, the rules and guidelines of polite conduct eradicated to reveal the restlessness beneath.

As I hovered in the station foyer beside a newspaper kiosk, I caught sight of a headline proclaiming *Hundreds killed in terrorist attack in Docklands' London*, and I glimpsed a photograph of our apartment block - now a burnt-out shell - which must have been taken earlier that morning. Standing transfixed in front of the picture for several minutes, I could hardly believe that had been my home until a few hours ago. It seemed I had stepped into a nightmare world where anything could happen.

For want of anything better to do I joined a queue of people in the Station Cafe, and had already ordered a cup of tea and a piece of cake before realizing I had no cash on me. The girl at the checkout gave me a hostile glower as I apologized and stumbled out of the building, intending to head for the nearest branch of my bank. The countenances around me in the queue were impenetrable masks, and I felt as though I'd stumbled into a performance where only I was ignorant of the lines.

Quickly finding a cash machine, I inserted my bankcard and punched in my PIN number. My actions were automatic, and my brain seemed divorced from my body as if I were watching all my movements from a great height. *How much do you wish to withdraw?* came the machine's mechanical voice, and I typed in the largest amount I could contemplate. Money didn't matter any more and Life resembled a game of monopoly where nothing had real value. I stuffed the wodge of notes into my purse and retrieved my card. My actions seemed inconsequential and meaningless but I continued, if only because the sensation of movement was the only thing keeping me from desolation.

While at the hole-in-the-wall I spotted a pharmacy across the street, and a thought occurred to me. Stepping out into the busy thoroughfare, I failed to notice the dark blue estate car belting along at speed, which practically knocked me senseless. "Look where you're going, you daft cow!" yelled the driver, swerving to avoid me with a screech of brakes. Too shocked to answer, I ran across the other half of the highway with a palpitating heart, and entered the chemist's shop.

I approached the counter immediately, and waited while the young Asian girl shop assistant served a buxom middle-aged woman in a bright green plastic mac. The woman complained in a strident voice about the shampoo she'd bought the day before which had been incorrectly labeled as being for dandruff and dry scalp when it was for dry hair. With admirable patience, the girl explained to her customer that the brand of shampoo in question didn't market a dandruff formulation, but the woman demanded her money back - turning and looking at me for moral support which I failed to give her, not wishing to draw out the argument by getting involved - and the shop assistant was finally forced to comply. It took an age for the girl to deal with her obstreperous client, and I shuffled impatiently from foot to foot, too distracted to entertain myself by viewing the other articles in the shop.

At last the woman shambled out of the shop, still grumbling under her breath, and I neared the counter. The shop assistant favored me with a weary smile: "Can I help you?"

"Yes thanks." I handed her the prescription my doctor had written me two days earlier, which in the excitement of preparing for the New Year's Eve celebrations I had neglected to fill before now.

"Won't be a moment" the girl said, disappearing momentarily behind the partition to give my prescription to the pharmacist.

While waiting, I regarded the perfume shelf. Having been bombarded by advertising for the new fragrance, *2020* - fantastic computer graphics epics involving people morphing into various dazzling creatures, shown repeatedly on television as an enticement to include the perfume in Christmas stockings and which many of my office colleagues had fallen for, claiming the perfume to be uniquely tangy and fresh - I experimented with a little from the tester on my wrist. I wrinkled up my nose in distaste at the acerbic smell, which didn't appeal to me at all, reminding me as it did of hospitals and men in white suits.

I had just moved over to the shelves stocking facemasks when the shop assistant reappeared, clutching a small white paper bag. "Alice Carpenter" she called out, reading my name from a label on the side of the bag.

I walked up to the counter and extended my hand for the bag. "Thanks. How much is it?"

"£10" the girl replied.

Fumbling in my purse, I located a twenty-pound note, unfurled it and held it out to the girl.

"I'm afraid we've only been able to give you one month's supply."

I stalled before the girl had a chance to take the extended note from my hand: "One month? But the prescription was for six months."

"I know. I'm sorry. I'm afraid we're only allowed to give out one month's supply at the moment."

"But...that's crazy!" I protested. "I need it. My doctor said so."

"I'm sorry," the girl repeated. "There's nothing I can do. We've been given instructions, I'm afraid. One month only for the time being."

"But why?"

The young shop assistant sighed, her brown eyes clouding with anxiety. Perhaps she'd been over this ground already with another customer. "Someone telephoned us this morning. There's a new policy from I.C.A.L. I don't know if you heard about the terrorist attack last night--"

"I heard about it" I interrupted miserably. "I was there. I work at...used to work at I.C.A.L."

"Oh, I see!" the girl exclaimed, clapping her hand over her mouth in embarrassment. "I had no idea." Now she took the note from my still-extended hand and, opening her till, gave me my change and receipt.

"What is this new policy?" I asked. "It must be something very sudden, because I haven't heard anything about it."

"I think it was fairly sudden, yes. Apparently, the whole factory where they manufacture the drugs was blown up last night and the entire stocks destroyed. I'm terribly sorry." She added this last sentence after seeing the look of absolute despair on my face. "Until the company can repair the damage and start manufacturing the drugs again, we're forced to rely on the stocks we keep in the shop, which aren't considerable. There are many more people like you who'll need the drugs and we're going to have to try and spread them around as fairly as possible. You do understand?"

"Yes, I suppose so" I replied, keeping my face downcast.

"I'm so sorry" the girl repeated. "There's really nothing else we can do."

"Do you know when there will be more stocks of the drugs?"

The shop assistant shrugged. "I'm afraid your guess is as good as mine. It depends on how quickly I.C.A.L. can become operational again. Perhaps you should ask somebody there, if you work there yourself."

I nodded glumly and left the pharmacy without another word. Outside, the weak winter sun was warm on my face but I hardly felt it, so preoccupied was I with my despondent thoughts.

The girl assistant probably didn't appreciate the full extent of the damage as I did. I'd seen the I.C.A.L. complex of buildings devoured by flames, knew most of my work colleagues must have been killed. There was no point asking anybody there for further information. There was nobody surviving to ask.

I shuddered at the memory of the devastation I had left behind. How could I go back? There was nothing to go back to.

I returned to the Station Cafe and rested my exhausted body on a hard plastic seat while I tried to think clearly enough to review my situation objectively. I had confidently expected to stock up with six months supply of the I.C.A.L. drugs, which meant six months relative wellness and freedom from symptoms, six months reprieve from the worst effects of my sickness in which to carry out the journey Genevieve had instructed me to take.

I felt desolate at the knowledge that I had just over one month's supply of the drugs. One month! Such a tiny amount of time. And in that month, the only way to save myself was to find the reincarnation of my brother Clair, who would be able to give me the cure for the disease. The task felt overwhelming. Utterly impossible. How on earth could I achieve it?

And yet I had to. What other option did I have? To wait in London until stocks of the drug were replenished, having no idea when that would be, and meanwhile wasting precious time? No, I had no choice but to begin my journey. There was no other way out of my predicament.

At that moment I felt desperate for a cup of tea. It seemed that one small piece of normality would help to calm me down and make me feel whole again. Having plenty of cash with me on this occasion, I ignored the checkout girl's rude stare as I paid her and took my tray back to the table. I must have sat and nursed my cup for half an hour.

Having attempted to spice up the tepid liquid by adding a couple of sugars, in my dazed and clumsy state I dropped my teaspoon on the ground and when I bent to recover it

I saw a ticket lying by my feet. I picked up the small white slip and studied the writing on the paper - *One way to Dover, January 1st 2020, second-class reservation.* The ticket hadn't been punched. I looked around, but could see nobody seeking a lost ticket. I wondered vaguely how the ticket had come to be lying beneath my table.

I reflected that I must take some action. I couldn't sit in the Station Cafe all day drinking tea. I wished I had someone to confide in, a friendly person whose advice to seek.

I thought of my friend Genevieve. She had enjoined me to take a journey. The night before I hadn't believed she meant my travels to start so soon. But what did I have to keep me in London now, with my mother dead and my home gone and my job nonexistent, now that I.C.A.L. had been practically destroyed? Everything had changed, just as I had wished when I'd pulled the chicken-bone.

I had no more idea where to go than a person swept along by the swirling tide. But I did have a one-way ticket to Dover and some money in my purse. So I joined a line of people and almost before I knew it found myself on a station platform and then on a train, standing squashed between banks of jostling passengers, bound for the Coast.

The people around me chattered, but their voices made no sense to me. I watched the English countryside flash past - the green fields and the sweet country villages so seemingly peaceful and serene on this unexpectedly beautiful winter's day - but none of these sights could cheer me now.

Chapter Four

A WAKING GRADUALLY FROM what seemed a deep slumber, I didn't immediately stir myself but lay immobile, enjoying the soothing rise and fall of the boat and the sounds of mingled near and distant voices around me. Flickering open my eyes, I mustered my strength sufficiently to take in my present surroundings, and gathered that I was lying outstretched on a hard plastic bench on deck and that someone had draped a blanket over my body which was insulating me nicely from a keen ocean breeze. Many of the people around me stood looking out at the grey sea and the cloudy sky, unconcerned with my movements.

I wrapped my blanket around me, surprised at how comfortable and rested I felt. I checked the date on my watch and ascertained that it was still the first of January, with the time now five o'clock in the evening. This made me think of New Year's Eve and all that had happened before and after the fateful I.C.A.L. party. When I contemplated the meeting with Genevieve and her mysterious gift, I remembered that I hadn't yet seen inside the box I'd been so keen to open the evening before. Retrieving the object from my inside pocket, I was glad to note that my jacket's waterproofing had kept it miraculously dry and undamaged.

For a few seconds I sat and ran my fingers over the smooth black surface, marveling again at the strange perception of life pulsing from within. Then, with escalating excitement, having no idea what I might find, I lifted up the clasps and opened the box.

On first inspection, the box appeared to house a sort of wooden chess set or scrabble board. Tiny cubes of dark-colored gleaming polished wood - several painted black, two with the letters C and A delicately carved on their surface, and the others plain - were fitted neatly into slots. When I examined the overall pattern more closely, I could see that it was meant to represent a blank crossword puzzle. The glossy wood was so beautifully carved, an intricate design having been etched around the edges of the pattern, I wondered whether the box was an antique. Certainly, it was a unique artifact, and not manufactured in any ordinary way.

Inside the top lid was a pocket made of strong blue cloth, which bulged a little, indicating the presence of something stowed there. I felt inside the pocket and carefully removed its contents: a piece of thick parchment paper creased in half, so that when I unfolded it a Kodak instamatic photograph fell out into my lap. To my disappointment the photograph was completely white, not having developed properly, so I replaced that in the cloth pocket, not wishing to discard anything Genevieve had given me. Then I regarded the parchment paper in my hands. But what I read there - written in ornate calligraphy as beautifully executed as the carved wooden squares - made my heart sink:

1. *Manic Alice helps (a bit) in the cure.*
2. *Sounds like Hugh Garrison is in this race.* (in German)

3. *Just like a family.* (in Italian)
4. *Ridiculously easy to be about right for some time.* (in Nepalese)
5. *Bring out of barbarism, being polite with looks, it is said.* (in Malay)
6. *Get nothing back and it's the beginning of the end - that's a short letter!*

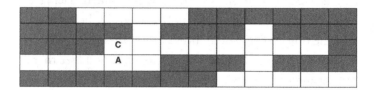

Unable to ignore the acute disappointment I felt at the discovery that this was the entire contents of my precious box, I heaved a sigh of exasperation. None of the "clues", which I had anticipated so eagerly, made any sense to me. I had never completed a crossword puzzle in my life - even those requiring nothing more than ordinary synonyms - and I wasn't proficient in any languages apart from English. The sentences I saw were not only in different languages but even the English ones were obviously and bafflingly cryptic.

I scrutinized the piece of paper and the wooden crossword grid again. Was this really all there was? This was the wonderful magical box, which was going to provide me with the solutions necessary to find my brother? All it consisted of was an incomprehensible puzzle and a damaged photograph. Was this some elaborate joke of Genevieve's? I thought resentfully of my faith in her predictions and my hopeful expectation on the previous evening. Perhaps Genevieve was simply a mad old woman who I'd believed possessed special wisdom because she differed from my other friends.

I gazed gloomily around me at the grey sky and the endless sea and the other passengers chatting to families and friends, and I felt depressed. A sense of my isolation suddenly oppressed me. I had no family, no job, no home, and no friend close enough to support me through my current crisis. What did I have left to me now, apart from this box and the search for Clair? Nothing.

I concluded that - trust in her or not - I may as well go along with Genevieve's instructions for the time being. And so I shook my head free of negative thoughts and resolved at least to make a start on the puzzle.

There were six spaces to be filled. I assumed the six sentences written on the paper were clues to the words, which should fill those spaces. I looked at the two English sentences until my head ached with concentration and the letters danced before my eyes, but no amount of thinking made their import any less obscure.

I felt the weight of bitterness and despondency settle on me once again. If my efforts with these two sentences were so futile, what chance did I have of decoding the clues in foreign languages? Even if I could get all the sentences translated, discover the solutions and insert them correctly into the grid, how would that help me to find Clair? The box was all I had. If it couldn't help me, I had no hope of ever finding my brother, not knowing what he looked like or even his name.

A memory from the evening before tapped me on the shoulder and rebuked me for forgetting it. *What did Genevieve say? His name begins with S and there's an S on his body.*

I recalled the wound-mark the coal had made on Clair's neck and I wondered if he would be marked again in the same way, with a birthmark that would strike me as familiar when I saw it. That was one tiny shred of evidence to go on. It narrowed down the list of potential candidates - to the thousands perhaps, I reflected bitterly - but still gave me no indication of where to begin my search. These unhappy musings reminded me that I didn't even know the destination of the ferry I had boarded.

I carefully replaced the parchment paper in the lid of the box, redid the clasps and returned the receptacle to my inside pocket. There was some consolation in the fact that I no longer felt cold. I threw off the blanket - folding it neatly and putting it on my seat to retain my place - then tottered down the steps below decks, struggling to keep my balance despite the slow rocking of the boat. As I had guessed, there was a map on the wall by the bar, which showed the boat's destination as *Dover to Rotterdam*.

Seeing the name of that town reminded me of Hanneke, a Dutch girl I'd kept in touch with since her days in the I.C.A.L. typing pool who now taught English at a high school there. She'd stayed with us on the Isle of Dogs for a few weeks the previous summer and had been inviting me to visit her ever since. I'd never imagined myself taking up her offer so soon, but now certainly seemed the ideal opportunity.

The thought of my friend cheered me and gave me renewed faith in the fruitfulness of my quest. It was peculiar and fortuitous how events occurred to me without my volition or intervention - the ticket to Dover planted under my seat in the café; the coincidence of this boat going to a town where I knew somebody - as if some guardian angel was extending a helping hand and pointing me in the right direction. Having always been someone who'd worked their life out beforehand with plans and schedules and never strayed from her pre-chosen path, here I was with no fixed destination in mind, knowing nothing about my journey in advance and forced to accept whatever happened to me. But perhaps - I concluded - whatever did happen to me on this journey, while I was dealing with it a solution would come.

It was dark now and a host of stars decorated our night curtain of black sky. I wrapped the blanket around my knees and let the gentle rise and fall of the boat soothe me. My heart felt lighter, now that I had decided at least what the first stage of my journey was to be.

Finding Clair was the most important thing in my life now. Not only because I had missed him so much all these years that I longed and needed to see him again. Not only because my illness gave me only a finite time to survive, and I knew from my experience of the disease's progression that the end would be swift and sudden, like a cat pouncing on prey it has stalked patiently for hours. But because of what Genevieve had told me, that my brother had a message that was important, not just for me but for all the others as well. A message about a cure for the terrible disease, which afflicted practically everyone of my generation in Britain.

Perhaps - having died from Level 3 himself - he had gleaned some knowledge that would help us solve the mystery of the illness: why it normally lay dormant for thirty years before developing into the symptoms which would prove fatal in practically every case; why it was ultimately incurable even despite the drug therapy so successfully manufactured by I.C.A.L.; how it was able to replicate itself so quickly and kill off its host cells so effectively. Many scientists and doctors had grappled with these questions but none had been able to offer a final solution or, ultimately, to save anyone destined to die. People like myself who contracted the disease had given up expecting the medical establishment to save them, relying on the drugs for a temporary respite from the agonizing symptoms while waiting patiently for the inevitable end, preparing themselves with practical resolution for death.

It was late that evening when Hanneke and I finally arrived at her tiny apartment in the center of Rotterdam and I had to reveal to my friend the less-than-palatable circumstances of my visit. When I told Hanneke about the death of my mother, she was at first too shocked to respond and sat staring at me over the rim of her wine glass momentarily transfixed, her lips parted. Silently she put her arms round my shoulders and hugged me, and the gesture released the emotions that must have been pent up inside me since the night of the explosion. I sobbed out my grief at losing my old life and the people and places I'd been attached to, grief mingled with fear at being thrust out so suddenly into an unfamiliar world.

Hanneke was smaller than most of her Dutch compatriots, her straight blonde hair cut in a neat bob to frame her round face. Her habit of pushing her steel-rimmed spectacles up the bridge of her nose when distracted was being used repeatedly this evening, as she offered again to refill my glass. I gladly accepted - believing that drunken oblivion would be one way to ease my suffering, at least only for tonight - and my friend disappeared into her little kitchenette to open another bottle while I absentmindedly scratched the surface of her corduroy sofa with a chewed fingernail.

"You know, you can stay here as long as you like, Alice," she said as she reappeared with more wine and filled my glass to the brim. "I know there's not much room but you're very welcome to the sofa. I'm out all day anyway, so you won't get in the way."

"Thanks" I replied, wiping my nose with a tissue from my pocket. "It's really good of you to put me up...put up with me, I mean. Sorry to dump myself on you with no warning and everything, but--"

"Look - I'm glad to have you here, no need to apologize. It's a good thing you caught me in, actually, because I was supposed to be spending New Year in Delft with my parents but I couldn't stand any more of the family reunion so I came home early. Also, I had to get back to work."

"Isn't it the holidays now?"

"Yes, but I'm going into the school a couple of days a week to do some administration before the children return."

"Wow - what dedication!"

"Oh, not really." Hanneke admitted with a small embarrassed laugh, "I love my work, you know."

"I wish I could say the same."

Hanneke perched in her armchair like a little doll, her feet curled up underneath her and her back as stiff as a soldier. She swished the wine around in her glass, making the ice cubes tinkle together. "You know, I heard something in the T.V. news about your A.L.A. terrorists. I even wondered to myself if you would be O.K. because I knew there was some argument to do with I.C.A.L., but it never occurred to me that they would...that they would go that far."

"Can you believe that I didn't know anything about it?"

"Well, yes I can" Hanneke replied in her customarily serious manner. "It's ironic, but you often know less about what's happening in your own neighborhood than-"

"But I hadn't even seen any reports about it on the news or anything. Other people had. If I'd known I could have been more prepared, maybe moved or something or at least got Mother out of there. But I didn't even read the papers! That'll teach me to take no interest in anything beyond myself..."

"Alice - don't blame yourself. What could you have done?"

"I don't know...something perhaps... It's weird that all this was going on around me and I didn't hear a thing about it, you know? I lived with my head in the sand, with my rose-tinted glasses on... I'm mixing all my metaphors like crazy, but you know what I mean. I can't explain... I just feel sort of responsible, or irresponsible, or something..."

"You're upset, that's all. It's understandable."

"Yes, I suppose so." I gulped some more wine and looked down at Hanneke's apricot-colored carpet.

"Maybe you should have gone to that bereavement counseling thing. It'll be hard to adjust to things, and--"

"Bereavement counseling!" I grimaced at the thought. "I wouldn't know what to say. I don't like those kinds of things, lots of well-intentioned people trying to work out what's in your head or saying what they think you want to hear. No, I'll be O.K. I've got you to talk to, anyway. Thanks for being such a brick." My eyes were starting to fill with tears again and I held them back, berating myself internally for self-pity.

"As I said, you've got a bed here for as long as you want - well, a sofa anyway."

I looked at my friend and smiled. The wine was starting to go to my head and I could feel the dark cloud of my despair lifting and being replaced by a hazy euphoria. I was lucky to have such good friends to fall back on.

"I knew there was something else to tell you. I haven't told you the most important thing...well, kind of the most important thing. I can stay for a couple of days but not for long because I'm going on a sort of journey." I proceeded to relate to Hanneke the story of my meeting with Genevieve and the magical box and my search for Clair - carefully editing out any reference to my Level 3 illness, because I didn't want to burden her with any more of my troubles, plus I had a sneaking suspicion she might try to stop me traveling if she knew I was unwell. As I spoke my friend made no rejoinders and I could see a slight frown begin to develop behind her spectacles, but I went surging on, confident in the belief that she would be infected by my enthusiasm about the journey.

When I'd finished, Hanneke paused a long while before replying: "Are you sure this is the right thing for you to do?" she asked hesitantly.

"Of course I'm sure, I'm absolutely sure. Genevieve told me I have to take this journey and I've got the box, and--"

"Listen, I'm sure Genevieve really cares about you and she believes what she tells you, but how do you know she's right?" Hanneke frowned, adding doubtfully: "It all seems pretty strange to me."

"Yes I know it seems strange, but what else have I got? And I trust Genevieve, I really do. She's not like everybody else, you know, she has a sort of special wisdom." Even as I said it, the words seemed hollow and I wondered if I really believed them myself.

Hanneke shook her head slowly. "You've had a big shock. You want to find your brother because you've just lost your mother--"

"No, it's not like that at all! I wanted to find Clair anyway, I've missed him for years..."

"But he's *dead*, Alice. I'm sorry," she muttered, regretting the harshness of her words. "But he can't come back, you know. He died a long time ago. I know you miss him and everything, but, sometimes people die and you just have to accept it..."

"I *do* accept it. That's not the point." I was starting to feel frustrated at my inability to explain myself to Hanneke. She seemed to be mirroring my own doubts with her skepticism. And I desperately wanted her to believe, so that I could convince myself as well. "I know it seems crazy, but--"

"Yes, it does seem crazy. I'm sorry to be hard on you, but I really think you shouldn't go on this journey. It's pointless."

"It's not" I rejoined listlessly, already half-defeated by my friend's arguments.

Hanneke sat beside me on the sofa and put her arm around me: "I know you want something to cling on to and that's why this box and everything seems so important. But I know that in a few days' time, when you're calmer, you'll realize that it's all a wild goose chase. Don't go rushing off now, when you're all upset. It's not sensible."

I started to sniffle. "Maybe I *could* leave it a few weeks." The more Hanneke talked in her calm and sensible voice, the more I felt foolish for having been seduced into this mad and unpredictable quest. "I might feel better in a little while."

"That's right." Hanneke patted my arm. "You can either stay here with me or you can go home and pick up the pieces. You're going to have to do that sooner or later anyway."

I nodded dismally. "But what about Clair? Do you really think that what Genevieve said was all...wishful thinking. That he's not here at all and he doesn't have a message for me or anything?"

Hanneke sighed and pondered her reply: "I know you loved your brother very much and you miss him. But you'll meet someone else to replace him, I'm sure you will. A nice man."

I giggled. "You sound like something out of *True Romances*."

"You know what I mean. Clair won't come back. People don't come back from the dead."

"Don't you believe in reincarnation, then?"

"No, not really. Do you?"

"I don't know. I thought I did." I rested my head on Hanneke's shoulder. I was so exhausted, I was almost collapsing. I had no more energy left to think or to argue. All I wanted to do was sleep and dream and forget. Hanneke arranged a bed for me on the sofa and that night I slept as soundly as a baby.

Next morning, by the time I awoke Hanneke had already left for work, so I made myself coffee and stepped out into the street, intending to buy myself an *Uitsmater*

(delicious ham and eggs on toast) from a local cafe, to save myself the bother of cooking breakfast. It was a gloriously sunny winter's morning - cold but bright - and the bustle of activity outside refreshed and revitalized me. I knew the route to Hanneke's local cafe, having been given instructions by her the night before, so I set off at a brisk pace.

As I walked, I noticed the bareness of plane trees lining my side of the road. They had a fresh look about them, as if they were newborn and waiting to be clothed in a clean suit of leaves. The main road was choked with traffic, and I hovered on the corner of a side street waiting to cross, thinking about my conversation with Hanneke the night before. Why had I trusted Genevieve and the things she'd told me? To my eyes she'd been a kind of guru, a wise woman with a special fund of knowledge. But looked at from Hanneke's perspective - and probably everybody else's - she was merely a dotty old woman who wore funny clothes and talked about karma. Had I been stupid to put my faith and trust in her?

Just as these thoughts raced through my brain, I glanced across the street and my eye caught sight of a sign over a video shop with a message emblazoned on it in flashing neon lights: TRUST it said in twelve inch high pink letters. I blinked and looked again but it was still there. TRUST it said as it flashed the message to me over and over.

I regarded the other shop signs in the street but they were all in Dutch and unintelligible to me. That was the only English word in the vicinity and it was exactly what I had been thinking about. I shook myself, spotted a gap in the traffic and ran across the street. Peering into the video shop, I saw that it was perfectly ordinary, with a common assortment of movies on display, some American, some English and some international. When I stepped back to look again at the flashing sign it repeated its bizarre motto, and I wondered if Trust was the name of the shop or a movie currently being advertised. At any rate, the coincidence had left me feeling most peculiar.

As I strode on up the street, I was no longer quite so sure of my convictions. Had I been foolish to let myself be persuaded out of my journey by Hanneke and her misgivings? I'd been so sure of myself a few moments ago, and now here I was wavering again. My friend had sown the seeds of doubt in my mind and I had let them lodge there. Far from sticking to my course I had been easily swayed by her well-intentioned but misguided advice.

What could I accomplish by going home and "picking up the pieces" - another flat just like the first (only this time with no Mother or Marmalade for company, and feeling their loss all the more acutely because of old associations and memories), another tedious job like the one at I.C.A.L., a life just the same as before only emptier, a few months to live before my illness claimed me? Stocks of the I.C.A.L. drugs, which were keeping me well, had been decimated in the blast anyway, so there was no reason to be in England for my health.

I had asked for change and change had been granted me. And now, at the first whiff of doubt, I was considering turning my back on my journey, staying in Rotterdam with nothing to do but get in Hanneke's way or heading for home with my tail between my legs.

Perhaps the search for Clair *was* fruitless. Perhaps it was crazy. It was certainly risky and potentially dangerous.

But if I *did* find him, if I *did* find him, it would be worth all the effort.

Dazed by these reflections, my eyes wandered again into the busy street and I saw a car go by with a registration plate, which read: AC 2 TRY. As I stood there thinking how odd it was that yet another word should spring up from nowhere to mirror my thoughts, this time accompanied by my initials, another car went by and the registration plate read: AC 2 GO. This was truly bizarre!

I found the cafe, ordered my *Uitsmater* and sat eating my breakfast, my head lost in a whirl of thought. Again I pondered the magical box and the sheet of paper with the clues. They made no sense to me now. But perhaps - if I were to take them to a crossword expert, or a language expert, or both...?

Half an hour later, I returned to Hanneke's with a firmness in my step that surprised me. Even if I were wrong, I would never forgive myself if I didn't at least try. Hanneke may think me crazy, but she might nevertheless be willing to help me purely out of friendship.

Back at Hanneke's flat, I took the box from its place of safety in my suitcase and gazed again at the beautiful object, its tiny pieces of wood so delicately formed. Surely something that had been so carefully constructed couldn't be all meaningless, all for nothing. I withdrew the instamatic photograph from its place inside the pocket of the lid and held it up to the daylight. To my amazement, there was a distinct change in its appearance. I felt certain that the photograph had been completely white when I'd looked at it before, but now, a darkish stain had appeared in its center.

Noticing that stain - even though I had no idea what had caused it and recognized that there could be a perfectly prosaic explanation - nevertheless seemed the final straw to validate my desire to commence the journey and attempt to find Clair with the clues Genevieve had given me.

To my surprise and relief, when Hanneke returned to the flat having completed her administration work for that day, she didn't continue trying to dissuade me from my resolve. In fact, now that I was so stubbornly fixed on the idea Hanneke acceded to it quite quickly, and was more helpful than I'd anticipated. She gave me the address of a Dr. Hans Becker in Gmunden, Austria, and suggested I visit him for advice on solving the crossword puzzle, saying he was an old friend of the family and she knew he was not only a devotee of cryptic crosswords but also spoke several languages and had a house full of dictionaries. Together we found out the times of the trains and Hanneke rang him immediately to tell him when I'd be arriving the next day.

I thanked Hanneke for her help and promised to be back in a couple of days, after my trip to see Dr. Becker. Later that afternoon we parted at the train station, I carrying my meager belongings (a few clothes hurriedly purchased in Rotterdam, most of my things having been destroyed by the fire, like the rest of my life) in an old suitcase Hanneke had lent me. She wished me well and waved goodbye with what looked like an expression of respect.

I felt sure - at least for the time being - that I'd done the right thing.

CHAPTER FIVE

T HE BUILDING WAS colored a dusky pink, fringed with a band of white. The facade above the upper story was an elaborate series of steps leading to a point and then coming down the other side. I saw that several of the windows on the upper floor had been painted in - not actual windows at all but two-dimensional representations - and the whole effect was to make the house look like some huge cake or a picture from a book of Brothers Grimm fairy tales. I wouldn't have believed anyone could actually live in such a house, if I hadn't seen many others like it in the rest of Gmunden. Gmunden was small and quaint and impossibly clean, with friendly but rather formal inhabitants and an atmosphere of old-fashioned gentility.

I looked a little more respectable now than when I had descended from the ferryboat three days before. With some of my savings from the bank, I'd bought myself traveling clothes in Rotterdam Town Centre before boarding the train for Gmunden, which were smart but comfortable enough for long journeys.

I lifted the brass knocker on the front door - which was in the shape of an owl - and let it fall three times with a hesitant tap. The weather was cold, there was snow on the ground, and I shivered slightly inside my fake fur coat as I waited for the hall light to be turned on and footsteps to approach. I must have waited for about five minutes - shivering and hopping about from foot to foot in my impatience - and then I knocked again, a little louder. Again I waited for what seemed an eternity, but no one inside the house stirred. Hanneke had told Dr. Becker when I'd be arriving and it seemed strange for him to abandon me now, but I concluded that he must after all have forgotten my visit and gone out. I was too cold and impatient to wait any longer and I turned away from the house and prepared to walk back down the street.

Just then, a noise made me turn around and I saw that the door had been opened and a figure stood there. "I'm so sorry. Have you been waiting long? I often don't hear the front door knocker, you know. I'm slightly deaf." The face that greeted me was that of a white-haired man, stocky in build and with a strong bone structure that showed he must have been arrestingly handsome in his youth. When I introduced myself, he beamed me a dazzling smile showing clean white teeth, clasped my hands in his and shook them warmly.

"I thought you must have gone out," I explained.

"Oh certainly not, when I am expecting visitors. But come through, come through. Are you feeling the cold? We are having quite an Austrian winter this year."

Dr. Becker had obviously noticed my shivers. He took my coat - which was wet with melted snowflakes - and hung it on the coat stand in the hallway. As he ushered me into what he referred to as the "music room" at the front of the house overlooking the street, I was aware that the air was full of a continuous thrumming noise I couldn't identify. I gazed around me and saw to my amazement that the whole house was full of birds. They occupied every available space, every ledge, every tabletop, every arm of every chair. Every windowsill held a bird of a different plumage or hue, carelessly preening or scratching or flapping its wings. The sound I heard was the constant rustle of a hundred birds, each occupied with some small personal movement, and their various tweets and cries to each other.

I looked about me in wonder and couldn't hide my surprise from my host. "This is amazing! I've never seen so many birds."

"It's my fetish I'm afraid" said Dr. Becker, in his careful Germanic voice, still smiling and waving me into an armchair. "You will have to - ha! - adjust." The ha! was a bark of laughter that sounded like a snort, with which he threw himself into the chair opposite mine.

"And now" he said, lacing his fingers together and leaning forward with relish, "Hanneke told me you have some little problem with the languages - is that correct?"

"Oh yes, I was hoping you could help" I said, eagerly withdrawing the precious box from my bag, ready to show him. "I don't know any languages at all, you see. They tried to teach me in school but I just didn't have any aptitude. And now, I have to translate these sentences. And then fit them all into a crossword puzzle. It's ever so difficult, so I'm sure I can't do it on my own..." I was gabbling in my excitement and pleasure at meeting someone who could potentially help me.

"And I am the language expert" he said, with a self-mocking smile that contradicted the conceit of his words.

"Well, you know, I have many dictionaries here from all different languages, but I only speak German, English, French, Italian and Spanish. It is not so much, after all. I am not quite the language expert that Hanneke is so kind to call me." As he said this, Dr. Becker was cleaning an old pair of spectacles he'd taken from a case in his pocket and placing them carefully on the bridge of his nose. "But it is true that I find languages fascinating."

"I'm glad you find them fascinating because I don't at all" I admitted, as I extracted the sheet of parchment paper with the clues on it from inside the box's lid and handed the paper to the professor. I had been going to say I thought learning languages was a stupid waste of time when everybody spoke English anyway, but I considered that might be tactless so I held my tongue and waited for my host to regard the paper.

"Ah yes, I think you will find that if I cannot solve your little problem..." Dr. Becker didn't bother to finish his sentence, but took the paper from me and began to peruse its contents. After a few seconds he said "hmm" in an interested manner, took off his spectacles and breathed on them, wiped them with a large grubby handkerchief from his pocket and replaced them on his nose. I sat chewing my nails and tapping one foot absentmindedly on the ground, as I looked around me at the birds and the peculiar old-fashioned furniture in the room.

When the professor had finished, he removed his glasses and looked up at me. "This is very, very interesting," he said slowly. I suddenly had the urge to laugh - the combination of his seriousness and the Austrian accent made me think of Henry Gibson in *Laugh-In* - but I restricted myself to curling the corners of my mouth. I was nervous about what he was going to say, because I needed his help so much.

"I don't think I've seen anything quite like this before. You will forgive me if it takes a little time?"

I nodded, feeling a little thrill of excitement run through me. "So, it does make some sense to you, then?"

"Why yes, of course, naturally. You see what we have here" he said, coming over to me and sitting on the edge of my chair - dislodging a squawking cockatoo as he did so - his ebullience giving him the agility of a man half his age, "is simply six sentences written in six different languages: the first is English, which you can see for yourself. The second is German, the third Italian, the fourth Nepalese, the fifth Malaysian and the last one English again."

I looked at him with some admiration, impressed with the speed with which he'd recognized the languages.

"The second and the third I can translate for you immediately, the fourth and the fifth may take some work. But certainly, I can have all the sentences for you in English within one hour."

"That's great!"

"But this is most intriguing. Can I ask you where you got this?"

"It was given to me by a friend of mine. She says it's some sort of riddle I have to solve."

"Yes, obviously it is a riddle. She must be a very intelligent woman, your friend."

I nodded, pleased to hear Genevieve thus respected. I wondered briefly what had become of her during the terrorist attacks, and whether she was still in London, although I couldn't imagine any harm coming to my friend.

"But I am forgetting my manners. You must be both hungry and thirsty. Did you eat anything on the train?"

"I didn't actually. I suppose I was too excited. But you're right, I'm absolutely starving." Hunger had made me forget politeness for a moment. As if in answer to my words, my stomach grumbled and complained.

Fortunately, Dr. Becker was charmed by my impetuosity, and he promised to provide me with a substantial lunch. I was left alone in the music room for a few minutes while he went to instruct his housekeeper to prepare me some refreshments. Later, he came back with a silver tray containing a pot of strong coffee, thick cream, dark bread, sliced wurst and cheese, and Bavarian chocolate cake. I helped myself to all these things with gusto, while Dr. Becker retired to his study to look up words in reference books. As I ate, a large black crow settled itself on the table and pecked experimentally at some of the food. I shooed the bird away and it flew to the other side of the room with a disgruntled squawk.

The atmosphere was pleasant in this room, and I had now got so habituated to the noise of the birds that I hardly noticed their presence. A collection of instruments occupied one corner, and I approached them to take a closer inspection. The largest instrument was an old-fashioned harpsichord, beautifully inlaid and with carved wooden legs. I touched one of the keys experimentally and was surprised by the sharp but sweet sound. I was used to electronically produced sounds rather than the real thing, and the only instrument I'd ever seen before was the synthesizer we'd played with at the Youth Club in my teens. Next to the harpsichord stood a large harp, and again I couldn't resist giving one of its strings a tentative twang. I was entranced by these things, which were completely novel to me. They looked so cumbersome and awkward to play and yet they produced such a delicate almost ethereal noise.

I felt sad that I'd never been interested in music before, or even considered it important. Music was heard as a sort of background to other events - like the taped muzak in department stores or the accompanying music in films that added atmosphere - but I'd never listened to music simply for the sake of hearing it. And my chances of learning to play an instrument at school had been passed up as boring without a second thought.

I decided that I could while away some time now by attempting to play the harpsichord. So I searched among the books of sheet music, which lay on top of a table until I found something, which appeared to be a simple set of guidelines. Of course the writing was in German so I couldn't read the instructions, but it did have pictures of the keyboard and little cartoons of fingers pressing the keys in sequence. I struggled for several minutes to make sense of the book - prodding each key with an experimental finger and getting a cold, blank noise - and then I gave up in exasperation. It was no good; I could never learn to play like this.

Just then, a yellow canary came and perched on the back of the harpsichord and launched into a full-throated song, which seemed directed at me. The sound was sweet and very beautiful. It cocked its head on one side when it had finished, as if to enquire whether I'd appreciated its efforts, and then began again to sing the same song. Sitting at the keyboard, I threw the instruction book on to the table and attended the birdsong with pleasure. As the canary sang, I tried to imitate its notes on the harpsichord, using the sounds to guide me. And this time, I produced a tune! A simple tune perhaps, but quite definitely a tune. For the first time in my life, I felt that the world of music didn't have to remain closed to me. I could appreciate it and even participate in it.

I was about to examine the other instruments - feeling excited and happy like a child with a new toy - but at that moment Dr. Becker returned, clutching the parchment paper I'd given him. His expression seemed to have turned serious, and he shook his head slightly as he re-seated himself in the armchair with a sigh.

My heart sank, my elation of moments before quickly evaporating. "What's the matter? Can't you translate the clues? Do you need some more time with it or something?"

"It is not going to be possible to translate all the sentences completely. I hope you will forgive me. I have tried my best, but..."

"You did translate some of them, then?" I asked hopefully, sitting opposite the professor as before.

"Oh yes, of course, the German and Italian were no problem at all, and the English sentences are self-explanatory. But the two middle sentences - well I must admit to you that my knowledge of Nepalese and Malaysian is fairly rudimentary. I can get a general idea of what they are trying to say, but that is not good enough for the purpose. All the sentences must be precisely translated, because they are clues in the crossword puzzle. Were you aware that...?"

"The whole thing's a cryptic crossword? Oh yes. Which is why I can't understand why Genevieve gave it to me, because she knew...she knows I don't know how to do crossword puzzles."

"So." Again, this was a bark, like a command. "I can help you thus far and no further. I am sorry. But at least I have been of some assistance. The first three sentences may even have some bearing on the others. It is up to you to find the answers, and then we shall see."

"But--" I was beginning to feel distraught at the thought that this was all the help I might get, and now I would have to deal with the puzzle alone. "Can't you help me to solve the clues? I mean, that's the bit I don't understand. What do they mean?"

Dr. Becker cocked his head to one side and looked at me pityingly, reminding me for a moment of one of his beloved feathered friends: "I will do all I can to help you, but I think you must solve the clues yourself. They have been written for you, I feel. After all, is not your name in the first one - Manic Alice helps a bit in the cure?"

I nodded miserably. "Yes, my name's in the clue but I still don't understand how I'm to solve it. It's all just words to me, jumbled up and senseless."

"Nothing is senseless. There is meaning in everything - we have only to find it" he replied with the air of one making an important pronouncement about life. "Take each word separately and then together, and then the meaning will come to you - how do you say it? - *clear as daylight*."

Dr. Becker laughed at this attempt at an English idiom, but I was in no mood for jokes. I put my hand out for the paper with a sullen expression.

My host hung on to the paper, smiling teasingly: "This first word, *manic*, often indicates that the word following is an anagram - that is to say, the letters have been turned around to form a different word. The secret there is to write out the word in a circular formation and see what other word could come from it."

I frowned and nodded my head, trying to remember these instructions. "How did you know that *manic* meant anagram? Is it the only word that means anagram?"

"No, there are many words which may indicate this... words which suggest disorder of some kind such as...let me think of them in English - crazy, stupid, mad, ridiculous, stirred up - can you say this?"

"Yes, I see what you mean. But how do you *know*?"

"You don't know for certain, but you guess that this might be the case and you proceed from there. So! In this case, *manic* suggests that the word *Alice* has been jumbled. But after Alice we have *a bit*, so maybe it is just a part of the jumbled *Alice* that we are searching for. Do you see?"

"I think so." My head was beginning to spin. "And the answer will be something to do with me, will it?"

"I believe so, since this is no ordinary crossword. It has been made specially for you and therefore the answers will have relevance for you alone."

I suppressed a yawn, not wishing to appear impolite. I had suddenly become very tired. Dr. Becker handed me the parchment paper, and I saw that he had inserted English words beneath the German and Italian sentences in a small, neat hand.

"Thanks ever so much for doing this for me" I said, suddenly aware of my debt to him. "Is there anything I can do to repay you? I mean, I don't have much money or anything, but perhaps - I don't know - there's some job I could do for you or something?"

"No, not a job. But perhaps there is something you could fetch for me, if you can find it."

"Yes, of course. Name it" I replied confidently, thinking the doctor meant to ask me for some particular brand of English tea or something.

"As you see, I am a lover of birds" Dr. Becker said, waving to indicate the flying beasts with his hands.

"Yes, you certainly have quite a collection."

"But there is one bird I do not have, and it has such a sweet song. I heard it once on a recording made by a great ornithologist who captured many bird songs from all over the world. I think it would not be an exaggeration to say that I fell in love with this bird and its song. And I would so like to have one - or two, in fact - to join my aviary here. It is a particular kind of magpie, the Australian magpie. I do not know what the Latin name is, but it is a rather large bird with glossy black and white wings."

As soon as he said the word magpie, I ceased to listen to him. I was so amazed that my host had mentioned the very bird that had a particular relevance for me. Perhaps it was this that made me so enthusiastic in my desire to help him: "I will try to find you one. I really will. And I'll find some way of getting it back to you here."

"But if you cannot, don't worry. It is not strictly necessary to repay me, in any case. I enjoy translation and since my retirement there is little for me to do." As if in response, a large black crow came and settled on his shoulder and cawed imperiously. Dr. Becker scratched the bird's head with an affectionate gesture. "This is Mahler. He is quite a character. Did he try to steal some of your food?"

I nodded my head and laughed, remembering my irritation when the bird had pecked at my chocolate cake: "Does he usually?"

"It is his usual habit, yes. Some guests find it disconcerting." And at this, Dr. Becker let out a great gust of laughter, as if at the memory of some particularly embarrassed recipient of Mahler's attentions.

It was after leaving Dr. Becker's house that I began to feel depressed and conscious of my loneliness in this solitary pursuit. It was the first time in my life that I'd ever been truly alone, and the full force of it hit me with a cold sensation that seemed to trickle through my body.

I crossed a little bridge over a river. I walked back to the railway station through the snow - which had started softly falling again, giving the evening a muffled stillness - and as I passed the little houses I glanced through lighted windows and envied the people inside with their lives secure like a blanket around them. I had nothing - no family, no job, no friends to share my journey - only a box and a piece of paper, which held the key to a dream, which would maybe elude me. My life was a big empty void, with no comforting routine to fill it. And the only person to make the decisions was me.

My heart started palpitating quickly and my hands shook. I'd never felt like this before, anxious and frightened for no reason. There was no monster pursuing me, no immediate danger. And yet I felt afraid of everything, almost of life itself. It was the loneliness and the sense of rootlessness that were disturbing me. The perception that there was no one to share my journey and no knowledge of its outcome.

I concluded that if I could at least sit down somewhere in the warm, that would comfort me for the time being. I began to look around me for a place that was open, but many of the shops had darkened doors and windows. It seemed that most of the little town had retired for the evening. But the street was crisscrossed with fairy lights, which twinkled their friendly welcome in the dusk. I looked at my watch and saw that it was five to eight. The hour wasn't late and I guessed I would still have plenty of time to catch a train when I was ready to leave Gmunden, so I wandered into the single coffee shop that was still open, and ordered a *Heisse Chokolade mit schlag.* I had little idea of what would be served me, and was pleasantly surprised when the smiling, white-aproned waitress returned with a huge mug of hot chocolate topped with a mountain of thick cream.

Sustenance revived my spirits considerably, and I took out the piece of parchment paper from the pocket in the lid of my box and resolved to attempt the first clue, following Dr. Becker's advice: *Manic Alice helps (a bit) in the cure.*

I wrote out the word Alice in a circle, in biro pen on my napkin, much to the waitress's amusement. Remembering Dr. Becker's instructions, it would be some of the letters in *Alice,* which would make up the new word. But how was I to tell which ones? Did it mean that the answer to the clue was something to do with *cure* - with *helping in the cure*? And why would that be relevant to me?

I rolled the sentence around and around in my head for over an hour, meanwhile sipping my drink impossibly slowly to make it last. The waitress kept glancing curiously in my direction to see if I'd finished yet. I was the only other person in the cafe. But I didn't let her consternation bother me.

Then - in a flash of lateral thinking - the answer came to me. My sense of joy and achievement was so great that I smiled hugely and let out a "Yes!" of triumph. The waitress looked at me aghast. I wrote down beside the sentence: ICAL. It was the only possible solution. The letters were contained in my name, and they stood for a company that helped with finding cures for diseases, Level 3 being one. And it made perfect sense, since I.C.A.L. was the company I'd worked for all my working life. So perhaps Dr. Becker had been right and all the clues would have some similar personal connection.

I felt an enormous sense of relief. If I'd solved one clue, I might be able to solve them all. It would take time, but I could do it.

The only question now was where to fit my word into the grid. I opened the box and lay it carefully on the table, studying the order of little wooden blocks so intricately carved. My first word obviously had to go in one of the three four-letter spaces. I didn't know which, but at least I'd made significant headway by successfully completing the first clue. I drew a representation of the grid on my napkin and filled in all three possible spaces with the word in pencil, just in case it would help with the other clues.

I was glad I'd made the decision to come to Austria and meet Dr. Becker. But now that I had got the advice from him and solved the first clue, I had a feeling of anti climax. I was returning to Rotterdam to stay with Hanneke. But what would I do there? And how would I continue to solve all the clues on my own, not to mention getting the Nepalese and Malaysian clues translated? I realized I hadn't really considered what I would do after meeting Dr. Becker, I had expected him to solve all my problems at a stroke and all my future plans had ended with meeting him. Perhaps that had been the reason for my panic attack earlier. I felt all alone now in my quest and I literally didn't know which direction to take.

Well, I would return to Rotterdam and try to solve all the clues, which would maybe give me an idea of where to search for Clair. At least my friend was waiting for me. I would simply see what happened next and let Fortune guide me. After all, what else could I do? I replaced the paper with the clues back in the lid of the box and put the box in the inside pocket of my jacket. I liked to keep the box there because it felt safe.

I paid for my drink and left, stepping out into the cold street with a warm stomach and renewed optimism. If I could solve one clue, I could solve them all. And all the words together would give me the answer I was seeking, the clue to Clair's identity and whereabouts.

I strode into the railway station and consulted the big departures board, to see when the next train to Rotterdam was due. I consulted the map of Austria and its adjacent neighboring countries on the wall, and saw that the next train for Rotterdam was leaving in ten minutes time, at 9.30 pm. I'd been lucky to get here just in time to catch it. I decided to buy a ticket for a second-class sleeper compartment.

There was a little queue outside the ticket office, and as I waited I became increasingly worried that I would miss my train. I didn't know how to say *please could you hurry up or I'm going to be late* in German so that the others would understand, so I gave worried glances around me, sighed heavily and tapped my foot on the ground. The lady in front of me seemed to get the message, because she moved aside and indicated that I should go ahead of her, saying something in German in a strident voice. I was grateful, but I didn't even have enough time to thank her properly. I bought my ticket and ran on to the platform.

There was a train either side - both about to depart - and I ran towards the one on the left. I caught a glimpse of the first two letters of the train's destination, Rotterdam on the front of the train - the rest being obscured by a large advertising placard with a picture of a fizzy drink on it - and I leapt into the first carriage just as the guard blew his whistle and the engine started to pull out of the station.

I felt relieved and elated. Everything was going according to plan.

CHAPTER SIX

WHEN I AWOKE it was still dark, and the rhythm of the train, like the steady beating of a heart, began to slow. I raised myself on two elbows and shook my head to clear the sleep from my brain. The compartment was in semi-darkness, only a shaft of light projecting underneath the door from the corridor outside. I peeled the sheet and blanket away from me and let my legs dangle down over the lower bunk bed. I couldn't remember if anyone else was sleeping there, but no noise such as snoring or deep breathing suggested a fellow occupant of my berth.

Carefully, I put one toe on to the rim of the lower bed and eased myself down to the floor. The train rumbled and juddered on, but a few flashes of light slipping through the drawn blinds at the window indicated that we were approaching a station. I pulled aside one curtain and peered out. Sure enough, I could see ahead of us the lights of a station platform. As we drew closer to the station, I was surprised to see a lot of people waiting for our train, most of whom clutched a quantity of suitcases, giving the impression that they were long-distance travelers.

The train shuddered to a halt and I strained to read the name of the station we had arrived at. It was not a name I recognized. I thought I'd made a mental note of the major towns we'd pass through before Rotterdam, but I had no recollection of this place.

A shuffling behind my head alerted me to a stranger's presence and I turned around. The light from the station coming through the window illuminated the figure of a man, who had sat up in the lower bunk bed. I wondered how I'd failed to notice him before. "Good evening" he said politely in a soft voice with a slightly Australian accent. He was wearing a suit and hadn't bothered to pull the bedclothes over him as he slept. I couldn't make out much about his appearance, but from his voice I deduced that he was in his thirties or thereabouts.

"Hello. We're pulling into a station, but I'm not sure where it is."

"Are we at St Polten?"

"Yes" I replied, surprised that he should know. The man reached into a capacious traveling bag by his side, pulled out a packet of cigarettes and proceeded to light one. "Are you traveling far?" he asked in a conversational tone.

"To Rotterdam."

"Rotterdam?" It was his turn to sound surprised. Then he gave a sort of low laugh, which was odd, because he didn't explain what he found funny about this. "I think you may be on the wrong lines."

"And you?" I asked, not understanding what he meant by his last comment and therefore ignoring it.

"I'll get off at the last stop" the man replied cryptically, puffing on the cigarette and sending up a cloud of bitter-smelling smoke into the room.

I found his attitude bemusing, so returned my gaze to the people on the platform, who had now started getting on to the train with a noisy banging of doors and shouting of departures to their friends. "Why are there so many people at this time of night?" I wondered aloud.

"It's not so late," responded the man behind me. "Seven o'clock or so."

"Seven? It must be much later - we left Gmunden at 9.30." But to my amazement, when I looked down at my watch, I saw that it was indeed seven o'clock.

"That's right," said the man, unconcerned by my confusion. "We've been traveling for about two and a half hours."

"Well then" I said, turning to him, "it surely must be about midnight by now, if we've been going for two and a half hours." I wondered briefly if my watch had stopped. But no, I had looked at it in Gmunden and read the time before boarding the train.

"No" the man replied firmly. "9.30 minus two and a half hours is seven o'clock, isn't it?"

"Minus?" I gasped.

"Of course" he said, smiling at me reasonably, "we're traveling backwards, aren't we?"

I couldn't think of anything to say to this, but stood staring at him stupefied. The man was talking complete nonsense. And yet, when I looked out of the window at the station clock, it also read seven o'clock. What on earth was going on?

"What day is it?" I queried.

"Wednesday."

"And we set off on Wednesday?"

"Of course." The man was so serene in the face of my mounting frustration, that I was tempted to believe I was the one who was mad. "Haven't you ever traveled backwards before?" he enquired affably.

"No!" I spluttered.

"It should be obvious that we're traveling backwards, if you look at the map." My companion pointed to a map on the wall, which showed the whole of Austria, with the train lines marked out in red. "We're on the train from Vienna to Rotterdam via Gmunden, right?"

I nodded, dumbly. He ran his finger along the appropriate red line. "Here. You got on the train at Gmunden at 9.30 and we've pulled into St Polten at seven o'clock." The place he pointed to was north of Gmunden on the way to Vienna. "The train has been going backwards, in time and location. Is that clear now?"

"But how will I get to Rotterdam?"

He seemed to think my question odd. "That's what I wanted to ask you. If you're heading for Rotterdam, why did you get on a train traveling backwards? It makes no sense. You're on the wrong lines, as I said."

"The guard said this was the Rotterdam train. At least, I think he did. He said platform five, and I got onto the train on platform five. That must have been right. It must be the Rotterdam train."

"Sure - it's the Rotterdam train going backwards. You should have got on the Rotterdam train going forwards, shouldn't you." He pointed again to the map, and I stared at it miserably, trying to come to terms with what he'd told me. I reckoned I'd been made to look a complete fool. And yet I'd behaved perfectly rationally, in my opinion.

As I gazed at the map, the towns and colors began to blur and I felt myself drifting off into a sort of sleep. Then I heard a loud pounding on the door.

With a jerk, I opened my eyes. The compartment was bright with early morning sunshine, and I was lying in my bunk bed. My heart thudded with the shock of realization that I'd been dreaming and this was reality. The door opened and a young guard in a pristine uniform poked his head around the corner: "Guten Morgen, fraulein" he said, smiling at my disarray. "It is seven o'clock in the morning. We are arriving at Villach in a few moments."

"Thank you" I said, quickly composing myself and returning his smile. He closed the door again. I felt so disorientated by my recent dream that I hardly knew which way was up. The place he'd mentioned didn't sound familiar to me, but almost anything seemed possible now.

I let myself down to the ground and looked out of the window. Somebody must have drawn the curtains earlier - the guard possibly - and I was the only person in the compartment. I remembered my dream and looked down at my watch. To my relief, this time the fact that it read seven o'clock made perfect sense.

Remembering another part of my dream, I looked at the map on the wall, trying to avoid catching sight of my sleepy face in the mirror beneath it. The lines were marked in red showing the destination of the train, just as in the dream, but the legend by the side of the map read not *Vienna to Rotterdam via Gmunden* as I'd expected, but *Vienna to Rome via Gmunden and Villach*. I traced the line with my finger as it headed downwards on the page, not northwards back to familiar Rotterdam but southwards to Italy. Villach lay on the southern edge of Austria in the Sud-Tyrol, almost in Italy. So that was where we were.

I realized with a shock the mistake I'd made the night before, in my confusion and hurry. Rather than getting on the train bound for Rotterdam on platform five, I had jumped on the train bound for Rome on the opposite platform, not stopping long enough to check the destination.

I could see through the window that we were indeed approaching Villach. Like everything in Austria, it seemed, the station was clean and pretty in a quaint old-fashioned way, as if it had materialized from the pages of a child's picture book and had no contact with the modern world of skyscrapers and crime.

Well, if I'd made my bed - so to speak - now I would have to lie in it. Perhaps the dream had been trying to tell me something, that I was not meant to go backwards but forwards. Not into the past, but into the future, however uncertain. At any rate, I had arrived at Villach and I didn't want to go any further for the time being. I resolved to get off the train and explore this place and see what happened.

To my surprise, I felt excited and happy and no longer anxious. I couldn't remember having felt such vigor since I was a child. It was as if I felt sure that whatever happened, I would be all right. The unexpected was no longer a burden to be borne, it was positively thrilling. A new adventure was just beginning. And I couldn't wait to pursue it. I grabbed my bag and quickly brushed my hair, splashed my face with water from the sink in the corner and patted my cheeks with a towel. Then I gathered my things and exited to the corridor, looking out at the scenery as we slowly approached the station.

When I left the train, I was surprised at how few other people there were. The air was crisp and fresh like new linen sheets. The mountains shone grandly in the distance. I saw on the information board that the next train for Rotterdam didn't come through the station for several hours. Then I dismissed my idea of going back so soon. I may as well stay in Villach for a few days, as it looked like a pretty place. Hanneke would always be in Rotterdam when I wished to return. I could easily call her and say I'd changed my mind. And this was an adventure, wasn't it? I didn't want to go backwards any more, did I? I wanted to go forwards, to new places and new experiences.

I strode into the little tourist office adjacent to the station and asked about places to stay. I liked the feel of Villach. The travel agent asked me if I'd mind staying in an old monastery that had been turned into a hostel for women. The women were part of a self-sufficient commune and they had a few rooms to spare for passing travelers. It was a very beautiful location, he said, by the shores of a lake. I said I thought that would be ideal.

CHAPTER SEVEN

THE AIR AROUND me was frosty white and it burned my nose and throat when I inhaled. Beneath my feet, tiny splinters of ice were cracking with the sound of impermanence: I was literally standing on thin ice. My legs tingled with the fear of imminent danger and the image of a rent forming suddenly into a gaping hole, which swallowed my body with freezing water, death's hands gripping me and holding me rigid. So I tiptoed across the ice sheet, giggling and clutching Sophia's hand.

Sophia was a tall girl, with a strong athletic body, straight sandy blonde hair cut short and an open face with blue eyes that looked on the world with no hesitation. Her voice was soft and high, but not shrill, and she had a ready laugh. The images conjured for me when I looked at Sophia were like something out of a muesli commercial - clean bright winter days, tall white-capped mountains and rosy cheeked chubby children playing with sledges in the snow. Her outgoing and generous personality surrounded me with its warmth, and the way she pronounced my name - "Elliss" - bestowed on me the perception of being somebody special, foreign and out of the ordinary, which was pleasantly unfamiliar to me.

We ran back to the shores of the lake - tiptoeing over the slippery surface, our hearts racing - till we reached the edge and pulled ourselves up on to the bank by clinging to the branch of a strong tree. We staggered through a tangle of woodland until we reached the road - lined with tall pine trees resembling a Christmas card - that led up to the monastery. From the road we could see the outline of the monastery in the distance, its white and gold blending with the pale winter sky. In the other direction, huge craggy mountains white with snow, jutted into the sky.

As we trudged up the path - thinking of the hot *gluhwein* and thick pea soup to be served for lunch that day - I felt warmed from my exertions and the company I'd found. The pine trees around us gave off a sharp resinous smell, and I breathed in the odor like a perfume. It was amazing how good it felt to be walking in the clear, open air amongst the clean-smelling pines. In my enthusiasm, I stopped for a moment and stroked the bark of a nearby tree, enjoying the sensation of its knobbly surface along my fingertips. Then I wrapped my arms around the trunk and hugged the tree lightly, drawing in its substance and strength. I couldn't remember ever having been this close to nature before. It felt at once strange and oddly familiar, as if I'd just come home after many years away in a foreign land.

Sophia laughed at my antics and called me a "city girl". She walked ahead, kicking up the snow with her big boots. It was a slight struggle to keep up with her as she strode out confidently, unaware that my illness made me weak and easily breathless. I hadn't yet mentioned to Sophia and the other women that I had Level 3. I didn't want sympathy and pitying looks barely disguised, as if I were dead already, and was determined to live my life like a normal person for as long as I could.

I had told Sophia something about Clair and the reasons for my journey. I could tell from her blank response that she didn't fully comprehend, but she'd tried to appear sympathetic: "So this brother you are seeking" she had said, "is he not some kind of a kindred spirit? A soul mate? Is that what you say?"

"Well, sort of, but he's also my brother."

"How can he be your brother if your brother is dead?"

"Do you believe that people can return to life in another body?"

Sophia had given me a quizzical look at this point, as if unsure whether to judge me crazy or merely misguided: "I've never thought about it. It's enough for me to think about this life, without considering any others there might be." And she'd given her hearty laugh and changed the subject.

But perhaps she'd been giving some thought to what I'd said. We were trudging up the hill, our footfalls muffled by the soft snow, and I was watching my breath form little clouds of mist in the cold air, when Sophia asked impromptu: "Do you not even know what his name will be?"

"Who? Clair?"

She nodded.

"Not the same name" I said, gasping a little. I had to talk in short sentences, to catch my breath, and my voice fell torpid on the still, afternoon air. "Maybe...I don't know... Steven? Stuart? Genevieve said...his name... will begin with S."

Sophia put her head on one side and smiled. "With S. There must be many people in the world whose names begin with S. And you're not even sure...with an S? Hey, it could be me - Sophia!" I chuckled, not taking this suggestion seriously, and watched as Sophia scraped a line of snow off a branch as we passed, formed it into a small ball and flung it high and far into the air. We watched the ball crash to the ground a few yards ahead of us. "Really - he may be a woman now. Had you thought of that?"

I considered this for a few moments and we walked on in silence. I stumbled over a fallen tree branch in the path, losing my footing, and Sophia put out her hand to steady me. "A woman?" I replied. "You know...I can't imagine... him being a woman...but I suppose it's possible. It never occurred to me. Not really. I had thought, but... I don't think so. I don't know why. But I think...he'll be a man. Genevieve said...he might look different, though. So I don't know what to expect."

Sophia pushed back her short hair from her face with one hand and I noticed abstractedly how red and large her hands were: they looked like workmen's hands. "Oh Elliss! What if you meet him and you don't know it's him? How will you recognize him?"

"I don't know." I turned to my friend and shrugged. Perhaps Sophia thought my search was absurd. Perhaps everyone did. But I had to look; it was all I had left. "You think I'm mad, don't you?" I said with a self-deprecating grin.

"I don't know, not mad. But it just seems to me impossible, to find someone when you don't know what is his name or what he looks like."

"I've got the clues, though" I said, attempting to bolster my confidence and ignore the sinking feeling in my heart that Sophia may be right.

"Oh yes. I meant to tell you. I thought of someone in the group who might be able to help you with the clues" Sophia informed me thoughtfully.

"Really?" Stirrings of hope prickled in my chest.

"Renata. She is very intelligent. An...intellectual." Sophia had to search for the word. "She speaks several languages. I'm not sure which ones, but certainly Italian as well as German and English. And she also does the cross words."

"Great! Could you introduce me?"

"She's not here today. I remember she had to go to Munich to visit her parents. But I think she's back tomorrow. I will ask Uta."

The next day, Sophia was as good as her word and introduced me to Renata at breakfast. She was an older woman with a large-boned, rather expressionless face and a stoical manner. I took to Renata at once and decided I liked her. But we only exchanged a few sentences before she had to leave for her yoga therapy group, which she was giving to some of the other women in the main hall. I had time, though, to show her briefly the paper with the clues and she nodded her head in a characteristically deliberate way and said she would speak to me about it afterwards.

Later on that morning, as I was walking in the beautifully tended garden behind the old monastery, which housed the women's commune, I came across Renata weeding a patch of hard dry ground, which she'd cleared of snow.

"Hello" I exclaimed in greeting, surprised and pleased to see the older woman here. "I didn't realize you did the gardening."

"Yes, it is my, how do you say? Special task. We all have to do something to help with the commune's activities, and I volunteered for the gardening. I like very much working in the ground; it is very therapeutic, no? And you can be outside in the fresh air." She rose and stretched her large arms behind her back with a grunt.

"Even if it's rather cold," I suggested.

"I don't mind the cold. Not when I have on my warm jacket."

Renata seemed the type of woman who could happily climb Mount Everest in a snowstorm without complaining. "What are you going to plant in that patch?" I asked, not really interested but wanting to please her with conversation.

"White roses. This will be very beautiful in the Spring and Summer."

"Yes, I'm sure."

"You have had much help with your crossword puzzle?"

I was delighted that she'd remembered this. In all the novelty of my stay at the monastery, I'd almost forgotten my principle reason for wanting to meet Renata. "Not all that much, actually. I went to see this professor in Gmunden, Dr. Becker, and he's a bit of a crossword expert apparently. He translated a couple of the clues for me - the ones in German and Italian - but he didn't speak the other languages. He told me a bit about how you do cryptic crosswords. And... well, I think I've solved the first clue. But I don't know where it fits in yet."

"Would you show me again the puzzle?"

"Yes, of course. If you'd like to see it." I was thrilled that Renata was taking such an interest. She wiped the mud off her palms, and I drew the box out of my side pocket and put the piece of parchment paper with the clues on it into her hands. Renata took up a stance with her legs apart, removed a packet from her jacket pocket and lit a cigarette, before she considered the paper.

"Do you smoke?" she asked, offering me the packet.

"No thanks."

"I take my opportunity when I'm outside the monastery building. Sometimes I find their rules a little too strict, do you know what I mean?"

I nodded, appreciating her rebellion. Renata didn't appear the same as the other women of the commune: she wasn't a sheep, slavishly following the rules. Perhaps that's why I'd taken to her so instantaneously.

"Ah yes, I have been thinking about this second clue since you showed it to me earlier" Renata murmured as she studied the paper. "You have solved the first clue already, you say?"

"Yes, I have. I'm not sure if it's right but it seems to make sense. I've filled it in here - see?" I took the paper napkin from my pocket on which I'd drawn a crude sketch of the crossword grid, and showed Renata my attempts in pencil.

The older woman nodded. "The second clue I noticed more because it is in German," she said in her methodical manner. "I think I can help you with this clue. The answer may be - *human*."

"Why is that? How did you work that out?" I was amazed that Renata had managed to find an answer so effortlessly, when I had studied the paper for hours with no success.

"Well, you have already the English translation of the German - *Sounds like Hugh Garrison is in this race*. I have done many of your English crosswords from the newspaper, *The Observer*, you know it?"

I nodded.

"When they say, sounds like, they mean literally that the word you are seeking, or the syllable, sounds like the one in the clue."

"Oh, right - you mean, like in charades?"

"I'm sorry, I don't know this game."

"Never mind. Go on."

"So, *sounds like Hugh*, that is the first syllable of the word *human*."

"Oh yes, I see. It all seems so simple when you explain it. I can't think why I didn't notice it before."

"It comes easier when you're used to it" Renata responded kindly. "And then the word *Garrison* is not only a name in English I think, but it can mean to man for example a ship or a town that requires fortification against an enemy."

"Ah - so *man* is a synonym for *Garrison* and that tacks on to the end of *hu* to make *human*? But what's the last bit mean - *is in this race*? I thought this Hugh Garrison chap was running in some sort of race and I had to find out which one."

"That is what you are led to believe. But a race is not only something you run. It can also mean a species of animal, such as the human race. Do you see?"

"Yes I do. I've been looking at it in completely the wrong way."

"That is the secret behind cryptic crossword puzzles. You must look at things in a different way. You turn things on their head and look at them through...crossed eyes, in a way. That's the fun."

"Yes. I get it." I was almost starting to understand why people might consider that word games were fun. I'd always thought of such puzzles as tedious intellectual nonsense.

"Of course, most of my friends think I am totally insane to like so much the crossword games," said Renata, tossing the stub of her cigarette deep into the trees behind us.

"I think mine do too," I admitted. "For different reasons."

Renata handed me back the parchment paper. "Does my answer fit into your crossword grid, do you think?"

"Yes, it maybe will. I'm not sure where. But there are two places it could go."

"I am sure you will find the right place for it" Renata replied, bending over to re-commence her weeding. "You are a lucky person, I think. The Gods are shining on you."

"I hope you're right. But in any case, thank you for helping. I'd never have solved the clue without you."

"You would. It would have just taken you longer, that's all. I have saved you some time. And with the others, you'll be able to work them out yourself."

"Do you really think so?"

"I'm sure of it. You're cleverer than you think."

"Thank you."

"You're welcome. You know, the women at the monastery call me the intelligent one." Renata laughed, a harsh rather mannish sound. "But I am not so intelligent. I just enjoy giving my brain some exercise. I don't allow it to atrophy, like some of them do. I like to think for myself and not allow others to tell me what to think. You are the same in that way, I think." She said all this as she weeded, not bothering to look at me.

I smiled not knowing how to respond, and looked at the paper napkin in my right hand, on which I'd filled in the one clue I'd so far managed to solve. The grid I'd drawn looked like this:

		I	C	A / I	L						
				C				I			
			C	A				C			
			A	L				A			
							L				

I had filled in my answer to the first clue in the three potential places, and now I could see a place where *human* would fit. When I pondered the answer Renata had suggested, it did seem to link in with the other and to make a sort of sense. If all the answers were meant to relate to me, *human* was certainly relevant, since that is what I am.

"Thanks again for helping me, Renata. You don't know how much this means to me." In my excitement, I probably came across as effusive. But I couldn't restrain myself from expressing my gratitude.

Renata remained calm, her solid temperament giving her an air of quiet dignity that reminded me of some slow-moving cow chewing its cud in a field. "There is no need to thank me. I am pleased to help" the older woman replied unsmilingly, her eyes fixed on the patch of ground she was tending. "I am sure it does mean a lot to you. But you are a lucky person. And so you will find what you are seeking, whatever it is."

It was the second time Renata had made that assertion, and I was starting to believe her. Happiness welled up inside me. It was extraordinary how things always turned out all right, how I seemed to make the right decisions almost despite myself.

Just before lunch, as I walked into the big communal kitchens at the back of the monastery to make myself a cup of herb tea, I chanced across a young man who was lugging large boxes of fruit and vegetables from the back of his van to deposit them on the flagstone floor of the pantry. He introduced himself to me as Ugo and told me that he made these deliveries every day from the greengrocers in town. I liked his cheerful demeanor and wide smile and the good-hearted way he carried the heavy boxes, as if there were no burden too great for him to shoulder.

Ugo determined immediately that I was English and spoke fluently in my language, which impressed me all the more because of my own lack of skills as a linguist. I was ripe for conversation with a member of the opposite sex - having had a surfeit of women's company at the commune - and bored with being on my own, so delighted at the opportunity to stand gabbing with Ugo for a while after he'd finished the delivery and we both stood and drank herb tea in the cold stone kitchen.

Ugo pronounced his name for me in English - stumbling over the h as he said Hugh - and I was struck by the coincidence that he had the same name as in the second clue of my crossword, which Renata had just solved for me. Ugo was short - only just taller than me - and slightly stocky, with curly black hair that seemed to spring away from his head, and small dark eyes that held you possessively in his gaze. He was Italian, he said, from the South of that country, although he was going to be studying art at a university in Perugia from the start of their Spring term in March. He had been working in Austria for a few months in the greengrocers shop as a delivery boy in order to save enough money for his studies. Ugo was full of praise for the wonders of the EEC and the way it enabled its citizens to work in European countries other than their own. There was such terrible unemployment in Italy - even worse than we suffered in Britain - that he couldn't earn a decent wage in his homeland.

I asked Ugo where Perugia was and he looked at me as if I should have known better and said it was in Umbria, the place they called the *Green Heart of Italy*. I was impressed when he described how beautiful Umbria was, telling me of lush green hills covered with vines and olive trees, and mediaeval towns filled with tiny ornate churches where Catholic women dressed in black, lit candles and made their confessions. I concluded that Italy was a place I would probably like, and I also thought about the third clue; the one written in Italian, and wondered if meeting Ugo was some sort of sign. The young man had a warm, sensuous voice and the kind of smile that made me want to laugh with him.

After about half an hour, Ugo glanced at his watch and said he'd have to be going, as he had another delivery to make before lunch. I watched him step up into his van, where the young man hesitated, turned around and came back into the kitchen. "I have an idea," he declared, his brown eyes twinkling. "Would you like to go to a party?"

"When? Tonight?"

"Yes. After dinner. At about nine o'clock, we should go."

"Where?"

"In Villach. The center of town. There is a most beautiful ballroom there, I'm sure you'd enjoy. It's going to be a big event. I've been invited because my *capo*, the owner of the shop where I work, has done the catering for the party. But I don't want to go on my own and I don't know anybody else I could ask." Ugo leaned towards me and whispered confidentially: "I don't think any of the women here at the commune are interested in going out with men, do you know what I mean?"

I giggled and nodded.

"It should be a lot of fun. What do you say?"

"Sure. I'd love to go. Thanks for asking."

"Great! Well, I will collect you - in my van I'm afraid, since I don't own a nice car - at around nine o'clock from the front gates. O.K.?"

"Fine. I'll see you then." Ugo gave me a kiss on both cheeks, continental fashion, and waved goodbye as he got into his van and drove away. Delighted at the prospect of a social event that evening, I wandered back to my room on the first floor of the monastery.

Earlier that morning, Sophia had told me there was to be a very special occasion, which I would enjoy. One of the women of the commune was getting married. Her name was Marisa and she was a young girl, only twenty-one, but she wished to get married so that she could bear children. Apparently, the sanctity of marriage was very important to her, and she didn't wish to have children out of wedlock. Thinking of my own mother and her disinclination to marry, I thought Marisa's ideas rather old-fashioned, but I appreciated her sentiment and anticipated the ceremony, never having witnessed a real wedding before.

The wedding was to be at two o'clock, in the main hall of the monastery. I heard that Uta - the head of the commune - was going to preside over the proceedings, and I puzzled over this choice. Didn't the women need to employ a priest? Although female priests were common, to my knowledge Uta was not herself ordained into any religious order. But perhaps the system of marriage was different here in Austria.

At a quarter to two, Sophia and I were seated in the Great Hall, waiting expectantly and listening to Bach organ music being played on a laser disc and transmitted through speakers. The atmosphere was almost like the real thing, as I'd imagined it, but not quite. As the Great Hall was where we normally had dinner, the long table in the center of the room had been cleared away and replaced by about fifty chairs in several rows. Someone had also put a sort of plinth at one end of the hall - for Uta, I assumed - with a wooden music stand on which a large book rested, already opened at a page. Most of the women from the commune were present, and all were dressed in their best finery and chattering excitedly to each other.

Sophia swiveled in her chair to look towards the door at the back of the hall, and she nudged me with a delighted smile: "She's coming! Do you see?"

I turned to see the girl I assumed was Marisa. She looked very pretty, in her traditional white wedding dress and with a band of fresh flowers crowning her fair hair. Marisa advanced slowly up the gap between the rows of chairs, which served as an aisle, her expression at once radiant and shy with all the attention she was receiving. As soon as the other women saw her, there were murmurs and gasps of approval, and to my surprise everybody started spontaneously clapping at Marisa's entrance. Since all the others were applauding I joined in, although I'd never heard of people clapping at a wedding before. I presumed it must be their custom.

Marisa completed her promenade and finished precisely in front of the podium, on which Uta was standing ready with fingers smoothing the open pages of the book on the stand. But where was the groom, I wondered?

There was a further flurry of gasps and murmurs, and I turned around to see another woman, also dressed in white, and also walking slowly up the aisle. I was astonished. Were two women getting married at the same occasion? But Sophia had mentioned nothing about that. Who was this other person, and what was her relation to Marisa?

I wanted to ask Sophia these questions, but she was obviously too entranced and delighted by the proceedings, so I simply followed the events with my eyes and determined to find out later. The second woman joined Marisa at the front of the hall, and the two smiled affectionately at each other. Then Uta began. I discovered afterwards what Uta's exact words were, when Sophia translated them for me. At the time, all I heard was a meaningless stream of German, which I could only understand by the expression of happiness on the women's faces around me:

"Women, sisters and friends, it gives me great pleasure today to be solemnizing the relationship between Marisa and Heidi. As you know, they've been companions for over two years now, and I know they will continue to bring each other a great deal of happiness. I'm always delighted when two women of the group decide to commit to each other in this way, but never more so than now, as I know that Heidi only recently agreed to join us. I'm sure she'll find that life here in the commune brings all that she expects and more. And I know that the happy couple will soon be blessed with children, which is want they want more than anything else in the world. Let's all join hands now in a gesture of solidarity and sisterhood and send our wishes of love to these two women on their day of joy."

As soon as Uta began her speech I realized what was happening, and that this second woman was the groom I had been expecting. In fact, I didn't know how I could have misunderstood Sophia so totally when she had first told me about it. Of course it would be two women being *married*, as men weren't even allowed inside the Great Hall. Since the ceremony wasn't recognized in Law, there wouldn't be a priest presiding. It was a marriage only inasmuch as the vows and the intentions were the same.

That evening, I sat at a long table with about twenty other women, in the high-ceilinged Great Hall, now transformed again into the dining area. Firelight flickered on the stained glass windows and our voices echoed off the stone walls. We ate huge portions of dinner served on wooden platters - *sauerkraut*, red cabbage with raisins and spices, boiled potatoes, thick grey sausages of *leberwurst* served with *senf* mustard, all washed down with dark cool beer in tankards. We talked together in the firelight glow, and the company of women felt comfortable and familiar, as if another sex had never existed or was some strange aberration that we had simply wished away.

The alcohol was making me feel so warm and uninhibited that - at the prompting of a couple of women who were intrigued at how an untraveled English girl should suddenly find herself in an out-of-the-way place like Villach off season - I began to relate my story to the assembled company. Gradually, the other conversations at the long table ceased, and the twenty heads of the other diners turned towards mine to hear my tale. I was enjoying the fact that for once in my life I was the focus of attention, having recently had some extraordinary adventures to relate. For this reason, I probably elaborated and exaggerated slightly to give me even more importance. I appreciated the oohs and aahs as I told my receptive audience about the bomb which had exploded and destroyed my workplace, wounding and killing most of the people around me while miraculously leaving me unscathed. In fact, it hadn't occurred to me before this moment to realize how lucky I'd been to walk away from that event without a mark on me, so distressed had I felt at the time to think of Mother and Marmalade trapped in the apartment during the fire.

Telling the tale in this fashion made me relive the experiences as they replayed themselves in my mind. Yet I seemed curiously distanced from them and emotionally detached, as if I were talking about an exciting film I'd seen or some happenings I'd witnessed but not been involved in. Perhaps my detachment was due to the fact that my current environment was so different from anything I'd known before that I felt as though I'd become a different person from the Alice who'd departed England only a few days previously - that old Alice had died and been reborn, still Alice but a different Alice with different feelings and attitudes.

In any case, I enjoyed entertaining my appreciative listeners. When I started to explain about trying to get my prescription for drugs filled at the chemist and only being allowed one month's supply, some of the women didn't understand me, not having heard of Level 3. "You haven't heard of it!" I gaped, astonished. "But it's already killed thousands of people in Britain. Surely your news coverage..."

"We don't have newspapers or television here at the commune," remarked one of the older women who'd been living at the monastery for some time.

"I have heard of this Level 3" declared Marisa, now changed into everyday clothes but still looking radiantly pretty. "My father is a doctor in Frankfurt and he told me about it. It's really terrible. Such a tragic accident."

"You heard about it from your father? But wasn't there anything about the disease on your television? I mean, it's been around for ages, for years. I know there wasn't much news coverage until fairly recently, well, about three years ago I suppose, but surely..."

"Oh yes" remarked Heidi. "We did of course hear about this on our news bulletins. When they first reported about the infected milk. And then I think I heard about how your medical experts were trying to find a cure. But you see, because it's not something that affects us here in Austria we probably are not too worried about this disease. I know it's terrible, but you know, you don't tend to think very deeply about something that is not affecting your own country or your own family and friends."

"Yes, I suppose you're right" I agreed, seeing her point. "In England, when they report about a plane crash that's happened somewhere else in the world, they always say something like *Only two Britons were killed*, as if the other seventy-nine people of other nationalities who got killed don't matter. I never thought about it before. But we're just the same as you, aren't we?"

"But if you are ill with this disease" Uta pointed out, her wide forehead wrinkling in a frown, "should you not be resting at home, instead of traveling?"

"Perhaps I should, but I've been told I must make this journey. And there's nothing much for me at home any more."

"And what are these clues you mentioned?" asked Uta. "Renata told me she helped you with one."

"Oh yes. I'll show you." I was pleased, not only to dispense with the rather morbid subject of my illness, but also to have the opportunity of showing the others my beautiful and valued box. I had brought my box to the dinner table with me, as Sophia had mentioned being interested to see it, and I withdrew the slim black object from the inside pocket of my jacket which hung over the back of my chair. When I undid the clasps and opened the lid to reveal the intricately carved crossword puzzle grid with its tiny blocks of wood in position, the women gasped in wonder and passed the box from hand to hand down the table so that they could all have a good look.

"It's so beautiful," remarked Sophia, as the box was passed to her. "Do you know when and where it was made?"

"No I don't, I'm afraid."

"It is certainly very old," remarked Uta, who passed the box to Mathilda sitting beside her. "I would say it is an antique."

"Do you think so? Maybe it is." I felt flattered to have my box admired so.

"It would be worth a lot of money" Mathilda commented in her dry voice, running her fingers covetously over the wooden pieces. "Have you considered selling it? You could probably get a good price from an antiques dealer."

"Oh no, I couldn't possibly!" I exclaimed. "It's not precious to me in monetary terms but because it has sentimental value. My friend Genevieve gave it to me. Apart from which, the box has clues to help me on my journey. How could I ever think of selling it?" I was horrified even to consider the idea.

"I only thought," replied Mathilda with little concern at my outburst, closing the lid and passing the box back down the line to me, since it had now been conveyed along the length of the entire table, "If you were needing cash at any time..."

Interest in my box had waned sufficiently for the murmurings of alternative conversations among the women to have begun. Heidi - who sat beside me on my right - was thus able to whisper in my ear without being overheard: "Mathilda only says that because she thinks of nothing but money herself. I have heard she has many debts and is always poor."

"Really?" I whispered back. "Poor thing. What happened to her...?"

Heidi did not have time to answer my question, because just then our attention was diverted by the sweet course being served by two women of the commune who were acting as cooks for that evening. This was delicious apfel strudel with lashings of thick cream, and as the bowls were passed around to us, I carefully slipped Genevieve's box back into my jacket pocket.

When we had eaten dessert, I glanced at my watch and realized I didn't have time to wait for coffee if I was to meet Ugo at the monastery gates at nine o'clock as arranged, so I made my excuses and hastened away from the dining table, grabbing my jacket from the chair and trotting out of the Great Hall. Outside in the empty corridor, the monastery seemed dark and forbidding, the candlelight issuing weakly from the master staircase being too dim to give much cheer. I shivered and returned briefly to my room to wash my face, put on my boots and exchange my jacket (leaving the box in the side pocket) for my warmer fur coat, then dashed out of the back door into the night.

Being certain I was already late for my appointment with Ugo - because as I raced down to the front gates of the monastery my watch was reading five past nine - I was nevertheless glad I'd taken the time to change into my warm clothing and thick "moon boots" which protected my feet from the snow. I slowed to a brisk walk and caught my breath as I paced down the long driveway, looking up into the sky, seeing the stars twinkling like my silent friends and hearing the odd hoot of an owl in the trees.

I need not have worried because once at the gates I had to wait a few minutes till the headlights of a car brightened the road in front of me. I squinted to look at the driver, and the car came to a halt across the road, a male voice calling my name. "Alice? Is that you?"

He had rolled down his window and I approached to the driver's side, feeling relieved to see Ugo's smiling face framed by the fur hood of his anorak "Yes, it's me under this big coat" I replied hopping into the car, grateful for the warmth of its heater, as we started off down the road. Through the window, I watched the trees flash past me in the moonlight, and Ugo edged down the steep hill, applying his brakes carefully at every twisting turn.

Ugo and I were in an enormous ballroom lit by dazzling chandeliers. Pairs of dancers skidded across the polished wooden floor and laughed, throwing their heads back in abandonment. The music of Strauss blared out through speakers set in the four corners of the room, echoing across the walls and bouncing off the high ceiling. A balcony at first floor level ran around three sides of the room and there more revelers stood, some hanging over the edge of the banisters and shouting to their friends below, some lounging in amorous couples with their backs against the railings, some eying the dancers while sipping cocktails or wine from huge goblets. The ceiling was painted - like a renaissance frieze, only gaudier - showing round-bellied women embracing creamy-skinned cherubs with golden hair.

The women dancers wore ballgowns, and the men tailcoats, the spectators who stood around the edges being also clad in evening dress. I must have looked slightly outlandish in my winter garb, which clashed with the splendor of the surroundings. I had taken off my fur coat and moon boots, and stood in stockinged feet, jeans and a huge woolen jumper. I felt distinctly embarrassed as I met the stares of the other people in the room, who eyed me in my bizarre attire as if I were some sort of mad clown.

However, I was not going to be fazed by a little notoriety, and I decided to relax and join in the party spirit. A large trestle table had been placed near the entrance, on which rested dozens of goblets already filled with wine, so Ugo and I helped ourselves to liberal amounts, and stood drinking in the liquid and our surroundings.

After we had chatted for a while, Ugo persuaded me to join him for a waltz on the dance floor. I told him I felt a little silly dancing amongst all those strangers so beautifully dressed, but he replied that the Austrians were far too stuffy and formal anyway, and my English eccentricity was refreshing. I'd never waltzed before and Ugo practically propelled me over the slippery surface so that my feet hardly touched the ground. I laughed and gasped for air and felt quite giddy with the movement, the wine, the warmth of the other bodies flying around us and the swirling notes of the music that seemed to float like feathers and goad us on.

I had no notion of how much time passed, but Ugo and I must have danced for ages, because when the music stopped and we collapsed panting at the side of the room, I heard a church bell outside strike twelve. Feeling a bit like Cinderella afraid to lose my glass shoe, I admitted this to

Ugo, and he laughingly said I was a romantic and should have been born Italian. Softer music was playing now, and we gathered my outdoor clothes from a heap by the entrance and sat in an alcove on the balcony level, sipping our drinks and talking more familiarly. When I told Ugo something of my story, to my disappointment he didn't appear very interested. But when I revealed that the third clue was in Italian, Ugo's countenance sprang to enthusiastic life: "So, now you must go to Italy!" he announced, beaming.

"Must I?" I teased.

"Well, not, you must but...sometime everybody should see my beautiful country, and why not now?"

I took a large gulp of my wine and burped loudly, covering my mouth with one hand. "You know, I'm on an important journey and I have to go to the right place. I haven't got enough money to go rushing off everywhere just because I feel like it." I thought I sounded remarkably English and uncharacteristically sensible, but I was actually trying to find excuses for not easily falling in with Ugo's suggestions. After all, I couldn't let a near-stranger tell me what to do, could I?

"You should relax, Alicia. Don't worry about money. Something always turns up when you need it. That's my motto. Life will provide."

I grinned. "Yeah, I bet it always does for you. You're that sort of person. But I've always had to sort of plan ahead, work for a living, that sort of thing. I'm not used to doing things spontaneously."

"You are not working now."

"No - I suppose not, but..."

"Now, you're on this adventure and you live every day as it comes."

"That's right. But it still feels rather strange, you know. I'm not used to it."

"So where is the right place for you to go?" asked Ugo.

When I looked at Ugo, he was regarding me with his eyebrows raised and his head cocked to one side, as though he expected me to have no answer to his question. "Well..." I hesitated. "I don't know yet...I had thought I would go back to Rotterdam and stay with Hanneke for a while, but I'm not sure..."

"*Perfetto*" said my companion, shrugging his shoulders and opening his arms to the side, to demonstrate his point had just been proven. "You don't know where next to go. So, go to Italy and stay with my friends."

"Where do they live?" I queried, deliberately stalling while secretly warming to Ugo's plans.

"In Gubbio. It is a small town in the heart of the mountains, very near to Perugia where I study. You will love to see this place, it is ve-ery charming. *Bellissima*! These friends of mine are a nice family who speak English, so you understand everything."

"Well, I suppose I could go there..." I deliberated.

"Not you could. You go, tomorrow" Ugo bossed, beaming once more.

His suggestion did sound appealing. But I didn't expect to find Clair in a little mountain hideaway. "I don't know, perhaps I should try Rome."

Ugo dismissed this proposal with a grimace of distaste. "No, Rome is so dirty, so crowded with people and tourists. You would not like it there. You should see the real country, the real Italian people. In the mountains, the air is pure, the food is good..." He waved his hands, indicating that the list of Gubbio's positive qualities was endless.

"I'd be a stranger there, wouldn't I?"

"Nobody is a stranger in Gubbio" Ugo enthused. "My friends there will be pleased to take you in. You will be, how d'you say, part of the family!"

My companion's zeal was infectious. Any other plans I had formulated were nebulous and vague. And part of me said that, on this voyage that had no known destination, where so much had already been dictated by Fate, I should flow with the tide of opportunity and take whatever chance provided.

That evening I sat in my room at the monastery, mulling over what Ugo had said. Italy did sound attractive, but I had to remain sensible. I resolved to return to Hanneke's as originally planned and continue trying to unravel the clues. Then, when I had some more precise notions about Clair's identity and location, I would travel to Ugo's friends in Gubbio, if it seemed appropriate.

I put thoughts of the journey out of my mind and concentrated on the parchment paper in my lap, penciling the word Renata had given me earlier that day into the makeshift grid on my napkin. When I came to replace the paper in the lid of the box, the edge of the parchment caught on something and I tipped the contents out into my lap. The photograph - which I hadn't looked at since Rotterdam - landed right side up, and I saw to my astonishment that it had changed. The darkish blur like an ink stain which

I had noticed before, had seeped even more into the white and now covered almost two thirds of the glossy surface of the print. I wondered if some strange chemical reaction was occurring due to the photograph's being held in a warm place next to my skin, but I wasn't knowledgeable enough about such things to be certain. I replaced everything in the box, with a perception of a fog very gradually lifting and enabling me to understand the messages Genevieve had given me.

The next morning, as I threw my clothes and other belongings into my suitcase - with the intention of catching the very next train back to Rotterdam, waiting at the station if necessary - I noticed something that filled me with alarm.

When I came to pack my jacket in the top of the suitcase - thinking that I would be better off wearing my fur coat for the time being, the weather being still cold - I folded it neatly and pressed gently down to squash the article into a tight space. I was surprised that my jacket seemed less bulky than usual, and I felt around in the inside pocket for Genevieve's box.

But it wasn't there. The pocket was empty!

I frantically scoured my memory. Surely that pocket was where I had left the box on the previous evening. Running over the events in my mind, I listed them on my fingers: I'd had dinner, excused myself early to go to the party and come back to my room. The box had definitely been with me then because I recalled replacing it in my jacket pocket after telling my story to the women. I'd exchanged my jacket for my fur coat and I'd hung the jacket on the hook on my bedroom door. I glanced at the door as if for confirmation. I'd decided not to take the box with me to the party, thinking it might not be safe there, so beyond any doubt I had left it in my room. The only other time I'd been without my jacket and the box, was that morning at breakfast.

Nevertheless, I searched my room thoroughly, just in case I'd made a mistake and unmindfully secreted the box somewhere else. I looked in every drawer of the dressing table, under the bed and in the wardrobe; I ran my finger along all the shelves and on the window ledge behind the shutters. But the box was nowhere to be seen.

Hastily, I unpacked my carefully packed suitcase and threw everything out on to the bed, then went through all the articles I had recently packed, in case the box had somehow got mixed up amongst them. But the box wasn't there. My search was becoming obsessive, but I had no notion what else to do. I paced up and down the floor in consternation, then I searched the room again, in all the places I had just looked.

It was no good. I gave up and sat down on the bed with my heart thumping, wanting to weep in despair. The box had gone. It had completely disappeared. How on earth could this have happened? Surely, one of the women couldn't have…? Surely it was unthinkable that in this tight-knit little community a thief lurked, a common criminal who would steal a valuable article from a guest? I could hardly believe that.

As these thoughts rushed through my head, there came a knock at my bedroom door and I went to answer it. Ugo stood in the corridor, smiling cheerfully as usual. "I wondered how you are feeling this morning? Not too hungover from last night, I hope. Did you have a good time?" Noticing my ashen face and despairing expression, Ugo asked: "What is the matter? Are you not well?"

"I'm not ill, but...Come in a minute, Ugo." I ushered him into my room, and my friend sat in the armchair while I perched on my low single bed, first clearing a space amongst all the belongings, which were scattered on the coverlet. "Something terrible's happened," I murmured.

Ugo said nothing but his brown eyes grew wide with concern.

"My box has gone."

"What? Your wooden box with the clues in it?"

I nodded miserably.

"Oh, *Dio mio* !" Ugo clapped his hand over his mouth in dismay and rushed to the window.

"What is it?" I asked, confused by his reaction.

"Come with me. Quick!" Ugo grabbed my hand, and dragged me out of my room. I closed the door and locked it, wishing I had thought to do as much the evening before, and followed my friend as he raced along the corridor, down the grand spiral staircase to the ground floor of the building and out of the front door. Once there, Ugo stood on the porch and scanned the grounds with his gaze, holding one hand up to his forehead to shield his eyes from the glare of the sun as he did so.

"What are you looking for?" I demanded.

"No, she is no longer here."

"Who?"

"Mathilda" Ugo declared, turning to face me. "I'm so sorry, Alicia. I should have said something but it didn't occur to me. I thought you must have given it to her to look at or something."

"What? My box?"

Ugo nodded. "I saw her with it this morning. It was when I was in the kitchen delivering the apples. I went back to the van to get another load and I happened to catch sight of her leaving the front door of the monastery. She had your box in her hands."

"And she was leaving the monastery?" I asked, horrified.

"Yes. You know, I almost did go up to her to ask why she had it and then I thought, well for some reason you must have given it to her. I couldn't believe that she would just walk out with it."

"Oh my God!" I stood and gaped at Ugo in horror. "What are we going to do?"

Ugo took charge of the situation and whisked me back to my room, ordering me as he did so: "Pack up all your things in your case. You were leaving this morning anyway, yes? Uta told me you are going back to Rotterdam today. Perhaps Mathilda has gone into Villach with the box, hoping to sell it. I will drive you to town. But we must hurry. As soon as possible."

I followed his instructions and threw all my hastily unpacked articles back into my suitcase, grabbed my coat and flung it on then followed Ugo out to his van which was parked by the side entrance next to the kitchen. On our way there, we encountered Renata.

"You are leaving so soon, Alice? I wanted to say goodbye and wish you good luck."

"I'm sorry, but we really must dash" I gasped, as we sped past her on the stairs. "No time to say goodbye." Suddenly,

I had a brainwave. I stopped and whirled round to face Renata. "Ugo saw Mathilda leaving the monastery just now. Do you have any idea where she was going?"

Renata nodded: "Oh yes. I overheard her telling Uta she was going to Florence for a few days."

"Florence?" I gaped in horror.

"Yes, there is some antiques fair there or something, that she wishes to go to. She is very interested in the antiques, I think. She used to have some large antiques business in Hamburg that her father owned and then it went, how do you say? Bust? Lost all her money at once. Very sad."

Renata's last words were said to my retreating back, as Ugo grabbed my hand and literally pulled me down the stairs: "Come on!" he urged.

"Thanks Renata" I called out to her. "We're in a bit of a hurry."

Once at the van, I threw my suitcase in the back and Ugo and I fastened our seat belts in a second. Then he started the ignition and we sped down the driveway and on to the winding road, which led down to the town. "If she's gone to Florence" remarked Ugo, "You'll have to catch a train there. I can take you to the station. I just hope there is one very soon."

"Oh no. What a thing to happen." I suddenly felt nauseous. "What an idiot I was! Why didn't I lock my door last night when I was out at the party?"

"She probably took it this morning when you were at breakfast. Have you thought of that?"

"Oh yes, you're right. I didn't see her at the dining table. I didn't think about her not being there because several of the women get up earlier than the others and go out before the main breakfast, to do jobs in town or whatever."

"It makes sense that she would go to Florence."

"Does it?"

"Of course. There are many antique shops and dealers there. She would know all the best ones, if she used to have a business herself. And she could probably sell your box quite easily."

"And then come back here as if nothing had happened, having stolen from a guest?"

"Maybe she won't come back. She doesn't have to."

"No, I suppose you're right. She could sell the box, use the money to get over her current money difficulties and disappear back to Hamburg or wherever she came from. Oh shit! What a bloody mess!" I hit the roof of the van with my hands in my frustration. "Sorry. But it's just such a dreadful thing to happen. I can't let that box go. I need it. It's the only thing that's going to help me. What am I going to do?" I moaned in despair.

"Don't worry" Ugo soothed. "You can get it back, I'm sure. It may be a little difficult and take some time, but you will."

"Do you really think so?"

"Certainly. All you have to do is go to Florence and visit all the antique shops until you find your box. If Mathilda has sold the box - and she will surely do that immediately she arrives - you can be sure the shop owner will have such a beautiful thing on display in his window."

"With a hefty price tag on it..."

"Yes, maybe. But you have some money, don't you?"

"I shouldn't have to buy it back. It is mine, after all" I complained.

"I know that but the shop owner won't, and it may be hard to convince him..."

"Oh God, it's so unfair..."

"But perhaps you will" Ugo reassured me. "You must just smile sweetly and wear your prettiest dress. You know how we Italian men will fall for a pretty woman." He grinned at me, and I gave him a mournful smile in reply. "Don't worry, Alicia. It will all be O.K. And just think, now you are really going to Italy, no? Perhaps this was God telling you to go."

"Don't joke about it, Ugo."

"Well, in any case, you will see the beautiful city of Florence which everyone must see. And you know, Florence is not very far from Gubbio."

"Really?"

"No. Only a few miles. So you could stay with my friends after all."

"Well, maybe I will then."

CHAPTER EIGHT

A FTER A LONG and grueling train journey I arrived at the station in Florence, and went immediately to the Tourist Information Booth to enquire about hotels for that night. Being too late to start looking at antique shops that day, I resolved to find the most comfortable hotel I could for a reasonable price, and enjoy the opportunity to rest and recuperate so that I'd be bursting with energy to begin my search in the morning. The girl at the desk was very pleasant and to my great relief spoke excellent English. She was able to recommend a very acceptable small hotel near the center of the town, which I made my way to at once. In the taxi on the way to the hotel I didn't even glance out of the window, my interest in the sights of this famous town being nil at that moment, my concentration focused on regaining my treasured box.

That evening, after I had taken a refreshing shower and hung up my clothes in the closet of my tiny room on the top floor of the hotel building, I treated myself to a pizza at the local *trattoria*, and was pleased to be able to change my diet from the heavy Austrian food I'd recently been consuming. My dinner was delicious, and that night I slept extremely well despite my anxieties about the box. I was so convinced that I would retrieve my box the next day and so filled with optimism about my coming success, that even the sounds of a rowdy Italian party happening in the room next door couldn't keep me awake for long.

The next morning, I awoke at eight o'clock and leapt immediately from my bed, unusual behavior for me, as I normally lie prone for a while before taking the plunge into a new day. I felt charged with hope and determination. Whatever Mathilda had done with my box, the precious article was rightfully my possession and therefore I was meant to repossess it. I could not fail!

I hurried down to breakfast in the small dining room, and sat alone at one of the lace cloth covered tables, gazing through the window out into the street. I was surprised that nobody else had made it down to breakfast yet, but concluded that the hotel was probably not very busy at this time of year. The noisy revelers from next door had no doubt gone to bed late and were currently nursing hangovers or too tired from their exertions to make an appearance this early.

The waitress brought me strong Italian coffee, white bread rolls and little croissants with a sweet coating. I wolfed down my food and guzzled the hot coffee, then collected my handbag from my room, handed my key into reception and strode out of the hotel. It was a fairly pleasant day, hardly sunny but not cold, with a few woolly clouds chasing each other across the sky and a blustery wind blowing.

The first place I entered was a *Tabacchaio* across the street, which I had noticed the evening before. I purchased a street map of Florence and enquired of the shopkeeper where the antique shops could be found. His English was quite comprehensive, but he knew little about antique shops. The only information he could impart was that not all the antique shops in Florence were concentrated in one particular area of the town. However, if I went to the center where all the museums and art galleries were located, I would be sure to find at least one shop displaying *antichita*. I thanked the shopkeeper and, using the map to guide me, walked the mile or so to the *centro*.

Sure enough, I came across quite a large antique shop almost at once. I felt enormously encouraged by this, and certain that my job was going to prove to be every bit as easy as I'd envisaged. I could identify the building as an antique shop by the carved statues and old wooden furniture I glimpsed through the window. Outside the shop was a sign proclaiming *Oggetti D'Arte Antichi* in bold red letters. Despite the absence of my box in the window, I entered the shop and approached the counter full of confidence.

"I'm looking for a box," I announced to the pretty girl with long dark hair who greeted me. She gave me a sweet and apologetic smile. *"Non parlo inglese. Mi dispiace molto."*

"Oh dear..." I murmured in consternation, looking around me for assistance.

In a few seconds, a portly gentleman in a dark suit came alongside the girl. "Can I help you, Signora?" he offered unsmilingly in a heavy Italian accent.

"Oh, yes" I replied with relief. "I'm looking for a box."

"What kind of box?"

"Well, it's about this big" I answered, indicating the size with my hands, "made out of some black material which may be metal or plastic, I'm not sure. And inside there are lots of little wooden pieces which fit together like a sort of... jigsaw, I suppose."

Appearing perturbed, the man shook his head slowly. "There is no box like that here. Perhaps you would like to see one of our other boxes. We have many beautiful things..."

"No, no thank you. It's only this box I'm interested in."

"When was it made?"

"I really don't know."

"What century? Eighteenth century? Earlier?"

"I've no idea."

"Are you sure it's an antique?"

"Well, not really but, I'm not certain where else to look."

"Where did you find out about this box? Did you read about it in a magazine?"

"Oh no. It's a long story, but...the box is mine actually. Somebody stole it from me and I knew she was coming to Florence and that she used to deal in antiques. There was an antiques festival here, or something, wasn't there?"

"That's right. Yesterday."

"I thought Mathilda...this person...might have sold my box to an antiques dealer here."

"I see." The man stroked his chin in thought. "There are many other antique shops in Firenze, but it's impossible for me to say whether your box will be there."

"Yes of course, I realize that but I've got to look anyway. Could you tell me where the other shops are?"

The man gave a short laugh and shrugged his broad shoulders. "Signora, there must be fifty other antique shops all over the town. You can try all of them, but you will get very tired."

"That's O.K. I'm prepared to try all of them. I need to get my box back." Privately, I hoped it wouldn't be necessary to visit all fifty of the antique shops but I was determined to do that if I had to. "Could you tell me where some of them are, at least?" I withdrew my street map from my pocket and laid it on the counter. "Could you show me on this map? I don't have a car, so I'll have to walk."

"*Sulla carta*? Certainly." The man took some gold-rimmed spectacles from his pocket and placed them on his nose before bending over the map. "The good thing is that Firenze is not a very big town so you could walk all around it in a day. But, to visit fifty antique shops..." He spread his big hands wide in a gesture I was beginning to get familiar with. It was an Italian gesticulation, conveying the meaning, *rather you than me*. "You can start here in this Piazza," he said, marking the spot in biro on my map. "There are three small shops here, two on this side and one on this side. I know the owners and they often have unusual items. Then, you could try..." And he proceeded to tell me about several more shops, until my map was covered in tiny crosses where he'd marked the places I should visit.

"Thank you so much. I'm extremely grateful to you," I spouted, folding my map and returning it to my pocket.

"Not at all. I hope you find your box."

I was on the point of leaving the shop, when another thought struck me and I turned back. "Just one more thing, if you don't mind. Could you teach me a phrase in Italian, in case I meet another shopkeeper who doesn't speak English?"

The man nodded his large head lugubriously.

"Could you tell me how to say, *I'm looking for a box*?"

"*Cerco una scatola.*"

I had to repeat the phrase several times before I memorized it. Then I thanked the man again, and the girl who was still hovering beside him smiling, and departed the shop, feeling that I'd achieved something, even if I hadn't found my box. It would have been fairly extraordinary to have discovered my box in the first shop I visited anyway, I reflected. I determined to visit at least five more shops before breaking for coffee, and set off at a brisk pace for the Piazza the shopkeeper had marked on the map, the one that contained three antique shops.

Two hours later, I trudged into a cafe and ordered a cappuccino, already thoroughly sick of antique shops. I'd visited seven and none knew anything about a box. Some shopkeepers spoke no English, as I had feared, and I had to repeat my phrase over and over - *Cerco una scatola* - and sift through dozens of unlikely receptacles before attempting to explain that it was a specific box I wanted. It was a hard and dispiriting slog, but I was determined to continue until I'd visited every antique shop in town.

That evening, I staggered into my hotel at 7 p.m., thoroughly worn out and dejected, having visited twenty-five of the town's fifty antique shops with a zero success rate. Some proprietors had suggested other shops or antique dealers I could try. Some had missed the point of my mission and simply commented with long faces that I was unlikely to find such an object in the whole of Florence, and I should be content with a different box. I began to wonder whether I'd been a fool to believe I could possibly find my box here. It was like looking for a needle in a haystack. But I'd assigned myself a task - to visit every antique shop in Florence - and I wasn't going to stop until I'd completed it, even if it took me a week and wore out all my shoe leather in the process. That night I slept as soundly as a baby, out of pure physical exhaustion.

The next morning I arose with somewhat less enthusiasm but no less determination, had my breakfast as before and set off to my next location. The whole of that day was also spent traipsing around shops in a similarly fruitless quest and with even less success than before, if that were possible. Arriving back at the hotel that night, I speculated whether to give up and call off the whole enterprise. But how could I?

That box was literally all I possessed in the world now, which linked me to my brother: it was my one hope of finding Clair as Genevieve had predicted. If I never retrieved my box, what could I do? Return to England and beg Genevieve for another, when I had so carelessly allowed her treasured legacy to be stolen from under my nose? The very idea was unthinkable.

I had to find the box if it was the last thing I did. There was nothing else on earth that mattered to me. I silently vowed to Genevieve that, if I did regain her precious gift, I would never again let it out of my sight. I would certainly never again display the box to a group of people in a manner which, I realized now, had been stupidly egocentric. This punishment seemed fitting retribution for my foolishness in bandying the precious container about like some conversation piece, in a bid for more attention. I had learned a hard lesson from the experience that I would never forget.

The next day, I trudged my weary route with a careworn face, seeking a shop that had been described to me by a shopkeeper I'd encountered the previous day as "full of interesting paraphernalia". The shop was housed in a tiny building, perched on the corner of a back street in an out-of-the-way situation that took me some while to locate, despite the precise directions I'd been given. When I finally came upon the shop, its dingy facade and unprepossessingly terse sign above the door announcing *Antica*, did not fill me with optimism.

Nevertheless, I marched up to the front door and peered through grubby windows into the dim interior. My eyes ranged over the peculiar assortment of articles on display - cracked China dolls, silver bowls, glove puppets with damaged faces, a tiny white child's nightdress in lace, a pair of brass candlesticks - then they came to an abrupt halt.

In the middle of this eclectic assortment of articles lay a small black box! Squinting through the window, I attempted to scrutinize the object more closely. Could it possibly be...?

With a pounding heart, I entered the shop and was greeted by a tiny elderly gentleman with white hair and wire spectacles. Commencing in English, I quickly realized to my disappointment that this gentleman was one of the shopkeepers who couldn't speak my language, so I pointed to the box in the window, abandoning my usual phrase: *Cerco una scatola*, having hopefully discovered the box I was seeking.

The proprietor lifted the box from its position, shook it free of dust and placed it into my eager hands. I lifted the delicate clasps.

To my enormous relief and joy, inside lay the little wooden pieces, undamaged and unchanged. Looking into the lid's cloth pocket, I confirmed that the partly exposed photograph and the parchment paper with the clues also remained intact. Even the paper napkin on which I'd made an outline of the crossword grid to work from, with my attempts at the solved clues marked into the appropriate spaces, was exactly as I had left it. Mathilda's preoccupation only with the financial value of the piece, and her necessary hurry to dispose of it before she was discovered as the thief, meant that she had not tampered with the contents of the box at all.

I was so overcome with elation, relief and gratitude that tears came into my eyes as I shut the box and clutched it to my heart. "Thank you God, thank you!" I couldn't help crying out, uncaring of the shopkeeper's response to this unusual outburst.

Now came the difficult part. Explaining to the proprietor that the box was mine. My stumbling report - in loud English punctuated by pauses and gesticulations - that the box belonged to me and had been stolen, was met by a mask of incomprehension, and the shopkeeper merely shook his old white head and repeated: *Non capisco, non capisco niente.*

There had to be an alternative way to make the man understand. I'd acquired a small Italian phrasebook during my two days in Florence and, opening it, I leafed through the pages, hoping to find an appropriate phrase. There was nothing precisely analogous to my current situation, but I made some halting progress.

After about half an hour of dialogue accompanied by frantic mime on both our parts as we tried to communicate, I think the old man gathered the idea that I was claiming the box to be mine. The trouble was that he would not believe me. I knew there was no way to persuade him, because I had no proof at all.

In desperation, I asked the shopkeeper the price he wanted for the box. He seemed to consider for a few moments, then replied: *"Cento Euros"*, with the air of one who knows he cannot lose. I was obviously so enamored of the object that I would pay almost any price.

I could tell from the shopkeeper's expression that he was asking far more than he had ever hoped to get for the box. And I knew that such a large sum of money would be a strain on my already overstretched purse. Nevertheless, I had no choice but to pay him. At least I had found my box, which was the most important thing. So, with no further delay, I handed over the money, collected my box and walked out of the shop.

Chapter Nine

"*GUARDA, GUARDA!*"

The little girl pointed to the spire of a church, which was poised on top of a distant hill. A fluffy white cloud hung in the brilliant blue sky and seemed to hover over the steeple, protecting the building like an amorphous blanket. I turned back to the girl to see that she was smiling and still gazing entranced into the distance, holding her arm extended. It was the first time I had seen anything like animation or joy on the child's face. Her black curls were lifted and separated by the wind, leaving her thin neck bare and making her appear fragile and vulnerable. I wanted to wrap a scarf around the little girl and keep her from the cold, but she seemed not to even notice.

"The church is the *Chiesa di Santa Maria degli Angeli*" came a voice behind me, and I turned and smiled at Paolo. "It is not the one we go to for Mass, but she likes it because of the angels."

"Angels?" I asked, imagining white-robed figures playing harps and dispensing wafers and wine.

"There are frescoes on the ceiling and walls. Renaissance, I think. Or mediaeval." Paolo gave a shrug of his heavy shoulders and continued to guzzle his Chianti.

"We don't know so much about history" laughed Mariella, topping up my glass as she passed by me on her way to the picnic hamper for more cheese and mortadella. I noticed that Lucia, their little daughter, had nothing to drink and had been offered nothing, not even a glass of orange juice like her brothers. The girl stood apart and gazed at the church, as if she thought it could provide an answer to the unknown questions in her heart.

"I suppose you take things for granted when you're surrounded by them," I said to Paolo, trying to make pleasant conversation. Lucia's father regarded me with a slightly mystified expression. "So much beauty here" I explained, "and history, but you never even think about it?"

Paolo grunted and bit into a hunk of *ciabata*, then replied with his mouth full: "It's not important."

I didn't know what to say in response, so I kept silent and watched the family conversing with each other in Italian. The two boys - Carlo and Stefano, who must have been about ten - played roughly with each other, tumbling over on the grass and shouting oaths thankfully unintelligible to my ears. Mariella continued to fuss over the assembled group making sure we all had enough to eat and drink, but as for herself, I had never seen her sit down long enough to consume anything. I imagined that eating was something Mariella did in private, like a secret vice she didn't wish to admit to in company. Paolo was normally concerned with gratifying himself alone and made little attempt to put others at their ease. After lunch, he habitually reclined on the grass, smoking furiously and reading a newspaper, unaware of anything that happened around him. When the boys accidentally knocked against him in play, he simply pushed them off without even a casual glance, and carried on reading.

I had nothing in common with these people and I found it a strain being in their company, but I reminded myself constantly how generously they had behaved in accommodating me for a few days, providing me with my own bedroom and all my meals - despite my guilty protestations - even though I was a complete stranger who had been sent to them out of the blue by Ugo.

I gathered that Ugo was some sort of distant cousin, and the family's code of honor or hospitality prevented them from refusing me. Although grateful to Ugo, I was embarrassed and unsure how I should act in this situation since being thrown on to their courtesy. Part of me wanted to invent an excuse for leaving and simply escape, to a hotel in a larger town where I would be beholden to nobody and free to do what I pleased, but another part of me wished to remain. The countryside was exquisitely beautiful and peaceful, and as each day dawned with a blue sky undimmed by winter and the sonorous clang of early church bells, I found it harder to stir. Added to which, I was worried about the girl, Lucia.

My concern for her surprised me, because I don't remember ever having had maternal inclinations. But I was touched by Lucia's isolation and sparky disregard for her abandonment, and I wondered why the child's parents cared so little for her. I considered Lucia far more appealing than her two elder brothers - with her delicate fine-boned face and huge soulful dark eyes - yet it was they who claimed all the attention.

The boys dominated the old stone farmhouse with their wild antics, perpetually fighting, shouting, and causing a stir. When they chucked food around the table at mealtimes, Paolo and Mariella would laugh indulgently, as if judging such boisterousness natural and even laudable. Meanwhile, Lucia would sit silently, sometimes tugging her mother's voluminous skirts and hazarding a question which Mariella would ignore, while brushing her daughter off like an irritating fly and continuing a dialogue with her husband, or doing one of the million and one chores which seemed to occupy her every waking moment. The only person who ever looked at Lucia and tried to fathom what lay behind the plea in her urchin eyes, was me.

Although I had been living with the family for almost a week, the first time Lucia had ever dared look at me or try to communicate with me in any way was today, as I and the Italians picnicked in the winter sunshine on the wild grass behind the rambling building that was their home, and with our view over the distant hills unimpeded by other signs of habitation. Perhaps it was important to the girl, this church in the distance that held her gaze. Moving over to Lucia, I squatted beside her, and pretended not to notice her wince as though she expected me to berate her. I smiled, pointed to the church she had shown me and echoed her word, *Guarda*, with a question in my voice.

"*Brava*" Mariella replied, complimenting me on my accent, "It means to look. She likes to tell people what to look at."

Lucia regarded me suspiciously, unsure whether to trust my interest. I smiled at her again. "*Bella*", I ventured, meaning the church. The child giggled in shy recognition:

"*Vuoi vederla? Vieni con me*" piped the shrill voice, the girl not realizing that her words left me baffled. Lucia grinned from ear to ear, delighted that a stranger was paying attention to her.

"She doesn't want to," exclaimed Mariella, cuffing the child lightly on the top of her head. Lucia continued to stare at me, waiting for my reaction. "Our guest has seen too many churches already."

"They all look the same anyway," muttered Paolo.

"What did she ask me?" I demanded.

"She wants to know if you want to see this church of hers," replied Mariella with a soft tut.

"I'd love to" I responded quickly, smiling again at the child. Gathering the import of my words, Lucia brought her shoulders up to her ears and hugged herself in a happy dance.

"It's quite a walk" discouraged Paolo.

"I don't mind," I countered, glad to call their bluff. "I'd like a walk."

"Just after your lunch?" said Mariella, frowning. "You will get the *mal di stomaco*, no?" She rubbed her abdomen and grimaced.

I laughed. "Don't worry. I haven't eaten that much." Rising from the grass, I took Lucia's hand gently. "Does she know where to go?"

"Oh, she knows all right. She's been there many times," replied Mariella, slumping on to a garden chair as though concluding she had better ways to spend her time. I marveled that these parents allowed their child to wander alone over the hills - a little girl of seven - but it was none of my business to question their behavior. At any rate, Lucia would have the benefit of a companion on this occasion.

Lucia and I skipped around to the front of the house, into the road and down the old cobbled streets of Gubbio, hand in hand. I was amazed once more at the exquisite beauty of our surroundings: walking around Gubbio was like stepping into the film set of a small mediaeval town, all the buildings exact replicas of edifices constructed centuries ago, the only missing item being the extras in historical costume. Yet all this was genuine. Gradually, the streets gave way to dusty paths with fields of leafless olive trees on either side, and I realized that we had left the town. We continued - skipping, part running, sometimes giggling at nothing, scuffing our shoes with stones - for the best part of an hour.

At first the journey was downhill and my calves ached with the strain of keeping upright, and then we started to climb and that stretched my thighs. I was glad that my companion was a child of seven, and couldn't go much faster than I, with a palpitating heart, throbbing head and stiff limbs which were proof that my illness had already weakened me. Despite the cold air, sweat was dripping in rivulets beneath my thick woolen jumper.

As we clambered up the side of the hill, I could see the church ahead of us: it was unlike any church I had ever seen and differed even from its counterparts in Gubbio. The building stood in its own grounds surrounded by a low wall, and was round rather than square, with a central steeple topped by a long spire being the only part projecting proudly into the sky. The walls were rough-hewn stone, and I guessed that the church must be very old, perhaps predating its mediaeval companions, although my knowledge of history and architecture was too limited to define the building's age more precisely.

As we entered the grounds of the church, I was surprised to note that we were the only visitors. Although on the whole Italians appeared to be keen churchgoers, I supposed that the comparative isolation of this little church made the building less frequently visited than others. Lucia skipped ahead of me and, using all her child's strength, pulled open the heavy wooden door. Inside it was cool and dark and my eyes took a few moments to adjust to the lack of light. I imagined the coolness and shade would be welcome in the height of summer, but now it made me shiver and I noticed that even Lucia trembled slightly with the chill. I removed the woolen sweater that I wore beneath my coat and hung it over her shoulders, as the girl had come out in only a thin sweatshirt and jeans.

Lucia grabbed my hand and dragged me to the center of the circular church, directing me to look up. It the center of the ceiling was a hole through which light was penetrating thinly, strained as it was down the length of the hollow spire. As Lucia continued to point and to babble in her high-pitched Italian urchin's voice, I gradually became accustomed to the dimness and began to make out shapes and figures on the ceiling and walls. These must be the frescoes Paolo had mentioned. They certainly were fascinating and strangely beautiful, so old that the colors had mostly faded and yet still vibrant with a kind of fierce energy that must have sprung from the passion of their conception.

The scenes were probably biblical, although my knowledge of the gospel was scant and I had no idea what the pictures were meant to depict. The human figures had the angular, two-dimensional look of mediaeval paintings I had seen in books, with heads slightly too large for their bodies and faces always pointing forwards and slightly to one side as if in perpetual consideration of life. There was a childlike simplicity about the pictures, and I could see why they appealed to Lucia.

As I stood gazing and taking in the frescoes, the child slipped out of my grasp and out of the door of the church, so silently that I didn't at first notice she had gone. I dropped my chin and looked at the plain wooden pews and the plaster Madonna by the pulpit, her virgin hands outstretched in welcome. I wandered up to the statue and examined the face with its spiritual beauty still unmarred by the passage of time and age. I thought about stories of statues such as this weeping blood-red tears and people more religious than I and more steeped in faith, accepting it as a sign of God's grace.

While I was thus engaged in staring at the carved face, a wispy mist seemed to float in front of my eyes and I rubbed the sockets with my knuckles, thinking I must be tireder than I'd realized. When I looked again at the statue, the hands were held together in prayer, the head slightly inclined towards them. Surely, it had been different a moment ago, or had my memory been playing tricks on me, as well as my eyes? As I hovered in mental confusion I heard a sound, which I couldn't at first identify, because it was so incongruous and unexpected.

I heard music. The sound of a flute or panpipes playing a mournful tune, which floated in the distance. It lasted only a few seconds and I swiveled my head this way and that trying to determine where the music came from. But the sound had no direction, seeming to exist everywhere inside the church at once.

The music sounded at once strange and familiar, but it had the familiarity of a dream long forgotten. I couldn't tell when it began and when it ended, because my ears carried on hearing the music in my head long after its vibrations had ceased.

I suddenly remembered Lucia and, anxious about her safety, I walked out of the church. Abruptly, with the rush of outside air on my cheeks, the music stopped, and I wondered if I had imagined the whole thing. It had been so peculiar, and yet I knew I had heard it with some part of my being. It was as though the music had been trying to tell me something or to comfort me in some way.

Seeing Lucia sitting happily on the stone wall, squinting into the winter sun, I approached and sat beside her. For a few moments we remained in silence, and then the child turned to me with a look at once curious and concerned: "*Chi cerchi?*" she asked.

I didn't know the answer to the question because I didn't know the question. I could only look perplexed and shrug and open my palms in a gesture of compliance. "Chi cerchi?" Lucia repeated more firmly, as if she suspected that I was hiding something important from her on purpose. Not knowing how to respond, I changed the subject, and I started a game of run-and-catch down the road, which made her forget her question.

But later, when we had returned to the house at Gubbio, I remembered Lucia's words and repeated them to Mariella. "She asks you, who are you looking for" said Mariella without interest, as she concentrated on making her passata for that evening's dinner.

I pondered this and wondered how a child, a virtual stranger I had only known for a few days who didn't even speak my language, could have known to ask such a pertinent question. It was a mystery to me. But I was also ashamed of my sloth. I had not been trying hard enough to find Clair or to solve the clues. There was no time to sit around beautiful Italian villages looking at churches, if I was to complete my journey.

Lucia herself appeared more composed and confident at dinner and grinned at me conspiratorially over her spaghetti, as she speared it with her fork and twirled it around her spoon as the children had been taught. I grinned back, but I also knew that I couldn't stay and be the child's friend forever. Soon, I would have to depart. Clair wasn't here in this place.

I hadn't spoken to the family about my mission, partly because it was too hard to explain in an English of which they had only a basic vocabulary, and partly because I didn't believe they would understand. It was difficult to hit on a practical way of finding Clair, when so many things about him were left unexplained. I reasoned that perhaps the only way of finding my brother would be by using my intuition, and although that appeared nebulous and unrealistic it was all I had to go on, except for a blurred photograph and a set of unsolved clues.

That night, I sat in my bedroom and pored over the parchment paper by candlelight. It was odd that the third clue seemed to have a relevance to my current situation: the English translation of the Italian sentence as Dr. Becker had revealed it to me was *Just like a family*. Did it have some significance, then, that I had ended up being looked after by this Italian family? I let my mind drift over my feelings of the day and of the days before, to see if some lateral connection would spring unbidden into my mind.

I thought about Lucia and how she didn't seem connected to anyone or anything in this her family. About how she needed to connect with someone, as any child needs to be loved and accepted for what they are. I thought about how the girl had chosen me as the person she could trust, simply because I had taken notice of her, when to everyone else her worth seemed questionable. I thought about the feeling I had had that we chose each other because we were both outsiders, both unaccepted, both strangers. How our differentness bound us together and made us seek each other's company for support. The words floated into my mind and I let them remain there while I considered them, enjoying the sound and feel of them: family, kin, alike, same, one, connected, kindred, clan, similar. I stretched the words out and mentally played with them, discovering their different connotations, dissecting them letter-by-letter.

Just then there was a knock at my bedroom door and as it swung slowly open I could see a childish figure framed in the light from the corridor. I smiled in recognition and Lucia bounded into the room, clutching a book, and flung herself on the floor at my feet, holding out the book to me with a delighted grin. As she chattered in unintelligible Italian, I leafed through the pages of the book, wondering what it was in particular she wanted me to look at.

It was a young child's alphabet book, with each letter represented by an appropriate picture. As I looked at the letter D, Lucia stuck her chubby little index finger on the picture accompanying the letter and pronounced the word beside it, enunciating carefully: "*Donna, donna.*" The picture was of a buxom Italian woman, cheerfully carrying a basket of washing. I chuckled in amusement, recognizing that the child was trying to teach me her language. I repeated the word after her and she clapped her hands together and put her head on one side, as if assessing my efforts. "Woman" I said, equally slowly. "In English - woman." Lucia frowned in concentration and tried to imitate my sounds, and we both giggled at the result.

We carried on to the next letter. E is for...*elefante.* Both Lucia and I were pleased that the English word was so similar. And then on to F... *famiglia* - family. I was impressed by the coincidence of coming across this word - although it was quite an obvious one to have in a child's picture book - because I had been thinking about it so much just before Lucia came in. The picture with the word had a mother and father standing behind two children, a boy and a girl. I was struck by how much the brother and sister looked alike. It was obvious they were kin...

Akin.

The word popped into my head and I stared ahead of me, my heart racing, no longer aware of Lucia's babble and her insistent pulling at my sleeve to encourage me to turn over the next page of the book.

Akin meant the same, alike, just like. It also meant a-kin, a family member, one of the same clan. *Just like a family.*

For a few minutes I helped Lucia with her book, feeling that it was more the child who had helped me. But now my heart wasn't in it, as I couldn't wait to get back to the crossword puzzle and see if my new solution to the clue fitted the grid. I was mightily relieved when Mariella came by my open door and noticed Lucia and myself sitting together on the floor. As it was past the little girl's usual bedtime, Mariella scolded her daughter and apologized to me for having been disturbed in my room. I assured her that I didn't mind, gave Lucia a kiss goodnight and hurriedly closed the door.

I rushed over to my jacket which was hanging on a coat hook on the back of the door, extracted the black box from its customary position in the inside pocket, and withdrew the parchment paper with the clues, spreading it out on the floor alongside the wooden crossword grid and the paper napkin with my completed solutions, beneath the light cast by my bedside lamp. My eyes rapidly scanned the empty boxes and mentally filled them in with the new letters.

Yes, the word would fit! I felt a rush of elation. At the moment, the grid looked like this:

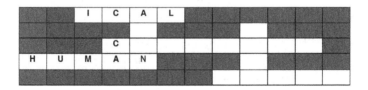

There were two spaces where a four-letter word could go. If HUMAN was in the correct position, AKIN could fit in to the right of it. So it would connect with ICAL on the top left. I filled the word in with pencil like so:

		I	C	A	L				
				K					
			C	I					
H	U	M	A	N					

That night I could hardly sleep, the excitement of having found solutions to three of the clues was so great. The words did have a kind of connection: ICAL the first; HUMAN the second; AKIN the third. Was it all something to do with families and children? Would the words represent the message Clair had for me?

Having solved three of the clues, I couldn't yet see how they would lead me to him. There wasn't a name for my brother or a town or country that gave his location. Perhaps the connection was more general, like that Clair was a HUMAN, that he was AKIN to me (i.e. like me in physical appearance) and he worked for I.C.A.L. as well.

I recoiled from that idea. If Clair was an I.C.A.L. employee that would mean I had been all wrong and should go back to London and look among the people there, my erstwhile workmates. My mind spun and spun on these problems, unable to clarify anything, or to rest and forget.

I awoke the next morning exhausted and confused. I was sure of one thing, however. My time in Gubbio was over. I had to continue to pursue Clair. For one thing, I had now been two weeks on the road, and I had used up almost half my supply of I.C.A.L. drugs. It was imperative that I get some more, if at all possible.

What if I.C.A.L. had started manufacturing the drugs again, back in England? I hadn't a clue what was happening outside in the world beyond this little town, as all the television and radio programs were in Italian, nor did I have access to any English newspapers. If I.C.A.L. were up and running again, perhaps I should return to England via Rotterdam and purchase more supplies. Although it would mean abandoning my journey for a while, at least I wouldn't have the threat of imminent illness and its attendant symptoms looming over me. I knew how difficult it would be to continue a journey suffering from the many painful ailments that went with Level 3, with no drugs to counteract them.

I wished I hadn't remained so long in this little town. Why had I wasted precious time here, when I had so little, and I never hoped to find Clair in this place?

I had to depart as soon as possible. I would leave today and make my way back to Rotterdam while deciding what to do next.

What to do about Lucia? I could hardly take her with me, although I would have appreciated her companionship. Even parents as offhand as hers would never let the girl go traveling with a comparative stranger on an unnamable expedition. Plus, a small child could only be a hindrance, in practical terms. Yet I hated to leave Lucia in this unloved state, watched over by nobody.

As though she'd read my thoughts, Lucia entered my bedroom, opening the door with a tentative creak and letting the sunlight stream in and light up my coverlet. I couldn't help smiling in recognition and pleasure at the sight of her face. When Lucia grinned she looked like any cheeky

Italian urchin, not the morose and timid child of my first acquaintance, and she was grinning now as she approached my bed and let something fall into my lap. While I glanced down at what she had dropped, Lucia took the opportunity to scamper off, with a giggle, shutting the bedroom door behind her and leaving me to wonder.

Something was packaged in heavy brown paper, and I carefully unfolded the wrappings and removed a slim gold ladies watch. I tried the watch on my right wrist and it only just fitted, having been made for more delicate arms than mine. The watch looked like an antique, at least a hundred years old. The tiny jeweled hands were studded with what looked like diamonds and the two gold wings on either side of the face had rubies set into their centers. Realizing that this must be a very precious ornament - both in monetary value and sentiment - I wondered where the child had got it from and why she had given it to me. How did Lucia possess such a thing? Did her parents know? And, more importantly, would they approve of the child giving it away? I was at once delighted and bemused.

When I went down to breakfast and informed Mariella and Paolo I would be leaving that day and taking the train to Rome, where I could catch a flight from the airport back to Holland, I took the opportunity to show them Lucia's present. I thought it would be presumptuous of me to wear it proprietarily on my wrist, so I kept the watch in its brown wrapping and placed the packet on the table.

"Lucia gave me this", I said, expecting them to react with horror and chide their daughter.

But Mariella, opening the parcel, only remarked, "Oh really?" with mild surprise. "She has it left to her from her grandmother. And she has given it to you, really? That's very generous." Mariella looked at Lucia - who had her head bent over her breakfast plate, devouring her food - and asked her a question in Italian, to which the child replied with assurance, "*E un regalo per Alicia.*"

"Yes, it is a gift she says," said Mariella to me.

"Thank you very much. *Grazie*" I said to the child, remembering the word, feeling suddenly embarrassed by this generosity. "But I can't possibly take it. It must be an heirloom."

"A what?" asked Paolo, speaking between gulps of coffee, as was his habit.

"Heirloom. Something from your family. Very valuable."

"Oh yes, it is worth a lot of money" Paolo replied, as if I had questioned the watch's monetary value, rather than my right to accept it.

"Of course you will take it," said Mariella, catching my meaning. "She has given it to you, so she want you to have it."

I realized that it would be rude to refuse the gift out of a misplaced politeness. So I thanked the child again, with feeling. "*Grazie mille.*" Lucia merely giggled and studied her plate in bashfulness. I reflected on what Ugo had told me about things coming to you when you needed them, and I carefully replaced the watch in its wrapping.

"Perhaps she would like to take you to the train station?" suggested Mariella to me, glad to encourage a friendship for her daughter. "*E vero? Vuoi prendere Alicia alla stazione?*" The child nodded vigorously and smiled at me.

So it was that we set out together for the station at about ten o'clock that morning, preparing for me to catch the 10.30 train, clutching my suitcase and with the precious watch on my wrist, having exchanged it for my old one which now lay discarded in the side pocket of my bag. Lucia clutched my hand tightly as we walked, and babbled inconsequentially, sometimes pointing things out to me, as was her way, and taking pleasure in my murmurs of interest. She was wearing a coat today, and it almost seemed the child intended to come with me if she could and stowaway on the train, never to return.

Although the idea appealed to me, I knew it would be wrong in many ways to take Lucia from the world she knew to live an unpredictable life with someone who couldn't protect her or provide for her. The girl had come out of her shell so much even in the last few days because of my attention, and she already had the confident air of one who could take her place in the world. She would have to learn to fight for recognition but she would survive, and her parents - although apparently uncaring - would offer their daughter a security that I never could. Perhaps, at any rate, I had managed to give Lucia something in the short time I had been there.

When the train arrived, Lucia stood looking lost and forlorn on the platform, and I picked her up and hugged her in a rush of affection. I told her to be good and, although she couldn't comprehend my words, she understood the meaning behind them. I waved from the window as the train pulled out of the station, and I believed that I would see Lucia again one day, although I didn't know when.

After the child had become a speck and disappeared into the distance, I reclined in my seat and pondered my future, and my journey seemed to stretch out endlessly before me. I knew where I was headed, right or wrong, but I didn't have a clear idea what I would do there.

The Stazione Termini which I arrived at in Rome was every bit as crowded and dirty as Ugo had predicted, and I fought off a wave of depression when I disembarked from the train. Something about the atmosphere of the place - the blare of announcements, the cacophony of constantly departing and arriving trains, slamming doors, guards' whistles, people shouting hellos and goodbyes, the grey uniformity of the building, the grey drizzle of the weather outside - all served to remind me of Victoria station and the day I'd left England feeling adrift and disorientated, as I did now. The memory depressed me because it brought back to me my loneliness and isolation.

But as I struggled down the platform with my suitcase banging at my heels and my open coat flapping wearily about my thighs, I determined to do the best I could to follow my journey to its conclusion. I had no time to waste on self-pity. I was resolved to catch the next flight back to Rotterdam, which left from Rome Fiumicino Airport in four hours. I'd already booked my ticket by telephone from Gubbio, and had been relieved to hear I could pay by credit card and pick it up at the departure desk at the airport just before the flight.

Glancing at the big station clock above the ticket desks, I saw that the time was only slightly after two o'clock. That meant I had quite a few hours to kill before taking the train from the station to the airport, so I elected to wander around in Rome a while and take in a few tourist sights while I was there. Shrugging my shoulders to shake off the weariness that the train journey had induced, I made my way to the exit doors, where a middle-aged Italian man with a swarthy face and a pleasant smile held one of the heavy swinging doors open to let me pass, and I thanked him with one of my few Italian words, my mood significantly lightened by this small act of kindness.

Using a combination of gestures, guesswork, slowly understood English and my minimal Italian vocabulary, I managed to hop on the correct bus to take me to the center of town, where I had ascertained that most of the interesting sights would be. I was amazed at the number of people inside the vehicle, most of whom were clinging precariously to the hanging straps or squashed next to each other too jam-packed to fall over, all talking ten to the dozen in loud strident voices. I had been lucky enough to claim one of the few seats, and I stared out of the window at this strange new city. The bus juddered and jolted its way down the wide streets until it came to a huge ornate white building with many statues, which was where I'd been instructed to alight. I pushed my way through the other passengers and out on to the street, wishing I'd thought to deposit my suitcase in a left luggage compartment at the station, rather than lugging the heavy article all over town with me.

I strolled past quite a large shop selling televisions and other electrical equipment, which displayed a tempting array of machines in its windows. As I walked by, intending to cross the road and make my way to the Trevi Fountain, my eye was caught by an image in one of the many television sets that had been tuned to a local channel. I stopped in my tracks and squinted into the window, hardly able to believe my eyes. There before me appeared my ex-boss, David Grainger. His arm was in a sling and there were great bruises on his forehead, but he was otherwise unscathed, and I felt unexpectedly overjoyed to see him. Although Grainger hadn't been a particularly considerate or pleasant boss to work for, the fact that he hadn't been killed in the bomb blast reassured me, because it confirmed that some of the I.C.A.L. staff other than myself had survived and gave me hope that the organization was getting back on its feet again, perhaps even trying to carry on as normal.

I pressed my face to the glass and gazed at the television screen. My erstwhile boss was being interviewed by a reporter - possibly for some news program - and I could see that he was speaking animatedly, although I wasn't able to hear his words and the Italian subtitles beneath the picture gave me no clue as to the subject of his dialogue with the interviewer. Something was different about Grainger's face: the old smug, self-satisfied expression had gone and been replaced by a sort of fear, almost a panic.

Now the picture switched to the I.C.A.L. building where I had worked up until only a couple of weeks ago, and I saw a picture of a burnt out shell. The reporter was standing in front of the building explaining something, and as he pointed to the windows, the camera zoomed in and came to rest on an I.C.A.L. sign which had come loose off its hinges and hung lopsided over a doorway. Then the picture switched back to the News Studio, and another item was introduced.

I stood in stunned stillness, unable to immediately assimilate what I'd just seen. Had the terrorist attacks completely destroyed I.C.A.L., then? Could the company pick up the pieces and start again?

Without thinking further, I raced into the shop. "Excuse me," I said breathlessly to the middle-aged Italian man behind the counter. "Do you speak English?"

The shopkeeper had the face of a doleful bulldog. He put his thumb and forefinger about half an inch apart and brought them up to his mouth: "Leetle" he said.

I sighed impatiently, and then ploughed on, desperate to know the worst. "You know that television program that was on just now, the news item? What were they saying?"

The man shook his head slowly, as if to deny all comprehension of my frantic questions.

"Television, television" I repeated in a loud voice, indicating one of the machines on the wall, which were still tuned to the same news channel, now showing pictures of a row of Italian beauty contestants smiling and waving at the camera.

"Yes" the proprietor agreed, nodding vigorously. "Television" he echoed. "We sell. You want buy?"

"No, no." I snapped in annoyance at his obtuseness. "This program" I said, going over to the nearest television set and tapping the screen with my index finger. "What did it say? Something about England."

The man gave an eloquent shrug before his telephone rang and he picked up the receiver, probably grateful to have a good excuse for ignoring me. Recognizing that it was no use pestering him further, I gave up and walked out of the shop.

I stood outside the window for a moment, gazing at the television screens, lost in anxious deliberations. What did it mean? Had Grainger been telling the interviewer that I.C.A.L. was completely destroyed and had no hope of getting back on its feet in the near future? Or had Grainger been explaining that they were going to start running the company again and start manufacturing the drugs for Level 3, which represented I.C.A.L.'s main livelihood? It was impossible to tell.

I carried on walking and after a while came to a large newsagents' shop, where I was delighted to see a newspaper in English. However, it was an American paper with no articles about I.C.A.L. I stood inside browsing through the paper for so long without actually buying it, that the manager approached me and shouted something in Italian, which probably meant - *Put that thing down unless you intend buying it,* so I left the shop as quickly as I could, feeling my face redden.

I must have spent over two hours trudging up and down the streets gazing at the sights to occupy myself, because by the time everything closed for siesta and I found myself in a small cafe ordering cappuccino and cake, it was a quarter past four. My earlier gloom had returned in double strength, and I stared morosely at the cup in my fingers and at my frazzled image in the mirror on the wall, wishing I'd never attempted this fruitless journey. I looked out at the steadily darkening afternoon sky and a persistent drizzle that reminded me of England, and contemplated returning there in the hopes that I might be able to buy some more I.C.A.L. drugs. But I knew it was a long shot. I wasn't even sure whether the drugs were being manufactured again yet.

I reflected that perhaps Hanneke would have some news to relate. At least I'd have someone to talk to when I arrived in Rotterdam. I resolved to telephone my friend as soon as I got to the airport to let her know when I'd be arriving.

It was pleasant to sit and relax in the warmth of this cafe. I stretched out my legs and enjoyed the sensation of not having to put any weight on my feet. My suitcase was tucked rather uncomfortably into the seat next to me, and I'd taken my coat off and hung it over the back of my chair. I felt in the pocket for my black box, then remembered that I never changed its position from inside my jacket pocket: the jacket was now packed securely in the suitcase. I was seized with a capricious desire to look inside the box and see if the photograph had altered again.

I tried to dismiss the desire from my mind, telling myself it would be far too much aggravation to rifle through all my clothes and locate the jacket with the box, disturbing my careful packing in the process. But it was no good. As soon as I had the impulse to look at the box, I knew I wouldn't be able to rest until my whim was satisfied.

I heaved my suitcase up on to the small table, moved aside my cup and plate, and proceeded to undo the fastenings and begin my search. The waiter regarded me with an amused smile from behind the counter, before coming to clear away my dirty dishes from the table, saying something to me in Italian, which I didn't understand. I smiled back at him, and then resumed my dismantling of the suitcase's contents. Of course, the jacket had been packed at the very bottom and I had to dislodge many of my other clothes in order to prize it from its position, but eventually I succeeded, retrieved the box from the inside pocket, repacked the suitcase rather clumsily and reset the case on the seat beside me.

I was always a bit secretive about opening the box in front of strangers, and now that the waiter had become rather intrigued by my antics and seemed to be staring at me wondering what I'd do next, I put the box on my lap where it was partially obscured by the tablecloth, and undid the clasps. I looked at the photograph, and to my extreme disappointment - considering the trouble I'd undertaken to locate it - the picture hadn't changed a bit. The same darkish stain covered about two thirds of the white surface, and that was all.

As I sat gazing at the photograph, a man approached me. He was probably in his mid-thirties, taller and leaner than most of the Italian men I'd seen, but with the same wiry black hair, swarthy skin and nut-brown eyes. He was dressed in a smart dark grey suit with a black polo neck jumper underneath it, and I noticed that on his hands - which were surprisingly small and girlish for such a tall man - he sported a couple of large and ornate gold rings.

"Is this seat free?" the man asked in perfect English, fixing me with his eyes and descending into the chair almost before I had a chance to give an affirmative nod. He lit a cigarette and inhaled thoughtfully, while I quickly stuffed my precious photograph back into the lid of the box, closed the container and repacked it in the bottom of my suitcase. I said nothing, but the man's silent stare was discomfiting me, and I wished he would either move away or open a conversation.

Seemingly in answer to my silent wish, he began: "Are you traveling alone?"

I nodded and put my suitcase down on the ground between my feet under the table, a combination of exhaustion and distrust having stifled my usually verbose nature. I sipped from my cup of cappuccino which had now gone very cold, then I remembered something and removed a little bottle of tablets from my trouser pocket, where I had put them earlier hoping to remind myself to take my customary daily pill with the teatime drink. I carefully unscrewed the top and tipped one tablet out on to my palm, then closed the bottle again and replaced it in my pocket. I had gone past caring whether this man or anyone else noticed that I took pills or what they thought about it. Plus, it was often at around this time of day that my energy started to flag and I felt in need of the temporary boost that the I.C.A.L. drug gave me.

The man's stare intensified, as he shadowed my actions with his eyes. I popped the tablet into my mouth, held it under my tongue for a couple of seconds and then took a large gulp of cold coffee to wash it down, tipping my head back to let the pill slide down my gullet. All this attention from the man opposite me was beginning to make me squirm like an animal in a zoo, but I didn't have the strength to ask him to leave, nor did I feel justified in asking him to stop his harassment, since he wasn't actually harming me in any way.

"You are not well?" he asked, leaning back in his chair and surrounding his head with a halo of smoke from his cigarette. His voice had a dry edge to it, like crackling paper.

"Yes, I'm ill" I replied rather curtly, not looking at him and hoping to discourage him by being blunt about my condition. "I've got something called Level 3, it's a disease that's affecting a lot of people in England. You've probably not heard of it."

"Oh yes, I have heard of it."

"Really?" I looked up at the man directly for the first time, surprised at his disclosure.

He gave a slow nod and narrowed his eyes, sucked the last bit of nicotine out of his cigarette, then stubbed it out in the glass ashtray on our table. "I work in the medical industry here. I know a lot about diseases and drugs."

"What - you're a sort of chemist or something, are you?" I asked.

"Yes." I noticed that his speech was slow and ponderous and heavily accented. Perhaps he was from the south of Italy, where I had been told the accent was much stronger. "This Level 3 is a very bad sickness, yes?"

"Yes it is," I agreed.

"And what are these drugs you are taking now? Can I see?" The man stretched out one jeweled hand across the table.

I hesitated, and then complied with his request. "I suppose so. Why not?" I took the bottle of pills from my pocket and handed it to him.

He turned the bottle over in one hand and studied the label carefully, before giving it back to me. "Where did you get this?"

"These pills are made by a company in England called I.C.A.L. They are...they were...a huge pharmaceutical company who provide the only drugs on the market effective against the symptoms of Level 3."

"And these drugs work?" he asked.

"Oh yes, they definitely work. Thousands of people have had success with them, including me." I almost didn't continue. But, to tell the truth, I was feeling lonely and glad of the chance to talk to someone, even this rather unprepossessing man. Besides, I judged, what harm could it do to talk to a stranger about medical matters? "The trouble is, you see, that I don't have many of the pills left. I'm probably going back to England to try and get some more but I don't even know if I.C.A.L. are making any now. The company were bombed a couple of weeks ago and all their stocks were destroyed. I don't really want to go back there and have a wasted journey if they're not making the drugs, but I can't find out anything about England from here, and I don't know what else to do." I broke off and shrugged my shoulders.

The man regarded me thoughtfully, and lit another cigarette. "There are other drugs available."

"No there aren't" I replied immediately. Then added: "Are there?"

The man nodded. "I see from the label on your bottle that this drug is made of ingredients I recognize. There is a company here in Italy that make a drug very similar to yours."

"But, how come I.C.A.L. drugs are the only ones people buy, the only ones doctors say are effective?"

"Doctors!" he sneered. "They work with the pharmaceutical companies, the company says here is my nice drug, will you prescribe it if I give you free holiday or free video or whatever, doctor says O.K., makes no difference to me." He gave a shrug of his large shoulders, as though to dismiss the entire medical profession.

"Gosh, that's a bit cynical, isn't it? Surely doctors prescribe what they think's best, don't they?" My voice sounded plaintive. I wanted to believe these assertions, but

I wasn't entirely sure of the validity of my argument. I knew nothing about medicine; simply trusting what other people told me was the truth.

"Listen." The man leaned towards me and blew noxious cigarette smoke in my face, making me wince. "I have also a friend with the Level 3, here in this country. She is an English girl, very nice. Like you, same age as you. It is just people your age that suffer, yes?"

I nodded.

"She came to this country three years ago, when she was first diagnosed with the Level 3--"

"Three years! She's lasted that long?" I exclaimed.

"Exactly. She has lasted this long time, longer than anybody else I know, or you know probably. And why? Because she did not take the English drug that is made by your doctors. She took the drug that is made here. And this keep her well all that time."

"But why haven't we heard about this in England?"

The man shrugged and opened his arms to the side, as if to say, *Don't ask me.* "Your company in England want everybody to use their drug, they don't want competition, want to make all the money for themselves. I don't know."

"But surely somebody would tell us. Somebody would find out."

"Who? How would they find out?"

"I don't know." I was staggered. I suppose it did make sense for I.C.A.L. to want to keep all the profits for themselves. But could it really be true that their drug was not the only one to be effective, and that I had miraculously bumped into a man who knew this?

"The trouble is, the drug they make here is very expensive. Made from very pure ingredients, much purer than in your drug. These ingredients more difficult to obtain, so..." The man made an eloquent gesture with his hands to complete his sentence.

"Is that why not much is known about the drug outside Italy?"

"Exactly. You read my mind. The doctor who make this drug here, he no want to make a very big profit, just a little profit, just enough you know? I know him very well because I got the drugs from him to help my friend."

"The English girl who's had Level 3 for three years?"

"Yes. I get the drugs for her. I buy them for her. They are very expensive, but because she is my friend..." The man withdrew a small bottle from the pocket of his expensive suit jacket. It was very similar to mine in size and shape, but when he handed it to me I couldn't understand the description on the label, which was in Italian.

"So these are the drugs?"

"Yes."

"They look very much like mine."

"They are very like yours. Only much more pure. So much better for you to take."

I fingered the bottle and asked experimentally: "How much are they?"

The man narrowed his eyes as if considering his reply, then said: "Five hundred Euros."

"Five hundred!" I echoed, my mouth agape in amazement. "For that bottle? That's ridiculous."

"This bottle..." he said, holding it between thumb and forefinger and shaking the contents slightly, "...has in it 300 tablets, enough for 300 days. It keep you alive for nearly one year. One whole year. Worth a million lire, no? To stay alive for one year?"

I took the bottle from him and peeked inside. He was right. There probably were as many as 300 tablets in there, because they were very tiny and the bottle was quite large. "They're very small. Do you really only have to take one a day?"

"Exactly. One a day is enough."

I screwed up my face in concentration and placed the bottle on the table.

"It is not so much" he replied. "Not much to pay for health for one year. That is priceless, no?"

"Are you sure this works?"

"Absolutely sure. Remember my friend. If you like, I take you to meet her. I am seeing her today at seven o'clock. She can tell you herself."

"No, no, it's O.K. I don't have time, actually. I have to go to the airport and catch a plane soon. But I don't think I have that much money on me."

"You don't have to give me the cash, if you have something…I don't know…quite valuable, that you don't need so much. I could take that instead."

I considered for a few moments and thought of Lucia's watch, now adorning my wrist in place of the old timepiece lying at the bottom of my suitcase. I hated to part with her gift, because of its sentimental rather than monetary value. But after all, the man was right to say my health was important. Wasn't it more important to be given the chance to carry on with my journey, rather than hanging on to an object that, however beautiful and precious, I couldn't actually use for anything practical? "I suppose I do have something..." I said slowly.

"Good" said the man. "Now I go to the gentleman's toilet at the back, leave this bottle here on the table while you make up your mind." He got up and walked to the back of the cafe.

I regarded the pills in front of me. It flashed briefly through my mind to grab the bottle and run out of the cafe. But I pushed the thought away. That would be stealing and theft under any circumstances was wrong. I gazed at Lucia's watch lovingly for a few moments, then unclasped it from my wrist and placed it on the table. I was convinced Lucia would want me to have any benefits the sale of the watch would bestow. And if these drugs really did give me a year's extra life, a year more to find Clair, what better and more valuable gift could I have?

When the man returned, we made our transaction. I was still reluctant to part with the watch, but I forced myself to go through with the deal, with inner chidings that I'd made up my mind and vacillation now would be pure weakness. I left the cafe and walked back to Stazione Termini, where I took the next bus for Rome Fiumicino Airport to await my plane for Rotterdam. Although unsure what to do when I reached Hanneke's now, I was optimistic that the new drugs would imbue me with new energy to solve the rest of the clues. After all, if they'd kept the man's friend alive for three years, the pills must be remarkably potent.

Upon my arrival at Fiumicino Airport, I went directly to the departures area and found the correct check-in line for the flight to Rotterdam that evening. There was a substantial queue at my desk, and I stared vaguely into space as I waited, ignoring the swirling crowds around me. I'd been unable to resist taking one of the pills the man in the cafe had given me, and had popped a tablet into my mouth during my bus journey to the airport, hoping to feel a surge of new energy almost immediately, as the man had claimed the drugs were very fast acting.

I certainly didn't feel myself, but the alteration was not as I'd expected. My head felt light and my body as weightless as if I rested on air. The surge of energy I had anticipated was more a kind of trembling excitement and my heart palpitated very quickly beneath my ribcage, in the same way it might if I'd suddenly consumed ten cups of strong coffee. I'd never experienced these sensations, either before or after contracting Level 3.

The events around me were happening very slowly, and life was taking on the aspect of a slow motion film. People's movements were made as if wading through a thick sludge of treacle, and I wanted to call out to them: "Hurry up, hurry up - why are you taking so long?" as though I were in a desperate hurry and everybody else was purposefully obstructing me with their infernal snail-like pace.

At the top of my queue was a young couple, who seemed to be carrying a truckload of bags and suitcases which all had to be checked in. The girl wore a bright pink coat, and the color hurt my eyes so much I had to shield them. Their voices wafted on the still air towards me, as if from a great distance away and echoing down a long marble hallway.

I looked down at my feet, determined to distance myself from the distractions around me, and contemplated the ground. The floor was covered in some sort of polkadot pattern and I gazed at it marveling at its intricacy, but the spots taunted me by dancing in front of my eyes, and I had to look up again.

And then, I saw them.

Two people were positioned with their backs turned towards me. The pair must have neared me while I was gazing at the floor, and they lingered in the queue next to mine, the line for a flight to - I glanced across at the board - Katmandu in Nepal. An elderly gentleman with thick white hair and a slightly stooped frame who was dressed in a well-cut dark brown suit of thick tweed, bent over his wooden walking stick. Beside him hovered a little boy of about six years old, who held his guardian's hand in his smaller one. As I stood regarding them, the boy turned his profile to speak in a foreign language to the man, and his granddad - or whoever it was - bent down slowly to hear what the child was saying.

The man replied to the boy in a low voice, appeared to make some decision, patted his grandson on the shoulder and pointed to the corner of the huge hall indicating a sign for toilets. The boy began to drift away, looking about him with curiosity at the other people in the airport. Maybe it was something in the way he walked - with a gait that was gawky yet cocky, at the same time hesitant and inquisitive - but I had a sudden and immediate recollection of Clair. It was like seeing my brother there before me, and I longed for the boy to turn around. At that moment, as if I'd willed it, he did so, and he seemed to be looking directly at me.

Now I saw the boy's face clearly, and I recognized him at once. I was absolutely convinced that he was Clair! The same white skin, the same dark hair cut in a bob, the same slender body, the same stance of mingled assurance and tranquility. But why here? Why now? Was this some sort of sign?

I had to talk to the boy, I knew that.

Abandoning my position in the queue, I raced over to the child in a state of nervous agitation. Reaching the small wandering figure, I tapped the boy on the shoulder and he turned to face me.

It was Clair all right. He had the same expression. Exactly the same eyes!

I wasn't certain what to say. The boy was obviously not English, but I didn't know what nationality he was. I bent down to the child's level, losing my balance and feeling my body practically topple over, so that I had to rescue myself with my hands on the floor. Almost before I knew what I was doing, I'd grabbed one of the boy's small hands. I felt as though my actions were happening without my control, as if I were standing outside my body and viewing these events as they happened to another person, some madwoman who accosted small children in airports for no reason.

But I was compelled to speak to the boy. Now that I'd found my brother, I couldn't let him disappear without trying to explain. My heart was beating so dramatically I was practically breathless.

"What's your name?" I managed at last, hoping that maybe the child spoke a few words of English.

The boy stood motionless - not, however, withdrawing his hand from mine - and fixed me with a bewildered stare. When he looked up in relief, I saw that the elderly gentleman had approached us. "Quest'ce que vous voulez?" the man enquired sharply, addressing me. I dropped the boy's hand and stood up to face my inquisitor, at the same time reeling under a spurt of extreme dizziness, which nearly sent me falling to the ground again. Putting a hand to my damp forehead, I shook my head in an effort to clear it. The man's voice sounded strange, metallic, like some kind of robot.

"Ramon" he barked at the boy. "Viens. Vite!" The old man grabbed the boy's hand and prepared to march away from me.

"No, wait" I cried in desperation. "I think I know your grandson. I think I know this boy." I pointed to the child with a trembling hand. "I mean him no harm. But I know him. He's my brother." Although I realized how crazy this must have sounded, the words blurted out of my mouth before I could stop them.

The old gentleman didn't comprehend me anyway, as he obviously spoke not a word of English. But he could understand the urgency behind my speech, from its tone of panic and anguish. He turned and addressed me more kindly, his thick eyebrows raising in enquiry: *"Parlez vous Francais, mademoiselle?"*

"French? Erm...yes, I think so..." I scoured my mind for some phrases of schoolgirl French. But my head felt full of cotton wool, and as though I was negotiating an impenetrable fog. The face of the old gentleman seemed to be moving in and out of focus, expanding and contracting like some monster from the deep. Surely, this couldn't be happening. He was just an old man, wasn't he? An old man, the father, the grandfather...of Clair.

"L'enfant..." I began, struggling against my confusion and pointing to the boy, *"Je connais."* The old man nodded,

having grasped this assertion at least. *"Je connais parce que, il est mon frere."* The man stared at me in total bemusement.

I couldn't think what else to say and stood gaping at them like some sort of turtle. After a few seconds, the man gave a terse nod and grasped his grandson's hand, moving away in an attempt to make their escape. *"Excuse moi, mademoiselle. Il faut que je part..."*

"No!" I halted them once more with my voice. *"Un moment"* I ordered, battling to make myself understood. *"Ou allez vous?"*

"Ou?" the old man echoed. He pointed to the board at the head of the queue where he and the boy had waited moments before. *"Katmandu. Nous allons on vacation. Excuse moi, encore."* The man inclined his head once more in a gracious nod, and dragged the child back to their previous place in the queue. The boy lagged behind, his eyes continuing to stare at me, and I took this as a token that he was drawn to speak with me as much as I with him.

But what was I to do? I couldn't let my brother disappear from my life forever, now that I'd found him. I had to follow them. To follow him. I'd make the old man understand. I'd find someone to translate for me so that we could have a proper conversation and I could explain everything.

I joined the Rotterdam queue once more and waited till it was my turn at the desk. Collecting my ticket, I asked whether I could exchange it for another flight. When the girl expressed surprise, I explained that I'd suddenly changed my mind and decided to travel to Nepal instead of Holland. She said it would be possible to exchange my ticket and, after a few hurried telephone calls, issued me with a place on the Katmandu flight. I checked in moments later at the

Katmandu desk, registering with little concern that there was now no sign of the old man and his grandson. I was due to board the same flight, so I was bound to meet up with the pair later. I would note carefully where they sat and make sure they didn't leave the airplane at the other end without me following them. As long as I kept the pair in my sights when we reached Katmandu, all would be well.

I achieved all these arrangements in a type of trance, hardly knowing what I did. My mind and body seemed to be divorced from each other and operating independently. My whole frame was atremble with the extra-fast beating of my heart and my face had broken out into a sweat. People looked at me strangely, leering at me, their faces distorting as the old man's had done. I began to imagine the world was against me, but planned to fight back if necessary.

What did it matter if the old man had warned people that I was crazy, that I had approached him with some story about knowing his grandson? I didn't care if he'd told the whole world and they tried to keep me from my brother. I was on a journey to find Clair, and now I'd found him nobody would stop me getting to him. Nobody!

Sitting in the departures lounge, I dwelled on these thoughts. I would kidnap the boy - I thought - and take him back to London with me. I would teach him enough English to be able to communicate with me and he would understand me immediately. Hadn't Clair and I been able to converse without words as children? Now I'd met Clair's reincarnation, the boy would surely accept who I was, once I could explain properly.

I reflected then on the mysterious circumstance that I was traveling to Nepal, and that Nepalese was the language of one of the clues (I couldn't remember which one), as Dr. Becker had informed me. Perhaps it was more than coincidence that I was going to that country, that Clair had led me there.

I knew little about Nepal, other than the fact that the main religion was Buddhism and the country had many monasteries. Our "religious experience" classes at school had touched briefly on Buddhism and I vaguely remembered pictures of monks in the Himalayas, with shaved heads and orange gowns.

Was I meant to go to Nepal? It did seem oddly coincidental that I had ended up going to Austria for the German clue and Italy for the Italian clue, so perhaps it was true that the languages were clues in themselves.

I was on a journey, wasn't I? And if it meant journeying to the ends of the earth to be with Clair, I was determined to go there.

CHAPTER TEN

I N THE DREAM, Clair was singing. He was an adult, as old as I am now, yet he looked exactly the same as I remember him. The same brown hair, the same white face, the same thin body, the same ingenuous slightly earnest expression. My brother was standing in front of an audience of people. I don't know who they were, perhaps relations. They were all smiling and clapping and enjoying his song. I was there too, watching with admiration, and sometimes Clair would look at me and smile. He was singing the song we used to sing as children - Sylvie.

Mother had an old cassette recorder (she always refused to buy CDs) on which she played a tape of some unknown seventies folk singer who sang in a whiny voice we children loved. Or maybe it was the words we loved best. At any rate we learnt them and we sang along:

> As Sylvie was walking, down by the riverside,
> As Sylvie was walking, down by the riverside,
> She thought on her true love
> She thought on her true love
> She thought on her true love, who'd gone from her side...

Clair was singing in his best choirboy's voice. He was wearing a suit and his hair was smart. Was he a child or an adult? I couldn't say. But he continued:

> *Last night in sweet slumber, a dream I did see,*
> *Last night in sweet slumber, a dream I did see,*
> *My own dearest true love*
> *My own dearest true love*
> *My own dearest true love, came smiling to me.*
>
> *But when I awoke I found it not so,*
> *But when I awoke I found it not so.*
> *My eyes were like fountains,*
> *My eyes were like fountains,*
> *My eyes were like fountains, where water did*
> *flow..."*

Then the dream ended and I awoke.

At first I couldn't remember where I was. The room was dark and there were strange sounds enveloping me. The bed on which I lay could have been anywhere: our flat in London with traffic outside, a boat crossing the Channel, the tiny bedroom at the top of the farmhouse in Gubbio. Opening my eyes I tried to make sense of the shapes I saw in the room, and gradually recognition dawned. I was lying on a bed in a hotel in the Thamel area of Katmandu in Nepal, and the noises outside were of cyclists' bells and hawkers selling their wares and packs of wild dogs barking and the bustle of a town that never sleeps.

Unpleasant memories were rekindled with my awakening, memories of the previous day. Sitting up in bed, I groaned at the thought of what I'd done. In reckless desperation at knowing the I.C.A.L. drugs I carried would soon be finished, I'd allowed myself to be tricked into purchasing drugs from a conman in a Roman cafe. So keen had I been to pay a huge sum of money for his worthless concoction, that I'd parted with Lucia's beautiful gift to me, the watch that had been her family heirloom, which she had bestowed on me with love. Cradling my aching head in my hands, I rued my rash folly.

What the hell were in those terrible tablets? I knew only that taking one tiny pill had created disastrous effects within me. An hour after the drug's consumption, I'd begun tripping as if on bad heroin. Never having experimented with recreational drugs, I'd had no idea until afterwards that the distorted images and thoughts that attacked me were due to a narcotic I'd pumped into my system. In my delusional state, I'd been so convinced of finding Clair that I'd pursued a strange French boy and his grandfather all the way to Nepal, in the opposite direction from where I'd intended to go.

I remembered little else about the flight except that I'd passed out for an hour or so, before coming to and spending the rest of the journey throwing up in the lavatory, much to the disgust of the other passengers. On disembarking from the plane, I'd been too sick and exhausted to even consider following the French pair I'd been so keen to tail. I'd fallen into a taxi at Katmandu airport and pleaded to be taken to the nearest reasonably priced hotel, where I'd collapsed for the night.

Recalling my actions depressed me unutterably, and I sat for a few moments staring into space, too wretched to move.

Then, sighing, I swung my legs down to the floor. I told myself there was nothing I could do about my errors now, except make the best of my current circumstances. I had a little money left, and I resolved to try and get a translation for the Nepalese clue, while I was here.

I rose and peered through the curtains at the street below. It seemed to be late in the day, as the thoroughfare was full of activity. I glanced at my old watch, which lay on the bedside table, and saw with dismay that it gave the time as a quarter to ten. I was already so tardy. At least I was feeling - remarkably under the circumstances - undeservedly fit.

My rage at the Roman conman spurred me to hurl his bottle of pills out into the street, but I was concerned that somebody else might try one of the tablets with ill effects, so I carefully emptied the bottle's contents into the toilet and flushed the chain.

After I had washed and dressed I went downstairs to the hotel restaurant and ordered a coffee and full breakfast, glad to observe that the Nepalese were relaxed about mealtime hours. My breakfast consisted of eggs and bacon, orange juice and Austrian pastries, delights I'd never anticipated eating in Nepal. In the lobby outside the dining room, a man sat with his long legs crossed, reading a copy of The Herald Tribune. As he was the only other person in sight, I imagined that all the other guests must have departed for the day to go shopping or on treks.

The newspaper reader was tall and thin with wavy mid-brown hair and a gaunt face. I couldn't account for a sharp echo of recognition on first sight of this man, so I dismissed the possibility of having met him before and attributed the feeling of familiarity he evoked to a fleeting resemblance to somebody in my past. His glasses and his narrow hands with their sensitive fingers and the way he drank in the contents of the paper with utter concentration made him appear an intellectual. Although I stared at him almost brazenly over my coffee cup, wishing to make contact with another person to cure my loneliness in this strange place, the man paid me no attention and continued reading.

Feeling full and invigorated after my breakfast I strolled out into the sunshine, appreciating the day's crisp freshness and winter cold. I meandered through the streets, finding it difficult not to be sucked into doorways by insistent traders urging me to buy their wares, who assumed I would find their cries of "Cheap", "Good buy", "Discount" irresistible. I tried to explain that I had come to look, not to buy. Gradually I learnt not to make eye contact with people and in that way avoid any harassment. The gaily-colored bicycle rickshaws with their young drivers so keen to offer me a lift for a few coins intrigued me, but I preferred to walk and drink in the atmosphere. The profusion of wonderfully old and ornate buildings and temples was delightful. By the sides of the road, women in gloriously colorful saris swept the ground with brooms made of straw.

I saw many bookshops selling all types of books calculated to appeal to the tourist: travel in Nepal, Buddhism, Indian cookery and general fiction that could be exchanged by weary hitchhikers with little space in their knapsacks. But

I searched in vain for the book I sought. There were simple phrasebooks and English-Nepali dictionaries, but nothing comprehensive enough to help me unravel the fourth clue's translation. I wondered whether the only solution would be to find a native Nepalese who spoke good enough English.

I wandered into a courtyard, through a narrow door, and was greeted by a scene of quiet and serenity in sharp contrast to the noise of the street a few yards away. In the center of the courtyard was the ubiquitous temple with its golden Buddha statue and food offerings placed outside. I made a slow promenade around the courtyard, and the Nepalese families who sat on the steps outside their small houses took no notice of me, indifferent to the fact that I was the only Westerner amongst them. In front of one doorway a woman sat, her long black lustrous hair being brushed by a small child. The woman was smiling, and I thought her radiant face the most beautiful thing I had ever seen.

I saw a youth herding a flock of geese in front of him with a stick. As he saw me regarding him with interest, he beamed and greeted me with a *Namaste*. I smiled back and noticed how happy he appeared, and with so little. How simple his life must be and how poor by English standards, yet his whole demeanor was so contented with life. I recalled how English commuters looked as they struggled to work on the underground - miserable and hard-faced, worn and old before their time. And yet their material advantages far outweighed those of this lad. It occurred to me then that contentment must be a product of inner peace and not of outer success.

In the street, outside another temple, stood a cow. Not tethered or confined, but simply standing as if it belonged there, safe in the knowledge that cows are worshipped beasts with nothing to fear from humans. As I meandered, lost in my musings in a kind of daydream, I became aware that somebody was waving at me from across the street and trying to attract my attention.

"Are you lost? English?" the girl called. She was Nepalese, in her twenties or thereabouts, wearing jeans and a t-shirt rather than the usual sari, but with decidedly Indian features.

"No, I'm not lost. I'm just wandering about." My first inclination was to suspect her of trying to sell me something, before I realized that she must have mistaken my aimlessness for confusion. The girl seemed genuinely keen to help.

She approached me, smiling. "I thought perhaps you wanted to reach the Durbar Square. I can direct you, if you like." I was surprised at her comparative lack of an accent, and pleased at her educated delivery.

"No it's O.K. I didn't have anywhere particular in mind."

"Do you need a map?"

So she was trying to sell me something. "No thanks. Really." I started to drift away.

"That's fine. But if you need anything, just call at my shop." The girl handed me a business card, maintaining her friendly smile, and walked away with no attempt to push me further. I felt a little guilty that I'd been so suspicious of her intentions and scrutinized the card. *Thamel Travel - for all your travel requirements: maps, guidebooks, trekking guides etc. Opposite the Himalaya Hotel.* I shoved the card into my pocket, and then recollected that I needed someone who spoke good English to help me with the crossword clue, and I wondered if this girl could assist me.

By the time I'd thus changed my mind about her offer the girl was already lost to view, but having the address of her shop I determined to visit there later. I had also considered asking the porters at my hotel, but their English appeared to be limited to a few stock phrases. There was that man, reading his newspaper, who had struck me as so intelligent. Perhaps he was English but spoke Nepalese, having lived here for a while? But that was unlikely, as a permanent resident would be living in an apartment and not a hotel. I recognized that my fascination with the stranger was such that I was already starting to construct a fantasy identity for him, and I chastised myself for my foolishness.

Later on that morning - when I returned to the hotel exhausted and footsore, asking for my key at the reception desk - I was surprised to be handed a slip of paper: "A message for you" said the smiling bellboy in the smart blue suit.

"Oh. Thanks" I replied casually in an effort to hide my amazement, wondering who on earth would contact me, since nobody knew where I was. I opened the paper and read the following:

Dear Alice, I hope you won't think me too forward, but I saw you at breakfast and I asked the boy on reception about you. I believe you're English and on your own here. I'm Australian and also on my own. Perhaps you'd like to meet sometime for a coffee and a chat? It would be good to have someone to talk to. Dan Armitage, Room 303

My heart started to thump with elation. This was the man I'd seen reading the paper. He had noticed me after all! I tried to restrain my excitement at meeting the stranger by assuring myself that I, like him, was merely seeking the solace of pleasant conversation. I wrote an answering message on a slip of paper and asked the bellboy to put it in the pigeonhole for Room 303:

> *Dear Dan, Thanks for your note. I'd love to*
> *meet for a coffee - say this evening at 7 p.m.*
> *downstairs in the restaurant? I'll look forward*
> *to meeting you then. Alice.*

Feeling significantly cheered by the prospect of my forthcoming date, I sat for a while in the foyer looking at guidebooks about Katmandu, which I hoped would inspire me with ideas on how to occupy the rest of my day. I was attracted by the picture of a Buddhist stupa at Bodnath, described as easily reachable by bus or bicycle. Bodnath possessed one of the largest stupas in the country apparently, and a large number of monks were sheltered inside the stupa's walls.

Perhaps I had been drawn to this place for a reason, even though my journey had seemed so futile at first. I liked Katmandu, and it was possible that the Nepalese clue had some significance of which I was not yet aware. Maybe I would find Clair in this country. If I tried to intuit the sort of place where Clair might be found, the idea of him being reincarnated as a Buddhist monk in Nepal seemed appropriate. Clair had always possessed a spirituality, in my remembrance of him, a quality that had sometimes caused Mother to teasingly refer to him as her "little monk" because of his serious demeanor and gentle ways.

I wondered whether it was my mission simply to find the place where my brother was, then wait for him to come to me. How was I to distinguish him from among hundreds of other monks - if that indeed was what he'd reincarnated as - when I had no notion of his physical appearance, apart from the mysterious S on his body that Genevieve had mentioned? As I sat ostensibly absorbing the guidebooks but actually working myself up into a lather at contemplation of the insuperable odds of my quest, I raged against the injustice of having been allocated this Mission Impossible. Why - I complained inwardly - did I have to travel all over the world looking for someone I may not even recognize when I found him, all on my own, with no help from anyone? My task was too formidable!

In my despondency and self-pity, a tear glistened in the corner of one eye and threatened to roll down my cheek. I brushed it roughly away with my sleeve and determined to put such negative thoughts out of my mind and take some action, whatever it might be. Weeping in a hotel foyer in Nepal was not going to get me any nearer to Clair.

Thoughts of Clair reminded me of my resolution to visit Thamel Travel and ask the girl I'd met in the street for help with the fourth clue. I set off at once, and was surprised to find the place with little trouble, Thamel being a small area where everyone knew the location of The Himalaya Hotel, which stood opposite the travel agent's.

Thamel Travel was a narrow building sandwiched between a tailor's - where three or four workers could be seen sewing designs of dragons and Buddha's eyes on to t-shirts - and a gift shop selling thangas, the beautiful mandalas hand-painted on to parchment and silk that Buddhists use for meditation. Outside the travel agent's were many posters advertising outdoor pursuits such as whitewater rafting, hang-gliding, trekking in the Himalayas and flying a light plane over Mount Everest. Being as unenthusiastic about sport as I'm disinclined towards physically dangerous activities, I disregarded the "excitement" promised by the posters and walked into the shop, inadvertently setting off the tinkling welcome chimes which festooned the front door.

The girl I'd encountered in the street was seated behind a desk serving another customer, but she looked up as soon as I came in and beamed me a warm smile. Either she genuinely recognized me and was pleased to see I'd taken up her offer, or she was simply happy to have another customer.

"Namaste" she said in greeting. "I won't be long. Please, take a seat over there and look at some brochures. There are lots to choose from."

I did as I was bidden and leafed through the pile of brochures on display, which were more or less similar to the ones I'd viewed in the hotel. Being only mildly interested in the sights of Nepal and more keen on making a direct query to someone who could help me, after a few moments I sat with my hands in my lap and gazed around me at the walls of the shop. Soft music droned in the background and I noticed the same strange musty smell as in many of the shops I'd entered in Katmandu, a not-unpleasant odor of old walls and earth mingled with incense. The light was dim inside the shop despite the bright daylight outside, and I observed only two small windows at the front and one bare bulb hanging from the ceiling to illuminate the room.

Within a few minutes the girl had finished with her other customer, and she motioned me to the chair in front of her desk. "I am glad you came back," she said, with another shining warm smile. "I thought maybe that you are looking for something I can help you with. We can organize any kind of trip you want here. Did you have a look through the brochures?"

"Yes, I did thanks, and..." I chose to begin with the easy request. "I saw some pictures of Bodnath. Do you know the best way of getting there?"

"The stupa? Sure. There is a coach trip that takes in the stupa at Bodnath and some other things too." She took a leaflet from a pile behind her desk and pointed out the relevant line about coach trips to Bodnath. "It's not expensive, only 150 rupees, and it goes every day at 2 p.m. You could go today if you want."

I looked down and considered the leaflet. It did seem very convenient and cheap, plus I would arrive back at the hotel in plenty of time to meet Dan. (Thinking of my date later that evening sent a shiver of excitement trickling down my spine.) "Yes. That sounds fine. Do I need to book?"

"No, just turn up at the bus stop." The girl indicated where it was on her map, and I saw that the stop was within easy walking distance of my hotel. "You can pay on the bus."

"That's great. Thank you."

She smiled as if to close our conversation and I realized she would think that was all I wanted. "Was there something else? A trekking trip, perhaps? I can help you with that - there are many groups going out now..."

"No, I'm not really interested in trekking trips. I'm not here for that..." I hesitated, wondering whether to trust her. After all, I had only met her briefly on the street. "It's something a bit more unusual, you see. I've looked at books, but they're not really very helpful." The girl regarded me with her pleasant, open face and I decided to risk it. What could I lose? There didn't appear to be any way of getting the clue translated properly other than asking a native. I took out the parchment paper from my pocket, and showed her the Nepalese script of the fourth clue: "I need to get this translated into English."

"Oh yes. I see. Well, that's fine. I have done some translation work." I felt relieved and glad that I'd trusted my instincts about her. She seemed an intelligent and co-operative person. The girl studied my paper for a few moments, while I again glanced around the room. I felt grateful that she didn't probe into my reasons for needing the sentence translated, but simply gave her best attention to the task.

The girl looked up. "It is rather a strange sentence. I'm not sure what it means, but perhaps it will make sense to you. It says: *Ridiculously simple to be about right for some time*." She wrinkled her nose. "Could that be right? Was that what you were expecting?"

"It could be right, I suppose. I wasn't expecting anything, really. It's a crossword clue, you see."

"A cross...word...?"

"It's a sort of game, a word game, we play in England."

"Oh, I see" she said with a little laugh, as if wondering why I would take so much trouble over a mere game, lightly penciled in the English words beneath the Nepalese script, then put the sheet of parchment paper back into my hands.

"But your clue is not in English?"

"No. It was given to me - by a friend."

The girl interlocked her fingers and regarded me serenely. "Your friend wanted to make it more difficult than usual for you" she guessed, "Because you are so good at this game."

Her suggestion made me laugh. "Oh no," I confided, "Quite the opposite in fact. I'm hopeless at crosswords. Although..." I recalled my recent success with the third clue, "I am getting better."

"We don't have anything like that here," the girl said with a slightly melancholy expression. "I think maybe I should like to play. I've always enjoyed words, in other languages I mean."

"Unlike me." She'd been so sweet, I couldn't resist revealing more. I pulled the box from my inside pocket and drew out the paper napkin where I had sketched the crossword grid with its partial completions. "The sentence is a clue to a word, and the word fits into a grid like this" I explained, showing her, "and it interlocks with all the other words, so you know that you've got the right one."

She smiled and shook her head. "Well, I don't know. It looks quite complicated."

"It's not so bad when you know the rules."

"But look" the girl said, pointing to my grid. "You say you are no good at this game. But here, you have filled in half - almost half - already."

I beamed with pleasure, flattered by her admiration for my less than remarkable efforts. Then a thought occurred to me: "Are you sure that what you said is right, the right translation?"

"What did I say?" The girl studied the paper again. "Yes, this first word is stupidly or ridiculously, something like that. This word means simple, easy..."

"But which is it - simple or easy?"

She shrugged. "I don't know, it could be either, it means both those words. Then ...to be...about...right...for some time, or a long time." I copied her words on to the paper napkin, so as to remember them precisely.

"It has to be exactly right, you see, or the crossword won't work, the clue won't make the right word."

"Yes, that is correct, I am sure: *Ridiculously easy to be about right for a long time.* Can you tell what is the answer to the clue? What is the word that goes into the grid?"

"Oh gosh, I can't do it just like that. It'll probably take me ages, and then I'll have to get other people to help me. But I'll do it. I did the others, so... I'm sure I'll do the rest." While pronouncing these words, I believed in the truth of them and had a rush of optimism that my journey would not be in vain.

The girl must have noticed the ardor of my expression because her face suddenly broke out into a cordial smile. "I wish you much luck."

"Thanks. Thanks very much." I replaced the papers in my box.

"You have brought this here from England, this cross word?"

"Yes."

"And one of the clues is in my language, so you had to come here to translate it" she divined.

"Well, sort of" I replied, guessing she must think me mad to travel halfway across the world on account of a word game.

"And anyway, it is a good reason to leave your work and come on holiday to an interesting place, no?"

I nodded, appreciating the irony of her suggested motivations for my trip.

"Are the other clues all in English?"

"Well, no actually. It's a specially difficult game, all in different languages."

"You must like speaking different languages."

"Me? Oh no, not at all. I couldn't even learn French at school", I replied, amused that she had judged me a linguist.

"I love languages. Especially English. That is the most... not beautiful, but sensible, harmonious language."

"Harmonious? Really?" I had never thought of my mother tongue as anything other than a means to an end, or considered what it must be like for people learning it for the first time.

"Oh yes. I know many other languages - apart from Nepali, I speak English, German, French and Urdu, plus a little Japanese but that is not good. For the tourists, you know, we must know some of their words, we can't expect them all to speak in our language."

The girl laughed self-deprecatingly, and I felt guilty. That was exactly what I'd always expected other people to do, converse in my language, and I'd never made the remotest attempt to return the favor.

"I have studied for a long time, for five years at University. In fact I want to be a teacher. I'm only looking after this shop during the holiday season for my cousin, to make a little...how d'you say... pocket money."

She was a lot more educated and talented than I. Yet I had dismissed her as a simple Nepalese girl who could do no more than smile and sell maps.

She seemed happy to talk to me, perhaps because there were no other customers in the shop and she was lonely, or maybe because she liked the opportunity to practice speaking English. She showed me her t-shirt, which had some English writing on the back: "This my brother brought back for me from London. He won a scholarship to study art at your famous school in Chelsea. We are all very ambitious in our family. I want to go to London too, when I've finished my studies. I want to see the whole world, but especially London. It must be a wonderful place."

"Not really" I murmured.

"Are you from there? Have you lived your whole life there?" she quizzed with bright eyes, as though I were a refugee from the Moon.

"My whole life, yes. I never much wanted to travel."

I realized with a shock that I had spent my whole life in one place and in one job, with no particular desire for change and with no spark of interest in a different culture or experience, until I'd been forcibly catapulted out into the real world of variety and diversity. What a different person I was from this girl. I'd been given all the advantages she longed for, and yet I had no impetus to use them. I'd sat all my life like an unthinking vegetable - working, eating, sleeping - every day just the same, and not even realizing how much more there could be. It suddenly struck me how lucky I was that that bomb had exploded when it did, lucky for me anyway, as one of the few survivors, because it had forced me to start really living before it was too late.

As these thoughts flashed through my mind, the telephone rang and the girl answered it, speaking in her strange staccato language, which sounded so odd and unfamiliar to my ears. I envied her ability to talk to people of her own culture, and then so naturally switch to me, shifting between languages with fluidity and ease. I realized what a bonus it was to be able to communicate with other people, whatever their language.

When she'd finished her telephone conversation, the girl replaced the receiver and turned to me with her amiable smile, resuming our talk with gusto. "So now you are here in Nepal. You must wish to travel after all."

"Maybe." I smiled. "But to be honest, that wasn't really the reason I started out."

I found myself telling her about Clair and Genevieve and the meaning behind the piece of paper in the box. She'd revealed to me something about herself, and had thus created a bond of trust between us that made it possible for me to tell her.

To my surprise, she reacted with less disbelief than other people I'd told. "I am a Buddhist," she admitted, "and you know, in the Buddhist faith, reincarnation is quite natural. Perhaps your brother is now a monk. But it will be hard to find him, I think. You know, there are many monasteries in Nepal and Tibet, with many monks in them."

"Well then, I shall just have to go and visit them all" I replied, with as much determination as I felt.

The girl smiled: "Then, I am sure you will find him in the end." Suddenly, she assumed a confidential air and leaned across her desk to me. "I want to tell you a secret I have never told any Westerner before. Do you promise not to tell anyone else?"

I was intrigued and felt thrilled to be invited into something normally kept hidden. "Yes, of course."

"I am an ex-Kumari Devi", she announced with a mixture of pride and regret.

"What's a Kumari Devi?"

"Have you not heard of this? Have you not read about it in the guide books?"

I admitted that I hadn't consulted any guidebooks before coming to Nepal.

"The Kumari Devi is the living goddess. She is chosen as a little girl of about four or five years old. When I was four some men came to my house and asked my parents if they could speak to me. They asked me all sorts of questions, and they seemed pleased with my answers. Then they showed me some articles of clothing that had been worn by the last Kumari Devi. I chose the right ones; I had passed the first test. They took me to a big temple and many other little girls were there, about my age. In a big room we all stood and the men made frightening noises and danced around us with masks on, beating the ground with sticks. I must admit now that I was frightened but I didn't show my fear, I kept my face always impassive. I never cried as a child, I don't know why."

"Gosh - I cried all the time, I seem to remember. Drove my mother nuts," I admitted with a grin.

"So, after this ordeal, the men selected me out of all the other girls and they prostrated themselves before me and said I was the new Kumari Devi, the reincarnation of the living goddess. I had passed all the tests and now I must live in the temple until I started my menstruation."

"Wow! What was it like living in the temple?"

"It was fun. I enjoyed it. I had all the food and toys I wanted and everyone treated me - well - like a goddess in fact. Every year there would be a big parade and I would be carried through the streets and all the people would cheer. I don't think I even missed my parents and my brothers and sisters, I was having too much fun being fussed over. Of course, I still had to have school lessons, but I had them at home, privately, not in a school with the other children."

As the girl spoke, her eyes shone brightly with the recollections of her past life, and I was carried along by the story. I couldn't imagine the sort of life she must have had, it was so different from mine in every way. Yet she was a girl like me, only a little younger than myself, and with a sort of innocence about her despite her unusual experiences. She didn't look directly at me as she spoke, but off to space, as though she were viewing there the images she recaptured for her audience. I began to notice, in the gloom of the room, a hazy light surrounding her, like a kind of halo about her head and shoulders. I blinked in confusion, wondering if my eyes had become strained by looking for so long in one direction, and let my gaze fall to my lap as I continued listening.

"Then, one day, to my disgust," the girl carried on, "I felt a wetness between my legs and I looked at myself and realized what had happened, and I knew that it was over. I had begun menstruating and now I had to go home to my family and let a new Kumari Devi take over. I was fourteen. I tried to keep it a secret for as long as I could. But of course they found out eventually. I cried and cried, I didn't want to go home, the people in my family were strangers to me now. And when I went home I had to be a normal little girl just like everyone else, and to go to school with the others and not have all the things I wanted, and I didn't like it at all.

But I adjusted. There was nothing else to do. People treated me strangely, though. Being a Kumari Devi is all right at the time, but when you are older everyone thinks you are unlucky and you can't get a husband. I couldn't be like other girls now, even if I tried. So that is why I have decided to study hard and become a teacher and look after myself. I don't want to marry after all. In England everyone isn't expected to marry, are they?"

I shook my head. "Not at all. In fact, lots of girls decide not to bother. My mother never married."

The girl regarded me enviously. "It's not like that here. Here, a girl is despised if she isn't married by the time she is twenty. But I'm not going to stay here, I shall go to the West and live like a Westerner."

"That's an extraordinary story. Truly amazing. You've really been through some things. Perhaps you should write a book - when you get to the West, I mean."

The girl laughed and shook her head, as if to diminish the importance of her tale. She seemed almost embarrassed by the attention I was paying her. Her large earrings tinkled and brushed the side of her neck, and I reflected on how modest and unassuming she was, compared to the majority of my English friends.

Her story had opened up a whole new world for me, a world where things were different from my expectations. For the first time in my life, I felt a desire to see this new world in all its manifestations, not for any other reason but to experience it and discover its different peoples with their different cultures and faiths. That curiosity, which had been so much a part of me when I was a child before Clair's death, was opening up again in me like the petals of a flower that had lain dormant for years and years. The real purpose of my journey was beginning to dawn on me.

"What an interesting life you've had" I said to the girl. "Hey, you know what? I don't even know your name. I'm Alice."

"And I'm Shama. Pleased to meet you." We shook hands and giggled at the formality of our self-introduction.

"Shama. That's a pretty name."

"And very common here in Nepal. It's the name of the song bird."

"What - you mean like a nightingale?"

"I don't know. A nightingale has a pretty song?"

"Yes, apparently, though I haven't heard it very often myself."

"The shama is really special because it has no tune of its own but it can imitate any tune. So we call it the songbird. And we like to call our daughters Shama, we think then they will imitate the tune their husbands sing." She laughed at this concept, and I joined in. I had a brief image of husbands ridiculously clad in bird costumes tweeting in the trees, and their wives responding.

"My mother used to call me and Clair magpies. But that's not such a good bird in England. The magpie steals things from other birds. And we have a saying in England when we see a magpie: *One for sorrow, two for joy, three for a girl and four for a boy.* Maybe in olden times people thought they could predict what sex their baby would be or something. Ridiculous really."

"Not necessarily" replied Shama, her expression serious. "There are lots of things we don't know about, but that doesn't mean they don't exist."

I screwed up my face in thought. "Well, I suppose you're right. Although I can't say I've ever thought about it before."

"But Alice, you should catch your bus" Shama suddenly declared, looking at her watch. "It leaves in ten minutes."

"Really? I forgot to bring out my watch - I left it on the table beside my bed in the hotel. I'm like that, I either leave things behind or I lose them." Looking at Shama's watch, I saw that it was indeed ten minutes to two. "Oh my God, you're right. I'd better hurry." I shot up out of my seat.

"Before you go, there is something I wanted to suggest to you. The bus will take you to Bodnath, which I'm sure you will find very interesting, whether or not you find your brother there. But there is another place you should visit too. It is quite near to the Stupa and I think you would like it very much." Shama pressed a leaflet into my hands. "This gives you directions for how to get there from the Stupa. It is not far away. And you would have plenty of time to go there afterwards."

I studied the leaflet. "Can I walk there from Bodnath?"

"Certainly. It is about a mile away. There is also a bus at half past six back to Bodnath, if you are too tired to walk again, and from there you can catch your bus to return to Katmandu."

"O.K. Thanks very much." Now, I was suddenly reluctant to depart. I'd enjoyed Shama's company so much that my enthusiasm for the trip had dwindled. "It's been great talking to you and hearing about your childhood and all. And thanks again for the translation."

"Don't mention it, it was my pleasure." Shama trotted out these trite phrases in such a fresh way, it struck me that she really meant them. "It would be nice to meet again, wouldn't it?" she suggested.

"Oh yes" I responded with enthusiasm. "You read my mind. I was just thinking that myself."

"We could have a meal together this evening. I know a nice restaurant where they serve local delicacies. I think you would like it..."

"Oh, I'm afraid I can't tonight. I'm meeting someone." I didn't want to elaborate about my date with Dan. I had a fleeting intuition that this Nepalese girl with her old-fashioned values might disapprove of my meeting with a stranger, even if only for a coffee. But I did want to leave the rest of the evening free, in case Dan also asked me out to dinner, as I rather hoped he would. "Could we meet tomorrow instead?"

"Of course." Shama wrote down for me on the back of my leaflet the name and address of the restaurant she'd suggested, and we agreed to meet there the following evening at 8 p.m. We parted with smiles and handshakes and I walked out of the shop feeling happier than I'd done in ages.

I'd made a real friend at last, someone I could talk to, and I had another potential friend to see that evening. I'd managed to get the fourth clue translated and I could work on solving it this afternoon as I traveled on the bus. Things were really looking up.

I decided that Nepal was a great place to be.

CHAPTER ELEVEN

I WAS BEHOLDING the most beautiful image I'd ever seen. The picture was enormous and covered the entire surface of a large flat table. I gazed entranced, allowing the vibrant colors to seep into me and infuse me with their warmth. The wealth of images it presented was so complex that it was impossible to comprehend or take in all the disparate elements at one glance.

In the center a rotund Buddha sat, legs crossed in the lotus position and one hand raised, a beatific smile on his face. Radiating out from his body like the spokes of a wheel, other Buddhas - slightly smaller but otherwise exact replicas of the central figure - were placed. All their torsos were encased in circles of blue and green and gold. Further down along these spokes lay other Buddhas, even smaller and encased in a square, leading to other Buddhas encased in more circles and so forth. On the outside of the largest circle were mosques, people, mountains and flowers, all in the most exquisite colors and all appearing to float on a sea of azure sky flecked with clouds.

And the most extraordinary thing about this picture was that it was composed entirely of grains of colored sand.

I was not alone gazing at this amazingly lovely work of art. Several other tourists like myself stood equally enthralled, making it difficult at times for me to see all aspects of the picture without having to peer over another person's shoulder or gently push them aside in order to gain a better view. But the effect of the picture was so engrossing that it made you feel that you were viewing it alone, or that the image had a special message to convey to you alone. It's possible that everyone else in the room felt the same way.

Outside in the courtyard the drone of monks at prayer and the sound of the long horn they blew with its single dirge-like note filled the air. It was a sound not beautiful or melancholy, but almost workmanlike in its precision and the intensity of purpose behind its execution. It conveyed the impression that the outer world didn't exist for these monks, that nothing existed for them except their religion and their faith, which bound them in a single unifying endeavor. I momentarily envied the monks their serene wisdom and their contentment in the face of existence without individual goals, a state of mind difficult for me to even contemplate.

As we Westerners stood appreciating the picture, a taller than average monk with a gentle countenance motioned for a space among the watchers to be cleared for him on one side of the table, and on the other side another monk appeared. They too were intoning, and the expressions on their faces were peaceful and benign. Both monks clutched long sticks, and as they raised them in the air with a practiced ceremonial gesture, I wondered what they intended to do. Their next actions, though, were so shocking that I could never have predicted them.

With a great sweep of their arms they each drew their sticks over the beautiful picture, dislodging all the grains of sand that must have taken hours and weeks of painstaking effort, swishing their sticks around until the colored grains melded together into a sort of undistinguishable soup. I was so horrified, that I literally stood with my mouth open for a few seconds. Surely, I surmised, this must be some kind of mistake.

But the elder of the two monks began to speak to our little group of tourists in a soft voice: "We always remember that there is nothing permanent in life" he declared with a slight smile which implied that he didn't wish to appear pompous but he believed what he believed. "Our life is no more permanent than a few grains of sand. And so, we spend a long time preparing the mandala, only to sweep it away and start again."

The monk bowed slightly and departed with his companion. The other tourists began to mumble to each other and exchange puzzled looks. I wandered to the archway separating this small antechamber from the main courtyard, which was currently occupied by a couple of hundred monks in orange costumes seated on the ground.

All of these monks looked exactly alike to me. If Clair were somewhere amongst them, how could I possibly ascertain which monk he was? Would my brother know that I was here searching for him? Would there be some sort of sign to reveal to me which orange-gowned man was Clair?

The monks faced away from me, intent on their task and paying us tourists no attention at all. It suddenly occurred to me that I should somehow disclose my presence at the Stupa; otherwise I might lose the opportunity of making myself known to Clair. Perhaps the head of the monastery might be willing to make an announcement to the monks. Although this seemed a crazy notion, I felt compelled to try something. I decided to enlist the aid of the monk who had previously spoken to our group, the tall one with the stick who had wiped away the sand picture. I had no idea what his status was amongst his community, but his air of quiet authority and his polite and approachable manner drew me to him.

At the far end of the courtyard I saw the man I'd privately appointed as my helper standing still grasping his stick in one hand, so I crept past rows of intoning monks to approach him. When he saw me, the monk raised his eyebrows and cocked his head to one side in a gesture that appeared surprised but not unfriendly.

"Thank you for showing us the sand picture. It was very beautiful. But I'm not just a tourist, you see. I've come here to try and find someone" I confided in a near whisper. The monk's silent and expectant gaze urged me on. "I think he might be here, but I'm not sure."

"Yes?" he said, inclining his head down towards me as though inviting further explanation. "Who is this person? A friend?"

"No... It's my brother."

I hesitated, wondering how to continue my story, and was surprised to see that the monk nodded serenely as if in complete acceptance of my tale. He clasped his hands together in front of his chest, his head slightly lowered and his eyes on the ground, as though meditating on my problem and waiting to hear more. The effect of the monk's response was thus to give me complete faith in him.

"You may wonder why I can't recognize him, if he's my brother" I continued. "The fact is...my brother died twenty-five years ago, and I'm looking for his reincarnation." Again, the monk didn't question this at all but continued his musing. "I've been told that he's in this world again and he wants me to find him. He's waiting for me. But it's difficult because I don't know what he looks like now or where he is. I only thought he might be here because...I don't know, really...I just thought he might. His name was Clair. But now his name begins with S. He's expecting me."

To anyone else, I would have felt an absolute fool making these declarations. I would have expected them to question my story and perhaps give me the look of ironic contempt or pity, which I had grown to anticipate when revealing the nature of my quest to a stranger. But this monk, who considered my tale with his eyes never straying from the ground, accepted my words without the slightest sign of disbelief, and his non-judgmental reaction made my ideas seem less preposterous.

"It is often thus" the monk replied thoughtfully in his quiet melodious voice. "A brother and sister should not be separated. You must find each other again. But it is not an easy task. I do not know if he is one of these here," he said, indicating the group of praying monks with a sweep of his hand. "Only your heart can tell you that. Look at them now."

I did as I was bidden and skimmed my eyes over the rows of orange-clad brethren. They all looked exactly the same to me - bowed heads shaven, thin arms brushing the ground.

"Only you can say whether one is your brother. To the naked eye they all appear equal. But to the clothed eye of one who surveys them with a heart full of purpose, the special brother would stand out. You would be able to see the light around him which is different from all the others."

"Light?" I didn't know what the monk was talking about. But I had a swift recollection of the strange light I had seen around Shama earlier. I had dismissed the phenomenon as a visual aberration, not knowing what it meant or even if I really had seen anything at all. Was this monk speaking about something similar?

The monk didn't answer me, seemingly lost in thought. The intoning of his fellows was starting to take on an eerie, otherworldly quality that affected me strangely. I don't know if it was the slow drone echoing from stone walls, the torpor of the still afternoon air, the sea of orange robes flowing in precisely coordinated movements before my eyes, or maybe the disorientation of my illness and the weakness it produced. But my body felt weightless and my head clear as crystal. The other tourists were forgotten, and I felt as though I had stepped into this alien world all alone, as if a veil had been lifted which allowed me to glimpse a whole other way of existence in which I was participating. Despite these sensations, I saw no light over any of the monks, no special sign that would mark one out as Clair.

"Do you think you see him?" asked my companion.

I shook my head, disappointed. "I suppose he isn't here after all."

"No matter. You will find him if you hold his image in your heart."

Feeling comforted by these words, I regarded the monk gratefully. I was about to make my apologies and leave, but he continued: "There are many monasteries where your brother may reside now. It may take you a long time to find him by searching each one. Otherwise...there may be some sign. Perhaps there is another way..." He stopped speaking, gazed into the middle distance and remained silent and lost in thought for so long that I was beginning to wonder if he had forgotten all about me and gone off into a kind of spontaneous trance.

But then, just as suddenly, the monk turned to me and his face broke into a boyish grin. "Come with me a moment." He put a tender hand on my shoulder and led me out of the courtyard, through the recesses of the Stupa and outside into the sunshine. I blinked in the sudden brightness, and then hurried after his rapidly receding figure. The monk took no notice of the milling tourists in front of the building, and he said nothing more but walked before me with light, confident steps along the dusty thoroughfare.

We must have walked a mile at least - me shadowing his narrow frame, and he never once turning to look and check that I was there. His bare shoeless feet didn't appear hampered by the stones underneath them, as we walked along the side of the road, occasionally overtaken by gaudily-painted lorries which sent up huge clouds of dust into the air. I noticed as the monk turned his head to one side to look at a lorry, that he held a fold of cloth in front of his mouth as protection against the dust. I hadn't thought to do that, of course, so the dust got into my nose and mouth and made me choke and cough. All around us lay mountains, some covered in a carpet of green and some with many terraces cut into their sides like steps for giants.

We walked quickly and on the other side of the road I saw what at first appeared to be a moving tree, but as we passed I saw that a man staggered under a huge load of branches that were bigger than him. I had seen other people carrying loads - mostly young women with bunches of straw strapped to their heads by a band of cloth - but never a stack this large, which looked like an almost impossible burden. The man, however, had no expression of self-pity but only one of quiet endurance, a toleration and acceptance of life, as he knew it.

The monk and I crossed a bridge over a river and I glanced down to see women in saris washing clothes in the water, their strong brown arms kneading the material like dough. Across the bridge, in a small quarry, men and women were breaking up rocks by hammering them with other larger rocks. Their task seemed slow and arduous, and the workers were glad of the opportunity to look up at us and smile and wave, shouting something in Nepalese to my monk friend. Outside a farmhouse, a woman sat sifting grains into a bowl. Beside her, two goats were arguing over a slice of watermelon rind as if it was some delicacy, but the woman ignored their insistent bleating.

At last we descended from the main road and along a sort of overgrown path, until we reached a large overhanging rock almost as big as a house. The rock had an opening in its center, about three feet high, and the monk started to scramble through the hole, without instructing me to follow although I recognized that was what I was supposed to do.

"Hey, wait a minute" I exclaimed, baulking at clambering through holes in rocks which led I knew not where. "I'm claustrophobic. I can't go in there." But the monk neither waited for me nor responded. Perhaps he hadn't heard me, having already disappeared through the hole. Or perhaps he realized that my curiosity would get the better of my fear and lead me to give a sigh of resignation, steel myself, bend down and follow him through the hole.

Actually I needn't have worried, because although the opening in the rock was small, the fissure opened out immediately into quite a large cave. The atmosphere was cold and damp, and I could feel and hear drips of moisture from the roof. The light was so dim that we wouldn't have been able to see much at all, if the monk hadn't lit a couple of candles which were lying on the floor. They were obviously left there permanently to help people see inside the cave, because any illumination that filtered in from outside was minimal even in broad daylight. Once my eyes had adjusted, I could see a narrow tunnel leading off from this cavern deep into the rock, through which the monk was now struggling on bended knees. I was horrified at the idea of following him, but I knew by this time that to complain was useless: my companion would carry on despite my protestations and expect me to either complete the journey with him or not, as I desired.

I watched for a few moments until the monk's retreating legs were only just visible, then swallowed the lump in my throat, gritted my teeth and plunged in after him. The smell of damp earth was almost overpowering and I could see practically nothing except the soles of the monk's sandals a few feet ahead. I tried not to think about how the dirt and mud must be staining my clothes and fought down feelings of panic that I might never reach the end of the tunnel.

Then, to my huge relief, after only a few minutes I glimpsed pale light ahead and the monk hauled himself to his feet. I followed him and stepped up into another cave. This time the room was quite small, consisting just of this one chamber and with no other tunnels leading from it anywhere else. This knowledge consoled me, as I didn't relish the thought of any more burrowing through underground shafts to reach our destination. It must be this very part of the cave that the monk wanted to show me.

Yet, I couldn't see much special about the cavern so far. Again, the monk lit candles, which were positioned on small boulders on either side of one of the chamber's walls. He held his hands together in prayer and I could see that he was staring intently at one particular spot on the wall, so I joined him and gazed in the same direction. At first, I could only distinguish a series of meaningless splotches and daubs, which had probably been painted some time ago, as the colors were very faded and indistinct. But as I continued to look, the outlines became clearer and very gradually I realized that we were viewing some sort of map.

"It's a map, isn't it? Where is it supposed to be?" I asked my companion.

"Nobody knows" he replied softly, turning to me for the first time. "It has a different meaning for everybody. It was painted many years ago, by one of our prophets. Everybody sees what they wish to see in the picture, what they need to see. Perhaps you will also see the answer to your question."

"When was it painted?"

"Again, we are not sure. But a long time ago. Maybe hundreds, thousands of years. Certainly, as long as we have been in the monastery."

I stood and gazed in silence at the map for a long time, so long in fact that the monk departed without another word and left me alone in the cave. I heard him making his way back through the tunnel to the larger chamber, and although in the back of my mind I was anxious about him leaving altogether and going back to the monastery without me, I couldn't tear myself away from the map on the wall.

I had a presentiment that the monk wouldn't abandon me. He had, after all, brought me here believing it was a significant experience for me. If there was a message to be read in the map, a message that would help me, I had to give it time to sink in. I had miraculously shed my fear of the tunnel and the small, enclosed space inside the cave like an old skin. It was important only to study the picture and read any knowledge it had to impart to me.

The picture represented a map, all right, of a very crude sort. Splotches of a sort of greenish-brown I took to represent countries, and between them lay a kind of sea of very pale blue, almost faded to white. There was also a very thin line; so narrow it might just have been a crack in the rock, which made a wobbly progression from one country to another. If I screwed up my eyes and blurred the image, I could just about imagine the blob in the middle of the map to be England, as it was a narrowish oblong with a sort of foot jutting out from the left-hand bottom corner and a smaller blob to the left of center. I've always thought the map of Britain bears a passing resemblance to a man seated behind a steering wheel and that's pretty much how this blob appeared.

Beneath Britain, a very large mass of greenish-brown could betoken Europe. But none of the countries had any names or distinguishable features, other than their general shape, which was roughly similar. The line or crack ran from the bottom of "Britain" down into the large "Europe" mass, veering to the right and down again a long distance until it ended at a large blob on the bottom right which could have symbolized Australia, painted in a slightly different color from the rest, with a more reddish hue. Something about this mass caught my eye, and when I bent down to look at it more closely, I saw that the rock had formed a natural crack in the center of the blob in the shape of an S. I smiled at the incongruity of this coincidence, stretched and stood up.

I could make no more sense of the map. My eyes were tired, my head throbbed and my body felt cold and damp from the moisture inside the cave. I daringly blew out the candles and struggled back in the half-gloom through the tunnel into the larger chamber, then retreated back through the fissure in the rock till I reached the outside, giving thanks for the sudden welcome warmth of sunshine on my face. The journey back to the outside seemed so much less threatening, that now I couldn't believe I'd been so afraid. I recognized the sensation of relief and slight strangeness from having been to see a film in the afternoon and stepping out into comforting daylight from a darkened room.

At first I couldn't see the monk anywhere, and anxiety began to prick me as I wondered how I would ever find my way back to the monastery, knowing no Nepalese with which to ask directions. Then I was relieved to notice a flash of orange through the trees, and I realized that he must have been waiting for me in a more convenient spot.

The walk back to Bodnath was shorter and less arduous, as return journeys often are. I thanked the monk for taking the trouble to lead me to the cave and show me the map. When he asked me if I had found an message in it, I answered truthfully that I didn't know and he smiled and nodded his head sagely and said that perhaps the answer would be revealed to me in time, "perhaps even in your dreams". The map was a sacred object of great significance - he said - and it was something few Western tourists got to see, but he had taken me to see it because he respected the fact that my journey was a quest rather than an idle holiday. I glowed in the knowledge that the monk had conferred a special honor on me by showing me something like that, so secret and normally hidden from public view. And I was glad that I had overcome my fears of the cave and the tunnel enough to allow me to have the experience.

"I wish you luck in finding your brother," the monk said, as we parted outside the Stupa. "My heart goes with you on your journey. Before we part, I wish to tell you of someone else who may be able to help you."

"Really? Who?"

"He is a great medium and spiritual healer called Rajan Mobley. I first heard of him twenty years ago when he came to Nepal to study Buddhism, although he himself is not a Buddhist. Many people have made pilgrimages to this man and found the answers they were seeking."

"Does he live here at the Stupa?"

"No, many miles away, in the jungles of Borneo. He lives as a hermit now, I believe. But he is a very wise man who has written many books, and his reputation still draws people to him."

"If I go and see this Rajan Mobley, will he be able to tell me where, or who, Clair is now?" I asked excitedly.

"He may. But your brother will tell you himself also."

"Clair? How?"

"Clair exists for ever in spirit. The spirits communicate in subtle ways that only they can know. If you heed the messages you receive, he will guide you. But remember, it is not only the destination that is important but the journey itself."

"What do you mean?"

"In the cave - it wasn't only the seeing of the map that was important, but also the traveling through the tunnel. You learned to conquer your fear and abhorrence. You put your faith in me and let me guide you. These are useful lessons for us all." The monk put his hands together in a gesture of prayer and lowered his chin on to the tips of his fingers: "*Namaste*. Our meeting was a pleasure. I wish you well."

I merely smiled, not knowing what to say in reply. Then the monk turned on his heel and wandered back into the recesses of the Stupa. I stood there for a few moments, feeling strangely peaceful and serene, looking at the tourists who were still coming and going, chattering and taking photographs. I knew now that Clair wasn't in this place. But it didn't seem to matter. Coming here had been an experience I wouldn't have missed for the world. I thought of the monk's words: It is not only the destination that is important but also the journey itself. Perhaps he was right. All the things that had happened to me so far were strange and extraordinary, sometimes difficult or frightening at the time, but always ultimately fulfilling. If I'd stayed at home in London, I'd never have seen Dr. Becker's house full of birds or met Shama, the Kumari Devi or heard unearthly music in the church in Umbria. This journey I was on, this quest to find my brother, was itself magical and full of events, which awakened my senses and opened my eyes to other worlds.

I silently thanked Genevieve for forcing me out of my safe and tedious cocoon and plunging me into this adventure. However unwilling I had been at first, I could now see the excitement in it, feel the thrill of it and enjoy the journey for its own sake, however long it had to last. My sense of euphoria was only dimmed by the knowledge that my illness set a time limit on everything and gave me only a finite period in which to find Clair before I joined him in the other world with no hope of retrieving his message. But now at least I felt optimistic that I would find him and that my goal was achievable.

It was something about seeing the map that had provoked this sudden change of heart. That and meeting the monk at Bodnath. I felt an urge to thank him for opening my eyes with his wisdom, and almost ran back into the Stupa to find him again. Then I realized that he didn't need my thanks, because he had taken pleasure in teaching me. But I wished that I had at least learned his name.

Shama had told me very little about what I was likely to experience in this place, and I approached the rundown farmhouse with some trepidation. In the distance, I could hear the Indian cuckoo warbling its four-note anthem over and over, the song the English tourists call *One more bottle.*

In front of the house, a woman was seated on a wooden bench, using a handloom to weave what appeared to be a large and intricately patterned carpet or wall hanging. She made a high-pitched wailing noise, halfway between a tune and a drone, which persisted without ever wavering or flagging. The sound was neither loud nor unpleasant, and it bestowed on the air around her an ethereal quality. She seemed to be imitating Indian flute music, the haunting melodies flowing into each other as seamlessly as the threads of the carpet she crafted. At first sight of this extraordinary woman, I felt that I already inhabited a dream or another world not normally seen, a place of infinite possibilities where I had no idea what would happen next.

The woman looked up and smiled when she heard my footsteps approaching, but continued her song without altering a single note.

"My name is Alice, my friend Shama sent me to see you," I declared, expecting the woman to cease her river of sound and offer me some response. But rather than speaking the woman carried on singing, ever the same tune, still smiling and weaving her colored threads in and out of the cloth with deft fingers. Only now, she seemed to be singing directly at me. Far from ignoring me or my question, she was using her voice to project whatever was in her head with her music. I wondered if the woman was a mute. But if she couldn't speak, how could she sing?

"Can I have a look around?" I asked, this time not anticipating a reply. I took the woman's smiling and singing for encouragement and decided it wouldn't be considered rude of me to leave her and wander inside the house. Pushing open the low wooden door of the thatched cottage - which was so tiny I was forced to stoop to get through - I entered a small, dimly lit room where several men sat hunched over swathes of silk, painting them with delicate strokes of the brush. All the workers looked up and smiled on my entrance but, as the woman had done, continued with their art despite my presence. I approached one man and looked with interest at his picture, which was an intricate and skillfully executed mandala.

"That's beautiful," I said with sincerity, while also hoping to stir some reaction from the artist with a compliment. The man smiled with evident pleasure and inclined his head in grateful acknowledgement of my appreciation. He placed his brush on the paper beside him - which, being covered with tiny scratches of color, I imagined he used as a sort of practice pad before committing himself to the silk - and made a couple of strokes downwards and upwards. Then he looked up at me and I realized he expected me to reply to him. I hovered in embarrassment, uncertain what to say, and he made the strokes again - the same strokes, which resembled a sort of wide tick symbol - before looking up at me and smiling expectantly. Suddenly it dawned on me that the painter was trying to convey something with his strokes, that he was actually talking to me with the strokes, as the woman outside had been talking to me with her singing.

Smiling in relief and new comprehension, I essayed further dialogue with the man: "How long did it take you to paint your picture?" I asked.

This time the artist furrowed his brow in concentration, before dipping his brush into one of the nearby tubes of paint and applying it to the paper. A long green line appeared, running from the top of the page to the bottom, which was executed slowly and laboriously. I was amused, having expected a more instantly recognizable symbol such as a number to represent hours or days, but recognized that this mark said everything about the length of completion time for the mandala, and the painter's attitude to it.

I decided it would be inconsiderate to keep the man from his work any longer, and said goodbye, to which he responded with wavy blue lines across the top of the page, done fluently and with a facility that led me to believe they were a frequently repeated emblem.

Stepping out of the back door, I found myself on a hillside overlooking a mountain. The ground was covered with lush green grass, daubed with swathes of gold by the dappled evening sunlight.

On the grass some men and women were dancing. At least, they appeared to be dancing, although they moved without the routine or repetition of a formal dance. Both sexes wore long billowing trousers and wide cotton shirts, which gave them great ease of movement. The only difference between them was that the women's figures were slighter and they had long hair plaited in a ponytail that hung down their backs, while the hair of the men was short.

I'd never viewed anything similar to this dance, which was at once comic and sinuous, performed sometimes carefully and sometimes with abandon. I longed for a video camera to capture the dancers, because they were truly remarkable and unusual. All I can remember now is that they used their entire bodies in the movements, and their torsos contained a powerful strength balanced by the grace and harmony of ballet dancers. The gestures were mostly slow and relaxed and enacted with no music to accompany them.

For some time I stood simply watching. Then one of the dancers spotted me and - as their companions in the house had done - all smiled at me but continued with their movements. Having had some experience with the woman singer and the men painters, I was intrigued to see how these people would respond when I addressed them.

"I come from England," I said. "I'm visiting Nepal for a few days."

Immediately, all the dancers made a circle around me and enveloped me with motion. It was an extraordinary routine, obviously one they all knew well and had done many times before. Again, I felt as if the dancers were speaking directly to me with the dance, that it was their form of language and they could communicate more easily with this performance than with words. After a minute or two, the circle disbanded and tailed off into a regular line of dancers, all facing me but still executing their individual movements, some almost still and some more energetic. One young man came towards me and drew me away from his companions. When I say he drew me, he didn't use his arms to touch me at all, but he used his motion and expression to convey to me that I should follow him, and I finished looking out over the mountains.

We were on a high point - higher than I'd realized - and a low cloud and mist had hung in the air all day, obscuring the distant Himalayas and shrouding the peaks from view. It was about six o'clock, the time when, as I had heard, on clear days the high mountains are bathed in a red glow as the sun sets over them. Now there was no red glow, just a line of white cloud enveloping everything. But as I watched in amazement, a bank of cloud on the left suddenly parted to reveal a jagged white peak which stood out clear and strong and much higher than the other mountains below, so that it seemed almost to be suspended in the air. It was a magical sight, to see the clouds parting like a curtain to reveal a glimpse of the miraculous stage set of the Himalayan Mountains. By my side, the young man danced a dance of joy, and now I felt that I could understand him. And I knew why Shama had wanted me to come here. I had always been obsessed with words. But here was a place where words didn't exist, and where language was neither a barrier nor a defense, but simply a means of expression. And I was suddenly filled with joy.

On the way back to Katmandu in the bus, I stared out of the window in a reflective daze, pondering on all that had happened to me and feeling a sort of mellow contentment, as the bus chugged over the winding roads and then through the narrow streets of the town. During my reverie the face of Clair came back to me, only for a split second. Or not just his face but his whole presence, his personality, the way he moved and spoke, the sense of him. It was such a fleeting impression that in the space of one breath my brother had come and gone. But even that was enough to fill me with happiness and the knowledge that my journey wasn't in vain.

When I arrived at the hotel and went up to my room, I glanced at my watch and saw with consternation that it was already ten to seven. My face and clothes were grubby from my exertions in the cave, so I had to wash and change hurriedly in order to be ready to meet Dan at seven. I surveyed myself in the one small mirror on the back of the bedroom door and wished that I'd brought some more glamorous clothes with me or that my hair weren't quite so straight.

Descending the stairs from my room, my stomach was jittery and I felt as nervous as a teenager on a first date. Silently I demanded of myself what all the fuss was about, because in the past I'd never been very concerned about the impression I make on men. I couldn't understand why this particular man should affect me so strongly. After all, he was just a stranger who'd invited me for a coffee out of loneliness. I knew nothing whatever about him. He wasn't the handsomest man I'd ever seen, although he was attractive. But there was something oddly familiar about his face. Could I have met him before, perhaps? Surely I would have remembered an earlier meeting, and so would he.

I reflected on how uncharacteristic it was for me to have agreed to meet a stranger for coffee. I would never have done anything like this in London. The men I'd been out with were always work colleagues or known through friends. Of course, throughout the journey I'd been behaving in uncharacteristic ways - in fact, traveling at all was quite out of character. Perhaps I really was changing more than I realized. After years of remaining the same, living in the same country and following the same routine, I was breaking out of the straitjacket of habit and becoming a different person. Perhaps when I had wished for everything to change, it was me that I had wanted to change most of all.

Dan was wearing a white suit and a flowery silk shirt like the ones I had seen for sale in nearby shops. I saw now that his skin was lightly tanned, giving him a healthy glow. Deep lines scored his cheeks, adding to the face's gauntness. I felt an unfamiliar flutter in my chest, like a sensation I'd read about in the kind of romantic novels I'd never taken seriously. As I entered the restaurant, he looked up and saw me and gave me a confident and easygoing smile. "Hi, you must be Alice" he said, standing up and shaking my hand. "I'm really pleased to meet you. Would you like to join me?"

"Yes, thanks" I mumbled, strangely tongue-tied, sitting down opposite him.

Dan ordered a coffee for me and we made conversation - rather stilted on my part - over our drinks. He told me that he was a journalist, recently divorced from his wife, and in Nepal for a four-week holiday. At least, partly on holiday and partly to get the flavor of the place for an article he was writing. He had a couple of days left before his flight took him back to Sydney. He said he'd seen quite a bit of the country - down to Chitwan on safari and across to the Pokhara valley - but he hadn't been tempted to go trekking in the Himalayas, as he wasn't really interested in the more strenuous activities. I laughed and admitted that I wasn't either. He told me that the most strenuous thing he'd done on this holiday was to take a long train ride across the country, and he described with relish the awful stink of the crowded compartments and the bone-breaking hardness of the seats. He said the only thing that made up for the privations of the long journey was the scenery, which was staggeringly beautiful.

As he related his stories, I suddenly had a flashback and remembered where I had seen Dan before. It was in my dream, the one I'd had on the train journey from Gmunden to Villach. He had been the man in my compartment, who'd smoked a cigarette and amazed me with his talk of traveling backwards. I stared bewitched at Dan as he spoke - fortunately, however, he enjoyed talking and didn't seem to mind my apparent absorption in his face - and felt more and more certain that he was indeed the same man.

The knowledge really startled me. Under the tablecloth, I couldn't resist pinching my arm to make sure I was awake. Could this really be happening? Could this man have stepped out of my dream and now be here, in this restaurant, talking calmly to me as if nothing extraordinary was taking place? Surely, at any rate, there could be no doubt that this was some sort of sign. There could be no clearer indication that we were in fact destined to meet. No wonder he'd attracted me at first sight, and had invaded my thoughts so quickly. Now I knew that it was not just the physical magnetism but also the familiarity of his presence that had drawn me.

Dan was leaning forward in his chair, having asked me a question that I in my reverie hadn't absorbed: "What did you say?" I stuttered.

"Do you believe in ghosts? You're looking at me as if you've just seen one." He laughed and sat back again. "That's what they always say in novels, isn't it? Don't worry - you just had this rather glazed expression. Not boring you, am I?"

"Oh no, not at all. Sorry to be rude. I've just had... rather a long day."

"Sure, sure. You went to see the stupa at Bodnath. That's quite a trek. I've been there myself, a coupla weeks ago."

To my relief, the waiter started hovering over us to ask if we wanted to order anything more, and Dan said no and offered to pay the bill. My earlier discomfiture was forgotten as Dan continued to tell me about some of the other sights he'd seen in Nepal and to advise me about the most interesting. As he spoke, he had a tendency to lean back in his chair, with his arms hanging relaxed over the back. His voice was deep and musical, with none of the nasal twang usually found in an Australian accent. He didn't fix his eyes on my face but let them wander around the room, as if everything in it were interesting to him. When people walked into the restaurant, he would glance at them briefly, as if checking to see if he knew them or they would be important to him. He spoke very openly and confidently about his life, like a man with nothing to hide.

When he in turn quizzed me about mine, my answers seemed tentative and equivocal by comparison. His confidence abashed me and made me feel gawky and naive. I'd never met an Australian before, and I was impressed and rather dazzled by his confidence and assertive manner. I was also aware that I was immediately very physically attracted to him - maybe more than I'd ever been to anybody before - and that made me nervous and shy. I wished again that I possessed some more glamorous clothes to wear, rather than the traveling outfit that had stood me in good stead for my journey but which seemed staid and unflattering now. I felt that he must think me a rather boring, old-fashioned English girl with no dress sense and not much to say for herself. My reticence was unusual for me, because normally I'm the one who loves to talk.

Whether or not he found me as unattractive as I felt, he invited me to have dinner, and I was pleased to have the opportunity of spending more time with him. We went to a rather up-market Indian restaurant in the Durbar Marg, which I would never have thought to patronize on my own, with its liveried waiters, purely Western clientele and quiet sitar music played by a handsome Indian man before a microphone. I made the assumption - correct as I later discovered - that Dan was not short of money. He seemed to know all the dishes on the menu and so I let him order for me, feeling like a child being taken out to dinner by her father. We demolished two bottles of wine between us, and I began to feel more relaxed and more and more lightheaded. I've always been easily affected by alcohol, and I was aware, through a slightly drunken haze, that I was smiling more than usual and holding my head coquettishly on one side without having intended to.

I started revealing more about myself, telling Dan without self-pity that I had a disease called Level 3, which was prevalent in Britain at the moment and for which there was no cure. On hearing this, Dan became animated and spoke with enthusiasm about the wonderful doctors and medical services that were available in Australia, the best in the world, he claimed. He felt sure, he said, that had such a damaging accident occurred in his country they would have found a way to cure it by now. I wanted to stick up for my own nation, but found to my chagrin that I was agreeing with him when he called England a "stick-in-the-mud" place where it was the norm never to alter the status quo if at all possible and the populace were far too resigned to putting up with incompetence from the authorities.

"It's kind of odd that we should meet up in this out-of-the-way location" declared Dan, melting me with his firm grey eyes.

I held my hands clasped together with my elbows on the table: "Almost as if it was meant?" I replied, staring back at him intently.

He gave a low chuckle. "I guess. If you say so."

"Don't you think some things are meant to be?" I hadn't told him much about Clair and my journey. I was waiting to find out more about him.

"What - sort of, preordained by Fate?" he asked in a mocking tone. "I doubt it. I think...you know...life is what you make of it. I could have stayed with my wife. But I chose not to."

"And you ended up here" I replied, as if that proved my argument.

"Coincidence." He caught my look of disappointment. "But a happy one" he added with a grin.

So Dan was a cynic. But it was possible, wasn't it, just possible that my brother Clair was not aware of who he was and who I was. Not until he discovered it for himself, or until I told him. Genevieve hadn't said that he would definitely recognize me when I met him. A little voice in the back of my mind reminded me that she had also said Clair's name would begin with S, unlike Dan. But I refused to listen to the voice, thinking that there must be some other explanation. Hadn't the monk said I would get messages in my dreams? And this was the man I'd seen in my dream.

The truth was, I wanted very much to believe that Dan was Clair. I felt a strong attraction to him that I'd never felt to anybody before. It was such a new sensation for me that

I felt I could be capable of anything. I wanted to have some reason to be there with Dan and to spend time with him, both then at the restaurant and also later, when I hoped our relationship would continue. I even felt - after a while, when the wine started to really intoxicate me and fill my head with delirious thoughts - that I didn't care whether he was Clair or not, I still wanted to be with him.

"So, where are you going next on your adventures?" he asked, with a slightly condescending smile.

"I'm not sure, to be honest. I might go to Borneo."

"Borneo! That's a bit of a hike, isn't it? Why ever do you want to go there?"

"Well, it's just something somebody said to me today."

"You certainly are a spontaneous little creature, aren't you?"

I said nothing, but simply grinned, delighted with this description of me as "spontaneous". I'd never before thought of myself as a free spirit but, I reflected, I supposed that's what I had turned into these last few weeks, and I rather liked the new me.

"You know, forgive me if I'm being forward here, but..." Dan leaned in and fixed me with his gorgeous eyes. "I've got a suggestion to make to you."

I raised my eyebrows. "Fire away."

"Why don't you come back to Australia with me?" He saw my look of amazement, and explained: "What I said about our doctors was true, you know. I have a strong hunch they could help you. And actually, I've got a few contacts in the medical world. I could do some research and dig out the best people for you to visit. What do you say?"

"Well!" I gasped, and put a hand to my throat in amazement. "I know I sound like something out of a romance novel, but, *This is all so sudden!*"

Dan roared with laughter at my imitation of a waifish heroine. "It is sudden, you're right. But you're the one who can make snap decisions about your future, so I thought I'd fling the idea at you anyway. There's no obligation. I won't be hurt if you turn me down. A little sad, perhaps." He glinted at me, his eyes twinkling dangerously. "Normally I might not be so impulsive myself but it's just that I'm going to be leaving Nepal so soon - the day after tomorrow in fact - so, if we're to carry on our acquaintanceship, it's really the only way."

He let this comment hang a while on the air and I digested its portent with a secret delight. The thought of spending more time with Dan certainly appealed to me.

After a few moments of charged silence, Dan remarked: "You're a brave girl. To be dashing about the world on your own." Lighting a cigarette, he inhaled it with evident pleasure. It had been a long time since I had seen anyone of my acquaintance smoke - any Westerner that is - as smoking had become such an antisocial and universally denigrated habit. But Dan smoked as if lung cancer had never been invented.

"Why am I brave? What could happen to me?"

"Oh, you know. You might get accosted by...some strange man." His mouth was curled in a smile, and I realized that he was flirting with me.

"That might not be so awful" I replied, flirting back. "Can I have a puff?" I asked, indicating the cigarette.

"I thought you didn't," he said in surprise, handing the butt to me.

"Just occasionally. I'm an occasional..." I coughed and spluttered as I ingested the smoke. I'd never let a cigarette touch my lips before, but all of a sudden, I'd just wanted to try. Dan roared with laughter at my efforts, and I was glad that my comic antics had brought us closer together.

It was at about midnight that I found myself in Dan's room, which was a room across the corridor from mine on the third floor of the hotel. It seemed that the Nepalese had a habit of housing guests from the same country on the same floor, and to them, Australia and England were pretty much the same country.

Dan had bought a CD of Indian flute music and it was playing rather tinnily on his portable machine on the windowsill. I imagined that this was a ploy to get us in the mood for seduction. As for me, I didn't really need any encouragement. The wine had already released my inhibitions, and I lay down immediately on the bed, feeling too tired and relaxed to bother with a chair. To my surprise, Dan didn't lay down beside me, but sat on the edge of the bed and started to unbutton his shirt with a slow smile.

"Are you comfy there?"

"Yes" I said, stretching out lazily to prove my point. The flute music wailed on and became louder and higher, then was joined by the insistent beat of the tabla. I closed my eyes and let myself be lulled and relaxed by the music and the soft feel of the sheets beneath me. I could hear Dan's steady breathing near me, and then his lips touched mine. As soon as he began to kiss me, I grabbed his neck with my arms and pulled him down, wanting his body close to mine. The force

MADISON C. BRIGHTWELL

of my emotion as I felt his urgent kisses on my neck made me breathe in quick gasps. His tongue seemed to be all over my face, my neck, my shoulders and then lower down. His hands were unburdening me of my clothes and I stroked the beautiful silky skin of his hard taut shoulders, marveling at the compact strength in his torso. As he launched himself on top of me, I scanned his lovely face with my eyes and reveled in the thick hair, massaging his scalp with my fingertips. I broke on the wave of an ocean of pleasure like nothing I'd ever felt before. This was the purest bliss my body had ever known. The purest physical bliss I'd ever experienced.

About an hour later, when I managed to stir myself, I got up and went into the bathroom, had a wash and rubbed toothpaste over my teeth. Then I got into bed beside the now-sleeping figure of Dan and pulled the covers over both of us. I reflected that I must have been drunker than I'd imagined, as my head was by now swimming quite badly.

I pondered on what Dan had said about the Australian doctors. Maybe he was right that somebody in his country could help me where the English medical establishment had failed. Perhaps I shouldn't dismiss the possibility out of hand. It was a large continent, a new continent, and Dan - with his money and his contacts - could probably find out who the best doctors were and get me an audience with them.

I don't know if it was the effects of the booze from which I was still lightheaded, or the intoxicatingly pleasurable experience I'd just had, but the idea of traveling with Dan to Australia seemed more appealing the more I thought about it.

I had to admit; I was also immensely flattered that Dan was so keen for me to travel with him. He'd only just met me, had only spent a few hours in my company, and yet here he was trying to persuade me to accompany him to his home, offering to let me stay with him, even possibly to aid me financially. Perhaps he had been as immediately attracted to me as I'd been to him. It was certainly true that Dan was a pretty special guy, in my eyes, and probably the handsomest man I'd ever slept with.

Could it be...could I be...falling in love with him?

None of the questions I was pondering could keep me awake for long, however. It had been a long, tiring and eventful day and blissful sleep closed over me almost immediately I switched out the light.

CHAPTER TWELVE

S HAMA AND I strolled along the streets of Katmandu the next evening, having had a delicious dinner in the Tibetan restaurant she'd taken me to, and enough intimate conversation to really get to know each other. As we embarked on a brief and thoughtful silence, we were passed by a couple of rickshaw cyclists who regarded me curiously and then cycled on when they saw that I was accompanied by a Nepalese girl. The street was fairly quiet, apart from the cawing of ravens that circled above the buildings high over our heads.

"Will you believe me if I tell you I've never...loved a man?" Shama glanced at me shyly.

"Of course I'll believe you." I laughed a little, though not enough to hurt her feelings. Shama was so open and the comments she came out with so ingenuous, that she reminded me of a child who hasn't yet learnt subtlety and cynicism.

"When you tell me about your experience with Dan, I'm a little frightened."

"Oh, but it's not frightening at all. It's lovely. Really." I wanted to sound convincing, but I didn't know how to discuss the subject without embarrassing her. I felt as though

I were explaining the facts of life to a younger sister, or a little girl who was innocent about sex. At this point I looked at Shama and received a sort of grimace that was also a grin. I made a stab at describing what sex with a man was like, but we quickly dissolved into adolescent giggles, covering our mouths with our hands.

After a few moments, Shama composed herself enough to remark: "I don't think it sounds very pleasant. I'm glad I have kept myself for my future husband."

"Well, maybe you have the right idea. You know, when I was a little girl we used to get loads of sex education in school, all about condoms and protection and that sort of thing..." Shama looked at me with incomprehension but I was unwilling to elaborate just then. "And there was lots of fuss made over how great sex was, but when we all grew up and had finished our...well...experimenting, we realized it wasn't that wonderful and got all blasé about it. In fact, I think monogamy's back in fashion in England. We've had our fill of free love."

Shama didn't respond to my conversation. I think I must have bewildered her. At that moment, it occurred to me that there was a divide between us, because of our different cultures, which conversation alone couldn't bridge. Perhaps such a bridge could be found eventually, but it would mean working out a common language where we understood each other. I'd been blathering on at her rather insensitively, as if she were just another girl from my background with the same experiences I'd had. But Shama's whole upbringing - about which I'd learned a lot that night - placed a value on fidelity, obedience and loyalty to family which I had never been taught to consider.

Being one of the few main arteries in Katmandu, this street was wider than most. On the pavement ahead of us some ragged children had gathered together bits of cardboard, which they were busy folding into a sort of bed on which to sleep. I wondered how they'd found themselves in that pitiful condition, and what could have happened to their parents. Even in England, where beggars and homeless people were numerous, I'd never before seen children forced to live in the street.

Shama broke my reverie: "So, do you still like this Dan?"

"Oh yes, very much. It's not just the sex, he's such good company, so interesting and talkative. He spent time showing me the sights in town this afternoon and I really enjoyed being with him."

"And will you go with him to Australia, as he asks? It is rather sudden, isn't it? I thought you said you were going to Borneo to find Rajan Mobley." Shama spoke hesitantly, as if she were secretly disapproving of my actions.

I reflected for a moment. "Of course, I am sort of altering my plans, but then what's wrong with spontaneity?" I remembered with pleasure Dan's comment of the previous evening about me being a spontaneous creature. "Yes, I think I will go with him. You know, sometimes things just happen and you should take advantage of the opportunity. Serendipity, we call it in English." I liked that word and was rather proud of having remembered it. I regarded Shama's downcast face. "You don't think I should go?"

"I'm only worried that you hardly know this Dan. How do you know whether...you can trust him, if he is a...good person?"

"I like him. Shouldn't I just follow my hunches?" Shama's caution was beginning to annoy me. Her attitude was that of a girl who'd led a very sheltered life - I concluded - and who had no thirst for adventure. But I'd recently rediscovered my thirst for adventure and was reveling in my newfound freedom.

"I think it is strange that he asks you to go to his country with him, when he's known you such a short time. And I hope there is no...trouble for you." Shama's voice trailed off, as though she was having difficulty explaining her anxieties.

"What trouble could there be? And anyway, I can take care of myself" I countered, wishing my friend would stop treating me like a child when she was in fact younger and less experienced than I.

Shama smiled at my hotheaded reply, and put her hand on my shoulder. "I'm sure you can. Don't be angry with me for considering your safety. I know I'm very careful and cautious - like the sloth bear, my cousin always says, always moving slowly. Australia must be a beautiful country. I'm sure you will have many wonderful experiences there. Although I don't think any city could be as beautiful as London. If I lived there, I would never want to leave!"

I laughed. "You may change your mind once you've seen it."

"Well, I will have to write to you and tell you what I think."

"Oh yes - let's keep in touch. I'll have to write to you first, of course, because you won't know where I am."

"And you will write to me at the shop?"

"Yes, of course. And tell you all about my adventures with Dan." I had images of Dan and I traversing Australia together in an old car, music blaring from the stereo, my hair blowing in the wind, like something out of a sixties road movie, and the vision appealed to me.

"I should like that. But please also promise me you'll be careful. You should be careful not to get drawn into things you don't want." Shama seemed melancholy. Perhaps, I thought, she's unhappy that I'm going away so soon, when we've only just become friends.

"I'll be careful, I promise" I replied smilingly, touched by her concern.

"At least, if he is a journalist and an Australian, he must have plenty of money," said Shama, with a shrug. "How old did you say he was?"

"He told me but I can't remember exactly. About forty-five, I think."

"Forty-five! And you are thirty-two? But that means he's years older than you. Years and years. I don't think that is so good. A man should be older, yes, but only two or three years."

As soon as Shama said the word "years", I had a peculiar sensation and then an instantaneous flashback, like a feeling of deja vu, only I knew that the experience I'd had before had happened not in reality, but in a dream. A dream that I'd had a couple of nights before, but which had been partly hidden from me till now.

In the dream, Clair had been lying on the bed, as he was the last time I'd seen him. Only this time I wasn't a child but an adult, and I knew my brother was going to die. I held his hand in mine and stroked it, trying to encourage him to hold on to life. But he looked up at me with his wise eyes and told me to let go. He said he would be back, and I must wait for him patiently. I asked him how long I had to wait and he said "years", and I remember my sadness at the thought of how long that was and how difficult it would be for me to wait that long. But I also felt amazed that I hadn't thought of this memory before, when Genevieve had told me Clair would return. It was as if I really had seen Clair, as if his ghost had talked to me and told me to be patient. He knew that I felt pessimistic about finding him, that the illness gave me too little time, but he was trying to comfort me and reassure me that my journey wasn't in vain.

My face must have betrayed something of the turmoil of my feelings, as Shama looked at me and asked me what was wrong. "You broke my dream," I answered.

"Broke? What do you mean?"

"It's what we say when...I had a dream the other night and I'd forgotten it but when you said years like that, it brought it all back to me." I told Shama about the dream and she agreed that I must be more anxious than I'd thought about the progress of my journey. She asked me again if I'd really made my mind up to go with Dan, and I said I definitely had, perhaps because her evident displeasure at the idea made me rebelliously decide that it was what I wanted to do. Shama couldn't hide the fact that she felt bad about it, and when pressed for a reason she could give none but that my decision felt "wrong". She said she had an "intuition" that this was a bad course of action for me.

But I didn't want to hear about any intuitions. To me, Dan was the future, beckoning to me like a lodestar. What could Shama know about what was good for me? I was the only one who could make the decisions, as Genevieve had said. I felt good about sticking to my guns and not letting anyone deflect me from my intentions. I hadn't let Hanneke dissuade me from setting off on my trip, and I wasn't going to let Shama stop me from pursuing the next stage of my journey.

Plus, I'd been thinking over and over that day of Australia. It was such a big country. And generations of people had gone there to follow their dreams, so why shouldn't I? The line I'd seen on the map in the cave had pointed to a large continent a long way to the East, and there the line had finished. If that meant nothing to me, why had the monk taken me to the cave in the first place? It was a message, and I was supposed to follow the messages sent to me wherever they might lead. I was so sure of the wisdom of my actions now that I wasn't about to listen to anybody else's advice, however well intentioned.

Shama and I said goodbye fairly hurriedly, when we reached my hotel. It wasn't that I had tired of her company, but I was in a hurry to get to my room. I wanted to follow a hunch, which had been pressing on my mind for the past few minutes.

"Shall we meet again tomorrow?" my friend asked me, as she kissed me affectionately on both cheeks.

"Yes, that would be nice. I'd like to see some more of Nepal before I leave."

"What time is your flight to Sydney?"

"It's in the afternoon, at 2 o'clock."

"Fine. We shall have time to meet again, then. Shall I come to your hotel tomorrow morning at about 8 o'clock and we can have breakfast together?"

"Yes, great."

Once in my room, I reached immediately into the inside pocket of my jacket for my treasured box, and withdrew the parchment paper with the crossword clues on. I gave my attention to the fourth clue, and regarded the Nepalese script with the English words penciled underneath in Shama's neat hand: *Ridiculously easy to be about right for some time.* As I looked at it, a slow smile of triumph began to spread over my face. I picked up my pencil from the bedside table and wrote a word into one of the spaces on the grid I'd sketched on my paper napkin. It fitted. The grid now looked like this:

		I	C	A	L					
			K							
			C	I						
H	U	M	A	N						
						Y	E	A	R	S

When I thought about the clue, the answer made perfect sense. *Easy* was the word that had been made into an anagram, as indicated by the word *ridiculously* before it. The letters of the anagram word were placed in a different order around the letter R, standing for *right*. And the whole thing meant *some time*, or a long time.

My dream had been trying to tell me something. Or so it seemed. I'd never thought much about dreams back in London, and certainly never seen any messages in them. But now, I had dreams all the time, sometimes bizarre and sometimes banal, but always vivid. What a strange way to impart information. The monk had told me to take note of my dreams.

Perhaps it would be a good idea to listen to my subconscious - however strange and meaningless the messages might appear at first - as well as my more practical conscious side, the self I'd always used in my job at I.C.A.L., for example. It was extraordinary how the word years had sprung unbidden into my head, been echoed by Shama, and turned out to be correct. Maybe all my dreams were trying to tell me something.

I thought back on the other dreams I'd had recently. The one of Dan on the train had had an obvious message, which I'd acted upon. But, thinking of Clair singing Sylvie, I couldn't figure out what message that might have had to offer, although the dream had affected me deeply at the time. Perhaps it was just trying to console me and tell me that I would find my brother before it was too late.

The next morning after breakfast, as I packed my suitcase ready for our flight to Sydney, a knock came at my bedroom door and I went to answer it. Dan stood in the corridor, tanned and handsome in a flowered shirt and casual trousers.

"I didn't want to disturb you in the middle of packing, but I wondered if I could ask a favor?" he asked smilingly.

"Sure" I replied. "Do you want to come in for a while?"

"No, it's O.K. I'm pretty busy myself at the moment, got to make a few telephone calls. I just wondered if you wouldn't mind taking this for me in your suitcase?" He handed me a large china figurine of the Buddha. "Stupid of me to buy it really, because it's such an awkward shape to pack. I've got so much bloody stuff with me, there's just not a decent space in my case."

I turned the figure over in my hands, examining its size and weight. "Yes, it should be O.K. I think I'll have room in my suitcase, as I haven't got much stuff with me."

"Great. I'd appreciate it."

"No problem." Although I would now be forced to begin my packing again to find room for the large object, I felt I could hardly refuse Dan this tiny favor, when he'd so kindly offered to help me with the price of my airline ticket to Sydney and had taken the trouble to book it for me on his credit card.

"Make sure you pack it at the bottom, surrounded by soft clothes or something, so it doesn't get broken. Not that I care about it too much, but it would be a shame if it got smashed in transit."

"Oh yes. Of course" I asserted. "See you later, then."

"I'll meet you in the foyer at 11.30" Dan replied, favoring my cheek with a quick, businesslike peck before returning to his room.

CHAPTER THIRTEEN

I AWOKE TO the roar of the airplane engine droning in my ears. The side of my face was pressed uncomfortably against the cold glass of the window, and my lower jaw had dropped, making my mouth hang open. When I opened my eyes, I was glad to notice that my face was mostly covered with the airplane blanket, which I had draped over my head and shoulders for warmth. There was a slight draught coming from the air ventilator above my head, and I reached up to close it. Looking across at Dan in the seat next to me, I saw that he was immersed in a book and hadn't noticed that I'd woken up.

"Are we there yet?" I demanded teasingly in a sleepy voice, nudging Dan softly with my elbow.

He glanced at me unsmiling. "You've been asleep a long time," he said, closing his book. "We've only a coupla hours to go. They came round with breakfast a little while back, but I didn't want to wake you."

"Oh." I rather wished he had woken me. My stomach rumbled with hunger pangs and my back and shoulders were stiff and sore from being hunched in the same uncomfortable position for too long. Dan retreated again into his book and I pondered whether the real reason he hadn't woken me was that he didn't want to make conversation with me. He'd acted with such coldness and indifference towards me throughout the trip; it was like being with a different person from the day before. I asked myself if I'd done something to displease him, or whether the truth was he'd simply grown tired of my company and bored in my presence. With a stab of hurt pride, I wondered if he was already regretting having asked me to accompany him. Although I had contributed to the cost of my ticket out of my few meager savings, Dan was probably aware that I had little more cash or chances of employment in Australia and was worried that I would be a drain on his resources.

These disturbing thoughts flashed through my head but I pushed them aside, determined to keep cheerful and optimistic. My consort was probably just tired. It was a long flight, and some people didn't like talking all the time as I did. He was no doubt more habituated to airplane travel than I was and therefore blasé and unable to get caught up in my excitement at the comparatively novel experience. Or maybe the book he was reading was important for his article and he had to finish it before reaching Sydney. He certainly seemed completely engrossed in its pages. "What are you reading?" I asked, trying to peer at the title on the cover.

"Nothing much" Dan replied abruptly, putting the book down on his lap so I couldn't see it. "It's just a story." He appraised me with cold grey eyes. "You look terrible. Perhaps you should go to the Ladies and freshen up a little."

I was hurt, but concluded that maybe he was right, so I obeyed his instructions and squeezed myself down the long corridor to the toilet. Gazing at my reflection in the mirror, I was about as impressed with my appearance as Dan had been: my hair was lank and untidy and my complexion - always pale - now looked positively anemic. Although the I.C.A.L. drugs alleviated most of the painful symptoms of Level 3, the effect of pumping my body full of a drug strong enough to kill off this incredibly durable virus put a strain on my body's resources which was evident enough for anybody to see. My eyes were bloodshot, the dark circles surrounding them giving me a haunted look. Although I didn't feel too bad physically, I wished I could appear more attractive than this.

A little voice in my head kept asking me why I'd decided to come on this long airplane journey to Australia, when I had no real inkling of the outcome. Why hadn't I gone to see Rajan Mobley as Shama and the monk had advised me, and obtained his help in finding Clair? That had been my original intention. But I'd been so keen to stay with Dan, so sure this was the right thing to do - having seen it predicted in the map - and so persuaded by Dan that my earlier decisions were wrong. I had left Nepal impulsively, prompted by the knowledge that if I didn't travel with Dan I wouldn't see him any more, and fuelled by the intense physical attraction that he still had for me.

In any case, it was too late to regret my actions: I'd made my bed and I had to lie on it, as I didn't have enough money to travel to Borneo now, even if I'd wanted to. I determined to make the best of my situation. When I got to Sydney - I told my reflection - I would get a job, any job, to support myself, so that I wasn't dependent on Dan. He would be proud of my endeavors and happy to have me with him. I'd carry on looking for Clair in my spare time, and maybe I would find him there. After all, it was a big country with lots of people. At the very least, I would be able to translate the fifth clue and finish the crossword and that would help me know where to search. I washed my face and splashed on some of the cologne in a bottle by the sink and, with my spirits revived a little, returned to my seat.

Dan looked up from his book and grudgingly squeezed out of his seat for a moment so that I could occupy mine by the window. He didn't smile or look particularly pleased to see me. For the next hour or so, we passed over some wonderful scenery and I could see acres of desert below, which thrilled and excited me. I kept pointing features out to Dan and trying to include him in my enthusiasm, but he remained singularly uninterested.

I concluded that he must have made this trip before many times and therefore found the sights unimpressive. I asked him about where he lived in Sydney: was it near the center of town and was it a nice area? Would it be hot at this time of year and what would the local time be when we arrived? His answers were polite but short, giving me information but resisting being drawn into conversation. Eventually, I gave up trying to talk to him and simply gazed out of the window.

Some time later, Dan nudged me. "We've started our descent. Should be there in a half hour or so."

"Great" I responded, but I felt more nervous than pleased, at the thought of yet another new country, and this time dependent on someone else to provide for me.

Dan took a piece of paper from his pocket and handed it to me. "Here - you might need this."

"What is it?"

"My friend's address. You know, the one I told you about who lives in Woolahra. In case we get separated at the airport, you should just go there. I've told her about you."

I looked at him vacantly, not quite comprehending. "Won't I be staying with you?"

"Sure, but this is just for emergencies. When we go through passport control, we'll be in two different streams. I'm a citizen and you're an alien. They might take a long time to check you out. And they'll want you to give them an address where you're staying in Australia, so they know you're not an illegal immigrant. So keep the paper in your pocket. OK?"

"Yes, of course. And where shall I meet you after we check in?" The prospect of arrival was making me feel more and more apprehensive. I hoped the officials wouldn't take too long with me at passport control, interrogate me or ask me lots of questions I'd find hard to answer: *Reasons for travel? What! You're here to find your dead brother? Who are you trying to kid?*

Dan shrugged: "Wherever's convenient. At baggage collection, I guess. Don't worry. We'll find each other."

Now it was Dan's turn to visit the toilet, so while he was gone I gathered up my things and filled in my disembarkation card with slightly shaky fingers. I still felt cold and small and more vulnerable than I had before on my journey. Although I'd been alone before, I'd never felt so alone as I did now.

I hated landing. Passing through turbulence on the way down, the plane tipped and tumbled and I gripped the edge of my seat with sweaty palms. The sensations of panic in my stomach didn't subside until we touched the ground, brakes were applied with a massive roar for a few seconds and we taxied gently down the runway towards the safety of the terminal building. Dan didn't seem to be concerned by any of this, in fact he read all the way through it.

After the plane landed, perhaps my fatigue caused me to walk too slowly as I trailed after Dan down the long corridor to the Arrivals lounge, but as I passed the Customs desk one of the officers stopped me and asked me to open my suitcase. I obliged, hoping it wouldn't take too long to rifle through my carefully packed suitcase, and rather annoyed that customs officials had chosen to swoop on me, probably the least likely person to be carrying anything contraband. As the uniformed woman bent down over my case to inspect its contents, I looked around to see if Dan was waiting for me and noticed with disappointment that he'd disappeared. No doubt, he'd elected to wait for me in the Arrivals lounge. It seemed somewhat churlish of Dan not to stick by me when I'd had the misfortune to be stopped, but I consoled myself with the thought that perhaps his large strides had carried him out of the area before realizing that I was no longer close behind him.

The black woman who was examining my suitcase rooted around in my clothes, ruffling everything a bit and to my irritation dismantling the careful job I'd made of packing Dan's figurine. But thankfully she didn't take long, and within a few minutes I was closing up my case again and treading the rest of the way down the corridor to Arrivals.

When I got into the huge hall, to my surprise, there was absolutely no sign of Dan. I raised myself on tiptoes and craned my head to peer over all the other bodies that were swirling about, but Dan's tall lean figure didn't materialize.

Bewildered, I went through to the main terminal building - wandering through the jostling and hurrying crowds in a daze. I searched in all the places I thought Dan might choose to wait, but could see him nowhere. I couldn't understand why he hadn't just lingered a few minutes at the Arrivals position for our flight. That would surely have been sensible. He must have realized I'd been stopped by Customs, so why didn't he wait for me? Why had he suddenly vanished into thin air?

Feeling confused and unsure what to do next, I steered myself on automatic pilot to the Information Desk, and asked the girl there to page Dan for me. I listened to the lonely little announcement over and over: *Please could Mr. Dan Armitage come to the check out desk for the 12.05 flight from Katmandu* - but nobody responded.

I flopped down on to a seat amidst the swirling crowds and waited, still unable to believe that Dan had simply abandoned me. I felt sure he must be somewhere. There must be some mistake: perhaps Dan had mentioned something to me on the flight or as we walked off the plane that I had subsequently forgotten, something about how he would meet me outside the Terminal Building or in a certain cafe. But I searched and searched my memory and could recall nothing like that. A horrible cold feeling started to seep down into my stomach.

I had a sudden brainwave, and looked at the crumpled piece of paper in my pocket on which Dan had written his friend's address in Woolahra. Perhaps, for some extraordinary reason, he had decided to just go on ahead and meet me there. Perhaps, indeed, he had said he would do that and I had simply forgotten. I was starting to go mad with my speculations. At any rate, there was nothing much else I could do. Dan could hardly be angry with me for just showing up at his friend's house, since he had invited me in the first place.

So - using the small amount of Australian cash I had acquired in Nepal - I hailed a taxi to the address Dan had given me. The journey took almost an hour, and I must have seemed a very taciturn passenger, as I could only manage monosyllabic replies to the cab driver's friendly chitchat. Speeding down Sydney's streets, I felt only half alive or as though the tall buildings, hazy mountains in the distance and metallic streams of cars in the other lanes were all part of some gigantic T.V. screen that I was watching with dreary disinterest. Perhaps it was a form of jetlag, or my confusion over Dan's disappearance or the limbo-sensation from the whole trip and my illness starting to catch up with me. Or maybe it was a combination of all these things. When we finally pulled up outside a neat little house with white wrought-iron gates and windows and the driver assured me that this was the place, I got out of the car with legs almost trembling with bewilderment, gave him too large a tip in a daze and watched him drive away.

As I walked up the driveway, through the immaculately tended garden with its lemon trees and mosaic of brightly colored flowers lavished by streams of water from the endless spray of a sprinkler, with the hum of unfamiliar insects soft in my ears, I think I knew in my heart the answer I would receive when I knocked on the door.

Nevertheless, I did knock, and a woman answered. At least, she had the face and body of a woman but she was dressed incongruously like a young girl, in a pretty flowered flock and with her tousled reddy-blonde hair done up with a big bow on top of her head. Her cheeks were slightly flushed and her eyes shone with a sort of vivid excitement. She smiled lazily as she saw me, which I, in my bemused state, took to be an indication that she recognized me from Dan's description.

"Hi, honey" the woman said, as if I was some relative who'd popped over for tea. "It's hot, ain't it? You look all washed up."

I hadn't noticed the temperature. There was only one thing I wanted to know. "Is Dan here?"

"Dan who, honey?"

"Dan" I said, stupidly hoping that by magical repetition of his name the woman would suddenly know who I was referring to. "Dan - Dan Armitage."

"Oh, that Dan!" She clapped her hand over her mouth and giggled like a teenager. "Silly me. I plumb forgot. He called just now," she said with an easy smile. "Told me you were comin'."

"Just now?"

"Sure. You must be Alice, huh? Come on in."

I nodded and stood motionless on the doorstep, feeling more than a little perturbed. "So, is Dan not here?"

"No, your friend ain't comin' over for a while. Not today anyways. Told me about you, though. Asked me to look after you for a spell."

"But where is he?"

"I don't know. He didn't say. I figured you'd know."

"No. I was at the airport; we'd just got here from Nepal. When we went through customs they stopped me to search my suitcase, then when I went into the terminal building Dan had gone. I looked all over for him, but..."

My voice trailed off into a plaintive whisper. Suddenly, I was too miserable to speak, the full impact of what had happened beginning to hit me. I don't know what set me off, but all at once I couldn't stop the flood of pent up emotions inside me from releasing in a torrent, as hot tears welled up in my eyes and started to roll down my cheeks. I didn't even have the strength to wipe them away, but stood foolishly clutching my suitcase on the doorstep of a stranger, feeling as alone as I'd ever felt in my life.

When she realized I was crying, the woman's smile vanished and her attitude was all maternal concern. Grasping my free hand, she pulled me gently inside the door: "Aw honey, it can't be that bad. Come on into the house and take a drink of lemonade. There ain't no man worth crying over, believe you me."

"My name's Mary Lou" the woman announced, as she handed me a full glass.

"Pleased to meet you" I replied, not knowing what else to say.

"Pleased to meet you, I'm sure." She giggled like a child at the formality of our self-introduction, hiding her mouth behind one beautifully manicured hand. Again, I was struck by the contrast between her dress and demeanor - which was like that of a naive schoolgirl - and her actual age, which I would have put at about 40. Nevertheless, I was grateful for her candid friendliness, and her gaiety must have been infectious, because that coupled with the effect of the cooling drink, made me start to feel much better.

"You're a stranger in these parts, ain't you?" she said, evidently proud of her perceptive deductions, "I guess you've come pretty far. Where you from, then? Darwin?" she asked, as if having hit on the furthest possible location.

"I came from Nepal."

"Nepal" she echoed, amazed. "Where in hell is that?"

"It's in the Far East. Between India and China."

"My Lord! So are you Chinese?"

It was my turn to laugh - she was so obviously ignorant of anything outside her own experience. "No. I'm English. From England. I'd been visiting Nepal."

"So how come you wound up here? Oh, I see" she said, before I could reply. "Your friend Dan. How did you guys meet?"

"I met him in Nepal. I was there because...well, it's a long story. Dan was doing some research for his newspaper."

"What newspaper is that, honey?"

"I can't remember the name. The *Australian Times*, or something. He's a journalist, isn't he? That's what he told me."

"I wouldn't know."

"But I thought he was a friend of yours."

"Of mine? Oh no, honey. I only met him the one time. He's some business colleague o' Chuck's. But I guess everybody in town knows I'm a sucker for a hard luck story, so when he told me you had no place else to go I said sure she can stay here a while. It's no skin off my nose. I got this whole big house to myself anyways, with nobody to talk to most o' the time, so I'm glad of the company to tell you the truth."

"But, I don't understand" I replied, confused. "He asked me to come back to Australia with him, and I agreed. I thought I'd be staying with him." Mary Lou shot me a sympathetic smile, and I continued. "You see, I had been going to travel to Borneo, but Dan persuaded me not to. He said you have wonderful doctors over here who might be able to help me with...I've got an illness, you see, a virus that's affecting a lot of people my age in England. And nobody's found a cure yet, so far as I know. Dan and I traveled over here on the airplane together. But at the airport, I... lost him. I don't know where he went. But he'd given me this address. So I thought he might have come here before me, for some reason."

"Well, ain't that the darndest thing. What a thing to do, to persuade you to travel over here an' all and then just dump you on me! Not that I mind, o' course" Mary Lou added, noticing the hurt expression in my eyes. "I'm pleased to have you, and you can stay here as long as you want till you get settled."

"Didn't Dan tell you anything else about me?"

"Nope. Nothing at all, save for your name and that you'd probably be arriving sometime today. I told him I'd be in all day, so it didn't matter none to me what time you showed up."

"Maybe there was some important business he had to attend to," I suggested, desperately seeking excuses for his behavior. "Did he say he would be telephoning again?"

"Oh, sure. He said he'd call and come over in the next couple of days. Told me you'd carried something for him in your suitcase."

"Oh!" I exclaimed, remembering the figurine. "Yes I did. He'll probably want that back. I suppose it must have cost him a bit of money - a Buddha statue he bought in Katmandu - it is quite big." Tears welled up into my eyes again, as the thought occurred to me that the figurine was all Dan wanted from me now. But surely, I reasoned, he wouldn't have gone to all the trouble of persuading me to travel to Australia with him and even paying for half my ticket, in order to save a bit of weight in his suitcase? No, there must be some other explanation. But I wished I knew what it was. I brushed away the tears and peered over my glass with red-rimmed eyes as I sipped my drink.

"He'll come back for you, just you wait and see" Mary Lou soothed. "You didn't ever twist his arm to come here, did ya? So he'll be wanting to see you."

"I don't know. Maybe" I answered miserably. "He seemed to really like me at first. When we were in Nepal together he was lovely and affectionate. But then he was a bit strange with me on the plane. I just thought he was in a bad mood about something, but maybe he's suddenly gone off me. I don't understand him. Why change his mind so soon? I don't know" I sighed. "Maybe he's like that with every woman he meets."

"Honey - men are a strange breed. I'm married to one, so I should know." Mary Lou gave me a wise look, as if she'd encountered my sort of story before and knew just what it meant. "Sounds like you need something stronger than lemonade." She poured me a large dose of Southern Comfort before I could stop her, and placed it on the table before me. I didn't have the heart to tell her I don't drink spirits, and I flung the liquid down my throat as quickly as I could to get it over with. To my surprise, the drink produced a warm sensation in the pit of my stomach, which was distinctly comforting. Mary Lou poured one for herself too, in a glass with lipstick stains around its rim, and I guessed the reason for her unnaturally flushed cheeks. She gulped down her drink thirstily and immediately poured another. "My guess is that you've been duped. Men sure can be skunks, I know it. Pretty much the same thing happened to me with Chuck - he got me to move here and then soon tired of me - only difference bein' that I wouldn't let go of 'im. Look where it's got me, though" she declared, waving her arms at the house around us, as though it were her prison. "I hate this country, this town. All the people in it are crazy. But I can't go back home now."

"Where's home?" I asked, surprised. Not recognizing the accent, I hadn't realized she wasn't Australian.

"Texas, in the Southern States of America" she said with a touch of fond pride. "I been here fifteen years and I still feel like a stranger. There ain't no place nice to go nearby, and I don't drive a car. Chuck's a good provider, I don't want for nothing on that front. But I don't hardly never see him. He works all day and comes home too dead beat to talk."

"What does he do?" I was being drawn into Mary Lou's world, intrigued by the difference between her experience and mine. It was as if we were two women at opposite poles. She'd constructed a life where everything was static and still and she longed to break out of her cage and fly. My life was one perpetual flight, full of misgivings and imminent danger, and I longed for a safe haven.

"He works in interior design, painting up fancy houses in Rose Cove. It's his life, you know. He designed everything in this house and had it built specially. It's just sticks of furniture to me, I guess one table's about as good as another, but he's totally obsessive about it."

"And do you work too?"

"Hell, no. I was a secretary for a while, but then I met Chuck and I got pregnant soon after we came out here. We got married on account of the baby. But then I lost it. We tried some more after that and I got pregnant again, but I couldn't never bring a baby to full term. I really wanted kids, but it just didn't work out that way. I guess God didn't think I'd be a good enough mother," she said cheerfully. "So I stay home and keep house and look after Chuck's precious things. They're my babies now." Mary Lou refilled my glass. "How about you, honey? I bet you're running away, ain't you. You got a husband and kids back home in England and you just took off one day and decided to go shoot the breeze with a trip round the world." She winked at me and flopped in the chair opposite mine, hitching up her flowered dress with one hand.

I couldn't resist laughing at her invention, which was so far from the truth. "Well, it wasn't quite like that. I don't have a husband, or any children, and I used to work for a company called Independent Care Association Ltd. They are...they were a great big pharmaceutical company and they made drugs which helped people like me with this disease I've got."

"In...dee...what?"

"We called it I.C.A.L. for short."

"Do they have a branch here?"

"No - in fact, the whole plant's collapsed. At least, I think so. You see, there were these terrorists on New Year's Eve -- oh gosh, it's a very long story."

"Well carry on, honey. I got all day."

Mary Lou was easy to be open with, and the Southern Comfort had loosened my tongue. We talked and talked, for what seemed like hours, as the afternoon sun dipped slowly behind the trees and the light in the little kitchen grew dim. I told her about my journey and the reasons for it and about the life I'd lived in England with my mother before then. I told her more about my illness, and she told me she had heard of the disease from the newspapers and she knew a couple of people who had died. But far from castigating me for traveling in my condition with only months to live and fast running out of the drugs which helped me, Mary Lou accepted my reasons as entirely valid and extended to me a warm and non-judgmental sympathy.

As I talked about these things, my problems seemed to lose their towering significance and appear like small hurdles I could easily surmount. The peculiar spell that Dan had put over me with his attractiveness, which now I could see as entirely physical in nature - leading me to follow him to Australia despite my misgivings and Shama's intuitive advice, leading me even to fool myself that he might be the reincarnation of my brother - started to unweave itself, and I saw more clearly what sort of a man he really was and what had happened.

Following our passionate night together at the restaurant and the hotel in Katmandu, Dan had asked me to travel with him on an impulse, which he had later regretted, it being too late to stop me once the airplane ticket was purchased. He had known all along that he would get rid of me at the airport, where it was easiest to do so. As for his "friend's" address in Woolahra, for some reason he had given the address of this woman who was virtually a stranger to him. It was fortuitous anyway - and maybe a twist of that strange and uncertain Fate which had me in its grip - that I had ended up here with Mary Lou. Because I think we both knew from very early on that our contrasting needs would draw us together and create a bond of friendship. Mary Lou needed so much to have a confidante, a mirror in which to see herself to cure her isolation. I needed a branch to grasp in the swirling current of my adventures, an oasis of security in this alien land.

So, although grateful, I wasn't very surprised when Mary Lou offered me a bed in their spare room, and said she and Chuck would be happy to have me stay for as long as I wanted. Chuck - she said - wouldn't object so long as I kept out of his way. That should be easy enough, since he got up at 6 a.m. most mornings and was in bed by ten o'clock at night. She hardly saw him herself. And they had more money than they knew what to do with, with no children to support and no time for holidays.

That night it wasn't hard to sleep. In fact, I must have been practically falling asleep at the table as we sat talking, and in the early evening Mary Lou showed me to my room and I collapsed at once into a deep slumber. The next morning, I woke at 10 a.m. feeling hugely refreshed and filled with renewed optimism by the bright sunlight streaming through the half-drawn blinds.

It being one of the rare Saturdays when her husband was free from work, Mary Lou said we should celebrate my arrival, and suggested a trip to the Blue Mountains, a beauty spot a couple of hours drive inland from Sydney. So, together with Chuck - who had accepted me immediately as part of the family, probably relieved that his wife had found a companion to fill her loneliness - we drove out into the mountains and spent the day walking amongst them.

I can't remember how we got on to the subject of Dan, but when I began to repeat what Dan had related to me with great detail and bitterness about his acrimonious divorce from his wife, Chuck startled me with his response: "Dan's not divorced, as far as I know. I saw his wife Helen last week, so they would've had to move pretty sharpish to divorce in a few days."

"But he told me--"

"He's been giving you a line, mate. Dan's about as divorced as I am." At this, Chuck nudged Mary Lou playfully in the ribs and she whined in protest.

"So why did he spin that whole tale about her having an affair and him finding out and telling her to leave and saying he wanted to keep the house?" I was starting to feel aghast at the extent of Dan's betrayal. Where would his duplicity stop?

"It's the oldest trick in the book, ain't it?" put in Mary Lou. "He wants to get you to bed with him so he spins a lie."

I nodded, glumly. "He didn't need to tell me all those lies. I probably wouldn't have asked him loads of questions anyway; it's not my style. And I was that keen on him, he could have told me he was an astronaut and I would have believed him."

"Don't beat yourself up about it" soothed Mary Lou. "We're all suckers sometime."

"That's another thing," said Chuck. "He told you he lives in a house, did he?" I nodded and Chuck laughed. "He probably told you he's got a lot of money. Well, he may dress smart and talk posh but that's just his image. He and Helen live in a high rise apartment in Summerfield - not the most salubrious part of Sydney - so it's no wonder he didn't invite you home with him."

"Isn't he a journalist, then?" I appealed, knowing in my heart that the reply would be negative.

Chuck threw back his head and roared with laughter. "Is that what he told you? He's certainly a good actor anyway, should have been on the stage. No, that guy couldn't string a decent sentence together. The nearest he comes to a newspaper is using it to wrap his hamburgers."

"What does he do for a living, then?"

"Well, that I couldn't tell you for sure because every time I see the bloke he's up to something else. Last I heard, he was dealing in used cars or spare parts or something. He's never had a regular job, as far as I know. In fact, I've often wondered how he makes a living at all, because Helen doesn't work. They've got two kids, you see, quite young still. She's got enough on her hands with that. But he seems to keep chipper, always got some money-making scheme up his sleeve that he's trying to borrow money for, *just to get it going*, you know what I mean?"

I boggled at this description of Dan, which was so entirely different from the ideas I'd assumed about his character. It was as though Chuck and I were discussing a different person.

"What I don't understand is," I remarked, having by now recovered slightly from having my entire perceptions of Dan blown to smithereens, "why he asked me to carry his Buddha figurine for him if he had no intention of seeing me again. I've still got the damn thing and I've no idea what to do with it. It's heavy and I don't want to cart it around with me for ever."

"He did say he'd call," replied Mary Lou. "He'll probably come and get it sometime, honey. I wouldn't worry. Just leave it in the house. We got plenty more room for junk" she added, with a meaningful look at Chuck which he ignored.

"You could smash the thing," suggested Chuck with a mischievous wink. "Tell him the thing got damaged in transit. That'd pay him back a bit."

Mary Lou's eyes widened: "Chuck, you're a pig! Dan's your friend, ain't' he?"

"I told you" her husband replied. "There's no love lost between me and Dan. I think he's got it coming to him."

To my relief, we stopped talking about Dan after that and moved on to other subjects. After a while, Mary Lou began to sing - old American folk songs in a voice as sweet and girlish as her manners - and to my surprise, I joined in. I'd never been one for singing, even in the bath, believing myself to be tone deaf. But here under the night sky with my good companions, hearing simple melodies I remembered Mother humming to me in childhood, I felt no inhibitions or strangeness and the music spoke to me more than it had ever done before.

Later that night - as I lay in bed after Chuck had gone to his room and Mary Lou watched a late night chat show on the television - I suddenly had the urge to look inside Genevieve's box. I don't know what prompted me, because I realized I couldn't unravel the next clue until I found someone who could translate it from the Malay. But I undid the clasps anyway, and drew out the parchment paper with the clues and the paper napkin with the grid and studied them for a while. These things gave me no more information than the last time I'd looked, in Katmandu.

But then I looked at the photograph, and to my amazement, that was different. Instead of an indistinct darkish blur in the middle of the shiny white surface, I could definitely make out the contours of a face. It wasn't clear enough for me to recognize the face, but a face is certainly what it was. It was the most peculiar phenomenon. Especially when I remembered how disappointed I'd been when I'd first seen the photograph and believed it blank.

Perhaps what was happening was a very very slow and gradual development of the print. I'd never heard of anything like that before. But what other explanation could there be? In any case, it didn't matter why it was happening, only that it was happening. Eventually the photograph would be clear enough for me to see the face, and even recognize it. Perhaps the face would be that of Clair. Or even of who Clair had become. I felt almost euphoric in my excitement at this thought. One day Clair's face would stare back at me from the picture, and I would know for sure who he was. How, then, could I not find him?

I lay back on the bed; the photo clutched to my fast beating heart, and attempted to imagine Clair's face as a little boy when I had last seen him. But, try as I might, I couldn't quite remember it. It was like a dream whose memory eludes you, like an eel you fail to catch with your slippery fingers - his face was almost there, almost there, but not quite. The shape of each of his features I could recapture with my conscious mind, but his quality, the wholeness of him, I couldn't recapture.

I fell asleep with tears drying on my cheek.

And woke up a couple of hours later, my heart thumping. All these dreams - so constant and so vivid - were making my sleeping life even more extraordinary and seemingly real than my waking one. I had been walking with Dan down a long empty corridor. We walked apart, not hand in hand like lovers, and when I looked across at him I noticed that he had a large hole in his chest in the shape of a heart. I asked him wasn't it painful and he said no, he thought it looked decorative and it was less painful than a tattoo.

Lying there in a state of half-wakefulness, I was suddenly filled with the most peculiar sensation about Dan. At first, I wasn't quite sure what the feeling was and then I recognized it. It was anger, anger at his treatment of me and the way he'd used my gullible nature to lure me away from my correct path and seduce me on to this one, only to abandon me. It simply wasn't fair, and I hadn't deserved to be treated that way.

I tumbled out of bed, switched the main light on and went to the chest of drawers, pulling open the bottom one roughly. There, still wrapped in one of my old jumpers, was the Buddha figurine that I'd foolishly lugged to Australia for Dan. I took out the statue and glared at it, now noticing how tawdry and cheap it was, the fat smiling Buddha's face seeming to mock me. A phrase Chuck had used earlier returned to me, and in a moment I knew what to do.

I carried the statue over to the dressing table with its heavy marble top, lifted the scorned object high over my head and smashed the figurine with all my might against the marble. There - that would show him!

Shards of china flew all over the floor, where the bottom of the statue had been broken, the Buddha's head and upper torso still intact in my hands. I felt instantly guilty and remorseful that I might have damaged Mary Lou's furniture by my sudden act of vengeance, so I laid the remaining statue on the table and scrabbled around on my hands and knees for a few minutes, retrieving fragments of china from the carpet. One of the smaller pieces cut my finger and I was forced to sit sucking the fleshy pad for a while until the pain abated. I found a carrier bag and dumped all the broken pieces of china into it, then picked up the main unbroken statue from the table, intending to put it in the bag also. As I picked it up, something slid out of the hollow compartment inside the statue and fell on to the table.

It was a small plastic packet filled with white dust and sealed with selotape. I stared at the packet in astonishment, then felt around inside the statue and pulled out another two bags exactly the same.

With a sudden stab of horror, I realized what the bags were, and all at once the explanation for Dan's actions became abundantly clear.

Trembling slightly with shock, I placed all the broken pieces of the statue in the carrier bag as I'd originally intended, then sat on the edge of the bed while I considered what to do next, still transfixed by the three innocent looking plastic bags on the marble top of Mary Lou's dressing table.

Dan had used me to carry a stash of drugs - I didn't know what kind, possibly cocaine or heroin from the look of the substance in the bags - unknowingly from Nepal to

Australia. It had obviously been carefully planned right from the beginning, maybe even as far back as when he'd first noticed me on my own in the hotel and sussed me out as a likely candidate for a courier. No doubt, if I hadn't been searched by Customs at the airport, Dan might have waited for me and retrieved his precious figurine immediately we arrived inside the Terminal Building. As it was, he must have panicked and done a quick disappearing act in case the authorities were on to him.

He'd made certain, however, that he would know where I was so that he could come by later and pick up the statue. He was sure I'd have to go to his friends in Woolahra, because I was a stranger in town with nowhere else to go and no money for hotels. He probably intended to lie low for a couple of days then casually drop by - maybe waiting until I was out, to save any embarrassment - ask for his statue, and then vanish into thin air with none of us any the wiser.

But - unfortunately for Dan - his plan had been foiled by my act of revenge. Now, I had to decide what to do about the situation in which I found myself.

I wasn't going to return to Dan the statue containing his drugs; that much was for certain. Neither did I want to hand the packets over to the police myself, as the authorities would maybe consider me implicated in the crime. I couldn't keep illegal substances with me in Mary Lou and Chuck's house - what a way to repay two kind friends, by involving them in a drugs hoard that could land them in jail! Neither did I want to take such a dangerous haul anywhere with me. But I didn't want to wait here, either, where Dan knew where I was and would doubtless be coming any day to reclaim his property. What was I to do?

I pondered for a while and decided that I had to leave this place, and the sooner the better. I didn't know where else to go and how to travel without money, but I would sort something out. It simply wasn't safe for me to remain here. I would get the drugs to the police anonymously. I would simply have them delivered in the mail. I wouldn't even mention Dan's name, because that might lead the police back to me in the end. I would just send the drugs, and the authorities could do what they liked with the packages, destroy them or whatever they thought best. Perhaps the police were already aware of Dan's activities. In any case, it was no business of mine.

I turned out the light and lay back on the bed, my mind racing. What a good thing I'd smashed the statue. What on earth would have happened if I hadn't? Nothing perhaps, just that I would have been unwittingly involved in a crime. It was a shame that I would have to leave Mary Lou and Chuck so soon, when I liked them enormously already and felt comfortable in their house. But there was nothing else for me to do.

Next morning, I told Mary Lou and Chuck the dreadful news, and they were both as horrified as I was. They agreed that I should leave Sydney as soon as possible and send the drugs anonymously to the police. I was worried that Dan might take out some retribution against them for allowing me to go and disposing of the drugs, but Mary Lou pointed out that Dan wasn't even certain that I'd arrived there. The last time he'd telephoned had been before I'd shown up. When he rang again, Mary Lou said she would simply claim

I had never arrived at their house, and Dan could think what he liked. Chuck would back up her story and how could Dan ever prove otherwise?

We wrapped up the three packets in strong brown paper and addressed the parcel to the Central Sydney Police Station, not wanting to draw attention to our whereabouts by sending it to the local branch. Chuck offered to post the package from the main post office in town. I wondered perhaps about writing a note, then we dismissed that idea.

The main problem now was where should I go? I had to hide somewhere out of the way where Dan wouldn't think to look for me, somewhere a fair distance from Sydney but easy for me to reach. Mary Lou offered to lend me enough money to tide me over for a few days, saying that I didn't need to pay her back until I could. I was touched by her incredible kindness, but I had no other option but to accept her offer.

Chuck wandered out into the mid-morning sunshine to wash the car in the driveway, while Mary Lou and I discussed where I could go that would be reasonably safe.

"You know what? I just had a brainwave!" announced Mary Lou, leaping up from her chair. "You wait there and finish your coffee. I got to go fetch something." She disappeared from the kitchen, and I sipped my drink, reveling in the warm sunshine streaming through the window and hearing the lazy drone of bees outside. It was hard to adjust to the change in climate, traveling from cold grey England in the grip of winter, to Austria with its wintry blanket of snow, to Nepal with its crisp refreshing air and hazy sunshine, to Australia in the Southern hemisphere, now in late January experiencing the height of their hot summer season.

Mary Lou returned after a few minutes. "I got such a cute card from Simon last year - look." She threw something on to the kitchen table. It was a postcard with a picture of a smiling little girl clutching a red balloon in the shape of a heart. "It was for Valentine's but he goofed up on the address so it arrived a little late - pity I couldn't make Chuck jealous. I guess that's Simon all over. He never forgets."

I looked at the card, then at Mary Lou with a question on my face.

"Simon is Chuck's cousin" said Mary Lou. "We've always sort of got along. He used to take me out dancing, when he lived here in Sydney - used to make Chuck mad, but I didn't see the harm in it. After all, Chuck don't like dancing and I do. Besides, Simon and I are just friends, just real good friends. It's a pity he moved out to Byron Bay, 'cos now I hardly ever see 'im. Anyway, there I go again rattling on about me. I showed you the card because that's where I think you could go. To Simon's house in Byron Bay."

"Oh, I see. Where's Byron Bay?"

"It's up the coast, a few miles north of here. I don't know how far exactly, Chuck could tell you. I've never been there, but I've heard it's pretty scenic and wild."

"Do you think Simon would be all right about me staying with him? After all, I've never met him."

"Sure!" Mary Lou exclaimed. "He is one sweet guy, and very friendly. He's got a big house up there, I think he lives with a few other people, but there's plenty of room. He's always telling me to come up and to hell with what Chuck thinks, but I guess I just never did. I'd like to, but I didn't want to face Chuck's temper if I went without him and he's always too busy to take a trip anywhere."

"How does Simon have this big house? Is he very rich?"

"Well, he's no millionaire but he made a lot of money as a record producer for some pop group that got really successful a few years back, and since then he's sort of retired young. He's a kinda hippy guy, into all sorts of weird stuff. I'm sure you'd like him."

"O.K. That sounds like it might be a good idea. Can I take a train to Byron Bay?"

Mary Lou laughed. "You don't wanna take the train anywhere in Australia, if you can help it. It's boring and expensive. No, you should hire a car and drive up. You can drop the car off at the other end, and gas is pretty cheap in NSW."

"How long would it take to drive there?" I didn't want to dampen Mary Lou's obvious zest for her project, but I didn't know if my health could cope with spending days driving on unfamiliar roads.

"Oh, just a coupla days I guess. It's only a bitty ways up the coast."

Suddenly her eyes got wide. "You will come back, won't you?" Mary Lou demanded. "After a few weeks, maybe, when Dan's forgotten all about you?"

"Of course I will" I replied, surprised by her question. I didn't know how realistic it was of me to reply in the affirmative - my priority was finding Clair after all, wherever that voyage took me - but I hated to disappoint her.

My friend regarded me with not a trace of bitterness. "Do you still miss your brother a lot?"

"Yes I do. Very much. It's like a sort of ache that doesn't go away. Do you know what I mean?" It was strange how putting my feelings into words seemed to make them more real.

"I can imagine. You can't just hang out, in Byron Bay or anyplace else. Not if there's a chance you might find your brother."

As Mary Lou said these things I began to realize how true her words were, and the thought made tears start to prick the corners of my eyes. "I can't forget him, you see. I think I've forgotten him for a while and then the ache comes back again and I realize there's something missing."

"Sure, honey. I understand. And it's O.K. Really." Now we were both crying, big salty tears splashing into our drinks. And then we looked at each other's reddened faces and started to laugh at how idiotic we looked, until we were laughing and crying at the same time, hugging each other and promising to stay in touch whatever happened.

I didn't know what else to say. I suppose that deep down I knew Mary Lou was right. No doubt the trip up North would lead me on new adventures to I knew not where. But I couldn't put down roots anywhere until I'd solved my mystery. I wouldn't be able to stop and stay anywhere, until I'd found Clair.

CHAPTER FOURTEEN

I REACHED THE motel in Armidale at around 8 p.m. that evening. The sky was steely grey and I was drained from hours on the road. My room was sparsely furnished but clean and functional enough, and I washed away the grime of the day in the shower, then slumped in front of the television with a chilled coke, trying to numb my mind with distractions. It wasn't until an hour or so later that I realized I was starving hungry, as I'd eaten nothing that day.

Outside my room and on the tarmac of the car park, the air was still and quietly expectant as though waiting for something. Although a light shone in the motel reception office, the seat behind the desk was empty. I wished I'd decided to stay somewhere with a restaurant on site, but I was too tired to change motels now. So I traipsed up the deserted highway.

About two hundred yards down the road I chanced upon a small restaurant, which described itself as Mickey's Mexican Eaterie. Although not my first choice had there been an alternative, I was too hungry and weary to walk any further. I entered the restaurant and ordered the cheapest and most substantial-looking meal on the menu, which was chili filled tacos with refried beans and salad. As the restaurant was too basic even to provide air conditioning the atmosphere inside was stiflingly humid, so I removed my jacket and draped it over the back of my chair.

I can't have been there more than an hour when - feeling sated and distinctly more cheerful - I asked the waitress for the bill and put the required amount on to a saucer. Outside in the street, I noticed a large ginger cat stalking along the pavement, his tail erect. He was the spitting image of Marmalade. All at once - perhaps because I felt lonely and isolated and Marmalade had been my most loyal friend and affectionate pet - I wanted to stroke that cat more than anything else in the world.

I exited the restaurant without waiting for the waitress to collect my money, even though it included quite a large tip. Outside on the pavement, the cat heard my footsteps and halted in its tracks, unsure whether I was friend or foe. I adopted my usual tactics and crouched down, my hand out in appeasement, making soft clucking noises to attract his attention. He trotted off a few paces and stopped again, looking at me, so I followed and repeated the procedure, emboldened by the fact that he hadn't completely rejected my advances.

This happened two or three times, almost as though the animal was leading me somewhere. When we got to the corner of the street I made a lunge for the top of the cat's head with my hand, hoping to stroke him there and gain his confidence. But to my amazement and horror, he sprang, not at my outstretched hand but at my bent knees, his claws out and his teeth bared in a vicious snarl. I leapt back, just in time to rescue myself from the attack, and he came for me again, with a low growl. I retreated immediately, and the animal ran off into the shadows and left me, confused and shaky.

A vision of Marmalade, trapped in the flames, came back to me. Then my guilt returned in full force, and the knowledge that I had been my pet's killer. All at once I felt that I could never be absolved from this sin, and that every cat I came into contact with from now on would be exacting retribution for the creature I had loved so well.

Hot tears welled up in my eyes and rolled down my cheeks, as I commenced dragging myself back to the motel. I hadn't gone more than a few yards when a little rush of cold air whipped my arms and I abruptly realized that something was wrong. I'd forgotten my jacket, which was no doubt still adorning the back of my chair in the restaurant. It was a red quilted jacket - the color faded now with age and many washings - and it didn't have much intrinsic value, but I kept it with me always because the inside pocket was where I stored the box Genevieve had given me. I couldn't imagine anyone finding the jacket attractive enough to steal, even if they'd had the opportunity to do so during the short time I'd been out of the restaurant, so I wasn't overly fretful as I looked through the window and attempted to locate my seat.

At a first glance round the tables, I couldn't see the chair with my jacket anywhere, and I wondered if the waitress had noticed the garment and picked it up, intending to keep it for me. Just then, I heard footsteps across the road and I swiveled my head to see a flash of red turning into a side street on the right. I bolted after a young girl clad in denim jeans, who was clutching my treasured jacket.

Hearing my approach, the girl turned her head to see me in hot pursuit and started sprinting along the road with steps as light as an athlete. I raced as fast as I could, shouting at her to come back, but I was gasping with the exertion and my legs felt as heavy as lead. I willed my body to move faster, but my limbs resembled metal parts that had rusted from under use and my feet seeming to be wading through mud. There was no one else in the street to help me. I kept running and shouting, but all the doors of the houses remained closed and the windows stayed shut. All the time, the girl was skimming over the ground and moving further and further from me, my jacket around her shoulders and the treasured box in its inside pocket being spirited away from me with every step.

Seeing her receding more and more into the distance, with a superhuman effort I summoned all my strength and raced as fast as I could, almost stumbling and falling in my endeavors. I clenched my face tight and willed every atom in my body to come to my assistance. Then, miraculously, the girl lost her footing on a loose stone and fell to the ground. I was twenty paces behind her, and before she had time to get to her feet, I was upon her and pinning her to the pavement with the full weight of my body on top of her. "Give me back my jacket!" I screeched like a wildcat. "Give it back!"

The garment was underneath us both, still gripped under her left armpit. The girl squirmed beneath me and I ripped the jacket away from her grasp, causing her to yelp as the metal zip scratched her bare arm. "Let me go, lady" she squealed. "You can have your stupid jacket. Just lemme go!"

I loosed my grip - still clutching the precious jacket in my left arm - and the girl scrambled undaintily to her feet. I rummaged around in the right-hand pocket and was overwhelmed with relief at feeling the sharp edge of the box, still where I had left it. The girl was staring at me, wide-eyed, her legs shaky. "Boy, you sure are something" she exclaimed in her high tight voice. "You aren't gonna tell on me to the cops, are you? I gave you back your jacket. It's only an old jacket anyway. I was just cold, you know? Just cold."

I looked into her eyes and I saw that she was frightened. Of me? No, I'd just given her a shock from which she'd easily recover. The fear in her eyes was something more permanent, the expression in them was wild, dangerously out of control, but like a beast that's just had a narrow escape from a trap. I wondered what had happened to make her so afraid of life, and in that moment I pitied her. I shook my head slowly, and the girl scampered away.

That evening in my hotel, I tended to the cuts and bruises on my legs with cotton wool, ointment and plasters purchased from the First Aid kid in reception. I felt quite drained and numb with exhaustion from the day's events. I didn't want to think about anything, or even look at the clues inside the box I'd made such a mighty effort to recover.

Just before collapsing into bed, I staggered over to the full-length mirror on the hotel wall, to examine my face for any signs of deterioration from my illness. As I stood back to look at my face the image started to blur, so I blinked several times - thinking I must be even more exhausted than I'd realized - and rubbed my eyes with my knuckles. When I looked again, my reflection in the mirror was hazy as if seen through a mist, and I wondered that I hadn't noticed this before. Perhaps the mirror was made out of some cheap glass that fogged easily, or the lights in the room were dimming because of a temporary reduction in the electricity supply.

As I regarded my face, it seemed to get darker and darker and the contours altered, becoming wider and larger. The strange thing was that I felt perfectly normal, and everything else around me was exactly as it had been before - the warm air on my body, the wall around the mirror which I could glimpse on the periphery of my vision - but the reflection that now confronted me was not of my face, but of another countenance I'd never seen before. It was a man's face, dark-skinned, with wide nostrils and a wide smiling mouth. Curly hair stuck out from his head in a wide halo. Frightened by the unfamiliar image, I shook my head with my eyes closed, hoping to dispel it. When I looked again at the mirror it was my own face that stared back, and a surge of relief overwhelmed me.

I wasn't going mad. It had simply been some kind of bizarre optical illusion, probably brought about by my extreme tiredness. I fell on to the bed, closed my eyes and was immediately shrouded in sleep.

CHAPTER FIFTEEN

A MONTH LATER, I was still living at the beach house in Byron Bay, which I had come to regard as my temporary home. Simon had been right when he'd told Mary Lou I'd find it difficult to leave: the beauty of the location and the easiness of my life there - surrounded as I was by good company - seduced me into staying longer than I'd intended, and the days slipped so gently one into another that time literally flew by.

Simon had a round baby face that often broke out into a wide grin, dark tufty hair cut short, and large sticking-out ears that gave him the demeanor of a genial clown. The money from his record producing days enabled him to indulge in his interest for all things esoteric without the daily grind of work, and to share his house with friends of a like mind. Ever since my arrival Simon had made a special fuss of me, and I quickly realized that his affection was more than friendship. I liked him enormously and was grateful for his kindness, but after Dan I couldn't readily contemplate another romantic involvement. Fortunately, Simon was sensitive enough to realize this and so our relationship remained happily platonic.

Concerned about my lack of money and wishing to earn enough to pay back Mary Lou as well as make the trip to Borneo I'd originally intended before being sidetracked to Australia, I had almost immediately found a job and started working in a wine bar in the tourist area of town. Although Simon had offered generously to provide me with accommodation and all the food I wanted and would accept no payment for these, I knew I must support myself as much as possible. I had been lucky: as soon as I'd made the decision to find a job and begin looking, I was hired on the spot at only the third place I tried, a wine bar on the main street. The proprietor said he could do with somebody to help out serving drinks, and I was employed with no questions asked and told to start the following day.

Although nervous at the thought of a new occupation of which I knew nothing - especially when I saw the rate at which most of the waiters rushed around attending to their customers - I accepted the job gladly and determined to do the best I could.

Working as a waitress in Henry's Bar wasn't as bad as I'd anticipated. Although it was exhausting and pressurized, I only worked for four hours on five evenings a week and in the daytime I could rest. I even began to eagerly anticipate the working part of my life.

On the plus side, my English accent made me popular with staff and customers alike, and I found after a while that I was quite good at the job. Perhaps because my normal attitude is to be polite and friendly to strangers, this endeared me to customers who were waiting for their orders, and I even built up a small clientele of people who would ask specifically to be served by me. Although the wages were not high, I made a surprisingly good income from the tips I received from my regulars. My quirky English mannerisms and figures of speech amused Henry - the owner of the bar - and the other waiters, and I was the butt of much good-natured teasing for my "pommy accent".

Among my colleagues, my special friend was Swee, a tiny Malaysian man whose smooth face kept his age a secret and who sported a permanent grin. He was so quick and light on his feet when taking orders that he almost seemed to be dancing, a quality, which earned him the nickname of "tutu". In fact, a jazz dancer was what he longed to be, his earnings at the bar being saved for his course fees to an illustrious performing arts college where he'd been offered a place to start later that year.

As a rule I got up late, and during the days I would watch soap operas on the television or sit in the sun-filled kitchen or the garden inhaling the scent of tropical flowers and basking in the summer sunshine. Simon said he enjoyed this time of year most of all, when it wasn't blisteringly hot and the sun wasn't too dangerously strong to sit out in for more than a few minutes. We would talk and sip from long, cool, ice-filled glasses and revel in the luxury of having nothing else to do. In the evenings, by complete contrast, the hectic pace of the bar enlivened me and gave me plenty of little stories and anecdotes with which to amuse Simon and the others the next day.

I also found that I was able to save some money, and after only a short while I had more cash than I'd begun my journey with. I had very little to spend my wages on, as Simon insisted on feeding me and the others on the vegetables we grew in the garden and accepting nothing for rent, asserting that he had plenty of money and our company was payment enough. In the evenings I never went out because I was always working, and I felt no need to buy any but the most basic of items. So, I amassed my Australian dollars in my burgeoning bank account and kept telling myself – only a couple of weeks more and then I would have enough to go to Borneo. Somehow, though, there never seemed to be quite enough money to commence my trip.

Maybe it was because subconsciously I was rather relishing the chance to stay in one place for a while and take the opportunity to relax from the relentless pursuit of my quest. Maybe it was because the earlier traumatic events in Australia had depleted me of my energy more than I realized. Or maybe it was because I had now completely run out of my I.C.A.L. drugs, and the Level 3 symptoms were beginning to appear, making me tired and low in energy. I realized now how bogus Dan's claims had been regarding Australian doctors: Simon confirmed for me what I'd suspected, that Australian doctors knew no more than English doctors about a cure for Level 3 and the only pharmaceutical company manufacturing drugs to combat the symptoms was I.C.A.L.

I noticed on the television news one day that the I.C.A.L. factory was back in action in London and stocks of the drugs were fast being replenished. I was glad, of course, but I had even less energy to contemplate going back to England at the moment than making the trip to Borneo. At least, the lights in Henry's bar were dim and didn't irritate my sore eyes, and I forgot the aching of my limbs when my mind was kept active by my job.

One night while working my shift at the restaurant, I was sitting quietly resting at a table until more customers arrived when Swee came and sat down beside me: "You OK?"

"Yes, fine thanks. I'm a bit tired, that's all."

"Tired already? We only just started the evening, girl. You ain't seen nothing yet!" Swee beamed at me, showing two rows of immaculate white teeth. He always enjoyed talking in stock American phrases, like a character out of one of the musicals of which he was so fond.

I smiled. "Don't worry, I'll perk up in a bit. Thanks for helping out back there" referring to the way Swee had earlier gallantly come to my rescue and offered to deal with a table full of stroppy teenagers demanding faster service.

"No problem. It's your loss anyway, they were good tippers. Hey - I got a present for you." Swee reached into the pocket of his jeans.

"What?"

"Don't you remember? You gave me it over a week ago. Sorry it took me so long, but I've had some friends to stay, you know, and there hasn't been time. But better late than never, eh? Here you go."

He handed me a slip of paper, on which was written the Malaysian words I'd copied from my crossword puzzle and underneath his English translation of the fifth clue: *Bring out of barbarism, being polite with looks (it is said).*

"Wow, that's brilliant. Thank you so much."

"I don't know what the hell it means, though. Sounds pretty far-out to me. Some kind of word game, huh?"

"A crossword puzzle."

"And you solved the other clues?"

"Well, four out of the six anyway. With a little help from...some people I've met along the way."

"OK, I guess you've got this problem licked."

"Oh, I wouldn't say that. I mean, looking at the sentence now, it doesn't seem to make any sense at all. Then of course the others didn't either. But I've no idea where to start. Usually, something just sort of happens to show me the answer or somebody says something significant and I take it from there."

Swee took out a small tortoiseshell comb and smoothed down his already flat, glossy, black hair. "Hey, you know what? I thought of somebody who could maybe help you."

"Really? Somebody here?" I folded up the piece of paper with Swee's translation and put it in the pocket of my jeans.

"No, he ain't here. He's an Indian guy, or half Indian half English, something like that. But he lives in my country. Pretty weird guy. He lives in the jungle, all alone, and never sees anybody. But he's some kinda guru. Or mystic. Something like that. He's written a lot of books. I never read any, but I've got this friend who's really into his stuff. His name's Rajan Mobley."

"Oh yes, I've heard of him" I replied, overjoyed at the coincidence that Swee had mentioned the very man I wanted to see, the man the monk in Nepal had told me about. "He must be very special. Two people I met in Nepal talked to me about him, and told me I should meet him."

"You don't say! My friend Carl raves on about him. Carl said this Mobley guy used to have quite a cult following here and in the States, because of his books. Then one day he got some bad disease and hid himself out in Borneo where nobody could find him and he's been there ever since."

"Really? I'm thinking of going to see him, if I can save up enough money to get to Borneo. D'you really think he'd be able to help me?"

"I don't know. But Carl told me he's some kind of heavy medium guy. Before he got sick, he used to do that thing called psychometry - you heard of it?" I shook my head. "It's where you take some object that belongs to a person and you can tell stuff about them. Have you got anything that used to belong to your brother?"

I recalled Clair's charm, which I always wore around my neck, drew it out from beneath my blouse where it lay next to my chest and reached over to show the amulet to Swee. "There's this. It used to be Clair's. I've worn it all the time ever since he died."

Swee fingered the charm, admiring the smooth blue stone. "It's really beautiful. You never take it off, huh?"

"Only if I have a shower or something."

"Yeah, that might be just the ticket. If it's still got your brother's energies on it, maybe Mobley could connect with your brother's spirit, you know, and find out where he is. What d'you think?"

"I don't know. Maybe..." We both sat in silence for a moment, willing the door not to open and let in more customers. "But how do I find Mobley? That's the problem. I've tried to find out exactly where he lives but nobody seems to know. I mean it's all very well going to Borneo, but the jungle's a big place."

"There's gotta be a way to find him. I guess Carl might know." Swee suddenly clicked his fingers and pointed at me, in a parody of the dudes he admired which was almost comical. "Hey, you know what? You and Carl should meet.

He's a really cool guy, and he hasn't got a girlfriend right now." Swee winked at me across the table. "D'you want me to set you up a date?"

"What - and make you jealous?" I teased. Swee and I were the greatest of pals but there was nothing sexual in our friendship. He'd never even made a pass at me and everyone tacitly understood that he was either quietly gay or was waiting for someone from his own culture. At that point, more customers walked into the bar and Swee and I jumped up to serve them. From then on, the evening was unusually busy and I got no more opportunity to speak with my friend.

The conversation with Swee had rekindled my enthusiasm to visit Rajan Mobley, however. I didn't see how it could be mere coincidence that the guru's name had cropped up again.

Not knowing how to discover Rajan Mobley's exact location, over the next few days I asked Simon and the other people in the house if they had heard of him. By a strange quirk of fate, Simon had a book by Mobley up in his attic. He got it down for me and dusted down the cover and I scanned it avidly, promising myself to begin reading the volume that very evening before going to sleep. The book had been published ten years before, and I could see why it had achieved cult status: it was an inspiring blend of philosophy and mysticism mixed with fascinating anecdotes about Rajan's early life as a medium and spiritual healer in India. The jacket cover said that the author had now moved to the jungles of Borneo near a place called Mulu to study primitive peoples, and the face in his photograph looked healthy and confident.

To my disappointment, the others in the house were extremely skeptical about my plans when I informed them of my intention to visit Rajan Mobley. Simon told me he didn't think there was any point spending a lot of time and money tracking down this supposed guru in the middle of the jungle, when there were plenty of other people in Australia who did things like psychometry and communication with spirits, if that was what I was really after. Jude told me that Rajan's body was now ravaged with a virulent strain of leprosy so he hid himself from all contact and lived as a recluse: he'd heard that Mobley didn't welcome visitors any more since the disease had scarred his face and made him a horribly disfigured invalid.

I felt my earlier enthusiasm for the venture begin to evaporate. Simon was pessimistic about my chances of finding Rajan Mobley in the jungle, even if I did make the effort to travel to Borneo, because as far as he knew nobody had any knowledge of his precise location. My nearest hope would be to stay in one of the tourist lodges near Mulu and hope that a native guide could direct me to Mobley's dwelling. When I stressed that I needed somebody to help me find my brother, as I couldn't go much further with the search on my own, Simon suggested he take me to meet a man who lived in Byron Bay, somebody he knew called Gedun Rinpoche.

I turned my face to the sun streaming in through the half-open curtains of my bedroom and tried to remember my dream, snatches of which returned to me. Swee had been parading me around a house I'd never seen before.

We'd entered a large circular room with no furniture in it but with many doors leading off from the center, all painted different colors. Swee told me that each door represented a "probable future" and that I must choose which one to take. I opened each door on to a different scene, not stepping through but simply looking and considering. One showed a garden in full bloom, one a snowstorm, one a space rocket being launched into the stratosphere, and there were others I couldn't remember. I felt dazed and confused and unable to choose which door to step through. Swee kept telling me to hurry up, that the doors would close soon and then I would lose my chance. And right in the middle of my agony of indecision, I'd woken up, my heart beating fast.

That morning, Simon took me to meet Gedun Rinpoche, who introduced himself as a Tibetan monk. He had a shaved head, which reminded me of the monk I'd met in Nepal, although this man was much taller and very slim. I was surprised to notice that he had Western features, although he dressed in the style of the Tibetan monks, with an orange cloth loosely thrown over his gaunt frame. Gedun lived in a small and sparsely furnished apartment on the second floor of a purpose-built block a few streets away from us. The largest of his three rooms overlooked the sea and one wall was entirely glass, so that all the light and sound and air from outside entered the room for the whole day. Gedun told me he loved everything, which gave light, and I noticed the many mirrors in his room and glass articles, including a small chair, which was made entirely of blue crystal. The most beautiful object in the room was an enormous mirror on one wall, which had a carved wooden frame depicting intertwined snakes and birds.

As we sat on the rush matting which served as the only seating arrangement, sipping green tea and listening to the sound of the ocean outside, I explained to Gedun about my journey and my search for Clair. "It's so hard to know where to look for him. When I was in Nepal I went to one of the stupas. I thought he might be one of the monks there. But even if he is a monk, I can't visit every monastery in the world, can I?"

"You are not going about it in the right way" replied Gedun.

"But I'm trying to. I've taken everybody's advice. I've done everything I can to find him. I've tried so hard and searched so long," I wailed. "Why are all these obstacles put in my path? It feels like however hard I try, I never get any closer."

Gedun regarded me with his small hazel eyes: "Perhaps your journey is one of the spirit rather than of the body."

"What do you mean?"

"Many things have happened to you, have they not, on your travels?"

"Yes..." I began, uncertain what the monk was hinting at.

"You search for your brother and this search leads you into many strange and uncharted waters, places where you wouldn't otherwise have ventured. You have made mistakes, perhaps..."

I smiled and nodded, thinking of Dan. Following him had been a mistake if ever there was one, even though it had culminated in positive things such as meeting Mary Lou and my friends here.

"...and you have learned the lessons from those mistakes, they were there to teach you. You have overcome hazards along the way, and that has made you stronger. Not in your body necessarily, but in your mind."

"Yes, I know the journey's as important as the destination. But what about Clair? He's still the person I want to find. If I don't find him, there's no point doing all this, is there?"

"You are trying, yes, and there is too much struggle. You are searching for your brother on the physical plane. But that is a mistake. He doesn't exist in the physical sense, only in your mind and your memories of him."

"But why am I on this journey?"

"There is no special journey for you, only the journey of life itself which we must all undertake. That is what your friend Genevieve meant. Go home and remember your brother as he was. Accept that he is gone now and he will not return. The past cannot be recreated. Go home and live your life from day to day."

I didn't really understand what Gedun meant by this. It all sounded like mere words to me, with no practical information that could help. In my frustration and impatience, I was glad when the monk got up to make more tea and I was left alone with the sound of the waves and my thoughts. When Gedun returned, I didn't want to receive any more advice about the lessons I had to learn from my experiences, so I thanked him politely and left shortly afterwards, thankful that he didn't press me to meet again. I was glad to return to Simon's house and my friends.

Although I had only spent a few hours in his company, Gedun's words had disheartened me more than any experience I had so far encountered on my journey. If he was right that Clair didn't exist on the physical plane, why was I searching for his reincarnation, why had I come on this journey at all, what was the point of everything? I could have remained in my safe and familiar world in England, helped by the drugs to live as long as possible, not weakened by the rigors of travel. But Genevieve had told me to come...

Now, I began to question and doubt everything. Gedun's words had opened my mind to the bleak possibility that this quest was only a miasma. The crossword puzzle was simply a game, interesting perhaps but possessing no mystical power to help me find my brother. My longing and eagerness to see him, coupled with my rootlessness when my home and job had been destroyed at a stroke, had caused me to set out on this bizarre and fruitless journey.

What exactly had I achieved so far? Nothing. I had had some interesting experiences, but even the clues I had managed to solve made no sense to me. It seemed crazy now that I had believed my brother to be alive again in another form. Even if he were, he wouldn't remember me and our life together, wouldn't be waiting for me as I'd expected. How had I expected a few words to help me find him, out of the billions of people in the world, with nothing else to help me? I had been a fool.

When I reflected on these things my desolation was overwhelming. It seemed that all my efforts had been futile, and I had nothing much to live for any more. I struggled to pull myself free of the black cloud that was enveloping me, threatening to drown me in depression. I puzzled over events again and again in my mind and asked myself the same questions: what had been the meaning of the messages I thought I'd received? Were they all figments of my imagination? Mere coincidences? Was there such a thing as a spirit world at all? Was Genevieve a well-meaning dupe who had no real insight? Should I have stayed at home? Should I never have come, never have longed for my life to change, never have embarked on this journey? The questions nagged me like angry accusers with wagging fingers. And I had no replies.

My despondency took hold of me by the throat and wouldn't let go. Over the next few days, the gloom of my mood was such that I couldn't even go to work. I called Henry and told him I was ill. I didn't realize how right I actually was. My depression and lethargy were in part caused by the fact that the Level 3 symptoms were every day becoming more acute. I slept longer and longer each morning, as it had actually become painful to move. The night when I had chased the thief in Armidale seemed a long time ago now, as these days my legs ached whenever I put any weight on them, making it uncomfortable even to walk far.

Gradually, the worst of the depression lifted and I began to smile again, but my energy didn't return. After a week, I called Henry and told him I wouldn't be coming back to the bar. I couldn't face the strain of working at all. It was more convenient just to sit around reading or to stroll down to the beach with the dog or do a bit of gardening or cooking. I knew now that I would never keep my promise to Mary Lou and return to Sydney, never visit Rajan Mobley in the jungle, never return to England and the friends I'd known there. Somehow everything seemed too much effort, and life was quite comfortable as it was. I no longer bothered to tax my mind with thoughts or questions about Clair or the clues or my journey. It didn't seem to matter any more whether I'd been right or wrong. I lived life from day to day, and became lulled by my comfortable and banal routine.

Nothing could have been more peaceful and conducive to contentment than that big old house, with its large airy rooms, its glass-fronted balcony with the magnificent views of the ocean, and its garden of medicinal herbs and exotic plants, which sloped down to the sea. In the living room where I often sat, strange works of art hung from the ceiling and decorated the walls, things which had been made by the occupants of the house: hanging mobiles made from polished silver cutlery, grotesque leather masks for commedia dell'arte characters, a huge bronze candlestick in the shape of a snake rearing up to strike its prey.

The sounds that filled the house filled my soul with ease: the soft roar of the ocean; the gentle snore of Tar, the old black Labrador, as he rested by my side; the plaintive cry of sea birds to their mates; the music of Tibetan drums and pipes which Simon liked to play on the CD; the gentle chanting from upstairs as Rowan practiced her mantras; the rhythmical tap of fingers on a keyboard as Jude wrote in his study; the soft plop of earth being tilled as Saul hoed and weeded outside. As I listened to these sounds overlapping upon each other, I would sit in the spacious living room and read from the huge library of books on all manner of subjects, or I would gather zucchini or tomatoes from the garden and chop them into a salad for our communal dinner, or sometimes take Tar for his daily walk along the beach, stopping every now and then to pick up an interesting stone and put it in my pocket to add to the collection which I was planning to make into a decorated lamp stand.

Rowan spoke to me one day of a place in Australia that bore my name: Alice Springs, a little place in the middle of the continent, in the middle of vast stretches of desert. I remembered the desert I had flown over for hours on end in the plane, all those weeks ago, when I'd traveled from Nepal with Dan. I looked up the place in Simon's *Encyclopedia of Australian Life*, and found a picture of the town. I became intrigued by it and drawn to the idea of going there one day. But it was a sort of fantasy idea, one that was nice to reflect on and shove into the storehouse of my mind kept for the indefinite future. Perhaps I could visit the place in some other life, because I didn't have much of this one left.

The days flowed seamlessly, one into the other, and I forgot all about the life I'd known before, forgot about my planned trip to Borneo and the reasons for it, forgot even about my illness and the fact that I knew I couldn't survive for much longer. Sometimes Simon and my other friends remarked that I was becoming thinner and hardly ate, or that I should do something about my continual cough or the redness around my eyes. But they realized there was nothing to help me but kindness. We hardly bothered to speak about it. Nothing seemed to matter now but the feeling of tranquility I had found and my desire to hang on to it. The house had weaved its spell around me, and I couldn't escape.

I felt at peace there, and yet it was a curiously unreal kind of peace. It was as if my real self had gone into hiding and left this cheerful shell of me, who was happy to live in a kind of bland vacuum where nothing significant ever happened, where people smiled and whiled away their days in pleasant recreation. I had no idea how false it all was, until a train of events occurred to shake me out of my dream...

One morning, I was taking Tar for a stroll along the beach, as I often did on fine days. The sea was calm and the warm air stroked my bare arms with a gentle breeze. There were few other people about, most of the tourists tending to congregate at the other end of the beach near the town. Tar and I clambered up a small outcrop of rocks, he more quickly than I and waiting at the top with his mouth open and his tongue out, breathing heavily. I rested on a smooth level stone and contemplated the waves, while Tar gamboled to the end of the natural pier and stood barking at the speedboats on the water, wagging his tail.

It was then that I noticed a large bird, which flew down to the rocks and settled a few feet away from me. There were many seagulls hovering overhead, which I took no notice of, but this bird caught my attention because it was larger than the others and had a glossy black coat. As it turned to the side to preen itself, I saw that its underside was white and I suddenly realized what kind of a bird it was. It was a magpie, rather larger than the ones I'd been accustomed to in England, but definitely the same species of bird. I clucked and stretched out my hand, hoping to entice it and wishing I'd brought some bread with me, but it ignored me and after a while flew off again. Then Tar returned and we descended from the rocks and walked back to the house.

Seeing the magpie had pricked my memory and made me think of Clair again. During the vision I'd had in Genevieve's house that night so long ago, she'd told me two magpies represented me and my brother. But now there was only one. What did it mean? Did it have any significance at all? Or was it just a bird, a random incident that had no connection with my life?

It was Saul who introduced me to Sarah. She was also a British expatriate, from Edinburgh, who had been living in Australia for about six months. Saul encountered the red-haired Scottish girl at a pottery class he taught at the local college, and her accent encouraged him to invite her round for tea one day, hoping to cheer me out of my current apathy with a potential companion. Saul was entirely correct in his estimation of Sarah: she and I shared an immediate empathy, which went far beyond our common nationality, and our friendship flowered even more quickly than he had anticipated.

Sarah was a couple of years younger than me and had squeezed far more experience into her life than I had in my longer time span. Although raised by a middle-class Scottish family, during adolescence she'd been seduced by the lure of drugs that were prevalent in her neighborhood, ending up living on the streets as a crack junkie at the tender age of sixteen. Somehow, a combination of her innate strength of character and her relationship with a man she met at a Drugs Rehabilitation Centre, helped Sarah to kick the habit, and she began the long and painful process of readjustment by moving to London and beginning a new life.

Despite an interrupted scholastic education, Sarah used her intelligence and drive to gain employment in a fiercely competitive environment. Having a strong interest in all things pertaining to health since her brush with the heroin using subculture, Sarah trained as an alternative therapist specializing in reflexology and shiatsu massage, paying for her studies by working nights in a restaurant, and after three years she was fully qualified and able to earn her living in a way which suited her temperament ideally. Sarah was not to benefit from the fruits of her endeavors for long, however, because only a few months after starting her successful reflexology practice in London, she learned that she - like so many people of her generation - had developed Level 3.

The news of her disease was more devastating to Sarah than most people. Because she was so violently opposed to any kind of drug therapy, she absolutely refused the I.C.A.L. medication that her doctors recommended. Having become increasingly disillusioned with all aspects of English culture - the corruption she despised being symbolized for her by the terrible and fatal accident, which was afflicting her generation - Sarah emigrated to Australia, and continued to work as a reflexologist.

Although Sarah had suffered from the disease for nine months, unlike me she'd managed to maintain her health sufficiently to work and support herself. Even she didn't know how long she could survive, but on that point she maintained a stoically philosophical attitude. One day when I asked to know her secret, Sarah smiled knowingly and promised to show me. She would bring round to my house the ingredients of the herbal concoction she was taking, so that I could try them for myself.

On a sunny morning in late February, Sarah stood in our airy kitchen, her face glowing in the steam from a large pan of boiling water over which she was hovering, and carefully dropping bits of what looked like tree bark into the water.

"What on earth is that?" I asked, wandering into the kitchen from the living room and gratefully cooling my bare feet on the tiled floor.

"It's a special herb that I got from a Chinese doctor. You can't get them in this country - my friend had to actually go to Hong Kong to get me supplies. I know it smells disgusting, but it really works."

"Really?" I sniffed tentatively at the pungent air, then wrinkled my nose in distaste. The herbs certainly did exude a disgusting smell.

"I take these every day. In the morning is best, after my meditation and before I begin treatments. I have to add just the right amount to the water, boil it for one hour until the water goes a very murky brown color, and then I drink the liquid."

"You drink that liquid?" I asked in disbelief.

"Yep" replied Sarah cheerfully.

"Is this part of it, too?" I enquired, poking about on the paper that Sarah had spread out on the work surface, and rubbing between my fingers some yellow powder, which looked a bit like flour.

"Hey - don't finger it. Yes, that's part of it. I don't know where they get it from. It's some sort of plant or flower that grows only in China I think, but the label on the packet's all in Chinese so I can't read it."

"Does this stuff actually make you feel better?"

"Of course!" Sarah frowned at me, disgruntled that I should doubt her, then added the yellow powder to her mixture, and turned the heat down as the liquid frothed in the pan and threatened to boil over. I hoisted myself on to a work surface and took up a position there, my legs dangling in mid air as I viewed my friend's actions.

"Now then, Alice, I want you to take this infusion today at 4 o'clock." Sarah ordered in the "mother hen" voice I'd heard her use to recalcitrant clients.

"Do I have to? It really smells awful" I whined, wondering if I could wait until Sarah had left and then tip the vile brew down the sink.

"Do you want to get better?" Sarah scolded, glaring at me.

"Ye-es..."

"You asked how I keep well without those stupid I.C.A.L. drugs you're so fond of. This is how. I've been drinking this mixture for three months now, and look at me. I've had Level 3 for nearly a year, and I look fine, don't I?"

I nodded, not wishing to disappoint my friend. Sarah didn't exactly look fine - her skin was blotchy and flaky like mine, her eyes were permanently bloodshot and her flame-colored fine hair was daily growing thinner. I also noticed how she never uncovered her legs or arms, even in hot weather when other people wore shorts and t-shirts. Sarah always sported a long skirt and an Indian blouse with long sleeves, claiming to prefer the hippy look. But it was true that she always had plenty of energy and kept very positive in spirits, unlike me. So the herbs had to be doing some good. I concluded that they'd be worth trying, if only for the increased optimism they might induce.

"Does it taste as bad as it smells?" I asked, pushing out my lips in a thoughtful pout.

"No, it's not too bad at all once you get used to it. And anyway, no pain without gain and all that." Sarah continued cheerily stirring her concoction, for all the world like some young earth mother making soup.

"I know you'll scoff, but I'd prefer to take the pills. If I could get any, that is."

"Yes, I will scoff. You know what I think about that," replied Sarah sternly, not looking at me.

I hopped off the work surface and went to lie down on the sofa in the front room, listening to the lovely roar of the ocean outside. "Do you want to go for a walk along the beach later?" I suggested, after a few moments.

"Sure" replied Sarah. "I don't have my next treatment till three. Mr. Parker, from next door, he's coming for his reflexology. He's such a sweetie. He's got cancer, poor thing, but I really think the treatments are helping."

"Good." Suddenly recalling something, I eased myself off the sofa and drew out my flower press from under the table where I'd been storing it. I unscrewed the four little bolts at the corners and examined the different dried petals to see if they were ready to be used yet. I was looking forward to the artistic part of the process, when I would stick the petals to brightly colored cards and cover them in cellophane.

"Are you really not going back to Henry's Bar at all, then?" asked Sarah, leaving her steaming pan for the time being, and joining me on the sofa.

"No. I just haven't got the energy these days. It's enough to get up in the mornings."

"Well, those herbs will help, I'm sure they will."

"Hope so." The petals were still too soft and moist. I tightened up the bolts on the flower press and replaced it under the table.

"You know, Al, it's not just me that thinks those I.C.A.L. drugs are a waste of time. I've got a friend who works as an osteopath in a doctor's practice in England and I got a letter from him the other day. He says that a few months ago - round about last Christmas I think it was, just before you left home - there were some reports in the papers about these experts who were saying the I.C.A.L. drugs weren't all they're cracked up to me. Back then, people dismissed them as paranoid cranks, but there's been new evidence recently and apparently they weren't too far off the beam. Ray sent me this article--"

"What sort of evidence?" I interrupted, folding my arms skeptically and leaning back against the sofa's soft cushions.

"Well, you know I don't know much about medical jargon or anything and I couldn't understand all the long words, but the general point they were making is that the drug somehow actually promotes the virus rather than stopping it."

"How can it possibly do that?" I scoffed. "It cures the symptoms--"

"You don't cure symptoms. You cure a disease, you relieve symptoms..."

"Well, whatever..."

"What happens is that for a while the drug acts on the virus by killing off the cells it's invaded. That's why you feel better and you don't have any symptoms."

"That's good, isn't it?"

"It's good in the short term, yes. But not in the long term. In the long term, the drug kills off the virus' host cells and it also kills off the body's natural defense systems, so that the body's own immune system is weakened. You see, the drug can't really distinguish. It's like a team of crack paramilitary police who go in to save a group of hostages: to get at the kidnappers they have to bomb the whole building and that kills the innocent hostages as well."

I sighed and stared out at the ocean. "So what happens in the long term, then?"

"In the long term, the body's weakened by the drug. The virus isn't entirely killed off; it's just lying low, and the body's natural defense forces are depleted. After a time, the virus resurfaces and this time it kills the whole of the host's body because it's in such a weak state. So you see, the drug actually kills people in the end."

"But that's ridiculous! You're talking about very highly skilled medical experts here, Sarah, people who've given up their whole lives to medicine and research. I.C.A.L. wouldn't have manufactured a drug that kills people--"

Sarah waved her hands in a peacemaking gesture to stop my tirade. "Look, I know you used to work for I.C.A.L. and so you probably feel some loyalty to them..."

"No, I don't feel any loyalty to them particularly, I just don't see how the whole medical establishment could have been wrong about this."

"Who caused Level 3 in the first place? The people who made the baby's milk product that had the virus. They were wrong, weren't they?" Sarah waited for an answer but I remained silent, having no explanation. My head was beginning to throb and I wished we could stop talking and go for a tranquil walk along the beach. Sarah continued: "Do you think the baby's milk manufacturers didn't have highly trained medical people who'd been working for years? They didn't want to kill off a generation of the British population, why should they? But they made a mistake. What I'm saying is, it's possible for these people to be wrong, they're not as infallible as they make out."

We both lapsed into silence for a few moments. I turned to Sarah, maintaining my skeptical expression. "So who are these people who are speaking out against drugs now?"

"Well, they're not speaking out against all drugs ever, they're just saying that this particular drug that I.C.A.L. have manufactured and made a lot of money out of isn't necessarily doing the job right, and the whole area should be looked into."

"I don't know," I replied shaking my head. "I really don't know."

"I don't know either," said Sarah. "Nobody knows anything for sure about this bloody Level 3 thing. But just give these herbs a try, will you? I mean, you can see what they've done for me, and I want to help you."

"O.K." I agreed, making a face. "I'll take them. Can I have some cake afterwards, though, to take the taste away?"

Sarah nodded and smiled. "Sure. Or fruit, even. I've got some great watermelon I found on the market. Really juicy. Let's go for our walk now."

We enjoyed our walk on the beach that day. The afternoon sun shimmered on the surface of the turquoise sea, giving it the sheen of a sheet of glass. We picked our way between shells and seaweed, relishing the warm sand between our toes, then sat on a rock and swapped adventure stories: Sarah told me of her travels further up the Australian coast to Mission Beach, beautiful but deserted due to the prevalence of the lethal jellyfish which lay in wait along the golden sands, poised to administer a fatal sting with one of their gossamer-fine tentacles.

When I came back to the house and Sarah returned to her flat for her reflexology session, I drained the liquid from the boiled herbs as she'd recommended, poured the brown stuff into a glass and gulped down the liquid in one revolting draught. Unfortunately, far from making me feel better, the mixture actually made me feel a lot worse for a few hours. Not only did it taste absolutely disgusting but it brought on a bout of nausea which prevented me consuming anything else till the next morning. I discarded the rest of the concoction by pouring it down the sink, intending to salve Sarah's feelings by claiming I'd drunk it all.

To my distress, I was never able to talk normally to Sarah again. I wish now that we'd spent more time together on that day, because it was the last occasion that my friend was reasonably fit and well. The very next morning, Sarah was rushed to the Casualty wing of the local hospital, having fallen into a sudden coma. Nobody knew the exact reason for her lapse in consciousness, but her doctor suspected it was some unexpected side effect of Level 3.

When I received a telephone call from Saul - who'd been informed by the college of what had happened - I hurried immediately to the hospital, devastated at his terrible news. Sarah had been placed on a ward with cancer patients, all terminal. If she'd been conscious I would have complained and demanded a private room, knowing that the presence of death could only depress her. But I saw instantly that there was no point. Sarah lay motionless and with her eyes open as though in a trance, unaware of my presence as I sat by her bedside holding her limp hand and trying to will her back to health. I remained there for the entire two hours of the visiting session. Nobody else came to visit. Her family was all in England and the friends she had in Australia were too frightened by the imminence of her mortality to sit and watch her die.

I had seen this all before. I had been through it with my beloved brother, and this time I wanted to be there at the end. If there was any chance, any chance at all of Sarah's survival, I had to will it into being if I could. Over the next two weeks I visited my friend every day in the hospital, morning and evening, and sat by her bedside praying that she wouldn't die, pleading stubbornly with God - even though I didn't believe in Him or His divine intercession - over and over not to allow Sarah to die. I took her flowers that she didn't see and grapes that she never ate. I made her a card out of the pressed flowers - my first artistic effort - with a poem that I'd written especially for her. I placed it on Sarah's bedside table and begged God to make her well enough to read it one day.

But it was not to be. One morning a couple of weeks later, when I visited the hospital, the nurses gently took me aside and told me Sarah had passed away peacefully in the night.

I hadn't even been with her. Like Clair, my friend had been taken from me, and I had been powerless to rescue her. It was ironic that Sarah had tried to save me, giving me the herbs which she said were keeping her well, yet in the end it was I who was left alone. It was always I who stayed behind while other people, my loved ones, died. Was I destined to outlive everyone I cared about, unable to do anything to help them?

Sarah's death impressed me more deeply than anything else I'd experienced since the night of the bomb. It wasn't only that she was so young and I was certain to follow her sooner or later. Months ago, I had been given a mission, whether true or false I didn't know, but that mission had been given to me. A mission to find my brother Clair. A mission to discover from him the message that would spell out a cure for this terrible disease. A mission to save myself and all the others who were afflicted and casting around in the darkness for answers.

Drugs were not the answer. Even if Sarah's "experts" were misguided and the I.C.A.L. drugs didn't ultimately kill people with Level 3, nobody had yet survived the disease, not one single person to my knowledge. Either everybody would die and a generation of British people would be wiped out. Or somebody would find a cure.

Even if Genevieve had been wrong and Clair didn't exist on the earth plane in another form, what could I lose by continuing with my journey and trying to find him? I was ill anyway and hadn't much more time to live.

My brother had gone, my mother had gone, my cat had gone, my friend had gone. What did I have to lose?

I needed to find my brother. I had nothing else left. I had only a few weeks to live. My friend Sarah had died and

I knew the same destiny was reserved for me. Why not make one last effort to turn my life around before it was too late? What did I have to lose? I cared no longer what anyone else might think, I had made my decision.

For some reason, I felt uncomfortable discussing my feelings with my friends. Maybe it was because my quest to find Clair was the closest thing to me, the real me that I had discarded when I had come to the house in Byron Bay. I'd mentioned my brother to Simon when he'd taken me to see Gedun, but I hadn't told the others much about my trip because it had seemed unimportant then, and now I was convinced that they'd never understand my quest.

Why did I feel that my search would be meaningless to them? Perhaps it was because none of the other people in that house had ever had to struggle against impossible odds or question their place in the world. Their privileged middle-class backgrounds insulated them from a perception of tragedy, or even a knowledge of its existence. I didn't realize it consciously, but intuitively I divined the truth. They would scorn my search, because the idea of a real mystery would appall and frighten them. They enjoyed the serenity of Buddhism, but it wasn't a serenity born of years of suffering, they had never known anything but serenity.

But serenity wasn't *my* natural state, nor was contentment, nor peace, nor tranquility. My life since the death of Clair was a quest, a long quest, and a restless search and hunger to find something and someone before it was too late. Peace was something I had known in this house, but it was just an oasis on my travels, not my final destination. I had let myself be lulled into oblivion, I had let myself be conned into believing that mere existence was all I needed. But, of course, it wasn't. I could never live a life that was safe and secure and free from danger and threat, and therefore from experience. Not now, anyway. Not since that evening when I had wished so strongly that everything would change, thereby releasing the forces of turmoil that were to sweep me along like a current.

All these thoughts whizzed through my mind and were compressed into a few seconds' contemplation. It was as though they'd been waiting on the edge of my consciousness, waiting for that moment when I was primed to accept the truth and to realize the falseness of the life I had been leading. Perhaps the briefest shadow flickered across my face to hint at the depth of my sudden revelations, but even if it did, nobody noticed. I knew all at once that everyone else in that house was a stranger to me. A friend, maybe, of a certain kind, but ultimately a stranger. There was only one thing to do, and that was to leave and resume my journey. It would be hard and tiring and fraught with difficulties. But I could delay no longer. Suddenly, I knew what I must do and what the next step of my journey was to be.

"I'm going to have to go" I announced suddenly one evening at dinner, interrupting the flow of conversation, which at that moment consisted of dissecting a new and not much appreciated sitcom on the television. "I'm going to find Rajan Mobley."

"Who?" asked Jude.

"You know," answered Saul, "That weird bloke who wrote the book everybody was raving about a few years back. There's a copy on the shelf, and I saw Alice reading it a few weeks ago."

"He must have really impressed you," said Rowan to me, taking a large swig of wine from her glass.

"Perhaps you could just write to him," suggested Simon, his eyes suddenly sad and betraying his disappointment. "You don't have to go all that way, do you?"

"Yes I do," I asserted. "I have to meet him. I don't think he can help me otherwise. And after all, I've got enough money. It's the only thing I want to do."

"Atta girl!" encouraged Saul, sticking up his left thumb and chuckling. "You follow your dreams."

"Where does he live, anyway?" asked Rowan, now tucking into her desert with one of the dainty teaspoons she favored.

"Somewhere in the middle of the jungle, in Borneo" replied Simon, rising from his chair to locate Rajan Mobley's book and grabbing the volume from the shelf.

"Don't you want your sweet?" asked Saul, noticing that my desert bowl remained untouched. "I thought you liked apricot mousse."

"I do. I'm not hungry. You have it." I pushed the bowl over to him.

"You're crazy," said Jude to me. "How on earth are you going to find this bloke?"

"I don't know" I replied, undeterred. "But I'll find a way. There must be somebody who knows where he is."

"Sure, if you can get someone who speaks English. I mean, aren't they all pygmies out there, or something. Totally uncivilized" scoffed Jude.

"They're probably a lot more *civilized* than we are," countered Saul, who was a pacifist. "But you're right about the language thing, that could be a problem. Why don't you take your friend Swee with you?" he suggested to me.

"I'd rather go on my own. I'll be OK."

"You're braver than me," said Rowan, darting me an admiring glance.

"That's not difficult," said Jude, and I saw him take Rowan's hand under the table and squeeze it and realized then that those two were more than friends. Saul kept his big bearded face bent over his rice and Simon held his nose buried in the book he'd found. I looked at them all with affection and knew I'd miss them. But I also knew I had to go.

Within a few days I stood at the airport in Sydney, where Simon had accompanied me to await my flight to Bandar Seri Bagawan. Simon wished me luck and extracted a promise to let him know what happened with Rajan Mobley, before kissing me on both cheeks and telling me to come back and see him any time. As I wandered through the gate into the departures lounge, I reflected on how different my parting was from my arrival in Australia.

I didn't know if I would ever return. I didn't know if my illness would claim me while I was in Borneo, so that I couldn't return to Australia. But nothing seemed to matter much now. Nothing but completing my journey.

My journey wouldn't be finished until I'd found Clair.

CHAPTER SIXTEEN

I FELT WEARY, SO weary. My whole body ached with a kind of ague that suffused my bones until they were thin and light as brittle twigs that may snap at any moment. My head pounded and throbbed, as though a huge drum inside was beating out an unintelligible message. The skin on my face prickled when I touched it, as if covered by thousands of tiny ants crawling over its surface. I had been unable to eat properly for days. The very sight of food made my gorge rise, and I had to struggle to consume a little plain rice and some hot sweet tea, just enough to give me the energy to keep going for a while longer. I knew I hadn't much time left - perhaps a couple of months at most - and so I was compelled by a mindless panic to find what I was seeking as swiftly as I could.

The boat glided across the smooth water, the only sound a rhythmic swish of the paddle as the boatman steered us expertly through the river's thin channel. Somehow he appeared to know exactly where there would be enough water for our boat to pass. Years of experience making this trip back and forth had given him an unerringly accurate map in his head, causing him to veer suddenly to the right and make a sharp course to the other side of the river, where his wisdom told him the water would be full and clear. I found his knowledge amazing, the twists and turns of the river and its progress ahead of us like an endlessly extended ribbon all appearing equal to me. Our narrow boat tipped precariously from side to side, but despite the bobbing water we remained upright.

A drop of rain landed with a heavy plop on my head, and I shivered briefly. The air was not cold but humid and close, covered by a pale grey sky laden with rain. Pretty soon the water from above would meet the water below, and we poor human creatures would be trapped in the middle. This whole area was a land of permanent wetness - the river, the muddy banks - the air full of moisture, the clouds hanging ponderously above us. The swish of the boat's passage through the river and the metrical drops of rain hitting surfaces, mingled with the ongoing sounds of the jungle around us to create a wetlands orchestra. If I withdrew from the pain in my body and let my thoughts drift into my jungle surroundings, I could be almost peaceful.

The water whirled by, green and frothy. On either side of us at the banks, a screen of fronds reached into the river caressing its surface with fragile fingers. Ahead of us a black mist hung over the distant mountains like a blanket. As we turned a bend in the river, a wall of rock came into view on our right, the edge of a limestone cave with stalagmites that hung down in curiously shaped points. On the side of the wall coral flowers perched, beautiful creations of nature caused by years of steady droplets.

The rain continued to drip on my head and on my shoulders now. The drops were heavy and warm and steadily increasing. I pulled up the hood of my cagoule and hugged my knees to my chest, still unable to elude the wetness, which surrounded me. My legs were bare and the socks inside my walking shoes were already beginning to feel damp. The rain was starting to really pour now, drenching everything underneath yet leaving the air still clammy and warm. We began to mingle with the wetness and become a part of it, swimming along in the current of the river on our narrow strip of wood, seeming to float like human flotsam.

All at once I became aware of a human voice. Stiffly I turned my aching body to face the boatman - realizing that he was attempting to converse with me - but failed to comprehend a word he said. He was probably speaking in Malaysian or whatever his language was. I knew he didn't speak any English, because I had tried talking to him when I boarded the boat and he had simply stared at me blankly. I smiled through a wetness of rain resembling a sheet of tears on my cheeks, and he grinned back, nodding his head as if considering we'd reached an understanding without the benefit of language. The boatman was looking ahead of us and pointing something out, and when I turned to follow his gaze in that direction I made out faintly through the mist and grey of encroaching dusk a long wooden house by the side of the river, and I realized this must be my destination, the Jungle Lodge I was aiming for.

I didn't know how long we'd been traveling, but it felt like hours. All I knew was that someone at the travel agent's in Bandar Seri Bagawan had booked me on this journey, given me instructions on which speedboat to take from the jetty to arrive in Limbang and arranged for an English speaking guide to meet me and take me by jeep to the mouth of the river, where he consulted in Malay with the boatman and presumably told him where I was to be taken. All this had happened and I had drifted along as though in a dream and unable to control the flow of events, feeling a passive passenger on the journey I had instigated myself. It was all a part of the illness, I supposed, this sensation of unreality and inability to come completely into focus, hovering on the edge of consciousness, a spectator standing outside myself and viewing events with disinterest as though they were being played out by actors on a giant movie screen. Trapped as I was in this daze, people had started looking after me and I floated on the ocean of their goodwill in this boat on the river.

As we pulled up at the bank and the boatman extended a hand to help me to shore, I rose shakily and prized my clothes from my skin where they seemed glued to my body with moisture. I was glad to be back on land, but even the land I encountered was nowhere near what could be called dry. My shoes squelched through the mud as I followed the boatman - who carried my bag on his shoulder - along the path to the Jungle Lodge reception. When we arrived, the boatman jabbered something to another Malaysian man he appeared to know - who I assumed to be the proprietor of the lodge - and they both pointed at my shoes. I frowned briefly in puzzlement, then realized they meant me to remove my wet shoes to enter the building. There was no door as such, just a long open wooden room with several tables sparsely set for eating. My feet now bare, it was pleasant to sit in the comparative dryness of the room and gratefully drink the hot sweet tea that the proprietor brought me. He was quite overweight, with a round smiling face, and he enjoyed spouting his few words of English in a high-pitched, singsong voice.

After about half an hour the proprietor led me to my room, which entailed putting my shoes on again and squelching through more mud almost up to my ankles, the rain not having abated one iota. In answer to my glance at the sky, he waved his large hands and declared "Rain, here, always rain." I nodded back in mute agreement. The boatman seemed to have disappeared now, and the boat was no longer tethered at the bank. I wondered where he had gone, and if he was ferrying more tourists back and forth in his little vessel.

My room was completely bare except for a bed (with a mattress, pillow and one sheet), a hole in the floor which was the only toilet in one corner and a tap, which was positioned over a small drainage hole. There was a tiny window at one end of the room with a tattered curtain slung across it, and a single light bulb in the center for illumination. Nevertheless, this shelter was very welcome. I thanked the man, removed my muddy shoes and attempted to wash them under the tap, then collapsed gratefully on to the bed and slept for a long time.

When I awoke it was the next morning. According to my watch the time was just after eight o'clock, so I must have slept solidly for over twelve hours. I felt much improved, enormously refreshed, wide-awake and ravenously hungry. I tried to persuade myself that perhaps it was only sleep I had needed, after all.

The morning sun was streaming through the window, making my room appear even barer with its single garish light. My clothes from the previous day remained damp, but fortunately I had some others in my bag, which I changed into. Outside, the soil was still muddy, but at least I could see now where planks had been placed to walk on which covered the worst parts of the ground. A shape flew past me and hovered on the stem of a flower, its wings fluttering. I thought it at first a small bird, but when I studied the creature more closely I realized it was a butterfly. The largest butterfly I'd ever seen, with huge black wings and an iridescent green pattern in the center of them gleaming in the sun. The butterfly - unaware of its exquisite beauty and my joy in seeing it - sucked a little at the sweetness of the flower and flew on.

The dining room was virtually empty, and I wondered if I were the only person staying at Jungle Lodge. The only white tourist, that is. Two or three Malaysians, who I guessed must be connected with the lodge, loitered outside the building drinking tea and chatting casually. I breakfasted royally on sweet tea, white toast with margarine and incredibly sweet jam that had a picture of strawberries on the jar, although it tasted of nothing but sugar. Little ants ran around my plate and I had to brush them off my cutlery before using it. A rustling sound alerted me, and I glanced to my left to see a swift-moving lizard scuttling up the wall and then hovering immobile in one spot, trying to attain invisibility.

When the overweight man I had met the day before came back to my table offering more tea, I tried to discover more from him about where I wanted to go, but it was difficult to converse, with his halting English and strong accent and my complete lack of knowledge of Malay. He said that I could go on an excursion to the caves that morning, if I wanted, that the guide would take me. I asked him about Rajan Mobley, the man I had come to see, the man I had been told could help me. But the proprietor's face immediately darkened when he heard the name. He said to see Rajan was impossible; that the place he lived in was inaccessible.

"But other people have come to see him, haven't they?"

"No, no people see."

"But I read about him in a book. And it said he welcomed visitors."

"Where is? A book?"

The man didn't seem to understand and so I started miming in desperation: "I read about Rajan in a book in Australia."

"Australia" he repeated, his eyes lighting with recognition and envy.

"Yes, I was in Australia, staying with some people who were interested in..." I decided it would be pointless to elaborate, since this man's English was so limited. "I heard that Rajan Mobley knows a lot about languages and about..." I struggled to find a simple way of putting it: "The world of spirits. I need him to help me."

The proprietor appeared unenlightened, so I decided to try another tack. "Rajan is half English and half Indian, isn't that right?"

"Half. Yes." He nodded with conviction, seeming to understand this.

"And he's a medium? He can speak with the spirits of dead people?"

Now the man appeared unsure. He shrugged. "Don't know...I...never...meet..."

We looked at each other, uncertain how to continue. "I need to find--" I began, but the man had already commenced speaking, a certain tone of warning having crept into his voice: "Rajan...he...takes no sound...he..." The man cupped his hands over his ears in a gesture, trying to explain.

"Hears?" I suggested.

The man nodded. "He hears no sounds."

"What? He's deaf?" The man shrugged, not understanding, but I think that was what he was trying to say. He mustered himself for another attempt: "He...no good...no nice...he have no..." The man struggled to find the words for a few moments, looking into space for inspiration, then gave up with a helpless smile.

"The book said he's disabled, is that right?" I did a rather inexpert mime of a person walking on crutches. The proprietor seemed to recognize this and nodded vaguely. "The book said that people don't visit him much because they're frightened of him. Because he's disabled. Is that it?" I fell into the old trap of talking loudly and slowly to try and make myself understood, even though I knew it was the words themselves that the man couldn't fathom.

Still, he seemed to have got the gist. His face suddenly lit up with the remembrance of something: "Leper" he said, and repeated it excitedly: "Leper".

"Oh, I see. He had leprosy and--"

"His face..." The man gestured to his own face and grimaced in a parody of disgust. "No face..."

"I'm sure he has some face doesn't he?" I said, but I was starting to feel apprehension creeping up on me. Perhaps this man was more disabled than I'd expected.

"No nice..." said the man.

That was the only way he could describe it. But - I ruminated to myself - this man had probably never actually seen Rajan Mobley. In the absence of recent photographs, he had no idea what Mobley looked like other than through stories and rumors he'd heard from other people, and rumors and stories about a disabled man who lives as something of a hermit in the middle of the jungle are bound to be somewhat exaggerated. Anyway, I reassured myself, I had seen a photograph of Rajan on the cover of the book about him, even if it had been taken years before in India and before the ravages of disease had maimed his face. I couldn't help feeling a certain fear about seeing him, but I had to quell my anxiety. I had to see this guru, because I knew he was the only person who could help me find Clair. In any case, I had come all this way to meet him and I couldn't turn back now.

The proprietor mentioned again an excursion to the caves, and I said I would like to go. I was interested to view them anyway, and I thought perhaps I could persuade the guide to take me to Rajan Mobley. Mobley lived somewhere in the jungle near Jungle Lodge, and I had to find someone brave enough to take me.

It was good to rest in the still warmth of that room, listening to the murmuring voices outside. After about half an hour, I was aware that I'd been joined in the dining room by another foreign tourist, a white man in his twenties who positioned himself at one of the other tables and smiled at me in friendly greeting as I looked up. I overheard him order a coke from the waiter, and a few minutes later, he approached my table: "Do you mind if I join you?" he said in a light voice with a strong accent. "I'm on my own here, and don't speak the local lingo, so I can't really converse with the natives."

"No, I don't mind at all." Relishing the opportunity for a chat, I was pleased to share my table with him. I felt lonely anyway.

"You been here long?" the young man asked.

"At the lodge? No, I just got here actually."

"I only just got here, myself. Looks a fascinating place. Have you been on any of the jungle walks?"

"I'm going on one today. With Ali. He's one of the guides, the best one I think because he speaks good English and he knows a lot. He's taking me to see some caves, and..." I didn't know whether to mention Rajan Mobley, "...on a walk into the jungle, where not many people go."

"Sounds great. You'd recommend this Ali, then?"

"I think so. I'll point him out to you, if you like."

"Thanks."

I leaned back in my chair and stretched out my arms. "It's so hot..."

"I guess the weather is pretty stifling isn't it" my companion remarked. I felt glad that the light was so dim in this dining room that he couldn't see how ill I looked. I was tired of pitying looks and concern from people who couldn't help anyway.

"I guess we should introduce each other. My name's Tom", he declared with a smile, leaning over the table to shake my hand.

"Pleased to meet you" I smiled back. "My name's Alice."

"Alice" he repeated, "that's a pretty name. Like the town. Only that's not pretty, of course."

"What town?"

"You know - Alice. Alice Springs? Haven't you heard of it?"

"Oh yes." I nodded my head. "My friend Rowan mentioned it once. It's in Australia, isn't it?"

"That's right. Right in the middle, in what we call the Red Centre. That's because it's all desert around there and practically nobody lives there except a bunch of aborigines."

"Is that where you're from, then? Australia?"

"Yep" he replied proudly. "It's a great country. Ever been there?"

"Yes, I just traveled from there actually. I lived in Byron Bay for a couple of months."

"You should go back to Australia if you get the chance. There's nothing else like it. I'm from a place called Townsville, on the East coast, north of Sydney."

"So what are you doing here? Are you on holiday?"

"Oh no, mate, 'fraid not. I'm studying botany at university back home, and I'm here to do a research project on the jungle flora and fauna. It's one of the few places in the world, you see, where the natural habitats are still totally untampered with by man."

"It sounds interesting. I'm from England, where I'm afraid there isn't any natural habitat totally untampered with by man."

"Ah, the Old Country. I've always wanted to go there, but never got around to it."

"Well, it's OK if you like old buildings and history. But I didn't see much of Australia - only Sydney and Byron Bay. Are there beautiful parts?"

"Sure are. Depends where you go, really. There's a lot of variety. 'Course there's also acres and acres of desert with nothing but scrub. That might appeal to you if you like flat earth and burning hot sun. Got to watch out for the flies, though. They're killers out there."

"And why is that place called Alice Springs?"

"Don't know how it got its name, maybe some bloke named the town after his wife."

We sat in companionable silence for a few moments, and then I wished Tom a pleasant day and went back to my room to change into my walking boots for my trek into the jungle with Ali.

I felt glad that I'd decided to come into the dining room that morning. I'd have forgotten about the town of Alice if I hadn't encountered Tom. And - as I discovered later - the significance the town held for me didn't only lie in the coincidence of us sharing the same name.

CHAPTER SEVENTEEN

A LI STROLLED AHEAD of me down the wooden walkway through the jungle, humming to himself and seemingly unconcerned about my slower progress behind him, although he did stop and look back from time to time to make sure I was still following. He was in his early twenties, with an agile nut-brown body and a small elfin face. I noticed that his jeans were faded and full of holes and his t-shirt was damp with the sweat of exertion. His leather sandals flapped against the boards of the walkway, and every now and again he would beat back the branches before him with the large stick he carried, "for protection".

Sunlight pierced the trees and fell in pools of light on to the planks under my feet and on to the leaves of plants, the roots of trees entwined around one another in fantastic shapes and the rock pools which shimmered with the interplay of water and light. All these lined the jungle floor beneath the walkway. Under this canopy of overhanging branches from trees so tall that their tops were invisible, the air was cool and moist and verdant with the smell of the rainforest.

We crossed a narrow river by means of a rope bridge slung across both banks, which jiggled with nerve-wracking instability under our feet. I clutched both sides of the rope as I crossed, but Ali flitted ahead of me with deft footsteps, so accustomed to the journey that it held no fears for him. Once on the other side, we only had to walk for a few minutes before the trees parted to reveal the mouth of the cave ahead of us. My guide paused briefly here to let me catch up with him, and to explain that it would be dark inside the cave and cold, and that I should put on my gloves and have my flashlight ready.

Ali's English was as good as the lodge proprietor had promised, and I was grateful for his reassuring presence there. I was also happy because he had agreed to take me to see Rajan Mobley, or at least to lead me almost to his house in the jungle. He had never visited Rajan himself, he'd said, had never wanted to, but he had led other tourists there in the past, curious people like myself. I didn't tell him that my mission was more than just idle curiosity. He'd said we could set off the next morning, very early, and that he would come to fetch me later on.

Now we entered the cave, and I was surprised at how large it was and how high the ceiling. The structure was like some huge domed castle, built by the gods. Inside, the air quickly became cool and dank, and I was glad of my cagoule, which had seemed like a hindrance outside in the warm sunshine. This was the cave Ali had referred to as the "bat cave", and I could quickly see why. All along the walls and ceilings hung hundreds and thousands of still black shapes, waiting for the night to come and awaken them from slumber. The stench inside the cave was unbelievable, the ammonia smell of bat droppings so powerful it made me nauseous. But we carried on, deeper and deeper into the grotto, down steps, which had been cut into the rock. The guide seemed to know where to go even without light, but I had to navigate myself with the aid of the weak beam of the flashlight.

As we progressed into another, subterranean part of the cavern, the smell of bats died away and was replaced by a musty odor of walls and surfaces that never saw the light of day. Here, Ali used his more powerful flashlight to send a strong beam over the walls and point out to me the fantastic shapes that had been created by stalagmites and stalactites over the years, each of which had a name and a significance, he said, to his people. It was like an art gallery of incredible statues, made by some eccentric genius to while away his time in the cave. Ali shone his flashlight on a block of limestone, which looked at first like a simple pillar, but when lit up, the shape it threw on the wall was that of a woman in a headdress. Another looked like a child carrying a pail of water.

As we came to the exit of the cavern, the light from the outside world caught a shower of droplets falling from the ceiling and lit them in a shimmering stream as they fell to the ground. We passed through the mouth of the cave and the sunlight temporarily blinded me with its unexpected brightness. The young man led me down some rocks and I followed him, not knowing where he was going, tearing off my coat in the sudden clammy warmth of the jungle air. I clambered down the rocks, clutching at passing branches to try and regain my foothold. My thighs were starting to ache with the exertion, and the sweat on my forehead made my hair stick to my head in damp strands.

Presently, Ali turned and shouted for me to join him. We had come to a large pool of clear water, which looked invitingly cool. "Good water" he said, "Cool and clear. This is called Clearwater Cave."

"It's beautiful," I agreed, resting myself momentarily on a rock.

"Have a swim," he suggested.

"But I haven't got a costume" I said, hesitantly.

"No need" replied my companion, and he lowered himself from a large rock into the water and dived in with all his clothes on. I carefully took off my walking shoes and dipped my toes in the icy water. It felt so refreshing, I sighed with relief and enjoyment. The sunlight fell through the canopy of trees overhead, making little blobs and blotches of light on the still surface of the pool. As Ali floated on his back, I saw a solitary creature circling round him and every now and then skimming the surface of the pool and taking a quick dip in the water. At first I thought it was a bird, but then I realized it was a bat, a refugee from the cave who had woken before the others and was cooling itself in the clear waters.

I lowered myself into the pool and immersed my body up to my chin. At first the water felt cold and I scuffed my toes on the stones underneath, but when I started to swim it was the most relaxing and refreshing sensation imaginable. All around us, the jungle animals carried on with their lives as though we didn't exist, and there was such an atmosphere of peace and tranquility about the place, it was like having entered some primeval world before the dawn of civilization. I reflected that the earth might all still be this way, if humans hadn't civilized it and tried to control the forces of nature.

Returning to shore after my swim, it didn't take long for my clothes to dry on my body, as I lay on the bank in a patch of sunshine. Ali had prepared a picnic of rice and meat, and as we ate I asked him what he knew about Rajan Mobley. He didn't know much, just the same old rumors. He warned me that it would be quite a tough walk to Rajan's house, through the deepest part of the jungle, and that I should be on the lookout for leeches. They didn't hurt much, he said, though there was a lot of blood. But all I had to do was take some matches with me and I could burn them off quite easily. Then there were various trees to watch out for, one with a bark that secreted a poisonous sticky substance, which could give you a nasty rash, that lasted for weeks. And there were enormous ants in the jungle, as big as beetles. The soldier ants had huge red heads, and they would sting if you stepped on them.

I was disquieted at hearing about all these dangers, but nevertheless determined to go on. I couldn't turn back now. I hadn't told Rajan Mobley I was coming - in fact, as he didn't have a telephone, he couldn't communicate at all with the outside world - but I hoped he would be amenable to me when I told him of my plight. From what I had read about him in Simon's book, I believed Rajan was the one person who could help me now. When he'd been a medium and psychic in India, many people had traveled long distances to see him, hoping to make contact with dead loved ones or receive guidance from the spirits.

It seemed everyone in these parts was frightened of Mobley and viewed him as a dangerous creature. But I had ignored all the warnings from people who'd tried to dissuade me from attempting to visit him. I didn't see what harm he could do me. If he really was a deaf leper who could hardly walk and who lived entirely alone, how could he hurt me?

Ali got up and told me to follow him. He said he had something to show me. We scrambled up some more rocks and found another path along the wooden walkway, where we trudged for some minutes. Then we came upon another cave, much smaller than the last one. For this grotto I didn't need to use my flashlight, as some lights had been installed to guide our way. We seemed to go deeper and deeper and the walls of the cave narrowed until we were practically crawling through a sort of narrow tunnel in the rock. I would have felt frightened, except that I had complete faith in my guide who seemed to feel no fear at all and who kept assuring me that we would soon come to a wider section. I remembered the cave with the map in Nepal: I'd managed to conquer my claustrophobia then, so this time it wasn't so difficult.

At last Ali was proved right, and we stepped into what looked like a vast cavern with a huge high vaulting roof overhead. We walked along in the absolute silence for a few minutes, and then Ali motioned to me and warned me to be careful. We were coming to a dangerous bit, he said, and when I looked down I could see what he meant. Suddenly, the ground below us fell away into an enormous gorge, which stretched many feet below. The path narrowed on either side of the gorge and I edged my way along it with shaking steps. My legs trembled slightly at the nearness of the drop and the horrible image of a fall into that ravine. The path was really quite narrow now - no more than a foot across - and we had to walk very gingerly. I found it impossible to resist the thrill of looking down at the abyss, while simultaneously keeping my left hand pressed to the rock face to reassure myself of its strength and security.

To my surprise, on the narrowest bit of the path, Ali stopped and looked at me. "Are you afraid?" he asked with a curious smile.

My heart was beating, but I didn't want to admit it: "No, I'm fine."

"Do you know, how far down is it?"

"I don't know. An awfully long way" I guessed, staring down into the vast black hole.

"As far down as it is up." Ali seemed amused by something, I couldn't tell what.

I craned my head and looked up at the ceiling, way above us. "I suppose so. Or even further perhaps."

"Do you want to try jumping to the other side?"

I looked at him in disbelief. It was at least twenty feet to the other side of the gorge. "No, of course not."

"Shall I try?" He was still smiling, and I wondered for a second if he was mad. It was such a preposterous suggestion.

Then, to my absolute horror, he jumped.

What happened next was so surprising, it was as if my whole world - or my conception of it - was suddenly shattered. Instead of falling hundreds of feet into a huge ravine, he landed in about two inches of water. The image of the abyss beneath us was suddenly broken into pieces, into ripples of harmless water. I realized that what I had been looking at was not a gorge at all but a pool, which was so completely still that it held the perfect reflection of the high ceiling above us. What we had been carefully walking around was nothing more than a very shallow pool and an image of the ceiling, which looked exactly as if it was below as well as above us.

I stood stupefied, numb with shock and relief. Ali laughed and laughed for several minutes, literally holding his sides with merriment and splashing about in the shallow waters of the pool to show me how innocuous it was. After a while, I began to laugh too, and I jumped histrionically into the pool pretending it was a suicide leap, and we both continued to roar with laughter until the tears rolled down my cheeks. I laughed with relief and with the abandonment of care and the realization that it is often the things we fear most that are the most harmless in the end.

Later that evening, we found ourselves again outside the Bat Cave, this time waiting for the creatures to awaken and come out of their hiding place. Ali lit a cigarette and smoked thoughtfully, and I looked at the trees stretching high above us and marveled at the beauty of this natural world. A dragonfly landed on the leaf of a plant nearby, a creature with two bright red propeller wings, like a tiny helicopter. Some plants had leaves so big that a human being could sit on one, curling it around them to give shelter from the rain.

When the bats finally did come, they flew in a snaking coil, which erupted, from the cave and into the sky. The air was filled with the rustle of a thousand wings and their high-pitched radar calls. Only after that did we head back to the lodge, and by this time the sky had darkened and night had almost fallen, so I had to pick my way along the wooden walkway with the aid of my flashlight. By night the atmosphere of the jungle was if anything more magical. The air was alive with a hundred noises: croaking frogs, humming insects, chirping night birds, the click of passing bat wings and the wind soughing through the trees. Around me the fireflies danced and lit my journey in little flashes. In the distance I heard the rumble of thunder and felt the ubiquitous drops of rain from the storm, which was a regular evening event. Every now and then a sheet of lightning would light up the whole sky, as if a spotlight had been suddenly thrown on this stage, and just as suddenly extinguished. By the time we reached the lodge, we were already wet through again with the rain, but I was happy.

When Ali came to wake me the next morning at 6 a.m., I was at first unwilling to get up and fought off the mists of sleep. But then I remembered the important thing we were going to do, and I grabbed my bag and slung it over my shoulders - after checking first that Genevieve's box was in the side pocket of my jacket - and rapidly joined him. He was already grinning and smoking his first cigarette of the day. He asked me if I'd slept well and I answered truthfully that I'd slept like a log after the endeavors of the day before. He said they would be nothing to the trek we were going to do this morning.

Ali wasn't wrong. When I checked my watch an hour later, I couldn't believe that we'd only come about half the way, and I was already exhausted. My legs ached and my head throbbed, but I was intent on carrying on. I didn't admit to Ali how I was feeling and I refused to take a rest. At least, we managed to avoid the tree with the poisonous bark, and I didn't spot any leeches on my legs, though I looked down often to check, fingering the matches in my pocket for reassurance. On the ground I noticed small balls of a white substance, and when I picked it up I was surprised at how fluffy and silky smooth it felt, like the finest gossamer. Ali told me it was kapok and that it grew on plants, which dispelled seeds like nuts, full of the silky down. I couldn't resist collecting it and stuffing it into my pockets until they were bursting.

We seemed to clamber up and up for miles, until we reached a high point with a view through the trees of distant mountains. Then we started moving down again, and this time the trail was even tougher and I had to clutch at passing branches to steady myself and my legs and arms were often scratched by undergrowth and prickly thorns.

I was even now entranced by the world of the jungle. I thought again of why it was so different from the world I was used to. Here, civilization had passed by unnoticed, and the animals were master, Man being just one of them. Here, where nature had not been tamed, I was just a beast like any other and at the mercy of any stronger than me. It was an exhilarating sensation.

After another hour or so, when the morning air was already starting to warm up, we came to a clearing in the trees and I could glimpse a low wooden house ahead of us. "This is when I go," said Ali. "Rajan lives here." He pointed to the house, but seemed reluctant to leave me. "You O.K.?" he asked.

I realized all at once that he was genuinely concerned for my safety. Perhaps he'd come to like me these last couple of days and to see me as a person, not just a tourist. I was touched. But I wasn't going to turn back. "I'm fine" I replied with a smile. "I'll see you later. What time are you coming back?"

He shrugged. "When you want?"

I looked at my watch, which said just after 9 o'clock. "This afternoon. About 2 o'clock?"

"I'll be here. At 2 o'clock. You meet me here. O.K.?"

"What if you're late? You won't come up to the house to fetch me?"

He grinned sheepishly and shook his head. "No, no. I don't go into house. I meet you here" he insisted.

I agreed and watched my guide plunge back through the trees. Then I moved forward, with some trepidation, to the house.

CHAPTER EIGHTEEN

I T WAS QUITE an ordinary house really, and not as strange as I'd expected. A plain, long, wooden house with little ornamentation. My heart was beating so hard I felt almost dizzy, but I forced myself to knock on the front door. I waited several minutes but there was no sound from within and nobody came to answer the door. Now that I'd come all this way and screwed up my courage to confront this man, I had a distinct feeling of anti-climax. I knocked again and waited, and then again. But nobody came.

Yet the house didn't seem empty. It seemed alive. I wondered if Rajan were in there but refusing to come out, peering at me through curtains or hiding in a back room. Well, he would just have to see me. I hadn't come all this way to be given the brush off. The book had said for certain that the guru welcomed visitors. Especially a visitor from England, the country of his father's origin that he claimed a particular fondness for.

I tried to peer through the windows into what must have been the living room, but it was so dark inside that I could make out very little. I walked all around the house in case there was a garden at the rear, and the back of the house was as silent as the front. But it was a silence of waiting, not of emptiness. I wasn't going to be deterred. I remembered how I had almost walked away from Dr. Becker's house in Gmunden, thinking it was empty, but the professor had been there all along. I walked around to the front again, gave one last rap on the door, and then gently pushed it. To my surprise, it opened with no trouble at all, and I entered the house.

There was a strong unpleasant smell inside, which I couldn't identify. It was a musty, old, dank smell. The odor reminded me of old people's rooms and rotting vegetation and dark cupboards that hadn't been used for some time. It was like a smell of decay. The light inside was so dim that I could hardly see, but I had an impression of worn furnishings in faded colors and bare unswept floors. The silence now was eerie and unnatural, and I had the sense again that I was being watched. I looked around me but could see no one. The house appeared to have rooms with no doors to separate them, so I wandered between them feeling lost and confused. I came to a kitchen area with a grubby white sink and a single tap. I noticed that a plate and cup had been freshly washed and a dishcloth casually flung over the draining board.

Just then I heard a sound behind me - a squeaking, rasping sound - and I turned in alarm. The squeaking sound grew louder and then through the doorway emerged a wheelchair, which its occupant was self-propelling along the floor. The squeaking was the sound of unoiled wheels being pushed along the floorboards. The man in the chair gazed at me for a long moment without speaking, and I couldn't tell from his expression whether he was surprised or angry at my intrusion, or merely curious. His mouth hung open in a sort of parody of amazement, but I gradually realized that this was his normal countenance.

I tried to explain my presence: "I'm sorry...I knocked and knocked, but... you didn't answer so I let myself in. Sorry if I startled you. Are you Rajan Mobley? My name is Alice. I've heard a lot about you and read one of your books. I wanted to talk to you. The book said you welcome unexpected visitors, so I thought... I know you wrote it a long time ago, but still... I would have called beforehand but you haven't got a telephone..."

I realized I was rambling, but his silence was disconcerting, and the way he stared at me with the unreadable expression and his mouth locked into that strange position always agape. At least I was no longer afraid. Something about his demeanor was completely unthreatening. There was a sort of pinkish glow around the top half of his body, extending about two or three inches and seeming to expand a little as I watched it. At first, I thought it was an odd trick of the light, perhaps a reflection of sunlight from the walls or the ground. Then I remembered that I'd seen similar lights before around other people, although in different colors. I wasn't sure what it was but it no longer frightened me, and in a curious way it made me warm towards Rajan and feel encouraged that beneath his wasted body lay a kind and intelligent soul.

He made what I can only describe as a vocal noise with his mouth, though it didn't exactly sound like a word. Then a string of similar sounds, with a jerky motion of his head as he ejected them in a continuous stream. It was like a sentence that consisted entirely of vowels. After I stared at him in incomprehension, he seemed to repeat the sentence, this time more slowly and deliberately. To my amazement, this time I understood some of what he was saying: "Come closer to me. I can't see you there. I want to read your lips." He was gesturing to me with his right hand, and I noticed that his left hand hung limp and lifeless on his lap.

So I approached him, and repeated my explanation: "My name is Alice. I've come to see you. From Australia. I'm from England actually, but I've been on a long trip for several months. I haven't got much time left, you see, and I'm looking for someone. I wanted to talk to you. I need your help."

He nodded and I could see that he was attempting to bring up the corners of his mouth into a grotesque imitation of a smile, that was somehow pathetic on his poor wasted face. It was when I was this close to him that I could see the full effect of the ravages of leprosy. Although the man at the lodge had been exaggerating when he'd claimed that Rajan had no face, what face there was had been lacerated by the disease, which had eaten away at the skin leaving the mere stump of a nose and hollowed out cheeks. But his eyes still burned with a fierce intensity, as if all his energies and powers of communication were concentrated there. He had a smattering of flimsy white hair, and his whole body was emaciated and thin. His legs were hidden by a blanket draped over his knees, so that the only limb that appeared to be functioning normally, was his right arm.

He used this arm to navigate himself into the living room area at the front of the house where the light was best, and I followed him and sat in a chair that had no springs, so that I sank down into it almost to the floor. Now that I'd got used to his face, it didn't seem so ugly or repulsive, and I even found his speech comprehensible, despite the odd jerky rhythms of the sounds he made. It was obvious that a man of extreme sensitivity and intelligence was captive in the deformed body. I felt no fear, and after a while no pity, but simply admiration for someone who could survive in such circumstances. When I told him of how frightened other people were of him and how they had warned me against seeing him; that even my guide through the jungle had baulked at actually approaching the house, Rajan laughed. At least, it was a sound like sawing wood, which issued from his mouth as his thin shoulders shook and the corners of his mouth moved upwards slightly.

"So Alice" he said at last. "I'm glad you read my book and that it impressed you enough to feel I could help you. But what was so important that you came all the way from Australia and braved the jungle and the stories you'd heard, just to see me?"

I took the charm that had once been Clair's from under my shirt, lifted the chain off my neck and held it out to Rajan. "This was my brother's. He died when he was six years old, that's twenty-four years ago. Does the charm tell you anything about where he might be now?"

Rajan took the amulet and held it in his good hand, his eyes closed for a long time in concentration. Then he handed it back to me. "Your brother is still waiting for you. He knows you are not far away. Your brother is in a place you have come from. He tells me you must go back, retrace your steps, and you will find him. He asks me to tell you to remember the name; the name will guide you to him. That is all."

I felt excitement well up inside me at Rajan's words. Clair was here, he was waiting for me, and he wasn't far away. I repeated the words over and over in my head so that I wouldn't forget them: *must go back, retrace my steps, remember the name.* Mutely, I extracted Genevieve's box from the inside pocket of my jacket, took out the slip of parchment paper with the crossword clues and showed it and the wooden grid with the letters to him. Rajan looked at these objects for a long time; in fact he spent so long with his head lowered over the box and the paper that I almost thought he'd fallen asleep in his wheelchair. But then he looked up again: "The fifth clue is interesting - *Bring out of barbarism, being polite with looks (it is said).* And translated from the Malaysian, which is of course partly why you have come here. Perhaps you have already realized that the clues were written in different languages for a purpose?"

"I wasn't sure if that was for a purpose, or just...I don't know...to make the whole thing more difficult for me."

"Nothing in life is without a purpose, that is something which your journey should teach you. I see you've already solved the first four clues. You've done well. This last one should be easy for you, as it's in English - *Get nothing back and it's the beginning of the end - that's a short letter.* Ah yes, I see. How very appropriate, very appropriate," he said musingly, stroking his chin lightly with his good hand. "The answer makes a lot of sense. But it's really quite easy. Haven't you thought about it?"

I was so startled at how quickly he had divined the cause of my visit, that I said nothing for several seconds, but mimicked him with my mouth open.

"I'm sorry if I appear smug. Crosswords are an especial favorite of mine" he said with that odd, grimacing smile, "and I've already worked out the answers to these last two. But I think you should do them, don't you?"

I frowned. "Yes, I suppose it's my puzzle to solve. It was written just for me. But the answers I've found don't seem to make much sense."

"Ah, but they do make a lot of sense. When you have all the words of the puzzle, it will become more clear to you. All the words have meaning individually, as representations of stages along your journey. And your journey will not last much longer in time, although you still may have far to go in distance. But remember that together, together the words have even more significance than apart. Together, they reveal the message you seek."

He handed the box and parchment paper back to me, straining his body towards mine with an effort that made his chair creak. I wanted to say, *I'm so tired, and I've tried so hard all these months, couldn't you help me just this once?* but I didn't want to appear defeatist. So I just let the words die away and said nothing. For the first time in my life - sitting here in front of this man who seemed to be able to read my thoughts, although he could hardly hear my words - I could think of nothing to say.

So it was good that Rajan appeared to want to talk. "It is funny, isn't it, that these people find me frightening, just because of the way I look. Years ago, when I was young and strong, everyone accepted me because I looked the same as them, and yet I was far more potentially harmful to them then than I am now. Now I'm just a weak old man who can't even walk, who can't hear a visitor when they knock on my door." Again, his body shook with ironic laughter, and I smiled as well. "But that is the way of the human race. Some years ago, when I was working as an anthropologist in the jungle studying the Pandan people, I thought I could understand mankind by looking at the differences in people, by immersing myself in their differences and becoming like one of them. But do you know, I think I understand far more now, now that I'm a leper and an outcast. I understand their fear and I pity them. Really - I pity them. It's just the difference that they fear."

"Let me tell you a story. This is a story that was told to me by a very old man I met in the desert once, he was one of the Masai people - have you heard of them?"

I shook my head and sank deeper into my chair.

"No matter. At any rate, I think it one of the truest stories I have ever heard. A long, long time ago, before mankind was what is called civilized, when we were little more than sophisticated apes, all human beings lived in Africa. I suppose you know that? Anyway, at that time, all the human beings that there were looked the same; they all had dark skin and black hair and black eyes and wide noses. They were all about the same height, and probably all about the same level of intelligence. They hunted animals for food and ate the berries from the trees, that sort of thing. The point being that they were all exactly the same. And they lived that way, in small groups, for hundreds and thousands of years.

Then, one day, perhaps there got to be too many human beings, and some of them decided to move away from the area and try their luck elsewhere. And so they wandered across the plains of Africa until they had gone as far

North or in every other direction as they could go on that continent. They worked out how to make boats and they set sail across the seas and they discovered that there were other continents, and they colonized those continents and adapted to the different conditions they found there.

And because they had to change to fit in with different climates, their looks changed. Their skins became whiter and their hair fairer and their eyes paler and their bodies became taller and thinner. Their habits changed, and their customs and their culture. And they spread out into all these different races, with different languages and different attitudes and different thoughts even. So that now they felt they were entirely different from the human beings in Africa.

After hundreds and thousands of years, these new white races went back to Africa and found the old black races and they didn't recognize their brothers. Now they felt that these black races were unfamiliar and frightening. They spoke differently and dressed differently and had a different way of living. And the black people were also afraid of their erstwhile brothers, and had also forgotten how it used to be. So between human beings there was fear, and therefore subjugation and control, and therefore anger and resentment. Until now, every man feels that he is right and the others are wrong. That when he fights, God is on his side and not on the side of his enemy.

But what every human being has forgotten and continues to forget is that we all started out equal and we all started out the same. We are all one. That is the simple lesson we must learn."

Rajan sat back with a sigh, seemingly exhausted by his long monologue.

"That's a beautiful story," I said.

"And now, will you tell me your story?" he asked.

So I told Rajan all about Clair and the meeting with Genevieve and the fateful night of the party and the bomb, and all my adventures since. As I related my adventures I almost relived the events as the memories were recalled, and it was as though I was retrieving each memory from the storehouse in my mind, looking at it anew and filing it away for future use. Or as if each memory was a picture in a photograph album that I enjoyed sharing with a friend.

I talked as slowly and clearly as I could, taking account of Rajan's deafness, and his head seemed to nod slightly as he drank in my words. He seemed to enjoy listening almost as much as he did speaking, and I reflected on how lonely his life must be for the most part, and how he must long for this sort of contact with a stranger. The only thing I kept back from him was my illness, because I didn't want to burden him with my pain when he had so much of his own. But the softness of the chair was comforting and I didn't relish the struggle back through the jungle with Ali, although I knew I would have to manage it.

"Your journey has been very eventful" Rajan remarked, when I'd finished my story. "You must have learned many things."

"I suppose so" I replied dubiously.

"So - now you are a mapmaker" he declared, with his odd twisted smile.

"What do you mean? I haven't been anywhere new, I mean, I haven't discovered a new continent or anything."

"Not a mapmaker of the physical universe, but a mapmaker of the soul."

I stared at the guru blankly. I remembered something I'd read in his book about mapmakers, but I hadn't really understood it.

"Most people - the majority of people - live small contented lives without much experience. But a few are chosen to be explorers, mapmakers, who discover not new continents but new ways of being."

"So I've been chosen? But why?"

"I don't know. Perhaps you chose yourself. In any case, the lessons you learn must be passed on to others, you must go back share your knowledge with those who have stayed behind."

"What - go back to England, you mean?"

"You will go home to England, when your journey is over, and share your knowledge. Only then maybe, will you make sense of your adventure."

"What knowledge? I thought it was just a message from Clair that I was trying to find."

"Perhaps you won't be able to express your knowledge in words, even to yourself. But you have gained strength and wisdom from your journey, and learned lessons, which will be revealed to you gradually. If it were not like this, why make the journey at all? Why not just find Clair immediately, if he is the only important thing?"

"I don't know. But - how can I help other people to be wise, if I don't even know myself? I don't feel like I have much knowledge at all. Where do I begin?"

"Begin with the things that matter to you. Take I.C.A.L., for example. How would you feel about working there now?"

"Oh, I'd never work for them again!" I declared with passion. "It's a terrible organization. I can't imagine how I stuck it out for so long. The work was boring and the people were mindless. I must have been half asleep most of the time..."

"You see how you've changed? You are like a young plant, growing every day by infinitesimal degrees, until one day you suddenly see your branches reaching for the sky and realize you have become a tree."

Rajan assured me again and again that I would unravel the final two clues, easily he said. I complained again that the clues made little sense and I didn't know how to solve them, and he said the fifth clue was something very relevant and in my mind at the moment. It was even something he had mentioned. But he refused to give me the answer. I had to concur that he was right. Solving the crossword puzzle was my task, and it was something I had to do on my own.

I had come with the intention of asking Rajan to try and contact Clair's spirit, using his mediumistic powers. But when I mentioned this to him he convinced me that I didn't need his help: he reminded me that I could contact Clair's spirit myself and in fact had already done so. I recollected the times when I had seen Clair in my dreams or felt his presence with me, and when I had mistaken the little boy at Rome airport for my brother. Perhaps it was at those times that Clair's spirit had been trying to reach me. "Your brother is here. You have only to open your heart, leave your heart empty so that he can enter it, when you are both ready." So

I had only to wait and his soul would come to me and guide me to him.

It seemed like no time at all had elapsed when I looked at my watch and saw that it was almost two o'clock and Ali would likely be waiting for me on the edge of the woods, already fearful of the outcome of my visit to Rajan. In my sudden nervousness, I stood up almost rudely to leave, about to make my apologies and explain why I had to hurry.

By the time I left the house, it was a quarter to three. I thanked Rajan warmly for his help and understanding, and he just as warmly thanked me for visiting him. I think he was genuinely pleased to have had a visitor and some contact with the outside world, which normally shunned him so totally. I asked him if there was anything I could do for him to repay him and he said there was nothing he needed, but that he would enjoy reading a letter if I could write to him from time to time. So I promised to do so. Before I left, I made a present to him of the small bundle of kapok I had collected and kept in my jacket pocket. He fingered the stuff eagerly and pressed it to his wasted cheek, delighting in the feel of its softness.

As I strolled back across the clearing towards the trees, my head still full of the day's adventures, I could see the dark face of Ali peering anxiously through the branches, too afraid to show himself. I laughed inwardly at his cowardice and ignorance.

"You are late" my guide admonished me, grabbing my arm to steer me immediately back through the jungle and perhaps also to check that it was still intact: "You come to no harm? You see him?" He was full of questions, at once curious and alarmed and partly respectful of me for braving an experience which he hadn't ventured.

"Yes, I saw him. I'm fine. He's very nice."

Ali looked at me with patent disbelief. "Nice" was not a word which one could apply to such an ogre, even if he had seen fit to refrain from actual physical assault. Perhaps Ali thought I had spent my time skulking around the house without daring to enter. Or that, just this once, the monster had not been at home. Anyway, I prattled on about my visit, full of its wonder and significance and the surprise I felt at finding Rajan so amenable. I didn't care whether Ali believed me or not, I just enjoyed telling someone of my escapade and hearing the sound of my own voice reliving the tale.

Ali kept his mouth stubbornly shut, as though he thought the strength of his skepticism could burst the bubble of my excitement. Perhaps he didn't even want to believe that Rajan was not the ogre of his imagination, because that would have made him feel a fool for believing all the stories and rumors about the guru all these years, as well as a coward for not hazarding to find out for himself when a mere slip of a girl like me was able to. It was strange that all of a sudden I felt I could read the mind of this young man I hardly knew. It was as if gradually some of Genevieve's powers of perception were beginning to rub off on me. Was it something to do with all the experiences I was having and the different people I'd met? Was I starting to see people as all part of one family, as Rajan had said in his story? So that the differences between us were being rubbed away, like the gradual erosion of wind and rain on a block of stone, to reveal the basic similarities underneath?

That evening, I sat in my room at the lodge and stared and stared at the parchment paper and the box with its crossword grid, trying to make sense of them. I recalled over and over the words Rajan had said to me: *Something he had mentioned - relevant and in my mind at the moment.* So the answers to the last two clues should be easy for me to find. I lay back on the bed listening to the rain falling outside and the lazy drone of a mosquito near the naked light bulb. I tried to let my mind drift over the day's events and the things Rajan and I had discussed. I thought about the story he'd told me about the birth of the human race and how the races had grown apart. I let his words as I remembered them and the words written on the paper meld together in my head, until I could visualize them floating about in a sort of soup of words and images.

It was clear that the answers I had found so far - I.C.A.L. HUMAN, AKIN, YEARS - did have a sort of relevance that linked them. Perhaps the last two words would also be linked in theme, and the whole would make a sort of sentence that would make sense to me. But even so, I couldn't see how a sentence could be constructed out of those four words and two others. Perhaps it wouldn't be a sentence as such, but just an idea or a thought that it would initiate in my mind that would help me to find Clair.

Around and around the words floated, and the sentence, which was the fifth clue: *Bring out of barbarism, being polite with looks (it is said).* Nothing had ever seemed as hard to me as solving that clue and the last one. Perhaps just because nothing had ever been as important for me to work out.

I went through the story Rajan had told me. I had the feeling that it had some especial significance, a key to unlock the mystery. In a self-induced hypnotic daze, halfway between waking and sleeping, his words came back to me: *Mankind - what is called civilized - thousands of years - adapted to conditions - looks changed - unfamiliar - erstwhile brothers - anger and resentment - started out equal.* With his words, I could see Rajan's misshapen face and hear the sound of his voice with its odd staccato rhythm, full of vowels broken up into the chunks of words by the glottal stop in his throat.

But then, the image of Rajan's face vanished and another face came to me. It was a face so dear and missed that I recognized it with an ache of longing in my stomach that was almost painful. The face of Clair, my brother. Not only his face but his whole being, his whole essence, came to me in that moment. It was as if he was in the room with me. Everything about him - his movements, the sound of his voice, the way he turned his head, his laugh, his hand in mine - was recaptured with total clarity and brilliance. I'd never seen him as clearly as I saw him in that moment, and felt the warmth of his personality surrounding me.

As I lay cocooned in this blissful recollection, I had the most curious sensation. It wasn't something I created myself or anticipated or even found particularly pleasant. It was as though a very strong force or current were pulling and pulling, willing me towards it. I was being sucked up and pulled along by a mighty wind or the flow of a river carrying me inexorably to some destination. I can hardly describe it, but it felt as if someone were willing me to come to them with a longing equal to my longing to see Clair. I felt that it was Clair himself who was doing the willing, that he was drawing me to him with all his might and with the power of his longing.

I didn't know what to do or what to say to answer him. Although the sensation wasn't pleasant, almost frightening in its intensity, I didn't want it to stop because it felt as if I was making contact with Clair, the person I wanted more than anyone to communicate with. So I just repeated over and over again in my mind - as though I was saying it to him - *I'm coming to you, I'm coming to you, wait for me.*

After a few minutes the sensation gradually died down and I opened my eyes and saw the room around me and came back to normal consciousness. I felt light-headed and rather dazed by the experience. All at once, the room felt oppressively small and I had to get out into the fresh air. I put on my walking boots and my waterproof coat, with the hood up to offer some protection from the rain, and went outside, taking with me a small flashlight to guide my way.

The night was dark and silent, but the air smelt fresh and the rain was warm and friendly. I stepped out and squelched through the mud, quickly leaving the safety of the lodge behind me and venturing deep into the jungle. Once there, the canopy of trees and the night sounds of animals and insects comforted me with the impression that I was not alone but surrounded everywhere with life, busy and permanent, with individual needs and functions and yet all joined, all linked in some grand plan like a huge jigsaw puzzle where everything fitted and had its place and no piece could be left out without destroying the whole picture.

I must have known that what I needed was this space around me, because it was very soon after stepping into the jungle that the answer to the fifth clue came to me, unbidden. It arose, as from the mist of words surrounding it, and dangled on the vista of my conscious mind, and I knew instantly it was right. CIVILIZE. Rajan had said: *Before mankind was what is called civilized.* That's what we had been talking about all along. That was what I was discovering now, in this place. What it was like to be in a place that hadn't been civilized by mankind, that was the same now as if human beings had never existed and sought to conquer the planet. It also meant to *Bring out of barbarism*, as the clue hinted. When I thought about it some more, I could see that this had to be the right answer. Being polite referred to the first part of the word, CIVIL, and the second part of the word, IZE, rhymes with eyes, which means looks, the rhyme being alluded to by the phrase, *it is said*.

It was extraordinary how - having spent weeks in Australia agonizing over the solution to the last two clues with no success at all - now, walking along under the trees with the drip drop of the rain falling on to leaves and then on my hooded head, the answer to the sixth clue also came to me, easily and without effort. As soon as I knew the answer it seemed obvious and I couldn't understand how I'd missed it before. The answer was: LINE. Being *nothing* back, or NIL backwards, plus an E, which is the beginning of the word *end*. And the whole thing could refer to a short letter, such as a note you might write to a friend. So simple when I thought about it. As Rajan had said. That answer also made a kind of sense, and fitted in with the other words. The line was the unbroken line stretching from the dawn of civilization to now, which connected me with the rest of mankind both living and dead. I remembered the dream

I'd had on the train from Gmunden to Villach, where I'd encountered the man who looked exactly like Dan who'd said I was on the wrong lines. It seemed again as if my life was one long dream, where I wrote the script and cast the characters in it and everything connected.

I recalled enough to be able to complete the answers to the final two clues on my slip of paper. Being certain now about the answers to the clues, I scratched all the letters on to their relevant blocks of wood and assembled them in the grid on the box. Now the crossword grid looked like this:

		I	C	A	L					
			K				L			
		C	I	V	I	L	I	Z	E	
H	U	M	A	N			N			
						Y	E	A	R	S

I glanced at my face in the little pocket mirror that I carried in my bag. I hadn't bothered to look at myself for days or even to comb my hair. My appearance shocked me; I was so haggard and drawn. My eyes were bloodshot and encircled by dark shadows and my skin was even paler than usual, so that it looked as though I was staring out of a death mask. A skin rash had started at my wrists and ankles, and my constant scratching was exacerbating the problem. Looking down now at my wrists, I could see the scales of loose skin were beginning to creep up my forearms. No wonder everybody stared at me with such concern. At last, the physical ravages of the illness were beginning to tell. I wouldn't be able to keep it a secret for much longer.

But I had to solve the mystery before it was too late. I had to find Clair. So I put away the mirror and forgot about my looks, concentrating on the six words I had in front of me: I.C.A.L., HUMAN, AKIN, YEARS, CIVILIZE, LINE. Perhaps the crossword grid was a red herring, or just a way to help me discover the words. In any case, Rajan had told me that the words were important - not only individually, but also together - so perhaps when taken as a whole they would spell out a sentence with a clear and meaningful message.

I took out all the little blocks of wood on which were written the letters making up the answers to the crossword and moved them back and forth on the mattress, rearranging them into different orders again and again. I was so exhausted. I fell back on the bed, unwilling to carry on with what seemed a hopeless task. The six words in whatever order made no sense at all. What were these damn words supposed to mean to me? Now that I'd gone to all this trouble to discover them, they had to have some significance.

Then I had a brainwave. I thought the key was something to do with things being separate and then joined. I rearranged the letters of the words into different orders, as I had done with the words themselves.

Suddenly, my heart began to beat faster. When I started rearranging the letters, two things stood out immediately, and they were the two names: CLAIR and ALICE. So what I was doing maybe *did* have some relevance.

I shuffled and shuffled the letters on their wooden blocks, moving them back and forth over the bed with trembling fingers but keeping the two names intact. And gradually two other words began to emerge, which seemed important: LIVES and NAME. Now I had these words in a sort of rough order:

CLAIR LIVES   NAME   ALICE.

Of course, this took a lot longer to do than to describe to you. In fact, I think I must have been there reshuffling the letters for more than two hours. Gradually, two other words began to appear, and to make sense as a link:

CLAIR LIVES IN   HIS NAME   ALICE.

I felt I was on to something, and that ultimately this was the sentence I had been searching for. But no matter how I regrouped and regrouped the final six letters, I didn't know how they fitted in. I felt they must spell out the name either of where he lived or what he was called. But in that case, what was my name doing there? It didn't seem to have any importance at all in the sentence. Surely, his name couldn't be Alice as well? That would mean he was a woman. Anyway, hadn't Genevieve told me his name would begin with an S?

I started to feel frustrated and tense. I was getting nowhere, and now I was beginning to go round and round in circles, like a kitten chasing its tail. My previous excitement and elation had evaporated, and now I merely felt impatient with myself for being unable to finish the sentence.

I had to do something different, start again somehow. I decided to tackle the problem again in the morning. I put all the blocks back in their original positions in the crossword puzzle board, closed the lid of the box and put the whole thing away carefully in my suitcase.

That night as I lay in bed tossing and turning and unable to sleep with exhaustion and excitement, the events of the day became a confused jumble in my mind and produced strange and incoherent dreams. Tom was talking about Alice Springs, and I was standing in the square in the middle of the town looking at a fountain with water gushing from the mouth of a little boy statue, and Clair was singing Sylvie again, and the words came back to me with haunting clarity: *My eyes were like fountains, my eyes were like fountains, my eyes were like fountains where water did flow.*

I woke suddenly and sat up in bed, my heart beating. Alice Springs. The place with my name. The place Rowan had told me about that had drawn me so much when I'd been in Australia. The place Tom had mentioned, reawakening all those memories and forgotten longings. Rajan had said that Clair told me to remember the name. My name. I had to go back and retrace my steps, to return to Australia.

With trembling hands I took out the crossword box again, withdrew all the little wooden blocks and rearranged the letters into one last sentence:

CLAIR LIVES IN ALICE HIS NAME...

...and then there was a collection of assorted letters left, which could spell out a name, although not one I'd ever come across before. But it could spell out somebody's name. Maybe Genevieve had been wrong about his name beginning with an S.

Then I took the photograph out of Genevieve's box and studied it in the dim light of my little room. It was still quite fuzzy and indistinct, although there was no question now that it was the face of a man.

There was only one way to find out who it was. I had to go back to Australia, as Rajan had advised me. I would use my return air ticket to Sydney and then take a plane to the center of the continent. To Alice Springs, the place with my own name.

CHAPTER NINETEEN

IT WASN'T UNTIL I was walking through the streets of Alice Springs, that I remembered the map in Nepal and the curious S-shaped crack in the center of the painted "continent" on the bottom right-hand side. I wondered if it had been merely a coincidental fissure in the rock or some symbol whose significance I had failed to grasp at the time. But whether or not it was a message designed for me, I had ended up here in Australia, roughly analogous in its position on the earth to the blob on the cave painting. Although the hot, bright weather and the strong accents of the townsfolk were unfamiliar to me, I felt as though I'd come home. The fact that I had the same name as the town increased my feelings of connection to the place, as if we were half-sisters meeting for the first time, from different cultures but conscious of our blood link.

Not that it was much of a place. It was really rather barren and lacking in beauty or character. A smallish town, with flat, uninteresting houses and a feeling about it that everybody was on their way to somewhere else, or longing to be somewhere else. Traveling there on the plane from Melbourne, we had flown for miles over flat, dry land with no towns and no distinguishing features. Like an oasis of

Western civilization in the middle of hundreds of miles of unfriendly desert, the town of Alice sat, small and squat and unpretentious. There were many hotels of varying degrees of comfort, and I found myself in a rundown establishment in the heart of town, mainly frequented by backpackers and young students on their way to do a "Red Centre Tour" or traveling through the outback in dangerously decrepit jeeps.

Once there, I was unsure what to do with myself. I had little money left: most of the money I'd earned from my job at the restaurant in Byron Bay had already been spent on my return flight to Malaysia, and I now had to start being more economical if I was going to last out. I had rather feverishly imagined that simply by being in this place, all the answers to the questions in my head would suddenly miraculously come to me and I would be inspired by a sense of purpose and direction. But I didn't feel inspired or confident about what I expected, or even very much in control over events. My main emotion was a feeling of subtle despondency which hung over me like a miasma, a sort of anti-climactic gloom that here I was at the other end of the earth, having spent months traveling without achieving or discovering anything of value. With no one to help me, I didn't quite know where to turn.

So I wandered about the streets in the blazing heat under a cloudless blue sky and fought off the little flies which buzzed around my nose and mouth continually, and felt more and more defeated and lacking in energy. Perhaps it was mainly the illness which had me in its grip almost completely now. I didn't dare look in mirrors to be confronted by my ashen face and painfully thin body, and I could see people glance twice at me in the street, not quite certain whether to offer assistance. I could hardly eat anything, as even the thought of food made my gorge rise. I would go to roadside cafes during the day and drink a coke or two to inject myself with enough caffeine to keep me going for a while longer. I would force myself to eat a sandwich or some chips, although my teeth were like a steel trap wanting to remain closed against sustenance, and I even managed to consume a roo-burger once. But it wouldn't have mattered what I ate, since everything tasted like cardboard to me now. My head throbbed so much that sometimes I could hardly see, my skin rash had now crept all the way up my arms and legs so that I daren't walk around in shorts even in that heat, and I coughed continually, sometimes even spitting up blood.

I reflected on how I had once been - perpetually hungry and active, with an appetite for different tastes and sensations - and I could hardly believe I was the same person now as I had been then. Who was that Alice of so long ago? What did she have in common with this gaunt creature, who haunted the streets of her namesake town like a ghost, looking for something she didn't know how to find? Sometimes I felt almost divorced from my body, like a pale spirit wafting above me, watching and waiting for my imminent demise. I felt no fear about the prospect of death. I couldn't summon enough energy to feel fear about anything. I only felt frustration at the knowledge that I was so close and I hadn't found what I wanted, hadn't closed the story of my life, even though the author wanted to put down her pen and call it a day.

I can't even remember how long I spent in Alice Springs in this disassociated state. I suppose it must have been a few days. At any rate, one day a train of events happened to me spontaneously, as though my guardian angel had looked down and seen that I might wander forever without a helping hand.

Not realizing it, I had wandered into the aboriginal area. Although there were many aborigines living in Alice Springs and they mingled with the whites when doing their shopping and going about their daily business, they tended to live together in what I assumed were areas designated especially for them. I didn't know this was their part of town, until I looked around me and realized that I was the only person on the street with a white face. It was a curious sensation, being for once in the minority. Suddenly, I was the different one, the stranger who attracted stares from passers by. But I wasn't afraid, only interested in this new phenomenon.

I passed by a wall on which several posters were displayed, and the picture on one caught my eye. It was a large rock, unbelievably red in hue, topped by the bright blue sky I had become used to, and surrounded by unending desert. I recognized the rock, of course, since it was the main tourist attraction in these parts, but I couldn't quite believe it was really that color and that the photograph hadn't been retouched by some artist wanting to make the object appear more remarkable. Perhaps I was meant to visit the rock. But the idea of traveling miles to reach it, the idea of traveling anywhere in my weak state, was unappealing.

Late that afternoon, there was a performance by an aboriginal theatre company in the basement of our hotel, which had been kitted out with a sort of makeshift proscenium stage. Only about twenty or thirty people had bothered to attend for the show and I felt sorry for the aboriginal performers at having to expend all their energy and enthusiasm on such a small audience. For some reason, I seated myself in the front row to watch, perhaps because no one else was sitting there and I didn't want to have to crane my neck over some tall head to view the performance.

I enjoyed the show, which was a mixture of music, didgeridoo playing, informational speaking directly to the audience about aspects of the aboriginal culture such as how they make fire with sticks, and enactments of the native myths and stories. At the end of the show, the performers stood in a long and straggly line and sang their song *Proud to be aborigine*, possessing a catchy tune with which we the audience were encouraged to join in. I was surprised at how different all the aborigines were from each other: some tall and skinny, some almost as short as pygmies and with a variety of skin tones ranging from light tan to dark chocolate brown. I liked their genuine demeanor and the way they addressed the audience so openly. One of the group, the youngish one who had played the good snake in the myth section - seemed to pay special attention to me and to direct most of his remarks at me in the audience, maybe because I was the only person in the front row, plus I was smiling and obviously enjoying myself.

As we straggled out of the theatre and into the sunshine, I walked past the performers - who were standing in a long line in the foyer waiting to shake the hands of the audience in a gesture of mutual comradeship - and I took the hand of the young man who had addressed me. He had a wide face and a flat nose, shiny black skin and fuzzy russet-brown hair. I wouldn't have been able to distinguish him in a crowd of his compatriots, except that he was smiling so hugely that his mouth seemed almost to engulf his face, opening wide to show surprisingly white and even teeth. I had never seen one of these people smile before, and certainly not at me. So I was touched that he'd singled me out for this demonstration of friendliness. The man gave me such a wide smile that I couldn't resist smiling back at him and making a comment: "I really enjoyed the show" I commented. "I'm English and I didn't know much about your culture, so it taught me a lot. And it was fun."

"I'm glad" he replied, beaming even more. "You seen much of our beautiful country?"

"Well, no, not really, I'm ashamed to say I haven't done much traveling around while I've been here."

"You see Uluru?"

"No - where's that?"

"He means Ayers Rock" came an Australian voice beside me, and I turned to see a middle-aged man with grey hair and a florid red face. "Uluru - that's what they call it." The Australian man wandered away, and I turned back to the aborigine at my side.

"That's right" he declared, his smile still wide. "Uluru our name for the rock. Our name come first." This time he was laughing, as though he thought it was a huge joke that the white man had bothered to rename the rock. "It our rock - you know."

"No, I haven't been there" I said, replying to his earlier question. "I've only been in Alice Springs for a few days. So I haven't had time. But why on earth did we - I mean, the white man who discovered it or whatever - name it Ayers Rock?"

He laughed again. "I dunno. They got some reason."

"After somebody called Ayers, I suppose" I reflected, thinking of the poster I'd seen earlier.

"You wanna go?"

I was a bit taken aback by the aborigine's sudden proposal. "Well, I...I'm not sure. I'm feeling...rather tired. And it's a long way, isn't it?"

"No. Uluru not far. Just across desert. You not tired when you go there."

"I'm sure it's very interesting, but...oh, I don't know. I hadn't thought about it, really." I didn't want to hurt the young man's feelings by being unenthusiastic about visiting the rock, which was probably a sacred place to his people.

"You should go. Special place." He nodded with conviction.

"But is it really that color? It's so red in the pictures I've seen. I can't believe it's really that red, is it?"

The aborigine's dark brown eyes widened. "You don't believe? Then, you must go see. It really red all right. But it change colors. This time of year it mostly red. Then, when the rains come, it change to grey. When storm coming, it change to black."

"It sounds amazing. Like a sort of weather meter?"

He didn't understand my comment, so carried on with his description. "Tourists come from all over, just to see our rock. At sunset, they all take pictures with their cameras. They want to see the rock glow."

"What do you mean - glow?"

"At sunset, the rock glow even more red, say goodnight to the sun for another day."

I couldn't help smiling at his childlike way of speaking. "I suppose I should see it too. I've come all this way, after all. It seems a shame not to see Ayers Rock when I'm this close -- sorry, I mean Uluru."

"You not go with your mob?"

"My...what?"

He tried to explain. "On trip with group. Like tourists. In a big bus."

"Oh no. I'm not with a mob. I'm here on my own."

"On your own? No friends here?" He said it without the pitying look I might have expected from a white person, but with a sort of practical air.

I shook my head in response. "And I think the organized trips to Ayers Rock are pretty expensive. I can't afford it, actually."

Maybe I looked a bit pathetic when I said that, although it was true. At any rate, he suddenly declared: "I take you!"

"Oh no, you don't have to. I wouldn't want to trouble you..."

"No trouble for me. I offer, so I want you to come. You come?" The young man wasn't aggressive but he was persistent, as though he would brook no argument to his suggestion.

"It's very kind of you, but..." I petered out and looked at him helplessly, unable to think of a really good excuse for saying no. I pondered whether I'd be able to manage a trip through the desert to reach the rock. I wondered if this man were trustworthy, if he had any ulterior motive for inviting me to travel with him. These thoughts rushed through my head and I couldn't express them, but just stood there in a welter of confusion and embarrassment.

"I see you tired, you alone, you not trust black man," he said with a perception that surprised me.

"Oh, it's not that, just..." I wanted to be polite, although I had an idea he'd be able to see through my hypocrisy.

"I want to take you to rock. Rock will help you. Help many people before. Rock will help you," he repeated.

"Help?" I wondered what he meant.

"You can go on tourist bus with other white people. Take photos," he said smiling, doing a rather clumsy mime.

"I don't have a camera," I admitted with a grin.

"Or you come with me. We see the rock as it really is. You learn about what rock really means, hear it speak to you. That way, it help you."

"Yes...but..." I searched my mind to see what else I could find against the idea.

The aborigine could tell I was practically won over. "Yes. You come with me. I go tomorrow. In my car." He pointed proudly to a very old and weather-beaten vehicle at the side of the road outside the hotel.

"How long does it take to get there?" I responded dubiously, feeling a little guilty for looking this gift horse in the mouth, but unsure whether I was fit enough to cope with a long journey.

He shrugged his shoulders. "Not long. Five, six hours."

I opened my eyes wide in amazement. I'd had no idea how far away it was.

"Take longer by coach" he assured me. "They stop off, make you buy tourist things."

I smiled. He obviously knew all the tricks tourists were subjected to. Maybe had tried a few himself. "Well..." I was visibly weakening.

"You must see Uluru. It very important." He suddenly had an air of wisdom about him. I reflected on why I had been drawn to this area in the first place, why Rajan had told me to come here and why the aborigine had been drawn to approach me out of all the other people in the audience. I considered how my entire journey had been one of accepting circumstances and trusting to my intuition to direct me. I had been seeking something to do, somewhere to go, and now it had been offered to me on a plate.

"O.K." I agreed.

His huge smile returned, and he shook my hand. "You happy you come with me. You enjoy. This Uluru good for you. Cure you and give you new life."

I was startled when he said that. How did he know I needed curing? I'd only mentioned being tired, not ill. But of course - I reflected - it was obvious I was ill from the wretched state of my looks. Perhaps the aboriginals thought their rock had some kind of primitive healing power. I didn't really believe that a rock in the middle of the desert could magically cure me of Level 3. But I had been infected by the man's enthusiasm and I wanted to see the place.

"We meet tomorrow. I come to this hotel in the car?"

I nodded. "What time?"

"Twelve o'clock."

"O.K."

"Then we get there by sunset. You see at sunset. It deepest red then." He laughed and beamed and I smiled back and we shook hands and promised to meet. It wasn't until after he'd joined his companions outside the hotel and I'd watched him drive away in his car, that I realized I didn't know his name.

It was strange. I almost didn't believe I was really going to go to Uluru with this man I'd met by chance at the theatre performance. But I was in that state of mind where I just accepted what Fate threw at me. I decided that I would go along with whatever happened the next day: if he showed up as promised outside my hotel at twelve o'clock, I would have no reason not to go with him, and if he didn't come, then I was not meant to visit Uluru after all.

The next day I went to have breakfast in the dining room, but the toast and jam tasted like cardboard in my mouth, and even three cups of hot sweet tea weren't enough to fully revive me. The waiter hovered over me with an anxious expression. Perhaps I really looked as ill as I felt. Although I was very thin and weak, I felt nauseous most of the time and was unable to eat much without vomiting it straight out again. I forced myself to eat, to give me as much strength as possible. I packed a small bag with a bottle of water, a fly net and some suntan cream, put on my shorts and t-shirt and walking shoes (not caring any longer about my unsightly, scaly skin), and positioned myself outside the hotel at twelve noon. To my surprise, my aborigine friend was already there, waiting for me in his car. I recognized the vehicle, because it was so much smaller, older and dustier than any of the others in the street.

I approached the vehicle and said hello, he smiled as before and told me to get in, and we set off through the dusty streets until they were overtaken by flaming hot sands. The aborigine and I didn't talk a lot as we traveled. I was entranced by the sight of the unremitting desert speeding by the window, with its vistas of red earth broken occasionally by thirsty looking scrub. But I did remember to tell him my name and to ask him his.

"Kuniya" he replied, with his usual wide-lipped smile.

I tried repeating it slowly. "Kuniya."

"It a good name. Mean snake. What your name mean?"

"Alice? Oh, I don't think it means anything. It's just a name. I was called after a girl in a book - Alice in Wonderland. Have you heard of it?"

Kuniya shook his head. I looked out of the window briefly, then added: "Why is it good to be called a snake?"

He wasn't offended by my bluntness. "My people, we all called after animal. Or bird. It our totem. You know what is, the totem?"

"Well, I have heard of totems. But we don't have them."

"Every little baby given a name. And then also a totem. Which an animal or a bird. And the totem special to him or to her. Special because they can kill any other animal or bird for food. But not their totem. They must protect it. Otherwise, they die."

"So you can't kill a snake?" He shook his head. "But, what happens if you're bitten by a poisonous snake? You do have poisonous snakes in Australia, don't you?"

Kuniya shook his head sagely. "There is poisonous snake, yes. But poisonous snake never bite me. Snake my totem. All snakes know this."

A few months before, or if someone else had made this suggestion, I would have found it utterly preposterous. The snakes know not to bite a certain man, just because he's decided it's his totem? But Kuniya said it with such authority and conviction, that I had complete faith in him. How he managed it I didn't know. But somehow he worked such a magic on the snakes that they refrained from attacking him.

At about five o'clock, Kuniya pointed to a shape in the distance, and I saw the distant red outline of Uluru, standing lonely and poignant against the sky. An hour or so later, we pulled up in the car park, alongside a couple of tourist buses that had just disgorged their contents, spilling out tens of excited passengers with cameras slung across their shoulders waiting to take that postcard shot. We were about a mile or so from the rock at this point, at what they called the "viewing area", which was far enough away to get the whole monolith in vision but close enough to see how the sunset affected its color. I asked Kuniya what all the tourists were waiting for, and he said that when the last rays of the dying sun hit the rock, for a few seconds it glows red, and that was what they had come to see and to capture with their cameras. He wanted me to see too, he said, so that now I could believe how red it was.

Now I had to believe, since the rock was standing right in front of me. But it still looked like a stage set, too strange to be real. We stood and watched as the sun slowly dipped over the horizon behind us, and sure enough there was a glow. At the moment it happened, there was a flurry of activity around us and a hurried click of camera shutters. But I was glad not to have a camera. I just wanted to experience the moment myself, without capturing it forever on film.

It was extraordinary how quickly all the tourists piled back into their coaches and drove away, once the sunset was over. So, in a few minutes, Kuniya and I were alone. It was then that he announced his next plan. "Now, we climb rock" he said simply.

"Climb it!" I said aghast. "But, it's huge. How will we ever get up there?" What I didn't want to admit was that I was very ill and didn't think I had the strength for a long walk, never mind a climb up a rock a mile high.

But Kuniya was insistent. "We will go. I am there to protect you. You not fall."

He didn't seem to realize that what I was worried about was not falling, but having enough strength in my legs to get up there in the first place. But he was so convinced about it that I was carried along by his enthusiasm and unable to refuse. We drove right up to the rock, and this time we were the only people there. The sky was dimming and in the dusk the rock looked impossibly vast and unconquerable, a sheer face of impenetrable limestone. I couldn't think about how hard it would be to get up there. I simply followed Kuniya blindly, trusting that he knew best.

"This good time to climb" he said reassuringly, as we got out of the car and walked up to the edge. "After sunset, no flies to bother us. No hot sun in our eyes. And no tourists." He laughed in his infectious way, and I joined in, trying to lighten my anxiety and pretend a courage I didn't feel. "On the way up, you go first. So I catch you if you stumble. On the way down, I go first. Down more difficult. Good plan, eh?" I nodded.

We scrambled up for a few feet, and I think it was the adrenalin of pure fear that got me started. Then, to my surprise, there was a heavy chain to grasp hold of, and I hoisted myself up with that over the steepest part of the climb. My legs ached with the strain and I was gasping for breath within minutes. But now we'd begun, I was determined to reach the top and nothing on earth would have stopped me. My face was aglow with perspiration and I could feel the sweat trickling between my breasts, even though it was no longer hot now that the sun had gone down.

After about a third of the distance, the chain was discontinued and there was a sort of level platform where we could recuperate for the final assault. I looked down and was surprised at how far we'd already climbed. The desert stretched away into the distance, silent and impassive. I was starting to enjoy myself. Somehow the climb, or maybe even the rock itself, was invigorating me and filling me with more energy than I'd had in weeks.

The rest of the way was not so steep. But near the top of the rock there were lots of ridges that we had to traverse up and down, with the knowledge that the very top was very close but frustratingly difficult to reach.

At last, we were there, and Kuniya smiled enigmatically when I told him how exhilarated I felt. It was almost dark and the moon was just visible in the night sky. All around us the desert lay flat and imperturbable. I felt as if we were the only two people in existence. Suddenly, despite my earlier tiredness and the gloom of the past few days, I wanted to whoop with joy. This must have been what Kuniya expected me to feel, what he meant when he said the rock would cure me.

I think he must have known I wanted to be alone for a while, because he wandered off and stood with his back to me, looking out at the vista. I sat myself down in a little hollow in the rock and looked out and felt the cool wind as it whipped around my face and blew my hair out in a stream.

For the first time in my life, I felt totally at peace. More than that - at one with the whole world.

At that moment, it felt as though the rock beneath me - so huge and strong and solid, like a monument erected by the gods in the wilderness - was a warm and protective father, enveloping me in his arms and telling me not to worry. It seemed as if the rock spoke to me, as if it had a message for me that it wished to impart. And the message was: *We are all one.*

I knew that was the message, although it wasn't a voice that told me. It was a presence, vast and dark. It was a force from nature, telling me that all of life is joined and whole. The rock-father was benign and infused me with his strength. And I felt completely whole and at peace.

On the way down, Kuniya went first as he had promised. But I didn't feel as afraid as I had anticipated, perhaps because of my newly found strength and courage. I hardly even needed the chain over the steep section, and I kept looking around me with wonder, although now practically nothing of the desert was visible, only the stars shining brightly above us in the clear sky and the moon, which was full and bright and seemed to guide our way.

For most of the time on the way down I was staring at Kuniya's back. I noticed that a small lock of his hair - most of which stuck out wildly from his head in a fuzzy russet mop - clung to the nape of his neck in a sinuous s-shape, almost like a snake lying on his neck. I thought how strange that he should have that when his name meant snake. And everything I had encountered seemed to make perfect sense.

I had thought that we would drive straight back to Alice Springs and my hotel, but it was not to be. In my rather dazed state, although I complained at Kuniya's plans, I went along with them. He drove us away from the rock but off the main road, through what seemed like miles of unrelenting desert. For some reason I wasn't afraid of the aborigine, even though I hardly knew him and we were alone in the vast Australian desert together, me a city-dwelling stranger and he a native. When we'd driven a long way, he told me that we were going on a "walkabout". Not knowing what he meant by that, I followed him out of the vehicle - which he parked at an alarming angle on the side of the road - and we set off through the desert. I had left my bag in the car, and soon discarded my shoes, which were uncomfortable on my hot and swollen feet. All I was wearing was shorts and a t-shirt, and my bare feet were scratched and bleeding from walking through the spiky scrub.

We walked all that night and the next day, just walking and walking with no rest and no food and no distractions, Kuniya a few feet ahead of me as though providing a focus for my attention in that vast desert which seemed to me to have no features by which to navigate. But my companion appeared to know where he was going, although I don't know how. At first I moaned and protested about my tiredness and my sore feet and my shoulders, which were red and burning from the sun, but Kuniya took no notice and after a while I gave up complaining. I tried to lag behind him or run away, but where could I run to? I had no idea where I was or how to get home, without his assistance.

So I just kept walking, in a trance, not knowing what would happen, my legs striding on and on as if they were part of some automatic machine that didn't belong to me. After a while, the walking possessed a sort of rhythm to it, which lulled me. I felt as though I was no longer in my body but floating just above it, willing it to continue with my mind but no longer feeling any pain. It was extraordinary. Even the pains from the symptoms of my Level 3 seemed to float away from me, as though they'd belonged to some sort of nightmare, which I'd only imagined.

I don't know how long we walked or for how far, but I know I saw another sunset. Then, all was blackness.

CHAPTER TWENTY

WHEN I NEXT woke up I didn't know where I was. Or hardly even who I was. Images swirled about my head like monsters on a tossing sea. Lights and colors came and went in bursts and bubbles, following one after another like an endless pageant with no meaning. Sometimes all around me was iridescent blue, as blue as the night sky from some lonely planet without a sun. Then that would gradually fade and be replaced by a red so violent it was as if a thousand fires had been lit in front of me, and I was watching the inferno of hell itself. Or sometimes there would be no color at all, just an infinity of black like space without any worlds in it.

All the time, whenever my eyelids fluttered open to catch a glimpse of the outside world mostly denied me, a face would float into vision and it was always the same face, smiling and kindly and ever-present. It was the face of Kuniya, my friend. He was about the only thing I could recognize or remember clearly, when I had enough strength to remember at all.

My body seemed to have shrunk inside me, until all my limbs and torso were pencil thin, just a fine line of energy pulsating inside me with the rest of me withered away. I felt only partly alive, clinging on to life with my bare hands, with my bare bones and with the help of my soul that wouldn't let go. I seemed to be floating on a white sea, and when I turned and faced the bed I saw that the white was the expanse of sheet underneath me and it seemed vast and limitless and almost to engulf me. Like the desert had seemed, all that time ago. How much time? Was it days or weeks or months? I had no idea. I didn't even have the strength to care.

Little scenes played out in my mind, snippets of all that had gone before: sometimes I would see my mother sitting in front of the television on that fatal night in London; sometimes I would see the circle of friends at the party and hear the crash of the bomb's explosion; sometimes I would see Marmalade struggling at the window and trying to escape, as had happened so often in my guilty imagination. Then I would see a silvery road up the coast of Australia, with its vista of sea and wave-swept cliffs; and myself traveling happily in a car with the top down. Or myself in a cave in Borneo and Ali jumping into the void that was really a shallow pool, and I would hear his laughter. Or I would see the ravaged face of Rajan Mobley staring from his wheelchair and trying to smile.

All my memories jumbled together and I had no notion of when they had happened or even if they had happened at all, at least to me. It was as if I was watching a film of events that had occurred in the life of Alice, a girl I once knew. Sometimes I thought fleetingly of what people said happened to them when they died, that they saw their whole life instantly flashing before them, and I wondered vaguely if that was what was happening to me. But only vaguely.

Then there were the sounds. Like music sometimes, a sort of distant keening, as of panpipes or women wailing for some lost soul. I don't know if it was real or unreal, I only knew I heard it. I decided that somebody was calling for me, and that I should follow. That I should stop fighting and give in. Then came peace.

I had a dream that was so vivid it seemed real. My brother Clair came to me and he held in his hands a fruit I'd never seen before, with a thick dark skin. He broke open the fruit into two even halves, like the twin sides of a nut, and gave me one, telling me to eat it. When I bit into the fruit the juice felt sticky and bitter on my tongue and ran out of my mouth and down my chin in a stream of dark red like blood. I saw that Clair had done the same, and he smeared the blood-red juice over my chest and his and the sun quickly dried it into a sort of pattern like a tattoo. When I looked at Clair again he was still my brother but he had another face, a face I couldn't remember, another face.

One morning the sunlight streamed through the window, and I opened my eyes and really woke up. This time I could see and hear the world as it really was, and it was as if all that had gone before was a bad dream. There were birds singing outside, and the lovely normal cheeping they made comforted me and brought me back into the world of the living.

I was in a small, dark room, practically bare except for the bed on which I lay and a chair on which Kuniya sat with his back to me, looking out of the window. There was also a low table under the window with some bits of chipped crockery on it - a plate and a couple of cups. I felt surprisingly happy to be in this poor disheveled shelter, and to see that Kuniya was still there watching over me.

I heaved myself up on to my elbows and the noise made Kuniya turn around. When he saw that I had woken up at last, he smiled hugely, came over to the bed and hugged me tightly, hoisting me up to a sitting position with his strong brown arms. He smelt of sweat and red earth, a warm friendly smell.

"Good morning, good morning little sister!" he said, beaming. "You been asleep for long time."

"How long?" I asked weakly. My voice sounded strange, new and croaky, as though it didn't belong to me.

"Some days. Nearly two weeks."

I sighed and let the fresh new air fill my lungs. "It's good to be awake."

"You very sick. Very sick." He shook his head and looked concerned, like a worried father castigating his child for running across the road.

"Yes" I admitted. "I've been ill for quite some time, really. I hadn't told anyone. But it must have got much worse."

"You have the white man's disease. Brought from England."

I was stunned, but too weak to express the surprise I felt. Did he know about Level 3? I sat and looked at him with my mouth open.

"I seen it before" he continued. "White boy come here before. He look all pale, like you. I take him up the rock, like you. He come down, collapse, like you. Stay asleep for many days, like you. But then, he recover."

"So -- you mean -- you knew all along? When you saw me in the hotel...?"

"You have white face, like this boy. Very thin, like this boy. Your arms and legs with the dry skin like crocodile. I know."

"And so, taking me up the rock, that was..."

"Climbing the rock, very hard. Many tourists come and climb rock. They want to show..." He clenched his fists. "Strength, power. My people, we don't climb rock." He laughed at the absurdity of it. "Rock to us is sacred. Protected by stories of the Tjukupa." I looked puzzled at this word. "Our myths and legends. Stories of how the rock is made in the dreamtime. Stories of our fathers and their fathers."

"So if you don't climb the rock, why did I have to climb it? And the other boy?"

At this, Kuniya gave his biggest smile. "Test your strength. Your will to live."

I still didn't understand. "To live is also hard. But you must want to live. To climb rock, some people, too hard for them. They die, have... attack of the heart, or fall off. I don't tell you this before." He smiled. "But if you reach top, you have will to live which is very strong. And when will is strong, you fight away death."

"And the walkabout, that was to test my strength too?"

He nodded and smiled. "Your will to live very strong, although your body very weak, weakened by the drugs and the life of the white man. But you need to live to finish your mission so you not give up."

"So..." I began, slowly coming to grips with what he was telling me, "what you're saying is that climbing the rock and doing the walkabout is a sort of test. And if I pass the test, that shows I'm strong enough to live?"

He nodded.

"But in that case, why did I collapse? Why did I get so ill? I thought I nearly died these last few days, didn't I?"

"You fight the rock. You win. You fight the desert. You win. You fight your own body, tell it to be strong. You no want to die. And you win. Same thing."

"So I'm sort of learning how much strength I've got, and how to use it", I mused aloud. I reflected on what Sarah had told me about Level 3 and how she believed the I.C.A.L. drugs were killing people in the end. The drugs killed off the body's own natural resources, the body's own ability to fight the disease. Was that it? Was that the cure? To fight and not give in? The Western doctors always said to rest and recuperate when you were ill with Level 3, but perhaps that was precisely the opposite of what was ultimately good for you. Perhaps what Kuniya meant was that you had to go through the pain, as I had done, break through the threshold of the pain until you floated above it.

Not to experience the symptoms was not to experience the disease was to succumb to it eventually. But if you stayed and fought, and you were strong enough, or your will to live was potent enough, then you could win. It seemed insane to believe that the mind could so influence the body. It went against all the truth that science held inviolable, that facts were facts and couldn't be changed, that nothing was real unless visible and apparent. I reflected on how depressed I had felt while wandering around Alice Springs, and how my body had responded and I had felt ten times more ill than before, and almost ready to give up and give in. When what

I should have been doing was fighting back and refusing to let the illness overpower me. I hadn't known that I had any control over things. As soon as I'd heard that I had Level 3, I had written my own death sentence, giving up hope and giving myself only a few months to live.

Now I felt completely strong and with a head as clear and light as a ball of crystal. When Kuniya offered me something to eat, I gladly accepted. In fact, I felt ravenously hungry. I got out of bed, washed in his tiny adjacent bathroom, and changed out of the white smock he had given me, into my shorts and t-shirt. I saw with relief that the redness had gone from my skin and it was almost back to normal.

As we sat and ate at the table under the window, I told him as much of my adventures as I could remember. For the first time in ages, I spoke about Clair and the clues and the things in Genevieve's box, and I told him all about my quest, although, for some reason, my journey didn't seem to hold as much importance for me as it had done before. I felt so at peace here and so sure that whatever happened would be right for me; that the universe would provide me with answers as long as I knew how to listen to them. I told him about the night of the bomb and my subsequent travels, and why I had decided to come to Australia to look for my brother. But that I hadn't yet found him.

Through my entire monologue, Kuniya sat listening intently but silently, his dark eyes watching my face. To my surprise, when I had finished, he didn't respond or make any comment about my stories. He just commenced one of his own:

"Last night I have dream. Good dream. I dream that one person come from each country, from every country in the world. Come to this place. And here is a big pot." He spread his hands. "Like cooking pot. Over a fire. And every person come with a coin from his country. One piece of money. And each put the coin into the big pot, and all coins melt and melt till make like river. River of metal. And then one person take the river of metal and make of it a big stone. And on the stone they write some words. They say *We are all one.*"

I wasn't surprised that Kuniya had used the same words I had heard in my mind on the top of Uluru. He had probably heard the same words himself. Why not? They were there, for anyone who cared to listen. The rock would say the same thing in any language.

When we had finished talking and eating, I said I would have to go. I gathered up my bag and my few little things, and thanked Kuniya for all his kindness. He seemed disappointed that I was leaving, but I didn't see how I could stay there forever. I had to get back to my life and my quest for Clair. Perhaps I would go back to England again, I didn't know.

On the doorstep, Kuniya gave me another of his big expansive hugs, and told me to take care of myself and not to forget the things I'd learned on the rock. I felt warmed by his embrace and his smile. I told him the memory of my time with him would always stay with me and bring me comfort, which may have sounded melodramatic, but I meant every word. Then I found myself walking away from his house and down the street, back to the heart of Alice Springs, perhaps to the same hotel I had left two weeks before, back on my journey.

I was walking past a large spreading Acacia tree, and thinking how beautiful it looked in the late afternoon sunlight. As I drank in the sunshine and the wonderfully invigorating feeling of being strong and healthy again, I noticed two birds that flew down and landed in the tree and began to preen each other. I watched, fascinated by their antics, and when the slightly larger of the birds turned its back and I saw the white stripe down the center of his glossy black coat, I realized that they were magpies. They were singing to each other and it was a beautiful sound, even more beautiful than the nightingales I had heard in England. I thought of Dr. Becker and his wish that I should send him an Australian magpie because of their sweet song. But I had no desire to capture these birds and send them anywhere. I just delighted in their presence and was glad that they were together, that they'd found each other, as I longed to find my brother.

Thinking of Clair made me remember my friend Kuniya. I recalled how hard it had been climbing the rock with him on the way up but how it had seemed so much easier coming down Uluru. I recalled how he'd insisted he go first down the rock in case I slipped and fell, and how I'd noticed as I followed him that little lock of hair that clung to the nape of his neck in an S-shape.

Then a thought hit me with such a shock it was like a blow in the pit of my stomach.

I dropped my bag on the ground and crouched over it. I tore open the side pocket and withdrew the black box with trembling fingers. My heart was beating so fast, I could hardly breathe. But I extracted two things from the box.

First, the paper napkin which I had carried from the cafe in Gmunden and which was now dog-eared and stained with many fingerings. I looked at the sentence I had created from the letters of the clues, which read: CLAIR LIVES IN ALICE HIS NAME, then at the letters left over, which were: U A K I N Y.

Again and again I looked at those letters until they swam before my eyes. Now I knew what they spelt: KUNIYA. "His name begins with an S" Genevieve had said. She was right. His name was Kuniya, which means Snake, and there was an S on the nape of his neck, as a final clue. How could I have missed it?

Now I looked at the photograph, which was finally clear to me. The face was so familiar. It was the face which had floated in and out of my vision all the time I had been ill, when I had spent those two weeks tossing and turning on my bed and he had watched over me as tenderly as any nurse. Kuniya's face. Smiling, as always, but with that wise expression in his eyes that reminded me so strongly of Clair.

The tears were streaming down my face. I could hardly see. Somebody passed me in the street, saw me huddling over my bag crying, and asked if I was all right. I replied impatiently that I was fine. Then I began to retrace my steps, back to the house I had come to know so well.

As I approached the house, I saw that Kuniya was standing in the open doorway, almost as though he was expecting me. I stood too, looking at him through my tear-stained face, and neither of us moved for a few minutes.

You know, I've often wondered why, when in *Twelfth Night* Sebastian and Viola discover that they are brother and sister and that they have each found the person they'd thought was lost, they don't immediately rush into one another's arms and embrace and weep for joy. They simply stand there looking at each other:

> *Do not embrace me till each circumstance*
> *Of place, time, fortune, do cohere and jump*
> *That I am Viola ...*

Now, I think I understand.

When the emotion is so strong, so overwhelming, it's as if the body can't contain it, and all you feel is a sort of numbness. A dumbness, like an animal. All you can do, is stand there and drink in the feeling that's washing over you like a cleansing sea, sweeping you along in its current.

Of course he knew. He'd known all along. He'd just been waiting for me to discover. Because I had to do it for myself, you see. That's part of what the journey had taught me. The message he had for me, which I had come so far to learn from his lips, I had already learned from my travels and the guides I had met along the way. He was the shining beacon who had lead me to this point, the light at the end of the tunnel, the inspiration for my journey.

And what else? What else had the journey taught me? Oh, too many things to mention here.

But the journey was not at an end. It never will end, until I die.

And when I die, that will be another journey.

THE END